Ashes

Chicago Heat Series — Book One

V.J. Gage

◆ FriesenPress

Suite 300 - 990 Fort St
Victoria, BC, Canada, V8V 3K2
www.friesenpress.com

ISBN
978-1-4602-6815-5 (Paperback)
978-1-4602-6816-2 (eBook)

1. Fiction, Mystery & Detective

Distributed to the trade by The Ingram Book Company

Acknowledgements

First and foremost, for all of my Chicago Heat series, Shelley McLellan has been my research assistant, medical advisor, and travel companion. Shelley has been my friend since the '70s and these novels are better for her help and inspiration.

As well, one of the best decisions I made was working with the editor assigned to me by Friesen Press who did her job with such great passion. You gave me the best suggestions about what would take my novel from good to a polished, fast-paced story with strong characters, dialogue, and lots of action. Like the editor said, "Show, don't tell." I look forward to many more edits and forming a great relationship. Friesen Press has been a joy to work with and I thank them and would recommend them to other writers.

I must also thank Sylvia Holcomb, whose line-by-line editing of *Ashes* taught me so much. As a brilliant writer herself, Sylvia inspired me and taught me – less is best.

Thank you to the many friends who have read the book and given me corrections and suggestions, to Wayne Stanyer, my step-father, for his ability to see even the smallest error, and to my mother, who thinks I am brilliant.

To the most important people, my husband Dennis Gramatovich, the inspiration for my novels and my children, Natasha and Katrina.

Ashes

CHAPTER ONE

Jade pulled back the faded floral curtain of her second-story bedroom window and took one final look through the dreary, rain spattered day, at the official scene below. Her head was still pounding from the torrent of warm tears she had shed during the police investigation that morning. Until now she had been unable to find even a second to absorb the full repercussions of what happened. She thought of her mother's body, cold and lifeless at the bottom of the basement steps. Her mother was gone for good, and however bad things may have been before the accident, Jade knew they were about to become worse.

She heard the wail of the ambulance sirens as they took her mother away. Even the closed window couldn't muffle the sounds of the official voices as people on the driveway below discussed the tragic events. Jade could see several of the police officers shaking their heads as they continued to make notes. Neighbors stood on the sidewalk hoping for a snippet of information they could share with one another.

"Jade, what will we do now? I'm scared," Crystal whispered as she looked to Jade for comfort. "This is the worst thing that could have happened to us. How will we cope without Mother? He might be passed out in his chair now, but what will happen when he wakes up? You have to do something!" said Crystal, her voice becoming louder with a hint of hysteria.

"Don't worry Crystal, I'll think of something," Jade promised, trying to keep her voice even, not wanting to alarm her youngest sister Amber, who lay rocking on the other side of the bed with her legs curled under her tiny body.

Jade thought again of their mother's body at the bottom of the basement steps and turned away from the window. The sun was just beginning to pierce through the heavy, gray clouds, a beam of light shining through the window encircled Crystal and Amber, giving them both an angelic look. As if from nowhere, a song her mother used to sing came to her mind.

"Don't worry, be happy!"

Her mother Jewell had loved that song from the first moment she had heard it in the 'eighties. It had become Jewell's theme song, like a lifeline through the hellish days of her life with Sam. Amber, the youngest, held her baby blanket tightly in her small hand while she stroked her face with the other. She rocked back and forth in her usual way. It was at times like this that Jade was glad Amber was so different. Amber seemed untouched by the outside world; her inability to attach herself to anything real sheltered her from its harsh realities. Amber continued to rock while Jade and Crystal talked in hushed tones.

"I wish I could just be like Amber and not have to think about anything!" Crystal moaned, moving closer to Amber, shaping her body into her younger sister's small form, finding comfort from her rocking motion.

Jade knew Amber would never be able to cry over their mother's death, a fact few children could comprehend. But Amber would be able to sense the mood of her two older sisters, and today's events would only make her draw further into herself. Jade always marveled at how a human being that looked so perfect on the outside could be so mis-wired on the inside. If it wasn't for Amber's remarkable talent you would believe there was very little going on inside her blank, but pretty head. Jade could never remember Amber making as much as a sound, even as a baby. Amber's eyes could fixate on an object while she rocked and stared for hours, an action that often made her father go ballistic. Jade loved her sister as she was.

Their father treated Amber like a freak. Even her musical gift didn't soften his hatred of his youngest daughter. However, when Amber played the piano the heavens would open up and wonderful music could be heard. Jade thought that if anyone was listening they would be transported to a place they could only dream of. This was when Jade knew her sister was perfect and that even in a moment of despair, there is hope. Jade walked over to the bed where Crystal made room for her, turning slightly so that she could face Jade while still gaining comfort from the rocking motion of Amber, who wiggled her bottom so that she would still have a connection to Crystal. Once Jade was curled up beside Crystal's warm body, they both pulled the worn old comforter up around their slim necks, making sure Amber was covered in the process. The room was warm with the window closed, but as was often the case, the comforter was more for emotional reassurance than real warmth. It also helped to soothe the gripping chill deep in the pits of their stomachs, as the two girls faced the future.

Crystal finally said what Jade was afraid to say. "You know with Mom gone we will never be able to live with Dad and survive."

To live with Sam you needed all the skill and guts you could muster. It was always Crystal, the realistic one, who would meet the challenge head on. The years spent with their brutal father made her the one sister most likely to survive. They say middle children are like that and Crystal certainly fit the mold. Once she got a hold of something, she seldom let go or backed down.

"I don't see how we can make it without Mom. She was the only one that could handle Dad and without her, we will suffer a lot more than we already have," Crystal said, a shutter running through her body at the thought of what her father was capable of.

She didn't say more. She didn't have to. It was the nightmare that Jade had been living since she had gone through puberty. It was bad enough that Jade always had to be careful never to be alone with her father, but she also worried about the possibility of future abuse when Crystal started to develop and blossom into a pretty young woman, and then there was Amber. Jade knew Crystal sensed the danger their dad posed and had done everything to be as unattractive as possible. It was her way of hiding the fact that she was maturing. Crystal would soon turn nineteen, but she looked no older than thirteen or fourteen. Sensing her father's sick looks made Jade shudder and she knew Crystal would fall prey to his evil taunts and touches that were unbearable.

"I know, but don't worry. I promise I won't let

anything happen to you or Amber." Jade reached over and squeezed her sister's hand. Trying to calm her own fears, she hoped it would never come to this, but now she knew that Crystal was right. They would have to deal with their father, but how? Jade put her trembling hand under her head and rested on her elbow. She looked over Crystal's body to Amber, who continued to rock, unaware of what was happening.

"Try and get some sleep because we need all of our strength," Jade said, pushing back her tears.

Jade knew Crystal needed reassuring. In a different environment Crystal would have been an outgoing, demanding child, but with Samuel Walker as a father, she was sullen and angry. The way she dressed said it all; black, black, and blacker.

Lips, eyes, even strands of her soft copper hair were covered in a washable black dye. Jade wasn't sure if it was just a disguise or a "Goth" stage, or if Crystal was deliberately trying to look as glum and dark as she felt. So far it seemed to have worked. Sam simply scowled at Crystal and moved away from her as much as possible. He was always afraid of the things he didn't understand. Jade turned back toward Crystal, cuddling into her small warm body, and the fresh, baby powder scent of Crystal's odor filled her nostrils. Jade liked the rocking motion. Both girls often found they slept better if they let Amber rock them both to sleep.

After a while Jade moved away from Crystal who was now motionless, having finally fallen asleep. She pulled the comforter further up under her chin. She loved the smooth feeling of the worn old comforter. It smelled clean and fresh the way laundry did for the first few hours after a wash. It was one of the last things her mother had touched before the accident and Jade was sure she could smell her mother's clean, floral scent on the comforter. Her thoughts of her mother brought a fresh rush of warm tears to her face. Her dear, sweet mother, Jade had never heard Jewell speak a harsh word toward anyone, not even Sam.

Jewell had stopped loving Sam years ago, but she bore the burden of Sam with silence. She had tried to leave once, and the imprint of the violence she bore was still visible on her hand when she died. Leaving wasn't an option; Sam took no prisoners. Jewell had learned to squeeze what joy she could out of each day and the love she had for her children. Jade knew it was Jewell's fear of what Sam would do to the girls if she were to step out of line that kept her with him. Now Jewell was gone and Jade would make a decision about her sisters' and her futures. She was the oldest and the care of her sisters would be her burden.

Jade tried to hold back the stream of tears that ran down the side of her face into her ear, while a few drops found their way to her pillow, which would soon be soaked. *Oh well, these tears won't be the last,* she thought. They would join the thousands of other tears she had cried during her brutal years with her father. What was she going to do? She had to find a way to protect her sisters and get away from her father. Samuel Walker was supposed to protect and care for Jade and her sisters. Instead Sam was a monster who kept an iron hand on his family, and only the soft, protective touch of Jewell had prevented their father from doing the unforgivable.

It had been Jewell's job to keep her daughters safe,

at least as much as possible. It had taken all of her wit and cunning to keep Sam's attention on anything but the girls. Now, without Jewell, it would be impossible for Jade to continue. Jewell had done all she could to protect them. In the end even she didn't survive. Jade knew she and her sisters were not safe. She took one final ragged breath and hoped that the evening would bring her some peace, at least as long as Sam was passed out. Memories of the day's events tumbled through her brain, and thoughts of Detective Dennis Kortovich kept flashing before her mind's eye. Thank God Dennis had arrived first. It had made what had happened to Jewell and the horror of the moment so much easier.

CHAPTER TWO

Detective Dennis Kortovich sat back in his old, but comfortable swivel chair, behind a large, functional desk. He had spent the last few hours updating several files. Dennis was noted for his attention to detail. At a crime scene his ability to note even the smallest detail was a marvel, even to the other successful detectives. Dennis's ability to recall statistical data in forensics, as well as places, names, and dates, even several years after a case was closed made him valuable to his colleagues. The motto, "When in doubt, ask Kortovich," made his partners over the years feel privileged. If you were lucky enough to get on a team with Dennis, your work would be noticed by the brass.

Dennis looked at the pictures above his desk, a slow smile crossing his face as he remembered when they had been taken. Dressed in full uniform, he and another man were shaking hands with the mayor; big Cheshire grins were spread on their faces. Dennis and his partner, Chuck O'Brien, had been given their first award together. Many more had followed, but this had been their first case and the beginning of a great friendship. Chuck, with his off-the-wall sense of humor had made the past several years more enjoyable.

Hearing someone approach, Dennis turned around. He knew who it was even before the man appeared in the doorway of his office. Partnerships were like marriages; after a while you got used to each other and once in a while you became so in tune you could finish each other's sentences. Dennis knew the lumbering footsteps could only belong to one person, his partner, Chuck O'Brien.

"What's up?" Chuck asked as he sat down across from Dennis trying unsuccessfully to cross his short, chubby legs. Dennis noticed he had a donut in one hand and a coffee in the other.

"We've been given an immediate assignment; it's Judge Switzer's daughter. She's gone missing." Dennis indicated a file that sat in front of Chuck. "He has asked for us. The superintendent agreed to assign us to this case at the judge's request. We're to be at his home in less than an hour." Dennis grabbed his jacket from the back of his chair while he continued to fill Chuck in on the details of the case.

Chuck and Dennis were usually involved in homicide cases known as heaters; the kind of cases that caused the press or the higher-ups to put unusual pressure on the police department. The latest case had involved a serial killer, and there had been more slayings within six months, other than in drug-wars, than at any other time. But when the request came from the superintendent, you didn't argue.

Judge Switzer was one of the most respected judges on the bench. Most of the police force loved having him preside over their cases. For those lucky enough to have him rule on the case, they were assured fair and impartial treatment.

"Judge Switzer's kid can't be more than fourteen or fifteen. He's nuts about her," Chuck said.

Dennis remembered meeting the judge's daughter at a birthday party the judge had thrown for his wife's fiftieth birthday. She was the youngest of four children, the only daughter. All of the boys were at least twenty and Mandy, his only girl, was the apple of her daddy's eye.

"How long has she been missing?" Chuck began to gulp down his coffee and make short work of his donut.

"Just overnight, but the family is beside themselves," Dennis responded.

"Whatever happened to the twenty-four hour policy before we become involved?" Chuck stood, throwing his empty cup into the wastebasket beside Dennis's desk.

"Policy is like an old pair of shorts, it gets changed whenever things get too uncomfortable or start to stink. In this city you know almost everything is done on the 'I'll scratch your back, if you scratch mine bullshit.' That may not seem fair, but that's the way things are sometimes. The rich and the powerful make great media. If the judge's daughter doesn't show up in the next twenty-four hours, her disappearance will make headlines and all hell will break loose. Let's hope she just has a boyfriend somewhere and spent the night out gazing at the stars." Dennis ran his hand over his moustache as he finished his summation.

He looked up at the clock on his office wall, a gift from his daughters for his fiftieth birthday. The face of the clock had a picture of Dick Tracy, the famous cartoon detective. Dennis felt a shiver run down his spine at the thought of anything happening to one of his daughters.

He knew that the Switzer family would be going crazy at the thought of anything happening to Mandy.

"You know if anything goes wrong with this case it will be our asses on the line," Chuck stated. "I hate anything political, and this has all the signs of a suicide mission."

Dennis gave Chuck a nod of agreement as he wiped the crumbs from his desk; the remnants of Chuck's donut.

"This is what happens when you're good." Dennis smiled.

Chuck lacked the same faith in their ability to navigate murky waters, but he knew his partner was right. This would be a tricky case. The Superintendent of Police wanted to talk to Dennis and Chuck first. It would be embarrassing if a regular team of detectives took the case and the press found out. Dennis and Chuck were used to the media and they would be able to side-step any questions until there were more answers. A phone conference had been set up. They would leave soon after the call had been made. Seconds after the first ring, Dennis picked up the phone. It was the superintendent.

"I'm at the judge's home now. I think you two had better handle things as if it's well past the twenty-four hour rule. I'll take any flack if the press finds out," the superintendent stated.

"Is there anything you need us to know before we get there?"

"Only that you need to get this solved before the press find out. I'm counting on you to get the job done."

After a few more instructions Dennis hung up the phone, a look of angst on his face. He hated the politics of the job, and being told he had to solve a case on a short timeline made him feel a tightening in his chest.

All a man could do was his best. Would his best be good enough? A young girl's life counted on it.

"If she is out drinking and having a little fling and then turns up all starry-eyed, the press will have a field day. Then again, if she turns up dead, the superintendent will demand our heads." Dennis gave one last look around his office as he continued his summation. "The superintendent believes the judge, who says his daughter would never stay out all night. Most parents think that they know their kids. I hope the judge is right."

The drive to the Switzer home gave both men a chance to mull the case over. The judge lived in an upscale suburb called Oak Park; the home was on North Oak Park Blvd. Frank Lloyd Wright had designed many of the homes and the area had become a tourist destination for many would-be architects.

As one of America's most famous architects, Lloyd Wright had spent over twenty years making this area a landmark of quality home design at the turn of the century. It was still a great place to go for a Sunday drive. Dennis maneuvered his car through the elegant entrance of the estates. This was a wealthy area and most of the homes were situated on a full acre of well-manicured lawn. The judge lived in the largest house in the historic landmark section; an example of Wright's classic Prairie style. Powerful limestone windowsills and overhanging roof lines, along with the horizontal layout exemplified Wright's quest to reflect America's Midwest.

The circular driveway wound past an impressive entrance. The flair and style of a Latin inscription had been carved into the door by a finely skilled craftsman, reminiscent of old money. Dennis knew the inscription translated into "Truth and Honor" a befitting motto for the judge who was known to live by those two simple words.

Chuck was the first one to reach the front door, Dennis arriving at his side. A tall, thin woman, well past seventy greeted them with a soft smile. She was obviously once a great beauty and carried herself with regal bearing. Her expensive Chanel Suit was a soft, pearl white, with contrasting gold and black braid running along its edge. Her slim legs were in nylons, and considering how hot the day was, her attire was very formal. But they both knew that this breed of woman wouldn't be caught dead with bare legs, no matter how hot the day. The family was definitely old money, which demanded refinement and good manners.

"Detective Kortovich and Detective O'Brien." She held out her well-manicured hand as she spoke. "Come in, we've been expecting you."

Dennis and Chuck were ushered into a large, elegant entranceway. Deep oak paneling encompassed the foyer, and a circular staircase led up to a second floor that was paneled in an off-white oak with deep oak wainscoting adding to the richness of the wood. The décor matched the nature of the owner; warm and tasteful. The tall woman slowed before she ushered them into the judge's study.

"I'm Marsha Phillip, Lena Switzer's mother. I came over as soon as I heard Mandy was missing." Marsha lowered her voice and turned her beautiful eyes towards the detectives. "We're all beside ourselves with worry. I've heard from the superintendent that you two are the best. Please help us. Mandy is our world and she would never stay out all night."

She turned and opened the door to the library once she finished her plea for help. Superintendent Tom Holland greeted Dennis and Chuck. He was a tall man in his late fifties. His thick head of dark, wavy hair framed an intelligent face that showed little of what he felt or thought. There had been a time that both Dennis and Chuck had respected Tom Holland, but lately it seemed he was more a politician than a cop. Most of the other officers felt he was no longer watching their backs. Maybe that was the way it was when you got to the top. You forgot where you came from and how you got there. Dennis was aware that some of the more senior officers were suffering from a bad taste in their mouths from the sour grapes they kept feeding on. It had become a divisive issue in the department, but Dennis and Chuck preferred to keep their opinions to themselves.

Tom Holland was an old friend of the judge's, so when Mandy hadn't come home the night before, Judge Switzer had called him, knowing that he could be trusted to keep things quiet and to bring in the very best to find Mandy.

As soon as Chuck and Dennis were seated Dennis asked, "Judge, can you give us some of the details?"

Judge Switzer spoke with a cool detachment, but Dennis could tell from the pain on his face and the fear in his eyes that it was taking all he had to give the coolly delivered report. "Mandy spent the early part of the evening at a rave with several friends. The rave was just off of Clark Street, a part of town you wouldn't expect to find a proper young woman, but we trusted Mandy's judgment. At well after six a.m. when we still hadn't heard from her, we began calling her friends. No one had seen her since about two a.m. One of her friends, a young man, said he thought she had gone out of the club alone to get some fresh air. He hasn't seen her since. I'm afraid I have few other details at this point. We thought it was best to call in expert help before we let too much time pass." Judge Switzer's voice remained steady. "I apologize for the political maneuvering, but I'm sure you understand why I want you two, and the superintendent to handle this situation."

A familiar hand was thrust forward giving a warm and thankful handshake to both men, a forgotten nicety, in the rush to report the events. Judge Switzer was a tall elegant man who wore his wealth and position with a simple acceptance of his position. Dennis had always thought Phillip Switzer looked like the James Bond type, minus the English accent. He was tall, slim, and dark. Phillip Switzer's bright blue eyes seemed to see all of life, finding what he saw most amusing. His colleagues were both his detractors and advocates. The judge was known to be obsessed with finding the truth, and relating the facts to the law.

His obsession could drive a legal mind crazy, especially if a lawyer ever decided to argue a case with Judge Switzer, without doing a ton of research first. Switzer was a detail guy and it could send you raving and ranting after spending any time arguing with him. He had a way of tying his opponent into a mental knot, but you had to respect his mind and his search for the truth.

Judge Switzer stood to introduce his wife Lena, who had been sitting by the window in a large, winged-back chair. She obviously got her looks from her mother. Tall, at least five foot eleven inches, fashionably thin, and graceful, her fine-featured face was surrounded by an abundance of rich, shiny, auburn hair. Her dark, piercing blue eyes, framed by dark lashes, were red rimmed from crying. Her worry over Mandy's disappearance was obvious on her face.

Dennis and Chuck sat back down after the formal introduction on the big, leather chairs that were drawn up in front of a large, unlit fireplace. The day was hot, a summer storm on the horizon. She gave a brief smile and pushed a list towards Dennis. "You will need this," she whispered softly, as she gave Dennis a list of all of Mandy's friends as well as a recent photo.

"We drove Mandy to the rave at midnight. I know that seems late to be letting a fifteen-year-old out, but Mandy is very responsible and the raves are alcohol free. Mandy is aware of many of the drugs that are available and the troubles they can cause. She was even open to us searching her room at any time and if need be, she would allow us to do drug testing," Lena stated, her eyes pleading. "I hope you can understand what it's like to be the wife of a judge and have a teenage daughter. I hear so much about crime and drug abuse, my first instinct is to just lock my daughter up in her room and not let her out until she's twenty-one. But that wouldn't teach her how to handle the choices she will have to make in the kind of world we live in." Lena's deep, but now shaky voice reflected her fears.

"I have two daughters, they're now in their twenties, but it was hard for me too," Dennis reassured her. "Go on."

"We were to pick her up at six this morning but she wasn't there. She has a cell phone if she wants to go sooner and she knew we would be only too willing to pick her up if she wanted to leave at any time. When we didn't get a call from her, we went to the prearranged spot – she wasn't there. However often we tried her cell, there was no answer. I asked whoever was lingering behind if they had seen her. There was only one boy who remembered seeing her somewhere around two a.m. After that he says he never saw her again. His name is Jackson Page. I took his cell number and home address. He said he would ask around and see if anyone could remember seeing Mandy after that time," Lena said, handing a piece of paper over to Chuck who seemed to be uncomfortable in the deep, leather chair.

"I've made a list of all of Mandy's friends, both in school and out. We belong to the Shore-Side Country Club and I've also made a list of everyone she knows there too." Lena gave Chuck a second list and handed Dennis a picture.

Dennis looked down at the 8x10 picture of Mandy. The girl in the picture was a pretty, young woman with bright, blue eyes and a sweet smile. Long, soft copper curls surrounded an oval face that held the same intelligent look of her father and the beauty of her mother.

"I've put her height and weight, as well as what she was wearing on the back of this photo," Lena Switzer said, as she indicated the information. "She takes after my maternal grandmother when it comes to stature, not me," Lena noted wistfully. "She's not very tall, something she bemoans regularly. She is five feet, two inches and weighs about one hundred ten pounds. She was wearing 'hip hugger' jeans and a tank top with spaghetti straps, in coral and green. She wore sandals. I know it sounds like she is dressed scantily, but it's the way girls dress nowadays." Lena looked sheepish.

"I assure you she hasn't any tattoos or piercings. We say no to most things. But going to the raves, meeting up with her friends, and dancing all night is the one thing we relented on. She loves to dance. Now I feel like it's my fault." Lena suddenly started to cry.

Judge Switzer was standing next to Lena when she started to weep; tears welling up in his eyes as well. "Don't say that sweetheart. Mandy is a responsible girl. We can't protect her from the world. She has to have a chance to be with her friends. We can't blame ourselves," he said as he put his arms around his wife.

Dennis looked at the way the family seemed to be handling the situation. He dreaded having to ask the next questions. And although he believed the judge about how responsible Mandy was, it was still his duty to ask all of the questions; even the tough ones. "Is there any way Mandy would have met up with a special young man and have been talked into leaving?" Dennis asked, looking the judge in the eye.

The judge responded, "I know you must hear this all of the time, but Mandy knows that all of her privileges depend on her doing what she says she will do. She would never take off with a boy. The only thing that concerns Lena and me is that maybe someone slipped something into her Coke. We told her to never leave her drink unattended because of the date-rape drugs. She promised that she would drink a fresh Coke if she felt someone else might have access to it."

"Is Mandy happy at home?" Dennis asked; knowing it was a question that had to be asked.

"I can understand you having to ask these kinds of questions," Phillip Switzer said as he stood, his wife standing up along with him. "Let us take you to Mandy's room. She has a diary. I've never read it, but at times like this, we need you to see what kind of girl she is. If there is anything that you have to know about our family and Mandy's feeling about us, it will be there."

Lena Switzer led Dennis up the stairs to Mandy's room; Phillip Switzer following close behind. Chuck stayed with the superintendent to go over the procedures he would like Dennis and Chuck to follow.

"This is her room. Look through anything you like. Mandy keeps her diary in the top drawer of the desk. She also has a bunch of letters and notes from her friends in that small trunk at the foot of her bed. I'll leave you alone. It's hard for me to be here, not knowing what has happened to my daughter," Lena said, choking back a second round of tears.

Judge Switzer kissed his wife tenderly as she passed. Lena gave him a tearful hug and quickly left the men standing in Mandy's room.

"My wife is a strong and intelligent woman. She knows what happens when young girls go missing. It's hard for her not to tap into her worst fears." Judge Switzer went over to the south wall of Mandy's room where a series of pictures hung in expensive frames. He took one from the wall, holding it tenderly in his hands. "She is very special. Our lives would be intolerable without her. Find her for us." Judge Switzer replaced the picture on the wall and turned on his heels, leaving the room without another word. Dennis knew it was all beginning to be too much for the judge.

Mandy's room was tastefully decorated in yellow and mauve, playful, but not too young. In the center of the room a queen-size bed with a grape-colored canopy dominated the space. Three-tiered bed tables reaching midway up the wall flanked either side of the bed. Matching lamps sat on the top of each table with a clock radio on one side and a gilded framed picture on the other. The picture was of the family; Lena, Phillip, Mandy, and three strapping young men, her brothers. They looked like a happy, well-adjusted family. But as Dennis knew, a good investigator must consider all family members as potential suspects. Mandy's diary would give him a better impression, one way or the other. He pulled the white, leather-bound book from the desk drawer.

As he read through it, he began to laugh. Many of the entries reminded him of his youngest daughter Katrina. Katrina was the spunky, quick-tempered one in his family. She had an opinion on everything, as only the young can, but as his wife was finding out, Trina was very wise and deep beyond her years. The problem between his wife and his daughter was that they both wanted control.

Mandy seemed to be cut from the same cloth. – So and so is stupid – This one thinks too much of herself – That teacher is an ass – This boy is a jerk…another might be all right if he "dressed differently and had better shoes," and so on and so on. Mandy had a few crushes; she liked to keep her options open. Most of the entries about her parents seemed to be nothing more than the usual notations about them not being hip enough. Mandy felt it was the "square, moneyed world" her parents lived in. She felt that if her mother were to ever wear jeans or a T-shirt, like some of the other mothers, she would faint.

Dennis thought if the only complaint a teenager had about her parents was the way they dressed, that wouldn't be motive to run away. He put away the diary. It didn't reveal any conflict or discontent. Not among her family, friends, or even teachers. He decided he would start with the list her parents had given him. Good old-fashioned detective work. Today being Saturday, the school was closed. He and Chuck would start with the friends that had seen her at the rave and would hope for a lead from there. He came down the stairs just as Marsha Phillip; Lena's mother was coming up.

"I was just coming to find you, Detective," she said. "We are just having some coffee and warm croissants and wondered if you would like to join us."

"No thank you, I'll wait until lunch."

As Dennis returned to the library, Chuck was gulping down the last of his coffee, a half-eaten croissant still in his chubby hand. Chuck had a sheepish look on his round face. Dennis knew he had enjoyed a donut for breakfast and that the croissant would only add to Chuck's weight problem. He gave his partner a big smile. Chuck didn't see it as a problem, but Shelley, Chuck's wife would give him hell if she found out.

As Chuck stood, wiping whipped cream from the corner of his mouth, he held out his hand for one last farewell. Dennis joined in the hand-shaking, letting Chuck close out the meeting.

"We will be on this case with as much discretion as we can, but if we need to we may have to put a task force together. If we do, we won't be able to keep it from the press. So we will handle this list first, and see what we come up with. Depending on the time that Mandy has gone missing, every hour that passes puts more pressure on the case. That is when we can make a decision about other detectives helping on the case. We may even have to appeal to the public," Chuck said softly, wanting the family and judge to know the steps that would be taken to get Mandy back.

After providing assurances and promises, Dennis and Chuck made their way to the car. From the front window, Lena Switzer stared out at the detectives. The strained look on her face told Dennis of the pain that would come if Mandy weren't found soon.

CHAPTER THREE

Dennis had finished work for the day. It was time to shut down the computer that sat on his desk and bid farewell to the other officers. He and Chuck had spent the rest of the morning following up with friends of Mandy's who had attended the rave. Not one of them could remember seeing Mandy after two a.m., just as Phillip had told them. They spent the afternoon at the country club asking other friends and acquaintances if they had seen or heard from Mandy. None had. So far they were at a dead end. Dennis decided to look into all unsolved cases involving missing teen girls in the area, going back at least seven years. Was Mandy's disappearance an isolated case, or had there been others? Dennis would get the report later that night. For now, a few hours at home would be a welcome diversion. As usual, he cleared his desk and put everything in its proper place. Even the paper clips had a special place and arrangement; 'an orderly desk, an orderly mind.' The small cubed office held twenty years of memorabilia and awards. He got a great deal of comfort from the familiar surroundings; the Dick Tracy clock on the wall, the plaques, and pictures of his family. A few inspirational words etched into wood to give him that 'edge,' a gift from his ever-helpful wife, Veronica. Even the rough sounds and tangy smells from the other officers in the 'pit,' a common area where the detectives had their desks, gave Dennis a feeling of stability and order. In a work world where anything could happen, Dennis's office was a touchstone of stability, and he loved it.

Although it was late in the afternoon, the August sun still hadn't been able to break through the thick layer of clouds. A thunderstorm had broken the hot afternoon, pelting blobs of rain onto the streets below, while a slightly cooler wind blew in off the lake making the day smell fresh, as only a summer storm can. If the storm passed soon, he could still accomplish a few more things around the yard before the day was over.

Dennis's station was in Area Three, on Belmont and Westlen, about twenty minutes from home. The brief drive to and from work allowed him to clear his head and be present, whether he was at work, or home. As a Chicago cop for over twenty years, Dennis held his job as something almost sacred. He couldn't imagine doing anything else.

Looking back at his roots, in the early days of Chicago many Eastern Europeans settled into a neighborhood known as the Ukrainian Village, where Dennis had lived all of his life. As the years passed, families from other cultures and origins had moved into this district, giving the neighborhood a rich 'Bohemian style' that many artistic types gravitated toward. Veronica, Dennis's wife, loved the colorful characters and ethnic diversity of the area as well as the new artistic atmosphere that seems to define the change. She had considered the Ukrainian Village to be the best place to raise a family and she wouldn't consider moving to the suburbs. Veronica owned a beauty salon that she operated out of their home and her clients were as diverse and as interesting the neighborhood.

When Dennis thought of Chicago, a city of over six million, his thoughts were of a city with a dramatic history and bigger-than-life personalities like Al Capone, as well as many other shady characters on both sides of the law. Chicago was a city made for drama. Many movies had been made of real-life characters that seemed to define Chicago, and not always in a favorable light. Throughout history, many headlines from the *Chicago Tribune* were of scandals, often involving those who should be beyond reproach. It seemed the brotherhood of cops had always been plagued by disgrace.

There had been more than one scandal involving members of the police force or the Justice Department. But for the most part, Dennis believed his fellow officers were men he could be proud of. Dennis grew up with stories of Elliot Ness and other great cops. Now, at fifty, he knew nothing was black or white. Everyone, the good guys and the bad guys, were just trying to get by. Dennis had never regretted any decision he had ever made as a member of the force. He had always been guided by the values instilled in him by his Slavic grandparents.

When solving a case, Dennis followed logic and common sense, using whatever information he had in the moment. There were times when Dennis's and Chuck's lives depended on it. The last case Dennis and Chuck O'Brien had worked kept popping into his head. It was the worst case involving a serial killer they had ever heard of, let alone worked on. What bothered Dennis was that he had really liked the guy who turned out to be the killer. He felt that he understood what had made the killer slaughter over twenty innocent people…which had been a little creepy. Now that realization made him believe that given the right circumstances, anyone could kill. Dennis believed that very few people were born evil. The motivations for their crimes could be as simple as the desperate cries of a child, now grown but left without the resources to handle his pain and rage. Dennis wondered what invisible scars he may have left on his daughters, Natasha and Katrina. And although he doubted they would ever resort to murder as a cry for help, anything could happen.

Dennis deliberately pushed the thoughts of his daughters from his mind. He had too many of his own demons to face, and right now he had a difficult case to solve. Family life had only recently returned to normal, and Dennis hated to think about some of the sins he had committed. He thought back to a moment in his life when self-doubt and personal frustration had led to misgivings about his marriage and life with Veronica. These feelings had almost led Dennis to make a catastrophic mistake that could have ended his marriage. The shame he felt at his momentary lapse in judgment, had been replaced with a renewed commitment and love for his wife and family. He would do anything to protect the peace he now felt.

The drive home allowed Dennis time to take in the familiar sights and sounds of the city. As usual, a brisk wind was coming off Lake Michigan, bringing a clean, fresh scent to the dusty concrete smell of the city. The late afternoon was still hot and Dennis felt he would have plenty of time to do a few things around the yard before he had to go back to work later in the evening. Traffic still hadn't reached its bone-crushing tide of homeward-bound travelers.

He was thankful for small mercies. As he pulled his car around the corner of the quiet, tree-lined street near his home on Wood Street, he heard the call over the police radio. It involved a family less than two houses from his home; the Walkers' residence. Dennis was directly in front of his cozy, brownstone home when he saw Veronica coming down the driveway toward her green Dodge van, which was parked on the street. The sight of his wife brought back strong feelings of love and appreciation. Her tall form was a sight of majestic beauty. Her bright face, big, green eyes, and red hair made her stand out in a crowd, but her shapely body would have been competition, even for Queen Latifah. Veronica ran to the side of Dennis's car, putting her head into the open side window.

"Veronica, there's a 911 from the Walker residence. I'm going to stop there first and see if I can help."

Veronica answered; concern evident in her voice. "I'm on my way to the market. If the girls need me call me on my cell. I hope Sam hasn't given Jewell another beating. When will she learn that she has friends that she can reach out to when he gets out of hand?"

Dennis gave Veronica an appreciative kiss on the lips. "There's nothing you can do if this is a police matter. But I will call you if the girls need a safe place to go."

As she withdrew she gave him a concerned wave.

Dennis knew his wife had a great deal of difficulty not putting her pretty nose in the Walkers' business. But over the years Jewell had stopped calling the police for help when Sam got out of hand. She repeatedly refused to admit to anyone that her husband caused the many bruises, wounds, and broken bones. Veronica had asked Jewell to drop by many times for coffee, but Jewell never came. So in order to keep tabs on the family, whenever Veronica baked, she always took some fresh baking over to the Walker household, using the treats as an excuse. Dennis liked the fact that Veronica tried to keep an eye on the family, especially now that Jewell refused to get help.

Old Man Walker was as mean as a man could be and then some. Even though he tried to be charming whenever the police came by, Dennis knew it was a façade and that when the cops left there would be even louder cries coming from the Walker home. Dennis hoped that Jewell and the girls were all right. The call said there had been an accident. The details were scarce. He could only hope Jewell hadn't finally taken matters into her own hands, as abused wives sometimes do. From what Dennis knew of Sam, no one would ever want to convict Jewell even if she did kill the son of a bitch. Most likely Sam had gone off again and hurt Jewell. Dennis pushed the gas pedal to the floor and made the last two houses in only a second.

As a metro cop assigned to Area Three, Berwyn, Dennis's home district was outside of his immediate jurisdiction. As such, he really couldn't do much in an official way. However, as a friend he could at least give some comfort and secure the scene of the accident until the area officers arrived. Dennis was the first to arrive at the Walker home. The main door was open and only the screen door stood in the way of Dennis accessing the house. He had no idea what he would find, but as an officer he still needed to follow official procedures.

"Hello, anyone home? It's Detective Kortovich. May I

come in?" Dennis called from the front step.

"Yes, hurry," a soft, feminine voice answered.

Dennis entered through the front screen door. The living room was empty and he could tell from the sounds of soft crying that the girls were in the back of the house, in the kitchen. As he passed through the living room, Dennis noted the simple surroundings. There were few knick-knacks sitting on the coffee or end tables that flanked the simple, but worn couch. It was a contrast with his home, where Veronica kept flower arrangements, crystal, and angels, along with a unique selection of candles and every other popular home decoration occupying every available space. In comparison, the Walker home seemed stark and cold. The worn carpet had been vacuumed recently as the streaks made from the vacuum head could be seen in the short pile crisscrossing the living room. The smell in the home was of Pine-Sol and furniture polish. Everything was sparkling clean and neat. There was very little color, most of the furniture being beige and tan. Only a subtle hint of moss green broke up the monotonous, flat tones that seemed to pervade the room. It was as if the room was trying to blend into the background, unseen, much like Jewell and the girls.

Samuel Walker was knockdown drunk when Dennis walked into the kitchen, which also seemed to express little other than a tired, but clean mood. The faded floor had been scrubbed clean. Its dull, white background gave little contrast to the beige and green. The beige stove and fridge blended with the patterned floral wallpaper of yellow and green, once popular in the eighties. Everything was spotless, but sterile. Knowing how tense things were in this house, Dennis knew that Jewell would be reluctant to do little more than keep her home clean. Jewell's home was just a place to live, since very little love, other than the love for her children, could exist within these walls. Dennis could hear the soft hiccupping sobs of someone crying. As he walked toward the basement door his heart sunk to his stomach.

Crystal, the middle child of three girls, sat at the top of the stairs, her knees pulled up close around her small pointed chin, blue eyes as dark as midnight stared up at Dennis as he walked toward the basement. Crystal's eyes were red-rimmed from tears that even now flowed steadily. Blotches of red on her nose and cheeks made her skin look ghostly white by comparison. Soft sobs slowly replaced the loud ones as Dennis approached her from the kitchen door. Dennis was chilled by the sound of a voice coming up behind him.

"She's down there," Sam said to Dennis as he walked to the fridge trying to stay steady on his feet, to get another beer.

Sam was only in his late forties, but his leathery skin had more folds than a basset hound. His jowls hung from his long face while his slack smile had a perpetual sneer, making him appear dark and menacing. Dennis noted that Sam's checkered shirt had snaps rather than buttons, a real benefit if you're a drunk.

Sam's red-tag blue jeans hung limply on his skinny hips, threatening to fall off if he moved too fast. He held a beer in his sun-speckled hand and his eyes were glazed. Obviously this beer wasn't his first.

"Stupid woman can't even bring up a load of laundry without falling down and killing herself." Samuel's words were flat, and emotionless.

Dennis was sure Samuel was one of the soulless beings whose only feelings were of anger or indifference. Dennis had often heard the man's loud ranting from his own home; foul, bitter ravings, which seldom went unnoticed by the neighborhood. But after years of trying to help, Dennis, Veronica, and other neighbors could only pray that one day Jewell would come to her senses and seek out professional help. Dennis looked down the basement steps to see Jade, the oldest girl, holding her mother's bleeding head in her lap. She held the cordless phone so tightly to her ear as she pleaded for help from the 911 operator that it seemed to melt into the copper curls of her long hair.

"Stay with me Jade, the police are on their way, it should only take a few more minute," the steady voice on the other end of the phone assured Jade who had yet to see Dennis at the top of the stairs.

Jewell's legs were sprawled recklessly off to the side in an ugly, twisted manner, making her look like a discarded doll. Laundry was strewn all over the stairs, and the plastic basket lay off to one side with a few items still tucked neatly inside. Jewell's eyes were wide open; their usual deep blue seemed dull and faded. Her skin was pale and her naturally-curly hair, which usually hung to her shoulder in soft waves, was matted with blood.

Dennis could tell, even from the top of the stairs, that the fall had been fatal. The basement stairs were steep and Jewell had obviously taken a bad fall, hitting her head on the second stair from the bottom. A final crack of her skull had occurred as she hit the cold concrete floor below. Or did Sam have a hand in it? An investigation would reveal the truth.

"Jade, are you all right? I came as soon as I heard the call on my radio. The police should be here any second and I think you should just stay where you are," Dennis said reassuringly, as he began descending the stairs.

Jade stared up at Dennis with the same blue eyes as her sisters and mother. All of the girls were petite, with small, fine, even features. They reminded Dennis of Dresden dolls, the kind his mother collected. The girls had a look of a time long past, when women had a delicate refinement and the young men wanted to protect and care for such beauties. Their copper-colored hair was a color you seldom saw unless it came from a bottle and even then you couldn't match its richness. Whenever the girls went out, which was seldom, all eyes turned toward their striking beauty. Now, the Crown Jewel lay dead at the bottom of the stairs.

Dennis sat beside Jade, gently reaching over to Jewell's cold hand to feel for a pulse – nothing. "I want you to know that you have friends who care what happens to you. Just know that Veronica and I will be here for you and your sisters." He tried to sound reassuring. "Everything will be all right."

Dennis knew he was lying. From the look of Jewell, nothing would be all right and he could hardly look at the pain-filled, blue eyes that stared up at him in disbelief.

"I'm going to be fine, but you've got to get some help for Mom," Jade pleaded with Dennis.

Dennis put a reassuring arm around Jade's tiny shoulder. It seemed to help.

Jade noted that Dennis always looked fresh, crisp, and reassuring, and he smelled good too. She could tell that he must have come from work; his navy suit was cut perfectly, accenting his broad shoulders and trim waist. His light-blue shirt had a contrasting red and navy tie that looked expensive and well thought out. He always looked like some big executive, rather than a cop. Jade knew that Dennis was someone important in the police department and that he had handled some of Chicago's biggest murder cases. Reporters were always interviewing him and he was often on the news.

Somehow Jade felt close to him. She blushed a little thinking of the times she had pretended Dennis was her dad, someone she could love and be proud of. Many times on her way home, as she reached the Kortovich house, she would pretend that she lived there. She would fantasize about how things would be when she went through the side door and was greeted by Dennis. He would ask how her day was and then insist that she do her homework while he helped. He would be the father she had always wanted; someone who would give a damn about her and would make her feel safe and loved. Each day as she passed Dennis's home, getting closer to her own, and a feeling of dread would engulf her. Jade always hoped her mom was safe and Samuel wasn't at home, or at least that he would be drunk and passed out in his usual chair. Her worst fear had always been that something would happen to her mom or baby sister while she was at school.

Jade was jolted from her thoughts by the 911 operator. "Honey, are you still there? Stay on the line – the police are nearly there."

From a distance, Jade could hear a siren, faintly at first, then slowly getting louder as they neared her home. A few minutes seemed to take forever.

Dennis stretched his long legs, which were beginning

to cramp under him. He didn't want to move Jade or the body. As a good cop he knew not to disturb anything. He also knew that Jewell was dead. If he touched anything at this point the evidence could be compromised, and therefore unable to reveal what really happened. Dennis had learned that often, even first-hand accounts by eye-witnesses were not always accurate. Evidence gathered at the scene, as well as crime-scene photos, could help back up or discredit any story told. It was important to keep the girls calm and Samuel semi-sober until the investigation was underway. Keeping Samuel sober was going to be the tough part.

"Lazy bitch never was good for nothing. Crap, what am I going to do now? Shit! I can't take care of this fucking family. Nothin' but a bunch of useless, stupid broads and then that slut of a wife has to give birth to a fucking retard. She doesn't even talk." Samuel waved a bottle of half-finished beer in the direction of a petite, curly-haired, little girl rocking in the corner. "I've a good mind to take all the money and run. Who needs to take care of a bunch of stupid girls?"

Dennis could hear the sound of small bells. It was Amber with her toy phone. As beautiful as the older girls were, the youngest, Amber, was as close to perfection as any human being could be. Her copper hair framed an oval face of pink complexion. Her expression was fixed and her blue eyes held a blank look, quickly alerting anyone to the fact that she was autistic. Her petite body rocked rapidly back and forth. She sat playing with the numbers on a toy phone. Dennis doubted Amber knew exactly what had happened, but he was sure she was able to pick up on the sounds of her sister's cries. The commotion had obviously worked her into an agitated state. She stared up at some unseen object, continuing her unbroken rocking motion.

Dennis decided he should phone Veronica and let her know what he had found. She would be worried until she heard from him. As soon as he dialed the number, he realized that Amber had imitated him, hitting the exact same number that he had called. She could hear the tones of the phone as he dialed his wife on his cell. He was amazed at Amber's gift.

There was no answer. It was typical of Veronica to take her phone, but not to have it on. He would try again later. Dennis noted Sam's look of disgust as he passed by his youngest daughter, muttering to himself as he went from the kitchen into the living room.

"Fucking little retard."

A comfortable worn recliner accepted Sam's small, scrawny form, his slack, weather-beaten face forming an ugly scowl. Given enough time, a violent outburst was sure to follow. Dennis hoped for the sake of the girls that Samuel would pass out, but he also needed him to stay sober and awake in order to give a statement to the police. Dennis thought it was too bad it wasn't Sam at the bottom of the stairs, but as luck would have it, it was not the case. Now there would be little to protect the girls from this depraved, little man.

Dennis yelled up the stairs, "Stay with me, Sam. You can't pass out on me now. The police will need your statement." He heard the beer bottle crash to the floor.

"Wake up you bastard." Dennis's deep baritone voiced sliced through the air, startling Sam.

"Fuck you, Kortovich and fuck her too!" Sam's face

screwed into a red-hot scowl.

Dennis heard sirens coming down the road as the police and ambulance drew closer. They would be there in seconds. The girls only needed to answer the police questions once. Dennis would wait with them while they told the police their stories. He was a friend and they would need a strong shoulder to lean on. When he looked up at Crystal, she had stopped crying and with her head resting on her knees, she was rocking back and forth, her arms hugging her legs.

"Now what?" she asked flatly without looking up.

"We simply tell the truth and let the police take care of everything," Dennis tried to reassure her.

When Crystal looked down the stairs, the despair he saw on her face was that of someone who had lived a dozen lifetimes. He thought of his two daughters, Natasha, twenty-five and Katrina, twenty-two. Their minds were still open and innocent, less aware of the world's bitter twists.

"The police," Crystal's tone sounded angry and full of contempt. "What good are they? We've never been able to count on them. We tried and look where that got us." She resumed her position, her head once again resting on her knees.

Crystal's small shoulders slumped forward; dejected, hopeless. Her bare white legs and arms only made her seem more fragile and helpless. Dressed in black denim shorts and a torn black T-shirt, she looked like a poor orphaned child, rather than a young girl about to blossom into a beautiful woman. What remained of her poorly applied make-up were now only a few streaks of black mascara under her blue eyes and fading black lipstick on her trembling lips. Strands of her hair still held a hint of faded black dye, a poor attempt to cover her copper curls.

Jade felt her mother's body beginning to lose its warmth as she held on tight. She knew her mother was dead. She could hear the exchange between Dennis and Crystal, but felt too drained of emotion to respond. Crystal had been right! The cops had failed them. Not once, but many times. She recalled the first time Jewell had tried to run away from Sam. Jade was very young, but somehow even years later the memories seemed sharp and clear in her mind.

CHAPTER FOUR

They had never planned to run away, it just happened one dreadful night. Amber wasn't born yet, and Jade and Crystal were still very young, only nine and five. It wasn't like they really understood what was happening. When you're that young you really never do. How could you understand at nine that what goes on in your home isn't happening everywhere else? How do you know that the slaps, foul words, and threats aren't acceptable behavior? How do you understand that the tears, bruises, and broken bones are more mendable than a broken heart and loss of freedom and dreams? How could you possibly understand a mother's dreams, as she imagines the gruesome, lifeless bodies of her children, murdered at the hands of her husband? The man she swore to love, honor and cherish. Or worse yet! See her babies left motherless only to be abused by their father. Protecting her most precious possessions, her children, had always been Jewell's number-one concern.

Jade may have been young, but she understood in ways beyond that of a child that her family was different. As her thoughts drifted back to past events, Jade knew that if they had been able to get away, her mother, Jewell, would not be lying at the bottom of the stairs. Sam had still worked back in those days – it was great. With Dad gone, the days were peaceful and full of love and joy. Their mother would blossom once Sam left the house. Jade didn't understand why he left. He just did. After he drove away in the old Chevy the dark mood would suddenly lift for the rest of the day. Her mother would change from a quiet, sad woman into a delightful playmate that seemed determined to make the next few hours full of fun and laughter.

They would bake cookies or fresh bread in the morning, then lunch would be a tasty treat of their own efforts. Their favorite game was making up funny songs that made no sense at all, but the game always made them laugh. Naptime was full of soft smells and gentle touches.

Jewell gathered her children tenderly into her open arms, holding them closely and for a while they were able to lay their fears and bodies to rest. After their nap, playtime focused around books, games and puzzles, anything that allowed their imaginations to run freely and go into unexplored areas of the wild and wonderful. As the afternoon wore on, Jewell began to watch the clock. The atmosphere would never transform in a way that was obvious to an outside observer, it was less tangible than that. They could feel the energy begin to change; it was a subtle thing and they slowly changed from this small happy trio, into cowering creatures. If you looked around, everything was still where it always was, but the transformation was as real as if the house was taken to another place or time. You could almost imagine an invisible hand painting the house black; black with fear; black with pain; black with desolation and isolation. As the clock ticked closer and closer toward five, Jewell began to withdraw and turn inward.

Jade and Crystal would pick up the games and put them away out of sight. They didn't want their father to find their stuff and put his dark, evil stroke on all the things that gave them joy. At the final tick-tock of the clock and the mark of five, they scrambled to their bedroom where they would stay until their mother would coax them down the stairs to supper. Children were not to be heard and if Jade and Crystal could have had it their way, they would gladly have chosen not to be seen as well. They would slip into their seats at the table hoping that their dad would focus on his food and TV and not even notice that they were there.

"Where's my supper, woman?" Sam would yell.

Jewell never answered, it wasn't necessary. All she had to do was to put a hot meal on the table and sit quietly waiting for Sam to give the cue. If he wanted conversation he would ask a direct question of whomever he wanted the answer from.

If not, the girls knew to say nothing. It had taken Jade a few rough lessons to find out all of the unspoken rules. Once, when Jade had been excited about her first report card, she jumped into an excited chatter about how much fun kindergarten was and how much she loved her teacher. "Did you like school, Daddy? Who was your first teacher? Could you do the whole alphabet? Miss Lane thinks I can read almost as good as a grade one," she said excitedly.

Without a glance in Jade's direction Sam swung his open hand across her face. "If I wanted to come home and listen to the useless chatter of children I would have signed up to work at a school cafeteria. Don't ever speak to me unless I ask you a direct question," Sam spat, never once looking at Jade to see the shock, humiliation, and fear on her small face. He simply dug into his food and continued to watch TV.

The kitchen was just off to the side of the living room and Sam's kitchen chair could be turned so he could enjoy his meal at the table and still focus his attention on the television. Thank God for that small box that blared out the scores and exploits of men who ran around a field or soared across the ice. Sam shouted swear words at the box and would shake his knife and fork at some athlete he deemed stupid or unworthy. He could go on and on about a score, completely forgetting his family. That was when the girls knew they could quietly sneak out of their seats and slip into their room to play until bedtime.

Jewell would stay with Sam, making sure he had his beer and that the remote control was close enough at hand, not allowing him to notice that she was still within slapping range, although the shouts and curses still managed to hit their marks. There were the times when the news or the score made Sam mad, and words turned to beatings, leaving Jewell a quivering, mass of tears and blood. It was on one such night that Jewell decided to flee. Jade now figured it must have been the breaking point, before her mother's spirit was entirely shattered. The mood that night was especially dark; Sam's day had obviously not gone well. Everyone could sense the danger as he walked through the door. Halfway through the meal Jewell forgot to ask for the butter to be passed. She reached past Sam's plate to pull the butter toward her. In a split second Sam's hand came down on Jewell's, his knife slicing through her skin like a spoon through Jell-O, leaving her hand impaled onto the wooden table.

"You fucking bitch, if you wanted the goddamn butter you could have asked!" Sam roared.

Jade saw the look of shock on her mother's face, noting that Jewell never moved a muscle; her blue eyes transfixed on her hand. Little blood flowed from the wound; the knife was jammed so far down into her flesh. Jewell's face was ashen and Jade saw her double over, grabbing her stomach as she tried not to vomit from the pain. Would Daddy stab Mommy again? Jade's legs went weak. She had seen Sam hit her mother many times, but never had she witnessed anything like this. Crystal sat across from Jade, her eyes wide, not daring to move.

For a few minutes Sam seemed to be frozen in time; a strange smile on his lips. Then he slowly pulled the knife from Jewell's throbbing hand, twisting it side-ways as he struggled to dislodge it from the table. He tossed the knife casually onto the table, took his plate to his favorite chair, and plunked his bony body into its worn frame, his attention once again focused on the television set while he mentally dismissed the pain and horror he'd just caused his family.

Jewell moved like a ghost to the sink to wrap her wounded hand, which was now bleeding profusely. The tea towel could hardly absorb the blood, most of it staining the front of her white dress. Jewell doubled over again as she grabbed the sink to steady herself. Jade could tell that she was in a great deal of pain; she was so pale. She had seen a ghost on TV once before, and she wondered if her mother was now a ghost. All of the blood made Jade think that maybe her mother was going to die. Jewell motioned for the two girls to come to her; it took only a second for them to cling to her blood-soaked dress.

The three of them moved to the back door, took their sweaters off the hooks, put on their shoes, and moved silently out of the door. They began to run. They ran, and ran, and ran, until they thought they could run no more. Jade tried to urge Crystal on; Crystal's small legs unable to keep up the frantic pace. Jewell finally picked up Crystal, pulling her close to her chest, still running. Jade's legs started to turn weak. She had to keep up. The late spring night quickly engulfed them. Jade followed closely, uncomplaining.

The blood continued to gush from the wound. Jewell tried to hold on to Crystal with her good arm and took a deep breath of the cold spring air. "Oh God, your father's after us, we are all as good as dead," she cried.

When Sam was in a rage there was no predicting what he would do. Jewell pulled the girls across the street, paying little attention to the red light that would keep them stuck on the corner, with Sam less than a few blocks away. Jade heard him racing towards his escaping family.

"You fucking bitch, stay where you are or I'll punch your face to smithereens," Sam screamed from a distance.

There was no mistaking his tone; Sam was deadly serious. Now that Jewell and the girls were on the other side of the street, Jade thought frantically, where would they hide? Finally they came to an intersection that led to an alley behind stores so old that they too looked like ghosts. It was a Monday night and all of the businesses were closed. No one was around to witness the event that was about to unfold. The alley was deserted except for the petite, copper haired woman, with two tiny girls clinging to the edges of her blood- soaked dress. With stars as the only witnesses to the terrifying night, they stood for what seemed to be an eternity. Jade's heart was beating so fast, she felt its pounding. Her lungs felt as if they would explode. What did it matter? Daddy would find them and hurt them like always. Jade could tell by the look on her mother's face that tonight was different. It was going to be much worse than all of the other times.

"Mommy, Daddy's coming! Run!" Jade screamed.

The tiny, anguished voice of Jade jolted Jewell into action and she started to run, Crystal still in her arms. Jade tried to keep up, doing double time, sweat breaking out on her upper lip and forehead. Jade could feel the warm blood of her mother on her hands. When she whipped some of the blood onto the front of her navy tank top, it seemed to soak into her skin, making her feel sticky.

Her mother stopped suddenly – they were behind the strip mall. Large, metal garbage bins were the only thing Jade could see. Where could they hide? From the corner of her eye Jade saw an old wooden boat that was tipped upside down. Jewell saw it too. There was no time to consider how good this small offering would be. Jade heard Sam's violent expletives as he roared out a string of foul words. His now taxed body was slowing down as he crossed the street. Running to catch up with his fleeing family had taken its toll on his skinny, out of shape form. The sound of his cowboy boots could be heard in the distance.

Jewell pulled Jade over to the small rowboat, still clinging to Crystal who was now whimpering softly.

"Hush Crystal, don't make a sound," she pleaded.

All three of them squeezed under the boat only seconds before Sam rounded the corner. The girls knew that even one sound would mean Daddy could find them. As they scrambled under the old rotting boat, a sliver jammed into Jade's upper shoulder. Her first instinct was to scream in pain, but her fear of Sam overpowered her, and not a peep escaped her trembling mouth. As they lay down on the cold tarmac, Jade heard the clunk, clunk, clunk of Sam's cowboy boots before she could see the scuffed, worn toes from under the raised edge of the boat. Sam knew where they were. He had walked straight over to the boat. The silence dangled in the air like cheap perfume in a small elevator. It was heavy enough to choke the life from even the heartiest soul. Suddenly a blast rang out into the night. It took Jade a couple of seconds before she realized it was the sound of a bullet. She had gone target shooting with Sam twice before, so she knew the sound. Once again, bang, bang, bang as three quick blasts exploded. This time the bullets found their way into the upper ridge of the bottom of the boat. A whooshing sound made her flinch as the bullet whizzed past her head. No one made a sound, but Jade's fear caused her to wet her pants. The warm liquid ran down her bent legs, spilling and splashing onto the asphalt parking lot, as it seeped out from beneath the small boat.

Sam said nothing and the silence was worse than any tirade. The sound of his boots clunking on the tarmac as he slowly walked around the boat made Jade feel as if her heart would burst. Any second a bullet would find its way into her mother. Jade imagined her red blood spilling onto the ground, seeping under the edge of the boat. It could be days or even weeks before anyone would move the abandoned rowboat and find them. Jade felt as if she would burst from the pain in her shoulder. Her panties were now feeling cold and a sudden itch made her want to scratch. But how could she? She had to be brave.

"I know you're under there. I'll give you less than a second to get out or I'll start shooting. If you think I won't, then just test me. Neither you, nor you brats will get out alive." Sam's voice was ice-cold as he stated the obvious.

Jewell slowly lifted the boat up several inches, allowing them to emerge from under its cover. Sam stood there in front of Jewell and the girls, his face a twisted mask of rage. The hate he felt was barely contained. It took two strides for Sam to reach Jewell, slamming his fist into her face. Just as her knees buckled he grabbed her by the hair, spun her around forcing her body to fall back against the boat. Jewell's bloody hand slammed behind her back, making the raw wound gush a fresh flow of blood. Sam pressed his body up against hers; his face only a few inches from her cold, clammy cheeks; his breath barely contained his murderous rage. Suddenly the barrel of his gun was thrust down into Jewell's dry swollen throat, choking off her air, as ragged breaths found their way out of her flared nostrils.

"Never, ever try to leave me you fucking bitch, or I'll make your brats watch you die. No one will help you!" Sam's statement was final and deadly.

Just then the sound of a siren blasting could be heard behind Sam. He quickly shoved the gun into the front of his pants. As he turned around he was careful to conceal Jewell as she cowered next to the boat.

The young police officer got out of his car. Sam pulled both girls forward, placing a loving hand on their shoulders, giving the officer a display of fatherly protectiveness.

"Having any problem here?" The officer walked forward trying to get a closer look at the family.

"No officer, we were just out for a walk. We saw this old rowboat and wanted to take a better look."

The officer looked back at his partner, still sitting in the cruiser. He gave him an all's well signal then started to turn on his heel to leave. Suddenly he stopped and turned back to face Sam. He strained to see who or what was hiding behind him. He then directed his question to Sam; "Who's behind you, sir? Maybe I ought to hear from her." The officer waited for a few seconds, but no one made a move or said a thing. "I said who's behind you?"

"Just my wife, and as you can see my daughters, we're all out on a walk. Do you have a problem with that?" Sam's tone was tense.

Jewell stepped out of the shadows and Jade hoped the police would see the blood on her mother's hand. They would be take them away and keep them safe. The officer looked Jewell straight in the eye. He was good looking in a slick, arrogant way. He had his hand on his gun as if to say, "Don't fuck with me."

The officer then looked at the two small children standing with their father. Silence hung in the air for what seemed to be forever. Suddenly he turned back on his heels, muttering a final statement to Sam as he retreated. "Well, don't hang around too long. We don't like anyone behind the shopping mall after hours. Have a good night." With those final words he got into the cruiser and backed the car up.

Sam gave a cocky smile and said, "You see what I told you. You're just too much paperwork. Unless someone calls in a complaint the cops hate to get into a domestic fight between a husband and his wife. I'm still the king of my castle and no fucking cop is going to get involved to rescue a bitch like you!"

* * *

Jade remembered her dad's words, and he'd been right; many times the cops had come to their home and only given Sam a talking to and a warning. Jewell had never made those 911 calls; it was always her word over the complaints of strangers and nosy neighbors. If they had known the extent of the violence, they would have arrested and charged Sam. Then the nightmare would be over. Sam's idea of over was death. At that moment, Jade didn't know there would be another time. It was only later that she found out that Jewell had planned their escape down to the smallest detail. When Jewell finally ran again she would have a plan and she would make sure Sam could never find them. The lives of her children depended on it.

CHAPTER FIVE

That was the beginning of secrets and for the next year Jewell made elaborate plans for a final escape. She never expected Sam to find out what she was up to. She was careful to tell no one, especially not the girls. They only knew there were many times that their mother told them she would answer their questions about the secret calls later, but 'later' never came. The less they knew, the less likely Sam would find out. The one thing Jewell never planned on was that evil has a way of finding its way and nothing is foolproof.

Jade was only nine and it was the spring of her third year of school. She had loved going to school from the very beginning. The laughter and fun in the class made her forget the fear at home. School was wonderful. The school halls had a feeling all their own, as though the energy of the children had been soaked into the brick and mortar, giving the walls a feeling of life that seemed to embrace Jade each day as she journeyed down the halls. Miss Dregar, her grade three teacher, was awesome and she remembered the first time Miss Dregar had bent down beside her to help her solve a problem she was having. She'd caught a whiff of something so breathtaking she burst out with a wondrous, "Miss Dregar, you smell!"

At first her teacher's face seemed stern. Then she broke out into a soft, but surprised smile. "Jade, haven't you ever smelled perfume before?" Then Miss Dreger looked at her with all the amusement a teacher could, making sure she did not embarrass her small ward.

"No…. I don't think so." Jade seemed to search her memory for anything as wonderful as the smell.

Miss Dreger said, "Well, I'm wearing perfume and it is something you spray on so that people will notice you when you pass them and think that you are special."

After that all Jade could do was think about was how she could get ahold of some perfume. She had asked her mother, but Jewell said Daddy didn't like it, and when Daddy didn't like something, you never did it, or you paid with your hide. On the day when her mom told her that she would not be going to school, Jade was broken-hearted and didn't understand. Jewell explained that they would be leaving that morning and not coming back. Sam had gone off to work and they would need the whole day to get as far away as they could. Sam had never allowed them to own any suitcases, but Jewell had managed to save some large paper shopping bags, big enough for them to take a few of their favorite things. Once packed, they quietly left the house, hoping never to return.

"Mommy, where are we going? Why can't I go to school? Can't we live here anymore?" Crystal asked.

At nine, Jade was the only one to really understand what the shopping bags meant. She saw the look on her mother's face and knew that this was taking all the courage she could manage.

"It's all right, Mommy, I'll help you. I have all my stuff in the bag and I'll carry Crystal's stuff too. Don't cry. We can do this."

Jade took her mother's face in her tiny hands and looked straight into her worried eyes. At that moment, she was more like the adult and Jewell the child. It was a tiny glimpse into her future, and the rest of her life. She was to take care of her sisters, a job that was impossible for a small child.

They arrived at the bus station at ten that morning. Jewell had been careful to take the local bus to a shopping center and then call a cab. She was hoping Sam would never be able to track her from a crowded shopping center. She even bought their tickets with cash. They were going to Gage-town, New Mexico. They had picked the location by rolling dice on a map. Wherever the dice landed was to be their new home. This was going to be a long trip, so Jewell bought lots of treats and games. It was only minutes before they were about to board the bus when Jade looked up at her mother, only to see a look of terror cross her face, while all of the blood left her pink cheeks, making her look once again like a ghost.

Jewell would rather have died than to have the day play out as it did. She would not be so lucky, although later that night the screams that echoed from the little house on Wood Street, did sound as if someone was being killed.

Jade turned to see what had caused her mother such alarm. She was terrified when she saw Sam and the triumphant look on his face. Sam calmly came up to Jewell, put his hand under her elbow, and escorted her to the parking lot where his car was waiting to take them back home. Jade found out years later from her mom that all the planning in the world couldn't outwit Murphy's Law. Anything that can go wrong, will go wrong.

Six months earlier, Jewell had found out that her parents had died. She hadn't seen them over the past two years. Sam had made it difficult for her to see her parents, who lived in Boston. They had stopped visiting, sensing how difficult life must be for their only daughter once they left.

Jewell's mother had begged her daughter to leave. "Jewell, your father and I are worried sick about you and the girls. Leave Sam and come to live with us. We have plenty of room and you could go back to school. We would take care of everything."

"No Mother, I can't and won't leave Sam. There is nothing to discuss. He's my husband." Jewell tried to sound firm.

"You can't possibly want to stay with a man like Sam. You come from so much better, and I know he hits you."

Jewell wanted to cry out for her mother for help more than anything in the world. To be able to move to Boston, away from Sam would be a dream come true. But she knew that the dream would turn into a nightmare. Sam would hunt them down and kill them all; her mother, father, and precious babies. No, she would have to stay with Sam until she could find a way to leave him so that he would never find her. The answer came with her parent's death.

They left her the financial resources to leave. Her parent's lawyer was able to get in touch with Jewell without Sam finding out. It was a provision of the will. Together they were able to handle the details of the estate and plan for Jewell and the girls' eventual disappearance, as well as a change of name. Everything was handled down to the last detail. It was the perfect plan, except for one thing… the one call that came when she least expected it. It was the call that Sam answered; the one that let him figure everything out in an instant. All he had to do was be patient until the day she decided to bolt. The rest was easy. Just follow along and show up just as they were just about to board that train, boat, car, or plane to freedom.

The call that let the cat out of the bag came from the lawyer's secretary, who had somehow been kept out of the loop. Everyone knows a good secretary does all of the work and always handles the details. Like that fateful day, when there was going to be a late release of money from the estate to the bank.

Because she was out of the loop, the secretary did what she always did and called the client to inform her that the transaction would be delayed. "Hello, is Mrs. Walker there?" The voice on the other end of the phone asked, sounding official.

It was unusual that Sam would be home at this hour but a raging headache had made it impossible to work. It was just as he came through the door that the phone rang. As usual, Jewell was downstairs doing laundry. She had to be the cleanest bitch in the neighborhood. He couldn't stand to hear the phone ring so he answered it with a gruff "Hello!" waiting for the caller to continue. It was for Jewell, not that she got many calls, but there were far more for her than he ever got, not that he cared.

"No, I'm sorry she's not." Sam didn't want to shout down the stairs for Jewell to come up, his head hurt too badly.

"May I ask to whom I am speaking?" the voice sounded official.

"I'm her husband, Samuel Walker."

"Are you sure you can't find Mrs. Walker? It is very important."

"No, she won't be able to talk until late this evening."

"May I leave a message?

"Sure, shoot." He kept his response short. It was easier on his head that way.

"Would you tell her that the money from her parents' estate will be delayed on the transfer by one day, also, tell her I'm sorry to hear about both of her parents dying so suddenly. It must have been a shock for you and Mrs. Walker."

Now it was Sam's turn to be shocked. You bet your fucking ass he was shocked. That was an understatement. This put a whole new light on all of the happenings of the past few months, especially Jewell's attitude. No wonder she seemed less stressed. There was a bounce in her step he hadn't seen in years and upon occasion Sam would see a faraway look in her eye. At one point he thought she might even have a lover, but a few weeks of spying uncovered nothing.

"Hello! Mr. Walker, are you there?" The secretary thought she lost the connection. There had been no response for so long.

"Yes, yes, I'm still here. I just had to have time to gather up my emotions, it's been such a sad event for us all." Sam tried to sound sincere, and hide the rage that was gathering just under the surface of his voice.

"The money will be sent to the first National Bank of

New Mexico and will be in the bank when she gets there tomorrow. Well, be sure to pass the information on to Mrs. Walker, as well as my condolences." The voice on the other end was gone while Sam still held the receiver.

He was still holding the phone minutes later when he heard Jewell coming up the stairs, humming an old '60s ballad. He hadn't heard her sing in years. Did she really think she was about to get away with leaving him? Sam hung up the receiver quickly and took up a relaxed position in his favorite chair. He would wait and bide his time. He would never let her leave him, unless it was in a coffin.

He was glad to see her shocked face the next day at the bus station. Sam would never forget that look of distress and surprise on her face as he walked up the platform. You would have thought the devil was at her heels instead of the man she married. Sam laughed to himself.

"Where do you think you're going?" he asked calmly as he approached her and the children.

Jewell said nothing. It would only make things worse. She looked around at the crowed platform. Families were boarding the many busses, heading in the hundreds of directions throughout the U.S.

"Don't even think of calling out for help. I'll knock you out cold and carry you out of here if I have to and not one of these do-gooders will even give you or your fucking brats a second look," Sam said his voice deadly calm.

Jewell let go of Jade's hand. She tried to hold the two big paper bags while still hanging onto Crystal's small hand.

Jewell walked silently behind Sam; her head lowered.

Jade looked up at her mother's face; tears were spilling from her eyes. Jade had seen her mother look afraid before, but she had never seen the look on her mother's face like she did on that day. It was as if Jewell's determination to leave had been sealed into a new resolution to stay. Her face was like stone and only her tears betrayed the fear she felt. Jade fell in step alongside of her mother and sister, knowing that from this day forward life would be even darker. That is how Jade thought; feelings had colors. Black! So far there had been few pink and purple days in her life…colors that she could never wear or enjoy in her limited life.

CHAPTER SIX

After Jewell's failed attempt to leave, she never again had that faraway look of hope in her eyes. When Sam beat her, she simply coped. If the beating was severe enough to put her in the hospital, she lied to the cops and doctors about what had happened. She kept the windows closed and doors shut. And never again did she let anyone in. Jade grew up trusting no one, especially not the cops. It was just like Sam said. Women and children weren't important. A man's home was his castle and he could do anything he wanted within the closed doors of his home. Years later, Jade learned only too well just how unimportant kids were to the cops, especially teenagers. Jade had been going through a very difficult transition both at home and at school. Her best friend Charlotte Kennedy had disappeared and Jade knew something awful had happened to her.

Charlotte had become her only real connection to the outside world. She had made Jade feel safe and accepted. Charlotte was a part of the 'in' crowd and she had taken to Jade at the end of grade twelve at Lincoln Park High, a school of over three thousand students. Jade had been shocked when the tall, athletic brunette showed an interest in her. Charlotte was always full of fun and laughter. She had good grades in school and was the star player on the high school basketball team. The thing Jade liked best about Charlotte was her relationship with her family. She envied them the seemingly happy, easy-going fun they seemed to have whenever they picked Charlotte up from school or attended one of her basketball games. Jade was at Charlotte's house on a Friday night, a rare event for Jade.

She had never witnessed a family that was so full of love and respect for each other, except on TV. Even then Jade suspected it wasn't real, just a bunch of Hollywood crap. Charlotte's mom worked part-time at the school library and her dad was an accountant. Each parent took turns cleaning the house, cooking, and driving the kids to sporting events and lessons. The result was a loving, close family where everyone was very much in tune with each other. The conversations around the supper table were full of genuine interest about what was happening for each member of the family, at school, with their friends, and the neighbors. Jade marveled at the total absence of fear within the family. It both saddened and impressed her. Everyone laughed and teased each other in a way that made her feel even more isolated and alone.

"Hey Charlotte, don't think just because you have a friend over for supper that you get out of cleaning the kitchen," Billy, Charlotte's older brother, said as he grabbed a platter of chicken, taking a second helping.

"You're not my boss. Mom, tell Billy to mind his own business."

"If you two don't stop this nonsense I'll tan both of

your hides and don't think you are too old for a good old fashioned spanking," Mrs. Kennedy said.

"By the way, how did your basketball game go?" Ken Kennedy asked, a smile spreading across his face.

"We won. I was the one with the most points, forty-two. It was the most points I've ever scored in a game," Charlotte responded to her father's question.

"That's because Jacob Smith was at the game and she wanted to impress him. Charlotte has a crush," Billy said, trying to bait his sister again.

Soon everyone was joining in on the conversation, filling Mr. and Mrs. Kennedy in on the details of their day. After supper Jade and Charlotte sat on the front step of their wraparound verandah and talked. Jade's mood shifted into low gear and Charlotte finally asked the one question very few had ever had.

"Jade, why are you so afraid and sad? What's happening to make you so withdrawn?" Charlotte's larger hand had grabbed Jade's small cold hand as she looked Jade in the eye for an answer.

Jade couldn't give her an answer. She had never trusted anyone before and couldn't find a way out of the dark, emotionless pit of fear, to feel safe enough to confide in Charlotte. As tears welled up in her eyes her only answer was a fearful, "I'm just shy."

"That's okay, I'm not," Charlotte responded. Together they enjoyed the rest of the evening, not knowing it would be the last they would share.

Charlotte was one of dozens of girls who had disappeared over the past few years. Jade knew her friend was most likely dead, because she would never have run away. The cops had given up; they said it was just another missing teen. They had failed Charlotte, as they had so often failed Jade, Crystal, Amber, and her mother.

The cops had said Jade's mother's death was an accident. They would never accept that it was their dad's fault. He had abused their mother so badly over the years that a recent bout with the flu had left her weak, unable to fully recover. Jewell hadn't been allowed to rest long enough to get well; her need to protect the girls from Sam's barbaric outbursts and physical abuse had made it impossible to stay in bed and get the much-needed rest. The result was a deadly tumble down the stairs. Jade couldn't count the times the police had failed her and she would never trust them in the future. The next time she would take matters into her own hands.

Jade abandoned her look at the past as the loud wail of a siren could be heard. With the arrival of the officers, Dennis could concentrate on the girls and their emotional well-being, taking the time to observe the scene of the accident a little closer. He wanted to see if Sam's cruel hands may have been involved, as he had always anticipated.

"What's going on Kortovich?" The familiar voice of Sergeant Tilley, the first officer to arrive at the home, was a welcome sound to Dennis. He had known Ken Tilley for several years. He was a nice looking man in his late forties with flaming red hair and golden colored skin, which reminded Dennis of Robert Redford; a pale, watered down version. Many of the women in the force took a second glance whenever Ken walked by. The police community was close and Dennis and Ken had attended many local events over the years. Their common profession had drawn the two of them together and Dennis had come to respect Ken's dedication and sense of fair play. Dennis tried to sum things up, knowing Ken would have to follow every angle. "It's an accident from the looks of it, although I suspect the husband isn't above tossing her down the stairs."

The paramedics were right behind Officer Tilley. As they descended the stairs it quickly became obvious that the pretty woman lying on the cold concrete was very, very dead. After a quick check of her pulse and other vital signs, they simply stood back knowing they were unable to do anything. As the other officers and Crime Scene Investigators began arriving, Dennis stood back as the investigative team began taking photos and prints while gathering as much information as they could from the scene. It was unusual for the special

CSI unit to be called in before the local police requested their presence, but with so many calls from the Walker house, the dispatcher had gone through channels to recommend that the unit be called, just in case.

"What do you think of the situation?" Tilley asked Kortovich.

"I think it's a damn shame that's it's not Sam Walker at the bottom of the stairs." Dennis's response was flat, but summed up his feelings.

Dennis knew the girls would feel safer if he stayed and maybe he could give them some comfort before a new day would begin. As he thought about the girls' futures, he knew that it would be even more terrifying living with Sam, now that Jewell was gone. The girls would depend on him and Veronica, and he vowed he would not let them down. This may not be his case, but he sure as hell could keep an eye on things as a good neighbor. If Sam thought he had full rein over the girls, he could think again. Dennis would make sure Sam never got too comfortable with his status as a single dad.

CHAPTER SEVEN

The girls awoke to the usual sound of Sam's screaming. "Jade, you whore, where the fuck are your sisters? What the hell happened yesterday? I remember cops coming. Where the hell is your useless mother?"

Sam was up and a new chapter in their lives would now begin. Without their mother it would have to be a short time. They would have to deal with Dad. They couldn't run away. But who would take care of Amber? If the two girls didn't come up with a permanent plan for Sam, they would never survive the added abuse. Could they frame him for a crime and send him to jail? They would have to think hard. The plan to deal with Sam couldn't surround domestic abuse, they knew from experience the charges would never stick.

"Someone get up and feed me." Sam leaned against the doorway frame trying to keep from falling down. "I asked you what the fuck happened yesterday."

"Mother is dead," Crystal said. "The cops will be by sometime today to question you because you were unavailable yesterday." Crystal's sarcastic remark didn't miss its mark and the scowl on Samuel's face let her know she was walking a thin line.

"Screw the cop, she did it on purpose. She never was any good for nothin'." Sam spit out his angry words. "She never did a honest day's work. Now she's gone and got herself killed just to spite me so it's up to you girls to keep me happy. Now get up, I want something to eat, now!" He turned and staggered down the hall. A new day had begun.

* * *

Crystal pulled the covers over her head. The thought of getting up and going downstairs to serve her father made her want to throw up. She knew her mother had always been there to make sure that she and her sisters could spend as little time around Sam as possible. "How could you leave us with him?" Crystal felt the familiar feeling of anger once again taking over her whole body. She had never expressed her feeling towards her father for fear of the physical retribution that was sure to follow. She had always harbored a great deal of anger towards Jewell. She felt her mother was a coward. Jewell had been too afraid to leave and too afraid to do something drastic. Not that she knew what her mother should have done. If Crystal had had her way, she would have pushed Sam down the stairs. Since becoming a teenager she had restrained herself from running away or screaming at her father. She would have loved to slap someone, anyone, when things got tough at home. But all she could do was to stand by silently and listen to the abuse. The only solace she could find was to retreat to her room with Amber, lie in bed, turn on her stereo, and rock back and forth, blocking out the sounds below. One day Crystal asked her mother what had drawn her to a man like Sam. A confused look crossed Jewell's face. "He wasn't always this bad, and I thought I could change him, be his rescuer."

For a moment Jewell's beautiful face had lit up as she remembered back to a time when a girl from the right side of the tracks met and fell in love with a boy from the wrong side of the tracks. He had been a James Dean lookalike. She recalled her first date with Sam and the few good months that followed.

"How come a pretty little gal like you can stand to be with a dirt poor guy like me?" Sam would ask.

It was Jewell and Sam's first date and he was dressed in clean blue jeans and a white shirt that looked crisp and smelled as good as the first day of spring; clean, bright and fresh. Sam's full head of hair hung below his collar, the sun catching the soft, golden highlights in his hair. His face was fresh and young. Jewell thought he was the most handsome boy she had ever seen.

"I don't care if your family hasn't any money. I'm not like that, nor are my parents. They would never judge you just because they have money and your family has hit hard times." Jewell lovingly looked up at Sam.

Sam said venomously, "My family never hit hard times; it would mean they would have to have worked to have good times. They are lazy, no-good drunks, every one of them. They're not worth the two cents they don't have to rub together."

"You're not your family. You can be anything you want." Jewell tried to comfort Sam who seemed to be growing angrier each passing moment.

"I come from trash. That's all my family has ever been; white trailer-trash. That's what I am. You should get away while you can. My family is a bunch of mean drunks," Sam shouted. "I'll probably end up just like them. It's in our blood." He pushed her away and started to walk to the car.

Jewell's heart broke when she saw how angry and dejected he seemed to be. She thought if Sam was loved and understood enough she could change him. She was wrong. The only thing that would change was that all the hopes and dreams of a young girl would be destroyed by the fear and isolation that Sam would create. After the birth of Amber, Crystal knew from conversations with her mother that Jewell felt there was no way out. That is until she had tried to run that one desperate night when Sam stabbed her in the hand. Then came the second time. Crystal couldn't remember much about either of Jewell's runaway attempts. But she knew of the stories from Jade. The beating that followed the second attempt had left Jewell with a broken jaw. But it was what happened after the beating that really broke her spirit. The rape had been brief but brutal. Nine months later Amber made her appearance into the world. It was only after Jewell discovered that Amber was mentally challenged that she gave up all hope of ever leaving Sam.

Jewell's parents were older and had moved from Chicago to Boston leaving Jewell even more isolated. After many frantic phone calls and visits they finally gave up trying to convince her to leave. She had become so reclusive that after a few years her parents were seldom allowed within the walls of her tiny home, a home that her parents helped Sam and her to purchase.

At the time, Sam was working with a Ukrainian immigrant, John Wakulchuck, whose hard work and quick mind allowed him to make a small fortune in scrap metal. He had been a blacksmith in the old country and had figured out a way to smelter down old scraps of iron into small and medium-sized iron balls, selling them back to the iron companies at a healthy profit. Sam was lazy, but John knew how important the money was to his family. John fell in love with the kind and gentle spirit of Jewell and her daughters, and wanted to protect them; feelings that others would experience after meeting the girls and getting to know Sam. For the years that Sam worked with John, things at home were at least bearable. But eventually Sam's drinking got more and more out of hand until he got fired. Sam no longer worked and for Jewell and her daughters, having him home all the time made life almost unbearable. It was a small inheritance that Jewell had received from her grandmother that kept a steady paycheck coming into the family. But it was never enough to allow Jewell to do more than the basics and the girls often went without extras that so many of their friends took for granted.

As they grew older, Jewell's parents seldom saw their granddaughters. Still, letters and presents conveyed their love. With their time running out, they came up with a plan on how to leave their only child, or their granddaughters the family fortune, without letting Sam get his hands on the large sum of money, stock, and property.

Crystal stretched and snuggled her pillow one more time. There was nothing to be gained by blaming her mother for the situation they were in; she had done the best she could. It would now be up to her and Jade to find a way out of the circumstances they were in. Crystal thought it would be easier if she could just stay in bed forever and never face what was waiting downstairs.

* * *

Jade moved off the bed into the bathroom to take a shower. She grabbed her housecoat, covering up her nightgown. As she passed the mirror attached to her dresser she noticed how dark the circles under her eyes were. She'd had little sleep and dreams of her mother sailing down the stairs hitting her head had replayed through most of the night. She felt the weight of the world sat on her shoulders.

"Crystal get up and get Dad something to eat until I get downstairs, and whatever you do hold your temper in check and don't provoke him. You know what he's capable of."

Crystal nodded seriously, letting Jade know she had no intention of making things worse.

Jade locked the door to the bathroom and as usual put the white wooden chair under the doorknob as a precaution; she had been only twelve when she'd found her dad in the bathroom watching her. Her body was just starting to develop and his newfound attention toward her made her feel dirty and ashamed.

At first she hadn't known why she was so creeped out, but as she found out more about boys and girls, she knew without a doubt he was capable of sexual assault. No wonder Crystal had started to dress in gothic style. Jade knew it was her sister's attempt to keep her father away from her. She remembered when Crystal first expressed the desire to dye her hair and change her looks. It was during a visit to Veronica Kortovich's salon for a haircut.

"What would you girls like me to do with your hair? Just a trim, or a new look?" Veronica asked.

"I want to dye my hair black," Crystal said.

"You and your sisters have the most beautiful hair color in the world. Why would you want to change it?"

"I'm too young looking. Everyone thinks I'm weak and can't take care of myself. I want a new look and I was thinking of gothic. People stay clear of you if they think you're strange," Crystal said, her voice gaining strength.

Veronica seemed to consider Crystal's request. "Look, I won't dye your hair completely black, but I will foil a few pieces. I'll use a wash-out dye and if you like it I'll sell you the product and show you how to maintain it yourself. If you like, I'll even show you how to do your make-up in a gothic style. But only if you'll promise me that you won't take things too far. No piercing or tattoos." Veronica's warm, hearty laugh let Crystal know she understood.

Crystal loved her black foils even though they hid amongst her copper curls. She wore more makeup at home than she did at school and Jade knew why. It bugged Sam. Still, somehow he sensed that Crystal's choice in fashion and makeup was directed at him. He only gave Crystal a hard time once, and then he left her alone.

"What the fuck do you think you're doing with your hair and that black crap you're wearing on your face? Your clothes look like you got them out of the garbage can. You look like a little witch rather than the little bitch you are," Sam yelled at Crystal.

Crystal stood her ground as she gripped the kitchen chair, thinking how much she would love it if her hands were around her father's skinny throat. "Don't be too sure I'm not a witch and that I won't make a poison potion. One day your beer might just have a funny taste. You wouldn't want to get alcohol poisoning," she said, daring Sam to do something, her small chin jutting out defiantly.

Sam got up from his chair, his right hand in the air ready to strike Crystal. She stood her ground and moved closer, staring him down. "Go ahead. You could hit my mother all you want, but if you hit me I'll make sure that all of us kids get taken away from you. Child welfare would love to find out what happens in this house," Crystal screamed. "If you ever touch me I'll tell anyone who will listen and I promise you, I am not my mother."

Jade stood, taking Amber from the kitchen table, fearing that Sam would turn his anger on his youngest. Sam stood with his hand in the air for a few seconds. As he lowered his arm the look on his face was such a twisted mask of hate, Jade knew her gut was right, without Mom, Dad would have to go. No one knew what Sam was thinking. The moment was so tense you could almost feel the air turn deadly cold. Sam simply left the table, picked up his remote, and sat in his chair with a cold beer in his hand, dismissing the moment as if it had never happened. Crystal had won a small victory and she was determined to push things as often as possible.

* * *

Jade took Amber upstairs to her room to get ready for school. Amber was picked up each day by a bus that would take her to a special-needs school for the mornings. There weren't many things that Amber responded to except certain sounds. If someone dialed a phone number that Amber could hear, she could instantly repeat the numbers on her toy phone, dialing the numbers backwards and forward continuously with a radiant smile on her face. But it was Amber's musical gift that made her special and everyone except Samuel made sure she explored it as much as possible. Amber never spoke or made any sounds at all. Often she would become engrossed in repetitive motions or would rock for hours. She never cried, but if touched, even as a baby, she would whimper and pull away. Jewell had purchased a padded jolly jumper in which Amber found a place of safety and joy, where she could rock for hours. Sam rarely directed his anger towards Amber, seeming to dismiss her totally. Jade remembered when Amber was very little and would be in her jolly jumper. This was before anyone knew for sure that Amber was 'special.' Sam would lean over her small body and pull on the rubber tubing, flinging Amber higher than her little legs could handle. After a few very harsh thumps on her head Sam would growl. "Fucking retarded frog."

Once or twice he even kicked her, sending her partway across the kitchen floor before the rubber of the jolly jumper brought her back to her original spot along with a few bounces along the way.

Sam would thrust his face into Jewell's. "I can't understand why you bothered having another kid. Two was enough. You can't do anything right. I don't know why I married a little mouse like you. It's your fault! I needed a real woman. Now all I have are too many mouths to feed and a life that looks like shit. You can't do anything but a bit of housework. Even your cooking is slop. To top it all off you give birth to a kid that's a retard." Sam, as usual, went to the fridge and got another beer. Along the way he tugged on the bungee-jumper, again giving Amber a couple of thumps on the head.

Rather than cry, Amber would hold her breath until Jewell's calming voice could lull her back into a dull, unaware state. "Hush my little baby, Momma's here to take care of you," Jewell would coo. Soon the movement of Amber's little body moving back and forth put her back into a world that only she occupied. Jade was glad that Amber would be unable to feel the terror and pain that she and Crystal felt at the loss of their mother. Hot tears streamed down her now-rosy cheeks, mingling with the cleansing water of the shower. She would dress and face the day as bravely as she could.

CHAPTER EIGHT

Tonight, Jade thought, she and Crystal would have to come up with a serious plan on how to deal with Sam. For now she would have to get him drunk enough to pass out before any harm could come to her or her sisters. She would have to go to the kitchen and make sure Sam had a few extra beers close at hand. Jade cleaned the kitchen, taking as much time as she could. It was important to keep Sam sitting in his chair. She made sure she had a beer to give him when he ran out; it had been her mother's mission, keeping Sam in his chair watching TV and now it was hers. As she handed him his fourth beer, Sam slipped his hands down Jade's blouse, cupping her tiny breasts in his skinny, cold hand. His foul breath assaulted her nostrils as he jokingly pretended to show an interest in her social life. Jade lost her balance, spilling the beer as she moved away from him.

"Well, Jade baby, anyone fuck you yet?" Samuel's tone was light, but menacing. "You'll make some young buck happy, just like Jewell made me happy all these years. Now who am I going to get to fuck me?" He slobbered in her ears, trying to drag her back towards his emaciated body.

Sam could see the disgust on her face as she pulled herself away from him. "Go get me another beer," he said angrily, dismissing her.

Jade quickly sidestepped him getting another beer. This time she put it on the coffee table in front of Sam, rather than handing it to him directly. She vowed he would never touch her again.

Crystal and Amber were in their bedrooms trying to avoid any contact with Sam. Jade was going to have to try to get her father to understand that they would have to attend to the funeral arrangements for their mother. But all Sam wanted was another drink. She had to try to keep the fear from her voice. If Sam found out she was afraid of him he would use that fear to keep her close, and being close to Sam was never good. She would have to talk to him, but with a taunting, angry voice, hoping he would not see how upset she was at his assault.

"Dad we are going to have to see to the burial arrangements for Mom." Jade tried not to break down and cry. "When the coroner releases her body you will have to call one of the funeral homes and decide what to do."

"Why should I bother with any of the fucking details? With your mother dead all the money belongs to you girls anyway, except for Amber. Now I will be her guardian and I can do anything I want with her and the money. I have a good mind to just go off into the hills and live off the land. That little fuck-head of a sister of yours won`t even know the difference. Besides, she can't talk much so she won't be able to say no. And a man needs caring for and she ain't good for much. Maybe she can keep me happy – know what I mean?" Sam slobbered at Jade knowing she understood his meaning.

"I don't think I should handle the arrangements. You are the head of this household. It's up to you." Jade's voice sounded as if it would break.

"I ain't got nothing. Your mother's fucking parents tried to fuck me over, but I got my lawyer to make sure Amber stays with me forever, and as her trustee, I will have control of her money. If she dies, I'll get all of her money. The fucking little retard isn't any good for nothing anyway. Who would even miss a little retard like that? So you see, if you stay or go it's of no concern to me. Either way I've got control of enough money to make me happy till the day I die. Not too stupid for an old man with a few burnt-out brain cells." Sam laughed, giving Jade an evil snarl while he slumped into his recliner.

"Dad, how can you talk like that?" Jade cried out.

"Because it's like I told your mother before she married me. I'm a no-good rotten bastard. It's all her fault. She should have listened to me when she had a chance and stayed with her snotty parents."

Jade stared at the recliner, thinking how much it was like her father; small, dirty and worn. It looked like it belonged in the dump, like a discarded piece of shit, foul and worthless. It had absorbed so much of Sam's energy that even when he wasn't slumped in it watching television it still seemed like an evil thing. No one ever touched his chair. Not out of respect but because it was a vile object.

"You girls handle the funeral arrangements. You turn twenty-one at the end of the month so you'll get access to a fucking fortune." Sam's eyes blazed at Jade. "Then you'll be 'Miss Big Shot.' So you might as well start learning how to face life now. I won't be around to protect and take care of you like always, but Amber will always be mine."

Sam stared her down for what seemed like forever, but was less than a few seconds. Jade could not mistake his intention. He was telling her the same thing he'd told her mother, but in a different way. The girls would not be safe if Jade left, so she would have to stay and protect them. They would never be free as long as Sam lived.

"I've taken care of this family long enough. It's time you decided what you are going to do when you turn twenty-one. Either move out or stay and take care of your sisters. I've done my share." Sam reached over for the beer and turned the TV up, dismissing her.

Jade thought, *Talk about blind.* Sam really did think he helped and was needed in some way. If he really saw himself the way others did, he might put a gun to his head and end it all, but that would be a dream come true and Jade had yet to see even one of her aspirations come to pass. It was always everyone else's fault and Sam was the victim. The world was out to get him and as usual he wouldn't go down without a fight. Too bad he didn't know there was no one left in his world to even care one way or the other if he lived or died. He had isolated himself for so long no one would even miss him. Jade was grateful for that little fact. Once she was back in her room, a plan was beginning to form in her mind.

CHAPTER NINE

Detective Ken Tilley stood outside the front door of the Walker home thinking about yesterday's events and the heartbreaking accident that had taken place just twenty-four hours earlier. He was glad Kortovich had been there, it had made his job a little less clinical. Now it was his distasteful duty to question Sam.

Sam answered the door still unshaven and dressed in his dirty, stained jogging outfit. Tilley almost wanted to slap the look of indifference off his skinny face.

"You can come in but I don't have much to say about the bitch. She fell down the fucking stairs bringing up the stupid laundry and now she's dead. Stupid woman probably did it on purpose so she wouldn't have to take care of me and the girls." Sam left the front door open, indicating that Tilley should follow. "She always was just a rich spoiled brat and never did understand the hardships of a working man." He staggered through the living room into the kitchen.

Tilley followed, hoping Sam would be sober enough to answer his questions so that this case could be concluded one way or the other. "Well Mr. Walker, I really have to get some background from you about the day and find out what factors may have played a role in the accident." Tilley wanted to drag Sam to the edge of the stairs and give him a good shove. Even if Sam hadn't done anything directly to cause the accident, Tilley knew that Sam had inflicted many beatings on his wife and it was a miracle that she had not been killed before.

"What do you remember of the morning before Jewell fell down the stairs?"

"I don't remember. All I know is I was sitting in my chair, and she was coming up the stairs with the laundry, like always. I was watching the White Sox play Toronto when I heard her scream. Jade was in the kitchen and she was the first one down the stairs. I never go into the basement. There's nothing down there but a washer and dryer. You'd think there was gold downstairs the way Jewell spent all her time doing the laundry. She was the cleanest woman I ever met. If she wasn't so obsessed with the laundry, she might have been doing something else and would still be alive."

"I must tell you that it seems suspicious that Jewell fell down the stairs. You know that the police have been called out to your house many times over the past fifteen years. You have a record of abuse and I am inclined to wonder if you pushed your wife." Ken Tilley watched Sam's face, hoping he would give him a clue one way or the other as to his involvement in Jewell's deadly tumble.

Sam began to shout. "No one has arrested me in years. Jewell never pressed any charges against me and if you ask any of my daughters, except the retarded one, they'll tell you Jewell was always hurting herself. It was never me!"

Sam was right, Jewell had always protected him from

the police after each beating, and no one in the family had ever spoken up about the abuse. Tilley could tell they were scared to death of Sam and now death was the final victor. In a way, he couldn't blame the girls for not trusting the system and the cops. The newspapers told of story after story of women who had been hunted down by their lovers or spouse. Many were brutally murdered even after they had sought out protection from the police and the courts. If a man wanted to kill someone, a restraining order couldn't stop him. The police were unable to protect all the women who needed safekeeping. Ken knew there were thousands of women like Jewell, feeling they had no way out, they learned to cope.

"Jade, get your ass down here!" Sam yelled up the stairs.

Ken Tilley heard the sound of footsteps coming slowly down the stairs. Jade came into the kitchen dressed in denim shorts and a red T-shirt. Her feet were bare and her hair was still wet.

"What?" Jade asked, her face showing little emotion.

"Tell this fucking cop that I had nothing to do with your mother's accident," Sam shouted.

"I told Detective Tilley everything I know yesterday," Jade answered.

"Well you must have said something to make this bastard think I pushed your mother down the stairs. What did you say?" Sam moved closer to Jade, trying to control his temper in front of Detective Tilley, but the tightly balled fist held by his side gave away the barely controllable rage that always ran just beneath the surface.

"Look Mr. Walker. Jade told me it was an accident, but it's my job to make sure that the truth is known.

Family members have been known to lie for one another." Fearing Sam's temper, Ken Tilley moved forward to stand between Sam and Jade.

"Well, she told you the truth. I never laid a hand on Jewell. If the little bitch could blame me she would. Then she and her sisters would be rid of me." Sam scowled.

Ken Tilley could tell the conversation was over. Sam moved from the kitchen back to his chair, picked up the remote, and turned on the TV. An afternoon baseball game blared so loudly that Ken knew talking to Sam was useless. It was time for Ken to do a once-over of the scene of the accident, draw his conclusions, and then make a report. He was just about to go down to the basement when he heard someone coming up the front steps. The door was open and as he looked up; the serious face of Detective Dennis Kortovich greeted him. Kortovich was a bit of a hero within the department and many of his peers said he was the finest officer they had ever worked with. Right now Tilley welcomed his arrival and even though this was not Dennis's case, Tilley figured two heads were better than one. "Come on in," he said. "I just finished questioning the master of the house and was going to have a look in the basement. Want to come?"

"Thanks, I'd like that."

Once they were down the stairs and out of earshot of Sam, Dennis leaned closer to Ken. "I've find myself doing nothing but worrying about the girls since this thing happened. Anything I can do will at least make me feel like I'm accomplishing something to make things better, although I doubt they will be very safe without Jewell."

As they turned the corner at the bottom of the stairs both officers were shocked. Just past the makeshift rumpus room was the laundry room and what a surprise! It was a magical room of absolute delight. The walls were covered in a thick layer of foam and a soft fabric. The color of the fabric was mostly white with a soft rose floral pattern, making it seem romantic. Along the wall were white wooden bookshelves that were neatly filled with what appeared to be romance novels. An old stereo lined a second wall and hundreds of records were piled neatly beside the unit. Dennis walked over and lifted the lid. Inside, a record still sat on the old turntable. He bent over and read the faded label – Tom Jones; a sensation of the 'seventies was just waiting to be spun for a romantic interlude. Along the ceiling were small, indoor twinkle lights that cast an idyllic glow inside the white lace that hung in delicate swags.

The washer and dryer were stacked on top of one another and beside them were white wicker laundry baskets, now empty and clean. In the far corner, away from the appliances and closer to the stereo, was a great big, overstuffed rocking chair covered in a deep rose floral. It was the only real color in the whole fanciful room and gave the appearance of a huge bouquet of roses, making it look even more inviting.

"The human spirit finds a way to make life more bearable in many unique ways and this room is probably what kept Jewell sane while she endured her life with Sam," Dennis offered as he continued to look around the room and admire the many little special items that adorned it, making it look like a treasure chest of feminine delights.

"I agree. It must have been a needed sanctuary for Jewell and the girls. From the looks and the size of the chair, all four of the little beauties could easily fit into that rocker and feel safe," Tilley commented with a wistful tone.

"Sam must never come down here. I bet he's usually too drunk to maneuver the steep stairs. It has to have been a blessing for Jewell and the girls to have had this room," Dennis said.

Tilley looked over at Dennis and without speaking, they both decided to leave the room, sensing that their presence was invasive to the soft spirit of Jewell whose presence seemed close at hand.

"The problem is that there really isn't anything here that will help us and most likely she really did just fall down the stairs. Jade said she was weak from her bout with the flu," Ken offered.

"Knowing that asshole husband of hers, the poor woman was worked to the bone. Her death will have to be ruled as an accident and that shit-faced excuse for a man will be all there is to take care of those innocent little girls." Tilley's summation of the situation was simple and he could tell by Dennis's scowl that Dennis didn't like it either.

Once back up the stairs Ken hoped he and Dennis could finish the final few questions of Sam and the girls. But Sam was passed out in his chair and the girls were nowhere to be seen. "I think I have enough to conclude that Jewell's death was an accident. The coroner's report will be finished Monday. If everything is alright, we can release the body," Ken said.

"I agree. It was an accident," Dennis said moving towards the back door with Ken.

Dennis's wife Veronica dropped by just as Tilley was leaving. "Hi Ken." Veronica greeted him with her warm inviting style. "I hope I'm not going to interfere with your investigation, but I wanted to make sure the girls had some good food for the next few days."

"You're just in time. We've done all that we can for the day. I'll have to go over things with the coroner and make sure that it all fits together. I'm sure it's an accident and there's nothing more that can be done." Tilley gave Veronica a thankful smile.

Dennis shook Ken's hand at the door. "Thanks for letting me go over things with you today. It makes me feel as if I'm doing something to help the girls, although for now I don't know what."

CHAPTER TEN

Veronica had cooked several casseroles and a pumpkin cake, a specialty of her sister-in-law Diane. She had also contributed cabbage rolls and perogies, a Slavic dish she'd learned from her baba. "Are the girls around?" she asked.

She had no sooner asked the question when the girls came down the stairs with Amber in tow.

Jade and Crystal were thankful for the food. Neither of them could cook very well. Their mother had never been a good cook. Jewell had never been able to teach her young children the fine art of food preparation. As a young woman of wealth, she had only visited the kitchen to be fed by the chef or steal some wonderful tidbit when no one was around. It had never really mattered much over the years. Sam had never seemed to enjoy eating. His eating habits were erratic and because of that he remained very skinny, albeit a small belly could be detected whenever he wore a T-shirt. Still, he looked half starved. Jewell had tried to cook for the girls but had always kept it simple. However her baking was passable and the girls loved to help in the morning and enjoy their treats for lunch. Once Sam was home the kitchen was no longer safe.

Jewell had made a special world of her own within the laundry room. She would spend her time waiting for a load to dry with a good book on the go to help pass the time. For some reason Samuel never complained when Jewell was downstairs. He knew nothing of how laundry was done and never descended the steep stairs to the concrete landing. All he knew was Jewell went down with a big load of dirty clothes in tow and a few hours later she came up with clean clothes.

The girls knew they had the cleanest, freshest laundry in the world. Sheets were changed every second day just to allow Jewell enough dirty laundry so that she could have a least two hours of peace and quiet each day while the girls were at school. On weekends they all took their time cleaning and grocery shopping, trying to stay out of Sam's way.

"Hi girls, how are you doing?" Veronica inquired as they continued their descent from the upstairs to the kitchen.

Crystal replied first, sounding a little sarcastic. "OK, considering what happened to Mom."

"Mrs. Kortovich, thank you for asking, we're just fine." Jade's response was added to Crystal's with a little more warmth and appreciation.

They both thanked Veronica for the huge box of food. Often it was Jade who commented on her friendly way. Over the years they had gone for a few haircuts at her salon; even though it was infrequent. Their curly hair never seemed to grow as fast as most people. Whenever they did go for haircuts, Veronica seemed especially kind, always commenting on their looks. "You girls will learn to appreciate your curl and hair color more as you grow older and realize just how special and pretty you really are." she said each time they came to her salon.

The girls could tell she was sincere and it always made them feel special. Just knowing that someone like Veronica, who was in the beauty business, would single them out to tell them how special they were seemed to boost their confidence just a little. And she somehow seemed to understand Crystal's need to look different.

* * *

For the rest of the afternoon all Jade could remember was a blur of small talk. She hoped neither Veronica nor Dennis would be able to tell that she was preoccupied. She and Crystal hoped Sam would just stay drunk and passed out on his chair for yet another night.

Eventually, the girls were alone in Jade's bedroom. "Jade, answer me! What's our plan?" Crystal's voice brought Jade back to the present and to the plan that was yet unformed.

Jade assessed the situation. "First we have to bury Mom. Then we can figure out what to do with Dad. I don't know how we will be able to get away from Dad, Mom never could. Maybe we could lock him up in a room and never let him out. We could just keep him in the basement." Jade was hoping for a plan of any kind that would keep Sam away from them.

"It's a good thing Dad's family are all dead, and no one can tell the police if he goes missing." Crystal must have read Jade's thoughts.

Sam's family had been gone for a long time and the girls barely remembered them. Both parents and his younger brother were killed in a drunk driving accident. Sam's father was the drunk driver. He had missed a sharp bend on a country road and went full speed into a half-frozen pond. They didn't stand a chance. The pond was less than six feet deep, but everyone was so drunk they couldn't figure up from down. Good riddance! They were just as mean and no good as their son; even Sam's mother was a fall-down drunk. Who knew? Maybe it was the only way she could cope. Jade was glad she'd never had to find out and at this point she certainly didn't care. Whoever and whatever Sam's parents were, they had produced a man like Sam, and the girls were not interested in finding out what had made him so mean. There was no excuse and the girls wouldn't give the memories of their grandparents any more thought.

"Money will never be a problem. I get my one third of our grandparent's estate and full access to the interest of yours and Amber's." Jade looked at Crystal. "Dad doesn't know any of that yet and if we're lucky he never will. He'd have a shit fit and we'll all be dead if he finds out. Mom told me that once I become of age, if she's not around, control of the money will go directly to me, and so Dad will be penniless without me. He thinks he can have access to Amber's share as her guardian, but he doesn't know that when I turn twenty-one I become her official guardian as well as yours. If we die everything goes to Dad and I think he's capable of anything! I will never feel safe if he finds out I have control of all the money. When he does, we're all in danger." Jade never doubted Sam would become dangerous if he felt he would lose the income from her grandparents' money. If she and her sisters were to die, Sam would get it all. That was at least a million reasons that Jade needed a plan and now!

"But how are we going get rid of Dad? I sure don't want to keep the asshole in the basement; I'd rather bury him in the backyard. But then again I've watched too many movies. When the bones turn up, someone discovers the body."

Jade's big blue eyes reflected her added concern about getting caught. If they locked Sam up or killed him, either way, they couldn't afford to get caught. Who would care for Amber if anything happened to the two of them? Murder was not out of the question but how would they be able to find a foolproof way of getting rid of the body? "The details will have to wait; we've got to handle Mom's burial. Dad says he doesn't give a damn, so it's up to us. We're all she ever had and she stayed to protect us.

Mom took his threats seriously and I know killing us would be easy if he thought we would leave him, or if he finds out the details of the will."

Jade moved toward the dressing table that sat off to the side of the bedroom window. The window was still closed, and although the day was much cooler than yesterday, it was still a little stuffy. Jade would open the window later after her dad was asleep. It was one thing to think of running away, but murder? Could they really do something deadly to their dad? Jade didn't think they could. That meant they would have to come up with another plan to run away, but what about Amber? How would they take care of her? Even with money it would be unlikely they could if they were on the run.

CHAPTER ELEVEN

Dennis and Veronica sat at their kitchen table. It was a beautiful warm August morning. It had only been yesterday that Dennis and Veronica had been over at the Walker house to help out the girls. Late Sunday evening Detective Tilley had called to say that the coroner had ruled that the death was accidental and the case was closed. But not for the girls who lived in the now motherless home; nor for the two concerned friends who sat and drank their morning coffee only a few doors down the street. Veronica was visibly upset, her large, slightly plump body trembling with anger.

"I don't care what anyone says!" Veronica's rich voice carried throughout the kitchen. "He killed her. He might as well have pushed her down the stairs himself. She was so frail and underweight." Veronica continued as she got up for a second cup of coffee; "If she was sick with the flu like the girls said, then his negligence caused it. Either way he should be charged. He's the meanest man I've ever met." Veronica's voice was getting louder. "I've often thought we would hear of some disaster at that house. It was only a matter of time." She sat back down, taking a sip of coffee and nudging Dennis for a response.

Dennis was always slow to voice his thoughts. It drove Veronica crazy waiting for his slow, deliberate answer. There was a part of him that was always amused by his overly dramatic wife as she waited impatiently for his answer. But today he nodded his assent quickly. "I know. There's been so little I could do over the years." Dennis held his coffee cup in a tight grip. "I've stayed in touch with other officers who have had to respond to calls of violence at the Walkers' over the years, and no matter how often she was hospitalized, Jewell never let us charge Sam. She was so scared that the charges would not hold, putting Sam in a murderous rage that might end her life. And who would protect her babies? She just put up with the beatings; the lesser of two evils."

Dennis stroked his moustache, a familiar habit whenever he was deep in thought. "Who can blame her? We fail a lot of women who are abused by their lovers or husbands, and things usually get worse. It's the hardest part about being a cop; knowing that you can't always keep people safe."

Veronica stared at her husband for a moment, noting his square jaw flexing back and forth. His grey-blue eyes were fixed at a spot on the table somewhere in front of him, his toast untouched. It was another sign of his personal involvement in this case. Veronica knew it was because of his paternal feelings toward the girls. The love for his own two daughters, Natasha and Katrina, made him especially vulnerable whenever kids were involved. Both girls were now grown, each happy with fulfilling careers. Katrina had just started real estate with RE/MAX while Natasha was building a successful clientele at the shop with Veronica. Tasha had completed an honors degree in Slavic language, but with the fall of the "Wall" in East Berlin and the dismantling of communism, the murder and crime spree that followed made going to Russia as a business attaché no longer safe. Both girls were dating brothers, Carlin and Steve; kind, intelligent boys who came from a great family. Steve's father was a doctor while his wife raised all four children and followed her passion of photography. It was hard to picture what it would feel like if either girl had married someone like Sam Walker.

"Let's take them something more to eat. They must be out of the food we took yesterday. No one should cook at a time like this." Veronica slid out of her chair and went over to the fridge. "I have several casseroles that are fresh, some pies, and fresh bread. At least this will help a little." Veronica's solution for many of life's problems was solved with good food.

"Good, it will give me an excuse to go over and check in on the girls." Dennis replied. He picked his empty coffee cup and untouched toast, slipped it off the plate into the garbage, and put the dishes in the dishwasher. "I don't like the thought of the girls being alone with Sam. I don't trust him in more ways than one. I guess I've just seen too much."

Veronica thought of the years Dennis had spent on the force and knew that in a city like Chicago you saw or heard it all. Murder, robberies, and drug-related crimes were taken in stride, but when it came to rape, domestic violence, or the abuse of a child, it made Dennis fume. Veronica knew that as a cop it was always hard to deal with these types of crimes, but as a father, Dennis was never sure what side of the law he would end up on. This added to the worry about the Walker girls and the judge's missing daughter. This new case was going to prove difficult, but Dennis knew he would stay involved in the Walker case; it was his obligation as a father as well as a cop.

* * *

Veronica showered first; it always took her longer to get ready. Once in the master bedroom she looked around. The green and wine colors of the comforter and drapes were both masculine and feminine; it was her favorite room. A huge, king-sized bed dominated the room. It looked like a picture out of *House Beautiful*; several floral pictures were arranged on the wall above the bed along with a huge floral bow done in wines, pinks, and several shades of green. On either side of the bed, hanging floral baskets drew attention to a

headboard that supported a variety of matching pillows and cushions, making the bed look like something from the movies. A large TV sat along the wall opposite the bed, with a high back chair in one corner.

This was the place Dennis would go to watch his favorite programs whenever Veronica was working in the salon. He found that the women got so loud the only way he could hear his programs was when he was at the back of the house in his bedroom. Large patio doors opened onto a deck where an oversized hot tub sat overlooking a spectacular back yard.

This was one of Dennis and Veronica's favorite things to do any time of the day whenever they wanted to relax. The hot tub was a great place to get together at the end of a long day, share a glass of wine, and discuss the day's events. Once out of the tub they would inevitably find themselves in bed for a round of lovemaking. Veronica took a good look at her ample body in the bedroom mirror and gave a sigh. It would be nice if she could take off a few extra pounds, but after a thousand diets with no results, she had given up and accepted the fact that not everyone is meant to be skinny.

Dennis had never once made a comment on her weight, he always seemed to love her just the way she was. Only once in all of the years that they were married did Veronica ever feel as if he had stopped loving her. As it turned out things were bad.

Dennis had almost gotten himself involved with another woman. It had taken a great deal of love and patience to work things out. After thirty years of marriage and two daughters, throwing all of that away seemed stupid to the strong-minded Veronica. After a year of counseling, things were better than they had ever been and Veronica was determined to never take life for granted again.

Veronica went into the closet and took out an Easy-Wear outfit of bright blue cotton. The day was going to be hot once again and Veronica loved the fit and feel of the lightweight fabric. Besides, it had a Velcro waistband that would allow her to find just the right comfort level. Her hair was easy to do; just wash and style and let dry naturally. Veronica would do her makeup while Dennis showered.

With the cleanup finished and Veronica almost ready, Dennis went to his bedroom to change out of his housecoat. A quick shower and he would take less than twenty minutes to get ready. He picked a new gray suit from his closet along with a freshly dry cleaned, crisp white shirt, and a black and red striped tie. Dennis's black loafers shone like the new leather seats in a Lexus and he smelled almost as good. Everything Dennis wore looked like money.

Once dressed, he thought about his day. First he would check in on the Walker girls and then he would meet Chuck and continue with the search for Mandy, the judge's daughter. Dennis felt a strong need to protect the Walker girls. They would have to handle everything with Jewell gone. Sam was useless and Dennis was sure he wouldn't lift a finger to help them with their mother's funeral. Maybe there was something he and Veronica could do to help.

As they walked over to the Walker house they were silent. Nothing more could be said about the incident and now they would have to try to keep the girls safe.

Dennis knocked on the back door of the Walker home. He knew that the family was usually gathered at the back of the house.

"Do you think the girls are home?" Veronica asked after waiting for a few minutes with no results.

"I can't imagine that they have anywhere to go. Jewell has always stayed close to home in order to protect them. I'm sure Jade and Crystal have taken it upon themselves to protect Amber. I know Jade is twenty-one at the end of the month and Crystal is already eighteen, although they look so much younger. With Sam as a father they never felt safe leaving their mother. It's a "Catch 22," Jewell stays to protect the girls and the two older girls stay to protect their mom. Now they have to stay to protect

Amber. Will they ever have a way out?"

Veronica knew her husband was right. Jewell seldom left the house and even when she went for groceries she would have Amber in tow. Dennis knocked again, this time with a great deal more force.

"What the hell is all the fuss about?" Sam came to the door, still in his underwear and an old stained T-shirt.

"We came by to see how you and the girls are," Dennis answered still standing on the back step landing, Veronica at his side. "We thought you might like some baking and casseroles."

"Come on in. I could use some food. The girls can't cook worth shit, then again neither could Jewell. What you got there?"

"I have a casserole and some homemade bread. I also have a pan of brownies and an apple pie. The pie is frozen, but I could show Jade how to cook it." Veronica stepped past Sam and put the food on the kitchen counter.

"Jade's not here, she had to go and see to Jewell's funeral. The coroner released her body this morning and it was shipped over to Greenhill's. It's the closest funeral home," Sam said.

"I would have thought that you would have wanted to handle the arrangements for Jewell's funeral. After all, she was your wife," Dennis said sarcastically.

Sam gave Dennis a dirty look. A few years ago he might even have taken Dennis on in a fight, knowing Dennis's remark was a put down. He knew he couldn't beat Dennis, who was at least fifty pounds heavier and seven inches taller. So he backed off, giving Veronica a dirty look instead. "Why should I handle the arrangements? She never loved me – just the girls. She was their mother. Jade will be twenty-one next month so she might as well get used to making grown up decisions." Sam walked past Veronica and plopped down in his recliner.

"I'll be sure to let the girls know you dropped by," Sam said, dismissing Veronica and Dennis by turning up the TV to a blaring level.

They exchanged looks and let themselves out through the back door. As they walked back to their home, Veronica was bristling. As soon as she was out of earshot she launched into a tirade. "I can't believe Jade has to handle the arrangements for her mother's funeral. These girls have already endured too much and now this. I could just slap that man. If I could, I would call welfare and have the girls taken away. But I know they would be separated and I just couldn't do that to Jade, she loves her sisters."

Veronica was shouting and Dennis had to give her a look that said 'keep it down.' "All we can do is keep an eye on the girls, this won't be the last visit and maybe I can use some of my contacts to see if I can get the girls out of there. We might be able to get Jade as a guardian for the girls. Don't say anything to them until I check things out. They must feel desperate knowing that they are trapped alone with Sam. I hope they don't think about doing something rash like running away."

"I hope Jade is able to handle making the arrangements for Jewell's funeral. We will have to make sure we're there for her," Veronica said.

Dennis's thoughts turned to his schedule for the afternoon and what he had to do with his new case; all of the footwork needed to find Mandy. He knew that it had already been well over twenty-four hours, the mandatory window for an official disappearance report. Chuck, Dennis, and six other officers had divided up the names. The club manager had also given a list of the kids at the rave. Because they were all underage they had to give their names, addresses, and parents' phone number. The detectives had worked the case all of Saturday and it was now mid-Sunday morning. If she wasn't found he would be hard-pressed to find time to go to Jewell's funeral.

CHAPTER TWELVE

Jewell's funeral service was as depressing as her life had been. The only ones who attended were Dennis and Veronica Kortovich and their daughters, Natasha and Katrina, as well as Dennis's partner Chuck and his wife Shelley. Not one other person was present, making Dennis even more aware of how alone and dangerous it would be now for the girls without their mother. It was early Tuesday morning and four days had passed since Jewell's fall.

Jade, Crystal, and Amber were all dressed in black skirts. Crystal however, had traded in her black locks and grisly makeup for a fresh, clean look. The light tops they wore, given the heat of the day were as conservative as possible. It was a hot morning and the day promised to be another scorcher. The two older girls looked drawn and tired while Amber was fresh and as beautiful as a Dresden doll – she could neither feel the loss of her mother, nor appreciate the pain her sisters felt.

Natasha and Katrina had wanted to come to the funeral when they heard about Jewell's accident. Although they were both a lot older than the Walker girls, each felt a great deal of sympathy toward them. They had watched Jade, Crystal, and Amber grow up over the years and even though the girls had only spoken to each other once in a while, they were at least on casual terms. Natasha had always felt the Walker sisters were the prettiest little girls she had ever seen. Katrina could remember wanting to babysit her younger neighbors, but even though she offered, Jewell never accepted. Veronica had to make sure that Katrina didn't take it personally. Jewell never had anyone babysit her girls and after a while everyone knew the reason.

Jade looked around at those who had gathered at the funeral home to pay tribute to Jewell. They were outside in a large gazebo for the service. It would have held at least a hundred mourners, but today the gathering was very small. If Jade had been able to, she would have had only herself and her sisters. She smiled at Crystal and tightly held Amber's hand. Amber rocked gently in time with an unheard beat somewhere in the dark maze of her brain. Her eyes were fixed on an invisible presence.

Jade wondered if Amber saw an angel from another dimension. It was as if her body was on this physical plane while her eyes and ears beheld an invisible realm unheard or unseen by others. She smiled a radiant smile, eyes wide, her face a vision of beauty. Jade hoped it was Jewell's face she was smiling at.

Sam was absent from the funeral. He was at home; falling down drunk, rambling on about Jewell's dying on purpose, and too angry to attend.

Dennis and Veronica had offered the girls a ride, but Jade was insistent that she wanted to go with her sisters in the family van. They would stay a little longer at the funeral home. It was another sunny, hot August day and when the funeral was over the girls would stay at the gazebo before placing Jewell's ashes to rest in a niche. They were not anxious to let her go, nor to return home to the abuses of their father. Jade decided they would spend the afternoon in the sun with Jewell's ashes and remember her sweet strength and all that she had endured for them. This would be her sister's and her private moments and personal farewells. Greenhill's was a beautiful place to spend a last moment with a loved one.

* * *

"I can't believe that there are so few people attending the funeral," Veronica commented quietly to Dennis, not wanting anyone to hear.

"I know," Dennis said, keeping his voice low, nodding in agreement. "It seems strange that there is no one else there. I never saw a notice in the paper, but I assumed that I had missed it." Dennis whispered his explanation for the lack of mourners. "It shows how truly isolated the girls are."

There was no minister to officiate at the funeral, only the senior mortician, Derek Hanson. Dennis thought Derek looked like Ichabod Crane from the Disney cartoon *Sleepy Hollow*. Tall, very thin, pale, and bony, he looked like a walking cadaver. His face was long, almost horse-like and his buckteeth emphasized the horsy quality. His hands were unusually large for such a slight-looking man. His fingers were long and tapered, while the nails were short and well groomed. Derek's hair was pulled back into a small ponytail, a left-over look from the '80s. If he thought it was cool, he was certainly out of touch.

The only thing that saved him from being a caricature was his sparkling white shirt and well-tailored suit that fit to perfection. If you stood close by, he emitted a slight smell of formaldehyde mixed with his fragrance, Drakkar. The nasal quality of his mono-pitched voice sounded flat and mournful. The words of comfort that should have made everyone in the little group feel better, only sounded shallow and too rehearsed.

"May she rest in peace!" Derek finished, closing his prayer book, and he stood off to the side.

As the mortician's final words were spoken Dennis looked over at the Walker girls – their small faces were drawn and tired. There was a look of determination in the girls' eyes that made him feel as if he were looking at two young soldiers on their final mission. Dennis hoped their youthful resolve would pull them through whatever lay ahead and that they would do what was necessary to survive. Dennis would have killed the bastard if it were him; Samuel was the kind of guy few would notice missing. Veronica gripped his hand as if reading his mind. He felt a slight blush creep up his already colorful cheeks. She always could read him. He quickly pushed the thought from his mind and went over to give one final hug to the girls. "Are you sure you won't come back with us?"

Both girls shook their head back and forth. No.

"Well, if there is anything you need, let me know. I'll drop in from time to time and make sure you are alright," Dennis said.

"That goes for me too," Veronica added. "I'll make sure you have a few good meals until you are on your feet.

If you need any help in the kitchen you can come over or call."

Crystal was the first to respond with a small smile, and she stood up to give a gentle hug to Veronica. "Thanks, but we'll be just fine. We have really appreciated all that you have done so far, but we will manage on our own."

"Yes," Jade added. "We're all right. Dad will probably stay drunk. We know how to stay out of his way and I can cook a few good things. If you come by it will only make things worse for us. So please call first. If anything bad happens I promise I'll come and get you." She gave Veronica a reassuring look.

"You promise?" Dennis looked both girls in the eye, seemingly checking back and forth to make sure they understood he was really there for them.

"Absolutely!" was the answer given in unison from both girls.

A look passed between the girls that Dennis couldn't quite read. He sure the hell hoped they would be all right. "Okay, but you have to be sure to call if you need us," was his final response.

As he walked off with Veronica, leaving the girls at the outdoor pavilion of the funeral home, Dennis had a gut feeling that something bad was about to happen, and he knew his gut was always right. Would he be able to use his skills to keep the girls safe? He put the thought to the back of his mind. He still had to find Mandy, Judge Switzer's daughter.

CHAPTER THIRTEEN

Crystal and Jade watched everyone leave. Dennis gathered his family on either side of him, his arms enfolding his wife on one side while Katrina nestled into one arm, holding her sister's hand in the other. It was a sight that made her feel sad and lonely. Why couldn't Sam be like Dennis? It was a question that seemed to have no answer.

"Do you think Dennis will call before he comes over? Crystal asked Jade.

"I hope so. If he comes over at the wrong time it will be the worst thing that could happen. With what we have planned for Dad we will need to make sure no one comes around for a long time," Jade answered.

"Do you think everyone thought it was strange that no one attended the funeral?"

Jade had been adamant that the funeral home didn't put a notice in the paper. She remembered the argument she'd had with Derek Hanson.

* * *

"Miss Walker, it would be highly irregular to not have a notice in the paper. You will never be able to contact your family and friends by phone. A notice lets everyone know the details of the funeral without you having to go over it again and again. It will save you a great deal of pain and grief," Derek Hanson said.

Jade tried to move back a few inches as Derek approached her, but the carpet on the floor prevented the chair from moving back with ease. Derek sat on the edge of the desk directly in front of her, putting little distance between the two of them. Although Derek was impeccably dressed, she still got a creepy feeling from him. As he leaned forward to make his point, he put his cold, clammy hand on her knee. A shiver ran up Jade's spine and as Derek moved closer, Jade got a whiff of his cologne. The fragrance was familiar, but on Derek it had a slightly 'off' smell. There was a strong chemical order about him that made her stomach churn. Was it the smell or something more? She wanted to get the arrangements for the funeral over and get away from the overly helpful mortician.

"Look Mr. Hanson. We have no living relatives on either side and as far as friends go, my parents kept to themselves and had few friends. I don't think anyone would know who my mother even was even if they see the announcement in the paper." Jade tried to sound assertive as she leaned in trying to make things seem more intimate and friendly. "The last thing my sisters and I need are a bunch of do-gooders that come by just because they feel sorry for us. Please Mr. Hanson; we don't want anyone other than the few friends we will contact ourselves. You know what its like; a bunch of strangers all gawking around hugging and kissing us saying they're so sorry. We just can't take it. Please respect the fact that this is how we want it." Jade hoped she was giving him her most assertive look.

A slow smile crossed Derek's long, bony face. His lips slipped past his yellow teeth, spittle forming in the corners of his mouth as he spoke. "I understand completely. I lost my own parents several years ago. All I had left was my baby sister and now she too is gone." He turned around and pointed at a picture of a lovely young girl hanging on the wall behind him. The girl was no more than twelve or thirteen. Her copper-blond hair and blue eyes shone with promise and life.

Jade felt a momentary connection; the girl's face seemed familiar. Suddenly a chill passed through her body, but she shook it off, concentrating on the details at hand. Jade didn't know why, but she didn't feel safe around Derek Hanson. There was one quiet moment when Derek stared at her with his pale, cold, blue eyes, and she thought she saw a look that was much the same as a wolf's, when it's sizing up its prey to see if it will be an easy victim. It made her blood run cold. She almost wanted to say, *A penny for your thoughts,* but at that moment she felt she would be paying too much. Whatever he was thinking she probably was better off not knowing. The way he smelled, walked, and talked was almost like a comic book figure; not someone of flesh and blood. Jade could see him stalking some poor girl who was dumb enough to be nice to him. You always knew the mentally unbalanced types.

"I will respect your wish and let you handle it the way you want. Just remember, I'm here for you if you need anything, and I mean anything." His hands lingered on Jade's bare knee.

Jade had had to make the trip alone, leaving Crystal to care for Amber. They had never trusted Sam and their little sister would be unable to protect her-self should he decide to try something.

After the usual formalities Derek took Jade on a tour. "Greenhill's is a state of the art funeral home. Whether you want to bury or cremate your mother is up to you. We have several affordable packages either way," he said as he walked Jade through a room full of caskets.

"I would rather cremate my mother." Jade choked out her choice, trying to keep her emotions under control.

"I must confess I'm partial to cremation. It seems degrading to allow a loved one to decay in the ground. Ashes seem to hold the essence of the person. Once they find a beautiful new home in one of our designer urns the relatives seem so much happier. I think it adds a sense of beauty to the death of a loved one."

Jade suddenly felt a chill run through her spine. The thought of this man touching her beloved mother was more than she could bear, but it was too late to turn back now. The coroner had shipped the body to Greenhill's that morning at Jade's request.

Greenhill's was new, with every amenity needed to help console those who faced the loss of their loved ones. The colors on the walls were a soft pastel green, the carpets an understated floral of yellow, rose and mint, giving the room a feeling of spring; a time of renewal and new beginnings. When Derek first entered the waiting room and introduced himself, Jade had to hide what must have been a look of shock. His face was too long, almost like a mule's; skinny, bony, pale, and very creepy. She had the impression he would be happier in a dark, damp cell somewhere in an old castle, rather than in this modern bright building.

At the moment, she had a difficult task ahead of her so she brushed off her unkind thoughts and got to the business at hand. All she had was her dad's credit card. If Sam had his way he would put Jewell in a box in the backyard, the way you'd bury a pet; cheap, and out of sight. "I hope credit is alright. It's my dad's. But like I said, he couldn't be here." Jade didn't want to explain why and she left it up to Derek to presume he was too distraught to help with the arrangements.

Derek remained courteous, but cool throughout their dealings. "A credit card will be fine. I can understand how your father must be feeling. Losing someone you love can do terrible things to a man. I know from personal experience."

She was unable to read anything into Derek's statement, but she presumed he was referring once again to his sister, the pretty girl in the picture. Jade was able to pay a portion if she wanted and wait for the final bill. After assessing the modest needs of Jade's request, Derek was certain she would need very little beyond the basic package. With the business and money details handled, it was time for her to go on a tour of the establishment. She had to pick out an urn and see the mausoleum where Jewell's ashes would be kept. The first stop was to see the crematorium, a free-standing chamber that Derek seemed to be very pleased with.

"Here she is," Derek said a sloppy grin on his face.

The crematorium stood sleek and cold in the middle of the room, not the usual square, recessed ovens that she had seen on television. It reminded her of a huge time capsule, all shiny stainless steel, with black, cast iron molded bindings at the ends and the middle of the sleek chamber. This 'dark duchess of death' stood on an independently raised concrete pad in the middle of a beautiful room. The carpet that surrounded the concrete base was plush with a heavy pattern of large rose buds, complementing the leaf-green walls and heavily draped windows. Straight ahead, at the front of the room a small nook was visible. It was draped on either side by a heavy, brocaded material that matched the carpet. Within the nook sat a small, ornate desk with chairs on either side. The occupant could close the drapes for privacy or leave them pulled back on either side, making a picture-like frame for the delicate little room. Jade liked the look. It offered privacy, allowing the occupant to stay out of immediate sight.

"This is where we will cremate your mother's body," Derek said watching Jade's face to see if there was any reaction.

Jade almost cringed. It wasn't the words, but rather the sound of Derek's voice that grated on her already overly stressed nerves. It held a tone of evil, making the high-pitched nasal sound of his voice send shivers down her spine.

"To operate the crematorium is simple." Derek stepped to the front of the crematorium, obvious pride on his face. "We turn two dials in opposite directions, after we place the body directly in the center. Then secure the doorway with an airtight seal." His bony hands pulled the cast iron handle down. "There must be nothing in the way to break the seal or the master switch will refuse to engage. This is the only free-standing unit in the world and I invented it. Its double coils don't allow for any smoke to escape into the atmosphere. It is environmentally friendly, and it would go undetected anywhere because you don't need a smokestack. It's foolproof and any child could operate it." Derek seemed pleased, like a kid with a new toy. "The contents are reduced to a few ounces of ashes. They are then retrieved after the cooling process, after which we put them in a standard box and later transfer to the urn of your choice."

Once again, Derek watched Jade's face in a way that made her feel like she was under a microscope. It was as if he was trying to figure out something about her that seemed to have him puzzled. Jade was sure he didn't handle all of his clients like this. He was a creep. If she could have prevented her mother from being cremated by this man she would have. But life must move forward and she was there to make her mother's funeral arrangements with as little attention from the outside world as possible. There was no time to shop around for a different funeral home.

Derek went over to the chamber and demonstrated the door. Next he went over to the double dials off to the side of the large oval opening. He turned one dial counter-clockwise, the other clockwise. "In less than an hour it's all finished. The oven heats to over twenty-four hundred degrees. Like I said child's play."

The final comment caught Jade for the second time. In a flash she knew this might be a perfect way to deal with her 'problem.' If she was somehow able to have Sam cremated it would be the perfect way to get rid of a body. No body, no evidence, no crime! Jade refused to mull over the tiny seed of an idea any further – after all, she hadn't completely decided how to deal with Dad. And as of now, she didn't have a crematorium hanging around the backyard just for a time like this.

"You are the last appointment of my day." Derek came over and placed a hand on her shoulder. "With all of the details handled I think we can safely say we have covered just about everything. I'll just get my coat and see you to your car."

Jade would have loved to say no, she could see herself out, but she had no time. Derek was already a step ahead of her and reaching for his black trench coat. "Thank you," was all she was able to say.

Once outside the large, white, double doors of the funeral home, Derek paused in front of an electronic keypad. "You'll have to stand a little to the side please. We lock up with a punch code number, and I would prefer if you didn't watch," he said with a self-important air.

Jade moved a few steps to the left of the huge double doors.

"It's not personal, but for security only you understand."

As his finger reached out to press the numbers, Jade could hear the audible tones as each number was pressed. Each key gave off a different musical tone, each perfectly pitched. It was at that exact moment that Jade knew she could get away with murder and no one would ever find out. It would be her little sister Amber whose gift would hold the key.

CHAPTER FOURTEEN

Sam's head hurt like it had never hurt before. It wasn't the dull ache that came most mornings before his usual morning beer. No, this pain was searing and hot. It came from a place in the back of his skull. The kind of pain you would feel if someone smacked you over the head with a baseball bat. He tried to move, he wanted to gather his bearings. He felt strangely disorientated. *What the fuck?* he thought. He couldn't move. His arms were bound tightly behind his back, and his shoulders were restrained as well. When he looked down at his chest he saw the gray duct tape wound tightly around the upper portion of it. His legs were also restrained. When he tried to lean forward for a better look, he almost choked. The rough fibers of a rope dug into his throat. Sam was able to lean back a little and gaze up. As he tilted back slightly, he recognized the black rubber tubing of an infant's jolly jumper. The hook secured tightly into the doorway frame, leading downstairs into the basement.

The chair Sam was sitting on was the old white chair that was usually in the bathroom. He had to blink a few times to clear his vision. For a moment he felt as if he would black out. He was startled by the sensation that he was about to fall backwards. It was then that he realized his tenuous predicament. He had a noose around his neck and his feet and hands were bound tightly, while he sat on an old rickety chair that was precariously balanced on two legs. Any sudden movement could send him crashing down the steep basement stairs. He found out only too quickly that if he leaned too far forward the noose around his neck would tighten, causing him to choke and gag. "There must be a robbery taking place, and the bastards must have tied me up," Samuel thought aloud. The memory escaped him; he couldn't remember a thing. It all seemed very professional – he was totally at someone's mercy, although at this point he couldn't see or hear a soul. At that exact moment, he heard the front door open. The voices he heard were not strangers'.

Thank goodness! Sam thought, relief spreading over his tired, sore body. "Girls!" he shouted. "Get over here, I need help!" Sam had to make sure he didn't move too far forward or back. "Where are you? Fuck! Get me outta here."

Jade looked at Crystal, her heart racing. The thumping in her chest felt like someone was punching her from the inside. Crystal's face looked pinched and full of determination. Jade knew that once Crystal made her mind up there would be no turning back. There was a part of Jade that still held a small hope that their dad could somehow redeem himself – maybe he could still say something to help her understand his deplorable behavior.

With Sam tied up, it gave the girls a sense of security. Crystal was the one who had come up with the idea of the jolly jumper and putting the chair at the top of the basement stairs; the place where her mother had fallen to her death. As they rounded the corner they were surprised to see the look of excitement and hope on their father's face. Neither girl could remember him ever having more than an evil scowl or being in a twisted temper tantrum, causing his face to distort.

"Thank God you're here. Hurry, untie me before they come back."

"Who?" Jade asked, not understanding what her dad was saying.

"The guys who tied me up, stupid!" Sam looked at Jade as if she were missing a few brain cells.

It was at that second that Jade figured it out. Sam thought someone had broken into the house and tied him up. Boy, was he in for a big surprise!

"There are no guys, Dad, it was us. We tied you up." Jade's statement was said so matter of factly, that Sam still didn't get it.

"You tied me up?" he repeated.

"Yes," Crystal answered.

"What the fuck for?" he shouted. "Let me go, for fuck's sake!" He struggled in the chair, but once again he began to choke.

"We can't do that, Dad." Jade's reply was soft.

"You sluts untie me now or when I get out of this chair you won't be able to walk for a week, I'll beat you so bad." Sam began to spit as he screamed at them, his face getting redder as he tried to shuffle in the chair without falling back.

Crystal exploded. "You stupid, mean old man! Do you think you're going to get out of that chair and ever lay a hand on us again? Not ever, ever, ever!"

Sam shut up, but only for a moment. "You can't keep me tied up like this, I'm your father. So stop this shit and let me go." He leaned a little too far forward after this speech and started to choke once again.

"Don't worry, Dad. We don't intend to keep you tied up for long. We're going to kill you. You haven't given us any other choice. It's you or us. Amber needs us, so it's got to be you."

At this point Jade was glad that Amber was upstairs in her rocking chair. She wouldn't leave her chair until one of the girls came to get her.

"Why? What have I ever done to hurt you?" Sam's face was pale. You could tell by his small, sneaky eyes that he was trying to figure out what to do next.

"What have you ever done to us?" Crystal repeated the question in a voice that sounded like fingernails across a blackboard. "Where should I begin?" she shouted, shaking her hands in the air in exasperation. "Let's start with you beating our mother for the past twenty years. Or maybe you're foul-mouthed ranting and raving. The slaps and punches across the head every day. The kicks and shoves if we didn't move out of your way fast enough. Or maybe the dirty little remarks made towards us and the inappropriate touching." Crystal started to choke. "Maybe it's just because you're a no-good sack of shit! Don't look at me that way; I learned all the foul mouthed stuff from you." Crystal's face was now only inches away from Sam's.

Sam's inability to move only fueled his anger. So when he spit in Crystal's face she was shocked. She slammed her fist into Sam's mouth as hard as she could, the full weight of her small body put into the punch. Sam's chair tilted precariously at the top of the stairs. The rope that was suspended from the rubber cord tightened around his neck, and the choking sounds weren't wasted on the girls.

"Just remember, you're in no position to push us around, or piss us off any more than we are already." Crystal spat back in Sam's face, wiping some of the dribble from her chin. Sam's spit was already smeared into her copper curls.

Jade moved forward. It was time to get things over. If anyone came to the door, Sam would be able to shout out for help. Jade lowered her face to her father's putting her hand over his mouth. "Don't!" she said, "or I'll kick you down these stairs."

When Jade removed her hand Sam gathered as much spit as he could in his mouth and spewed it out in full force. After the warm wad landed on Jade's face, he shouted out with all the hatred he felt. It wasn't personal; he hated everyone. "You little slut, I'll kill you when I get free. I'll slit your fucking throat!" Once again he almost choked, forgetting his precarious perch as he leaned a little too far forward.

That's it, Jade thought. *It's time to end it all.*

She kicked at the legs of the chair as hard as she could, breaking one of the spindly legs at the halfway point. The chair started to buckle, pitching back. Sam tried to stop the chair from falling down the stairs by putting his full weight forward, which allowed the rope that was attached to the rubber tube to tighten around his throat. With his eyes wide he teetered at the top of the stairs for a few seconds. It looked like he would be able to steady himself, and he sat holding his breath choking back tears of pain and fear. The chair balanced precariously on its three legs. It was a very old chair, cheap and worn. Even on its best day it was never really strong. Suddenly a second leg cracked. Time seemed to slow down as the leg buckled. The chair crashed completely under Sam's weight and although he wasn't a big man, his full weight caused the rope that was suspended by the jolly jumper to tighten completely around his skinny neck. Jade and Crystal instinctively moved toward each other. It was something they'd always done when things started to go wrong between Sam and their mother. This was different, though. Their hearts beat together in an off-beat rhythm that kept pace with the sound of Sam's thrashing, as he tried to find some ground to steady himself. It was impossible.

With the chair still taped to his body, he struggled fiercely at his awkward position, twisting as hard as he could, hoping the tape would break. His ankles were secured to the two remaining legs of the chair. As his body arched awkwardly forward, the rope from the jolly jumper cut into his flesh, and as the full weight of his body pulled him down, his head bounced a little from the elasticity of the cord. He fought back the choking feeling as he instinctively pulled back. That final movement was all that was needed to break the last two legs of the flimsy old chair. Sam now hung fully by his neck. He was not a big man, only five feet two inches and about one hundred and thirty pounds, but even so, his weight was too much. The door-jamb suddenly gave way, causing him to tumble backward with a force so intense he flew over the first few stairs, tumbling heavily down the remaining steps.

The girls watched, still holding each other tightly as Sam tumbled head over heels down the basement stairs, landing on the cold concrete floor where Jewell had landed, almost exactly a week before.

Sam's body didn't look nearly as twisted as their mother's had after the accident, and both Jade and Crystal stood transfixed at the top of the stairs, not knowing what to do next. It seemed like forever before anyone spoke, but as usual it was Crystal who made the first move.

"Now what?" was all Crystal could whisper. The fact that they had actually done it was just sinking in. "Do you think we really killed him?"

"I can't tell. It's so dark at the bottom of the stairs and I'm almost afraid to turn the lights on." Jade quivered, still holding Crystal tightly.

Crystal was trembling as she pried Jade's fingers from her upper arm and then her own fingers awkwardly found the light switch. Sam lay perfectly still at the bottom of the steps. The only sound they could hear was the beating of their hearts and the ragged off-beat sound of breathing. They couldn't tell if Sam was contributing to the soft swish of their breaths. They would have to descend the stairs to the basement below to find out if he was indeed dead. Jade seemed unable to move, so Crystal took the first tentative steps toward their father.

He now lay at the bottom of the stairs, the rubber cord still hanging awkwardly around his neck. Crystal could tell from her view at the top of the stairs that Sam's face was a twisted mask of hate. Slowly, step-by-step, she put each tiny foot firmly on each descending stair. She hesitated for a few seconds as she continued, trying to make sure her footing was secure. Crystal felt a wave of nausea hit her in the pit of her stomach and her knees felt weak. After what seemed to take forever she finally stopped two steps away from her father. 'Daddy Dearest!' What was that movie she had watched? Some movie star, that was mean to her kids, but she didn't even compare to her dad, funny how at a time like this you would think of some stupid old movie. Crystal noticed that the banister had been broken by Sam's fall.

Her hand found a small portion of the railing still loosely attached to the crumbling drywall. She instinctively latched on to it, pulling it from the wall. She was now only one step away from the cold cement floor where Sam lay unceremoniously. She lifted the broken portion of the ragged wood high over her head and brought it down on Sam's head. She could hear the crack of the deadly tool as it connected with his skull. *One more time for luck,* she thought as she went for a second whack. A small trickle of blood had formed under Sam's skull. Crystal was pretty sure he was dead.

"That's for the movies!" Crystal said. Her voice sounded confidant, even a little smug. As she marched up the stairs she looked up at Jade who stood on the landing, looking stunned.

"What did you think?" an annoyed Crystal declared. "That I haven't seen a few movies where the guy isn't really dead? I always thought it was stupid when the girl just stepped over or around him and then he grabs her. I only did what anyone with a few brains would have done. Made sure he was really dead." She looked back over her shoulder at Sam's broken body. "He won't be getting up for a second round!" Crystal's fears had been completely overcome by that final, personal act of liberation.

Jade smiled weakly at her younger sibling. God help anyone who messed with Crystal. Tears welled up in her eyes. Too bad Jewell wouldn't be there to join in. Suddenly a feeling of great calm descended over Jade.

When she looked over at her sister's determined face, she could tell Crystal felt something too. Maybe their mother was there. Tonight they would set an extra plate and celebrate their freedom. The spirit of Jewell would always be with them. They had finally done what their mother had dreamed of for years. Sam would no longer be able to terrorize them. They would now be able to live the life Jewell had prayed for, but only if they could get away with murder.

CHAPTER FIFTEEN

Dennis was staring at a stack of files of faces of young girls that had gone missing over the past seven years and had yet to be found. There were dozens of girls who had gone missing over the past ten years, similar to Mandy Switzer. Dennis's request for more information on missing teen girls had yielded dozens more, but these particular girls were different. They were all honor students with many friends and good families. Dennis hoped that he and Chuck could come up with something that might link Mandy's disappearance with one of them, thus providing them a lead. It had taken both Dennis and Chuck the better part of a week to get profiles on all of the missing girls, in order to narrow the list down into profiles similar to Mandy's. The girls who remained on the list appeared to be well-adjusted teens who had only gone out for a night of fun.

So far, Chuck and Dennis had followed every available lead that could help establish what might have happened to Mandy. No one had seen or heard from her since the night of the rave and with each passing hour, Dennis knew Mandy's chance of being found was growing dimmer. It was now Wednesday and Mandy had been missing since Friday. The time lapse was too big to ignore, and the chances of Mandy being found alive were now very slim. Judge Switzer was calling morning, noon, and night, and who could blame him? His only daughter seemed to have disappeared into thin air. Dennis knew that the total disappearance of a young woman usually meant foul play. Whoever was responsible for taking Mandy on the night of the rave would likely not have any ties to her. Dennis had no idea if they would get a lead that could help them to find Mandy safe and sound. Hard work and determination was all he had to offer at this point.

Dennis had gone to the office to pick up the files on the girls. Chuck and his new wife, Shelley McPherson, a medical examiner for Cook County, would be joining Veronica and him for supper tonight. He wanted to take the files home to review them again and see if maybe Shelley and Veronica could help shed some light on the investigation. Sometimes, a fresh set of eyes could see things that may have been overlooked.

Shelley was brilliant; she had a way of interpreting information in a file that was both analytical and precise. Veronica, on the other hand, offered a more unconventional view. It was as if, right out of thin air, she could come up with some idea that at first might seem a little off the wall. But often, Veronica's weird way of looking at things could deliver a small gem of an idea that led Dennis and Chuck to a new twist in an investigation. Several times over the past many years, difficult cases had been solved after Veronica gave her assessment of the case. Her flashes of brilliance often came from listening to her early morning radio shows that covered everything from aliens, the Bilderbergers, government cover-ups, past lives, and every conspiracy theory and strange plot that involved secret societies.

Veronica's many talents, her singing, and her many stories made her quite the attraction at cocktail parties. Dennis was grateful that her humor and charm could get her through the raised eyebrows and condescending smiles. Good solid detective work always laid the foundation of any case, but inspiration, although only one percent is often the catalyst needed to bring an investigation to an end. When it came to inspiration, Veronica had her share of it and then some. Her ability to think outside the box often made her helpful. Actually, Veronica never thought inside the box.

Chuck had yet to see the many files that Dennis had reviewed. He and the other detectives had been busy all week doing follow-up with Mandy's circle of friends. Whenever Dennis thought of Chuck, he'd send up a silent prayer of thanks for his partner and friend. Dennis was grateful to have found a partner with just as much personality as brains. That made his job a lot more exciting than it would be if he hadn't been lucky enough to find a guy like Chuck. Chuck was a lot different than the analytical Dennis, who liked to follow the rules. Chuck would be willing to bend a rule or two and his cockeyed way of looking at the world had yielded some interesting results on the many cases in which he had been involved. Dennis had decided that when Chuck had a hunch, if he had to open a locked door or tell a white lie to get a confession, then so be it, Dennis would let him take the lead. Bend – don't break.

Chuck, although the same age as Dennis, had many years of seniority in areas that Dennis had yet to experience. After a decade on Gang Crimes as well as five years in Intelligence and then Narcotics, Chuck was one of the most experienced detectives assigned to Area Three. Now with homicide, Dennis was the lucky guy who got Chuck as a partner.

Chuck knew everyone personally; a career in the Chicago P.D. still seemed to be traditionally Irish although not as much as at the turn of the century. Being an Irish cop in Chicago meant that the word 'brotherhood' had roots a lot deeper than it would for a guy like Dennis, with almost no roots to speak of. Many of Chuck's family, both past and present, had grown up as members of Chicago's finest throughout the years. Dennis felt closer to the other officers because of Chuck. The thing that made the partnership work was that together they created balance. Chuck was the kind of cop to rush in where 'devils fear to tread' although with his innocent face he didn't look like a dare-devil. Often Chuck would want to take action, while Dennis always looked ahead and noticed every small detail in a millisecond, summing up the situation before making a move. Chuck's real name was Charles Patrick O'Brien the Third. At a young age his favorite show was *The Rifleman* and the name of the star was Chuck. From then on, he wouldn't let anyone call him Charles or Charlie, only Chuck. And when it came to loading a gun and taking a quick shot, Chuck was the best. "Lock and load" was his mantra. The last case had been unforgettable and Dennis, Chuck, and Shelley were glad was over, but it had been Veronica who accidentally came up with the idea that inspired Dennis, thus solving the case. It was while working to solve that killing spree that Chuck and Shelley had initially been brought together. They'd often had supper at Dennis's home, but just as friends. Shelley's work as a medical examiner also put them together professionally. It was Shelley's lack of luck with men that finally brought them together on a personal level. Several really bad dates, to say the least; one with a stalker, another with the serial killer, had made Shelly realize that a nice guy like Chuck would make for a better, more solid partner. Dennis smiled, thinking of how much he loved the two of them. They were perfect for each other.

Dennis put the files of the missing girls into a large brief case. A little brainstorming wouldn't hurt. He laughed at the thought of the interesting evening that lay ahead as he walked through the pit, where three other officers were sitting at their desks, working on cases of their own. As Dennis walked by, one of the officers looked up from his desk and gave him a smirk. He turned his swivel chair toward Dennis and spread his long legs out in front of him, preventing Dennis from passing.

"How are things going with the Switzer case?' Juan Sosa asked, his Spanish accent still heavy, even though he had lived in Chicago for over thirty years.

Juan was the kind of cop that made you think of Geraldo Rivera. He always seemed to be looking for an angle or a way to sensationalize any case he seemed to be working on that might catch the media's attention. Dennis, over the years had become the media's darling. Dennis's ability to speak to the press and seemingly give his cooperation without compromising a case made the upper brass sit up and take notice. Over the years he and

Chuck had been assigned the cases that were known to draw media attention, making Dennis and Chuck police celebrities; something that seemed to tick Sosa off.

"No real leads so far," Dennis answered curtly.

"It's almost been a week. By now I figured you would have tied this case up. Maybe you're slipping. If you need help you can always ask me. Don't be shy. You're not the only one who can pull a trump card out of his ass, even though the superintendent thinks you walk on water."

"I'll keep that in mind the next time I'm in hot water and I feel that I need your help. Mind you, if that stack of files on your desk is any indication of how well you solve your cases, I would think you might need my help." Dennis nodded toward the huge pile of files on Sosa's desk.

Dennis knew only too well that in one's yearly review, the number of cases that you solved compared to how many you were assigned, set your reputation amongst the other detectives and police personnel. Dennis and Chuck's rate of solved cases was the highest on the force, while Sosa lagged far behind. Dennis knew the remark would hit home. Dennis stood in silence for a few seconds while Sosa scowled at him, unable to think of a response. Sosa turned back to his desk and grabbed a file from the top of the large pile, indicating that the conversation was over.

On the drive home Dennis wondered if Sosa was right. Would he be able to find Mandy in time? He doubted he would; a week was much too long. If he didn't get a break soon he would be willing to ask the devil himself for help. Dennis smiled at the thought. He held no such belief in a devil or a god. Strange how at the times in his life when he felt his back was to the wall, he was willing to pray to some unknown entity and bargain his way out of trouble.

CHAPTER SIXTEEN

As Dennis approached the driveway of his home on Wood Street, he noticed that Chuck's SUV was already parked out front of his home. *Shit,* he thought as he looked at the time on his car clock. *I'm late, oh well!* It wouldn't be the first time and Veronica was a great hostess.

"Hey, everyone!" Dennis shouted as he entered the back door that led to the family room. "I'm home."

"In here, sweetheart!" replied Veronica from the kitchen. "We were about to start without you. We're starving."

Dennis chuckled. The one thing Chuck and Veronica would never do was starve. Both were food obsessed and it showed. Chuck was a solidly built guy with a big round face that given a little time would make him begin to look like a Santa Claus stand-in. His full head of hair was already beginning to show signs of graying at the temples. Chuck's bright-red complexion shone out under a full beard that although dark, would one day turn silver. Once gravity got a hold of his chest and sunk it below his belt, he would make a fine St. Nick. His nature was jovial, upbeat, and full of laughter and it only added to his overall impression. At fifty, he was a solid guy who was the best partner Dennis ever had.

Then there was Veronica. Still beautiful, but as always, fighting an ever-losing weight problem; one she was destined never to win. The extra pounds only added to her sense of power and presence. Ever the entertainer, she seldom missed the chance to be the center of attention. Her wit, charm, and intelligence made her a star at any gathering, small or large. No, Dennis decided. Neither would starve.

"I don't think you two will waste away just yet, and besides I'm only twenty minutes late, so no guilt!" Dennis hugged Veronica, and slapped Chuck on the back as he came into the kitchen.

Shelley, Chuck's wife's, smiled up at him, as she seemingly read his thoughts, giving him a conspiratorial wink; one neither Chuck nor Veronica witnessed.

Shelley was one of those girls whose figure didn't look any different twenty years and one child later. Her freckled face and turned-up nose made her look perpetually young. Shelley would never get fat or grow old, a fact that made most of her friends, curse her great genetics.

"I hope that after we eat a quick supper, especially so that you two don't waste away to nothing, I can get some insight from the great minds that are gathered at my humble table," Dennis said with a laugh. "But seriously, we need some help with Mandy's case and quick. I think time has run out and I can't bear the thought of telling Judge Switzer that we've hit another dead end."

Being a cop in Chicago, a city of color and with a diverse reputation, meant everyone had a different opinion of the police; some good, most bad, depending on who you asked. From the city's beginnings, Chicago's association with organized crime and the likes of Al Capone left many of its good citizens feeling that city officials, as well as the cops and legal system, were often in bed with the very disreputable but colorful citizens that they were supposed to be putting behind bars. This distrust continued to be a major stumbling block to the police department. Even with many attempts to dispel those fears, it was still a hard sell. Especially with the many scandals the city had to endure.

One scandal in particular that got Dennis's attention was the Dianne Masters murder in 1982, around the time that he had joined the force. Although it was a case that took place outside of the city proper, it still intrigued Dennis.

Dianne had been a stunning blonde whose disappearance kept the press and public speculating for years whether or not her husband, a successful attorney with known police and underworld connections, was guilty of her murder. The most bizarre part of the case was just how deep the corruption of the police and legal system went, and who was in bed with whom.

When her body was finally found; in an underwater dumping ground that was well known to many a dirty cop, and in the years of investigation that followed, political blood flowed freely through the streets. The reputation of many of suburban Chicago's cops was under a light that showed just how raw the underbelly of the city really was. With all the Grand Jury Investigations in Chicago during the early to mid-eighties, it was widely believed that the monkeys in the city's zoo could do a better job than the cops. At least the monkeys could be paid off with bunches of bananas, rather than the wads of cash that were needed to pay off dirty cops.

It was rumored that if you wanted a criminal case to go away, all you had to do was hire Allan Masters. Pay enough cash and presto – Allen could get anything to disappear. The problem was he had to pay everyone along the way, all the way to the top. Depending on the charge, you had to pay cops, clerks, attorneys, and judges. No one was exempt from the graft. It was rumored that the local police 'helped' many of the clubs that were involved in prostitution, simply by turning a blind eye and collecting a few bucks for doing so. Allan Masters had a hand in many of those operations. The question on everyone's mind during the first few years after Dianne's body was found was whether or not Allan could make a person disappear by himself or if he had help.

It was during this time that Dennis had joined the force, the fulfillment of a boyhood dream. It was also during this time that Dennis got a good look at the world of good cop/bad cop. In Chicago when kids played cops and robbers, it was difficult to tell the good guys from the bad. Very often in real life, the cops were the robbers. In the early 'eighties, many of the good cops found it hard to face the negative press coverage that seemed to pervade the entire force. A few of the police that were indicted over the next several years were friends of Dennis's and close to many of the officers. The cops that managed to stay clean felt tainted and betrayed by the corrupt high profile cases, especially the Masters murder.

One cop in particular, Sgt. John Reed, stood out at the time for Dennis. He and his partner turned out to be good cops, the sort of police officers that can give a profession back its pride and reputation. Homicide detectives Sgt. John Reed and Paul Sabin, under the direction of Thomas Scorza, a federal prosecutor, were assigned to the Masters case. It was now 1986; four years after Dianne's body had been pulled up from her watery grave. The case seemed to have gone cold, mostly due to what seemed like sloppy police work. John Reed's reputation was one of the best in the Chicago Suburbs. Like most of the players in the Masters case, John grew up on the south side and knew all of the people involved on all sides of the law. Reed's involvement was unofficial and he did most of the investigation on his own time. It had taken thousands of hours, patience and good solid police work, but eventually the case was cracked. Allen Masters was put behind bars for a very long time, along with a few others who were identified.

Reed was a guy Dennis could relate to and everything about him made Dennis want to follow in his footsteps. At seventeen, Reed had almost become a priest. Lessons learned from childhood became the cornerstones of Reed's principals. As an Irish Catholic and former marine serving under the chaplain, Reed knew his duty to God and Country. It made him a great cop. Dennis liked his professionalism; every inch a cop, even in street clothes.

Reed was able to set an example for other officers without even knowing it. He and Sabin cracked the case even at the expense of the reputations of many police officers that were either directly involved in the Masters case or had helped stall many areas of the investigation. They won the admiration of the rest of the force. Over the next twenty years Dennis had tried to model himself after officers like Reed. Now Dennis enjoyed a similar reputation and there were many young rookies who watched *him,* hoping to be like him one day.

* * *

The meal Veronica served was one of her best. Her pork ribs could rival any southern BBQ-king. Slow cooked for several hours with brown sugar, garlic, chili, and a tangy hot sauce, the meat fell off the bone. It was the special sauce made from a tangy hickory smoke, and several secret ingredients that Veronica refused to share, which made for a mouth-watering, but rather messy meal that all four friends seemed intent on finishing to the last rib. Corn on the cob, potato salad, and a fresh apple crisp from apples of the tree in the back yard completed the feast. When all was said and done, the topic on everyone's mind was served up with hot gourmet coffee.

"Here's what we have so far," Dennis began, with little formality. "There have been over two dozen girls that have gone missing over the past seven years. They seem to have no reason for leaving; they were good students. Their parents had no problems with them, nor did they have any boys in their lives, and there were no drug or alcohol problems. Many of the girls had part-time jobs or volunteered for local community groups. Here are the dates they went missing." Dennis handed Veronica and Shelley a computer list. Chuck was sitting next to Dennis and he took the original list from Dennis to give it a look over. Chuck hadn't seen this part of the information yet.

"Wow! It seems that several of the girls went missing on one of two dates. One date is May the eleventh and the other November twenty-fourth. The last girl went missing November twenty-fourth and Mandy on the eleventh of this month, August," Chuck said simply, as he went over the printout.

"Let me see that list again," Dennis said excitedly as he lay down the files that had the same date; twelve in all. "Shit, you're right. And Mandy went missing in last week, August 12th. As did five other girls. It's six for six. The odds are against this many girls going missing on the exact same two dates are improbable. I should have noticed right away, but I was in a hurry to get home." Dennis smiled at Veronica. "Your cooking is a great motivator for not staying at the office."

"I agree there is little chance that this is a coincidence," Shelley added.

"Let's pull the files of the girls that went missing on these two dates and see if there is anything else they have in common," Chuck said to Dennis.

Dennis pulled the large briefcase out from under the kitchen table. Within a few minutes he had the files spread out on the table, placing the pictures of the girls' faces up on the top of each file. By the time Dennis laid out the last file, the room went deadly silent. Finally, Veronica stood up and pulled several of the files closer to her, lining them up vertically with only the pictures showing.

"Do I have to paint a picture or do you see what I see?" she said softly.

Chuck went pale, a rare feat considering his high coloring and rosy cheeks. The familiar lock of unruly hair that never seemed to find its place fell over one bushy eyebrow. "Each one of these girls looks alike and they could all pass for Mandy's sister, except for this one," he said as he pulled one file from the rest.

The picture of that girl showed a large boned, good-looking brunette.

"Look at the other eleven. They all have blue eyes, copper, natural curly hair and are no more than fifteen. Shit, three of them were only thirteen. " Chuck looked up at Dennis with a grim look on his face.

"This isn't a coincidence. All of these girls were abducted just like Mandy. We may not have any conclusive proof, but it doesn't take a rocket scientist to figure out that these girls represent something to their abductor," Dennis mused.

"What makes you think that they were abducted? Maybe they went willingly," Veronica asked.

"If anyone of them went willingly, then there should be a common link for all of them. No one just walks away with a stranger, not this many times. Either they were taken against their will, or if they knew this person, he would have to be in their circle of friends or acquaintances. Chuck, we will have to interview the families of these girls starting first thing in the morning."

"I agree. I'll take the list and make appointments from home, and then I'll come and pick you up," Chuck replied.

"This means you two boys may have another serial killer," Shelley said as she slid her slim hand down the files over the lovely young faces of the girls.

"How do you know they're dead?" Veronica asked.

"It's been six years according to the date of the first abduction," Dennis said. "If any of these girls were alive someone would have heard from one of them by now, if they didn't run away. And that's what it looks like, someone took them. Few girls are abducted and not sexually assaulted. If so, they are likely dead and dead girls don't tell. Or the killer may have had a more sinister motive than sex. With all of the girls looking alike, our killer has some kind of psychosis around young, blue-eyed, copper haired girls. Maybe it's an obsession? Who knows what drives a man mad? I don't see how the brunette fits in. It may just be a coincidence that she was taken on one of the dates. Either way, this is the file we will start on. What makes her a part of this group?" Dennis pulled the file from the other eleven.

Mandy's file made an even dozen. The brunette was the only file that didn't add up and Dennis knew in his gut that this was the place to start. He looked over at Veronica's wide eyes; he could see the wheels in her head turning, so it was no surprise when she blurted out her final comment.

"If some bastard tried to take either Natasha or Katrina, heaven help him. I'd hunt him to the end of the earth and there wouldn't be a punishment in the world harsh enough to satisfy me. I'd flay him alive. How must it be for the families of these girls not to know what has happened to their precious daughters?" Veronica lowered her face into her hands, tears slipping down her clear, smooth skin onto the files.

Dennis moved the files and took one of Veronica's well-manicured hands into his, kissing her on the forehead before he spoke. "The families are the hardest parts of our job. It's never easy. It's only when we solve a case that a family gets closure. Although I don't really think there is closure when it comes to a loved one."

Veronica smiled back at Dennis and kissed his hand tenderly before she removed it from her face. "I think

I will get busy doing dishes, while you two go over the files."

It wasn't that the girls felt it was their duty as women to clean up; Dennis and Chuck had done their fair share of dishes over the years. Rather they wanted to give the men the time to go over the files and make a plan for the next day.

"Can you imagine anything happening to Tiffany?" Veronica asked Shelley.

"There have been times over the years as a medical examiner that I have had to see girls that looked just like Tiffany laid out on a stainless steel table with horrible wounds inflicted by some madman during a rape or domestic beating. It has brought me to my knees. The only way that I've been able to stay sane is to divorce my feelings at work from my life at home. The boys have learned to do the same thing. It's hard for you because it's not a part of your daily life, but it's a reality for us," Shelley whispered softly, trying not to think of her eighteen-year-old daughter who was currently at home making a new dress for an end of summer party.

"I think I'll stick to cutting hair. It's a good job. At least all of the heads I see are still attached to their owners. I'm sure you've seen a few headless customers." Veronica turned her big green eyes on Shelley who started to laugh.

"Veronica, you have a strange way of looking at things. I wouldn't call the people I see on the job customers. They're dead by the time I have to deal with them and I usually refer to them by a number. Remember last winter when we had so many corpses with their throats cut I was beginning to think I was in the middle of a bad, grade-B slasher movie with Freddie Kruger as the star. As it turned out, I was," Shelley said as she remembered the case of the Vampire Killings.

CHAPTER SEVENTEEN

The phone rang and Dennis turned to Veronica with his usual look, even though he was sitting right next to the telephone.

"I don't know why you don't pick it up," Veronica said as she leaned across his chest and picked up the phone, giving him a nasty look.

"It's never for me," Dennis responded defensively.

The call was from Katrina who was checking in to share the happenings of the day and to say she loved them. Soon the conversation was over and Veronica hung up with a contented smile on her face.

"It's true what they say: 'A daughter is a daughter all of her life, a son is a son until he takes a wife.' I'm sure glad we have girls." Veronica laughed. "Speaking of the girls, have you checked in with the Walker girls lately?"

"I stopped by once." Dennis looked a bit guilty. He had promised the girls he would be there for them.

"Sam answered the door. He was just about ready to pass out from drinking. Jade signaled behind his back that everything was okay, but I'm not too sure. Maybe we should go over tonight and check." Dennis looked at his wife knowing full well she would not think that the past effort was good enough.

"It's not too late. Do you think we could take some dessert?"

"It's the neighborly thing to do. I'm sure it's not too late. It's summer and who goes to bed before nine in the summer?" Dennis answered, trying to make up for not seeing to the girls more.

The evening was warm, the stars in the sky barely visible above the city lights. Even so, you could still see some of the major constellations and enjoy the breeze and the magical smells of the August night.

"Dennis?" Veronica asked as she looped her arm through his on their way over. "Don't you sometimes want to take justice into your own hands and just get rid of a guy like Sam?"

"You don't know how often I've wished it was Sam who lay at the bottom of the stair not Jewell, but it's not the way things went." Dennis put his hand to his moustache, a gesture he always made when he thought deeply. "Every day I see good people suffer at the hands or actions of pieces of filth like Sam." He looked up at the sky trying not to break the mood. "It's at those times I wonder if there is a God or if this whole world is just full of crap that will never make any sense to me."

Dennis's neck began to stiffen as he continued. He hated getting into things this deeply, but he was driven by something unexplored inside and the need pushed him on. "But then I think of all the pain and hurt that usually goes into making these creeps and I try to find a little compassion. It's hard, but if I don't then the one part of me that can love and forgive would die. Then what would

I be able to bring home to you and my girls?" He looked down at Veronica and squeezed her hand. "No. I try not to think about these kinds of criminals and when I do, I try to see them as little kids."

Dennis once again stroked his mustache a sign that he was puzzled. "Few of us are born evil. Some are unlucky enough to have parents who have lost their way in order to survive, and shut off the part that makes them feel. If I judge and hate, then I'm one of them. I've got to be able to hurt." Dennis felt like he needed a real cleansing of the heart and sharing his feelings with his wife seemed to help. "When I'm in the middle of an investigation I need to stay focused, but later, by myself, then I hurt for everyone, the Sams, Crystals, Ambers and Jades of the world – everybody. Often as the result of a bad family life, victims become victimizers." Dennis blushed at his little sermon.

Veronica beamed up at him, feeling privileged at receiving a rare insight into her husband's thinking. She leaned her head on his shoulder. Veronica loved him more now than ever. It was hard to believe that love could continue to grow, but hers certainly had. It wasn't that they hadn't had their share of problems, because they had. But at some point you begin to let go of the little things and concentrate on the things that matter.

You begin to have faith that your relationship can endure anything and that love's light won't be extinguished, even if you don't agree with everything.

* * *

The three girls were sitting at the kitchen table when they heard the first knock. A wave of fear quickly engulfed Jade and Crystal while Amber sat oblivious to her surroundings, still able to enjoy her favorite food; macaroni and cheese. Jade was up first, her thoughts quickly reverting to the events earlier, and to the dead body of their father, still lying at the bottom of the stairs. As Jade rose she quickly tried to close the door to the basement. The frame had been pulled away during Sam's twisting and struggle, before his fall had prevented the door from closing.

The second knock got Crystal to her feet as well. She tried to help Jade secure the basement door but it was impossible. No matter how hard they tried it simply would not shut. It drifted completely open. With the light off in the basement it was difficult to see down to the black recess below. All the girls could do was answer the door and pray everything would be all right. If ever their prayers would need to be answered, it would be now. They looked into each other's identical blue eyes, squeezed each other's hands and crossed their fingers in silent prayer. When Jade opened the door, her heart almost stopped. Standing there was Detective Dennis Kortovich and his wife Veronica. What the hell should she do now? Hadn't she asked them to call first? She stood still saying nothing, only looking at them with what she felt must be the guiltiest look in the world. "Hi Jade. Sorry we never came sooner, but the last time we came over Sam answered the door and didn't exactly welcome us with open arms so we thought we would try again." Veronica spoke first, thinking maybe the reason Jade stood there so silently was her fear of Sam. Jade looked so small and frightened. Veronica wanted to reach out and enfold her into her motherly chest. "Are you girls all right?" she asked. "Here, I thought you might enjoy this lemon pie."

Jade knew she looked a little strange just standing there, but at this moment she could hardly think of a thing to say and if she invited them in, it would all be over for her and her sisters. "I'm grateful and yes, we would enjoy the pie, thanks." Jade still stood in the doorway not wanting to move.

Crystal came up behind Jade, hoping that if the Kortoviches saw that they both were all right they would leave.

"May we come in for a moment? We won't stay long; we just want to make sure you are all right," asked Dennis.

This time Crystal jumped in trying to prevent the couple from entering the house. The door to the basement was directly across from the back door and one step forward would allow anyone to see down to the bottom of the stairs.

"Dad's in the basement and he's all tied up. If we upset him it won't go well for us." Crystal tried to think of a way to send Dennis and Veronica away. Suddenly a brilliant idea hit her. "Can I walk you back home? It will give me time to tell you how we are away from Dad."

Crystal pushed past Jade, took the pie from Veronica, and gave it to a surprised but thankful Jade; meanwhile starting down the back steps, hoping their uninvited guests would follow.

Dennis could tell the girls were scared. That bastard Sam had really done a number on them. He and Veronica had no choice but to follow Crystal and hope they could be of some help.

"How are you girls holding up without your mother?" Veronica asked in her usual straightforward manner. "Is there anything we can do for you?"

Crystal's mind was working overtime – she needed to get Dennis and Veronica to stop worrying. If the couple came over again before tomorrow when they got rid of Sam the girls might not be so lucky. Then what would happen to Amber? Crystal answered hesitantly at first trying to find just the right words. "Dad seems to be going off the deep end without Mom."

Crystal's mind was keen and she had a small idea starting to form, one that just might help them explain their father's future absence. "I think he's overwhelmed by all of this, and I'm sure he'd like to just give up. He always talked about leaving us. He says we're just no damn good. I always felt he talked like that to make Mom feel bad, but now I think he's just had it. It wouldn't surprise me if he just took off on us." Crystal looked over at Dennis and Veronica to see if they believed her.

* * *

Dennis got a strange feeling something was up. The tone in Crystal's voice was the same as his daughter Katrina's when she wanted something or was about to confess to some minor sin and wanted to set him up for it.

"Don't worry. If anything happens we'll be here for you," Veronica responded, her motherly instinct kicking in. Veronica always took things at face value. She never held anything back, while Dennis listened for the things that were and weren't being said. Dennis had an instinct for being set up or if anyone was lying. Something was up with Jade and Crystal. He would have to follow his hunch over the next few days and make sure they didn't need him.

* * *

As Crystal walked back to her home she was suddenly overwhelmed by what was ahead. If they were to get away with killing their father, they would have to be very careful. Dennis and Veronica were well meaning, but it would be very difficult to hide it from Dennis. It was his job to catch people who did what she and Jade had done. But really, they had no choice. It was either them or their dad, and after this afternoon's events, Sam had lost. She found it amazing that the picture of Sam dead and sprawled at the bottom of the stairs caused her to feel carefree and relaxed for the first time in her life. She felt absolutely no remorse. Maybe she was evil, just like daddy said, 'No good for nothing!' Crystal dismissed her thoughts as she opened the back door after saying good-by to Veronica and Dennis. Tomorrow would be a long day. She and Jade needed a good rest if they were going to pull it off. She would have to try and figure life out at another time. For now, she was just too tired.

CHAPTER EIGHTEEN

Jade rose to an unusually hot day. Clear, blue skies spread out over the city of Chicago as far as one could see. The air was still hot from the day before when the usually cool evenings of late summer had taken a vacation like everyone else did in August. Even the breeze that came off Lake Michigan seemed to have deserted those who were forced to stay within the city limits. It would be stifling by noon, but if a cold front moved in later on in the day, a severe thunderstorm was sure to brew up. It was Monday and today the girls would have to face the gruesome task of pulling Sam's body up the basement stairs and loading him in the old, blue van. They would make sure all of his belongings were taken with him as well. This would be his final journey. If there were an afterlife, Sam would likely be in Hell. Destroying everything that had ever meant anything to Sam along with his body somehow seemed appropriate, especially after the miserable life Jewell had to endure.

Jade and Crystal had felt a kind of justice when Sam died in the same spot as Jewell. The girls had made him feel some of the fear that their mother had felt all of her married life. The look on his face as he tumbled back over the edge of the steps down to the cold basement floor was one they would never forget. Sam had never shown any fear and it came as a shock and surprise to see his face twist in fear and horror as the chair tipped backward. The sound of the chair legs crushing and buckling under his weight was all that could be heard just before Sam's cry of despair, as he tumbled backward. The girls could finally take control and no one would ever hurt or abuse them again. It was a promise they made to their mother.

"Jade, how are we going to get Daddy up the stairs?" Crystal asked.

Jade looked over at her sister. Crystal stood before the bedroom mirror raking her long copper curls with her fingers, a frown on her face while Amber, already dressed for the day, sat in her rocking chair moving back and forth at a leisurely pace, staring at the back of the wall at nothing in particular. Jade had always wondered what made each human being so different. She had been given the soft, giving nature of her mother while Crystal was more pragmatic and sensible, seeing everything exactly like it was, not as she hoped it would be. Dad on the other hand was mean and nasty, so you just stayed out of his way. You didn't try to make things better; you just took care of yourself and survived the best you could. Amber, however, was not even present until she heard music. Then she did what no one thought possible. She played what she heard note for note with sheer perfection. The old piano that had belonged to their mother's family had never been used. It wasn't until Amber was five that anyone knew she had the gift. One day, Jewell accidentally turned the radio on to a classical station. A piano concerto by some famous dead guy was playing. For some reason Jewell didn't switch the station, she let it finish. Jewell was impressed by the piece and went over to the piano and played the scale, something she hadn't done since she left home. For the first time ever, Amber seemed to focus, really focus. She turned to the sound coming from the radio, listening intently. When Jewell went to the piano Amber moved toward her mother and watched her fingers as they danced across the keys, performing the basic scales. Never before had anyone ever witnessed Amber acting as if she was really aware. When Jewell's fingers left the piano keys, Amber sat down beside her. Then Amber's fingers touched the keys. It was shocking. Everyone, including Sam, sat down in total disbelief. Amber played the scales note for note, just like her mother. Then she played the song she'd heard on the radio, note for note. Later, they discovered Amber could not only play anything she heard note for note, but that the numbers on the telephone could also provide a diversion for her.

Soon Amber was trying to use the phone all the time. If they dialed out when she was close enough to hear the musical tones of the numbers, she would rock back and forth until she could reproduce each tone on the phone for herself. Finally they bought her a special toy phone that could match the real telephone, tone for tone. It made life much easier and kept Amber happy. The piano and phone became the only objects that ever connected her to the real world. Without them she simply stared off into the distance and rocked.

They were all very different girls, Jade, the pleaser, Crystal, who pleased herself, and Amber who would never really know pleasure at all, except with her music. And now Amber's gift would save them, but only if they could get Sam in the van and waylay Derek Hanson at the funeral home before he locked up.

The girls sat outside the Greenhill's funeral home for at least half an hour before they saw the big, double white doors open. Jade was out of the van instantly, gift in hand. Crystal pulled Amber close behind, following Jade up the large stairs that circled the front of the impressive building.

"Mr. Hanson," Jade called up, before Derek could hit the seven digit key code. "We would like to thank you for all the help you gave us."

Derek Hanson's gaze rested on the girls, but it was Jade who got the full force of his icy stare; his pale, blue eyes resting on her face in a way that sent shivers down her spine. For one moment it was as if all the evil that once embodied her father now belonged to this stranger. Jade couldn't get this encounter over fast enough.

"There is no need to thank me girls, I was only doing my job, but I appreciate your gesture." Derek's voice was unnerving, a sinister tone creeping into his nasal flat-pitched voice.

"You were very professional and we sure needed the support." Jade thrust the gift she held in her had forward, indicating to Derek that it was for him.

"You didn't need to do this. As I said it was my job." Derek's voice took on an added tone of disbelief, even a little suspicion. It was as if he doubted their sincerity.

"It's not much, we hope you like it. It belonged to my grandfather." Jade's heart started to pound. She hoped he didn't become suspicious about their reason for being here, or wonder about the insincerity of the gift. Jade gave herself a scolding. "Get a grip!" she thought. "He can't know anything! He's just a very weird guy." She hoped that her thoughts didn't show on her face.

Derek began to open the gift. It wasn't very big so he was able to unwrap it easily. Inside the small case was an antique boy-scout knife. It was the only thing the girls could find to wrap up and give to Derek as an excuse to catch him before he closed the morgue. The knife hadn't belonged to their grandfather, however, it had belonged to Sam, and so giving it away was no problem.

Everything personal Sam had was in the van. Soon it all would go up in smoke along with his scrawny body. A wind could be felt on the girls' faces as the sky in the distance started to darken. The wind was a welcome relief from the still heat of the day. It was coming in from the northwest and from the look of things; a violent summer storm would soon be upon them.

Derek looked up at the sky, his long bony face screwing up as few large drops found their way to the top of his head. His ponytail, tied tightly to the nape of his neck, stuck out from the back of his collar like a directional sign. He put his bony hand on top of this greasy head. "Looks like a big one coming this way." Derek said, referring to the impending storm. "You girls should get going now, I have to lock up."

"Okay." Jade's brain pounded. She wanted to scream out, "Just hit the keypad!" willing Derek to get on with it.

"No time to argue with such beautiful young girls." Derek looked deliberately at Jade as he spoke.

A chill ran down her spine as Derek's pale eyes met hers. Jade seemed to sense the danger as she looked away from Derek's intense gaze.

"Let me lock up and we'll get out of here before we get drenched." Derek turned to the security pad outside of the doors.

As he hit the numbers and the individual tones rang out, Crystal moved Amber a little closer, making sure she could hear each key as it was being pressed. This was their song of freedom and as Derek's bony fingers hit each number, Amber's face became focused and alive. When the sequence was finished she began to rock. Crystal quickly grabbed Amber's hand, pulling her towards the van.

"We'll let you walk Mr. Hanson to his car and I'll get Amber settled before it begins to rain any harder." Crystal looked up at the sky as she spoke, noting the large thunderheads that had gathered overhead.

While Jade walked the creepy mortician to his car for final thanks, Crystal pulled Amber into the van. It was difficult. Amber wanted to go back to the keypad to repeat the sequence. She would continue to obsess about the numbers until she could complete them. Until then, Amber would rock quietly and move her fingers in a continuous motion, mimicking the sequence of the numbers.

When Jade returned to the van, her pale face and taut features spoke silently of the revulsion she felt towards Derek Hanson. "Boy, he gives me the creeps!"

"Yes, he's almost as scary as Dad."

"We better drive away from the funeral home and make it look like we've left, or old creepy face might become suspicious," Jade said, in reference to Derek.

The girls followed Derek as he left the funeral home and cemetery grounds. When Derek turned right they took a slow and deliberate left, checking their rear view mirror as they continued a short way down the road. At the lights Derek took another right and within a few seconds was out of sight. Jade braked suddenly, heaving both girls forward.

"Ouch!" Crystal shouted as she placed her hands on the dash, preventing her small body from being flung onto the hard plastic. "Next time warn me!"

"If you both had buckled up you wouldn't have hurt yourself" Jade snapped back, checking her rear view mirror to make sure Amber was all right.

Amber was oblivious to everything except the notes that played in her head. Even the short plunge forward into the back of the front seat did little to stop her small fingers from their continuous motion as she repeated the pattern in the air. She would not stop until she was able to touch each number in a perfect repetition.

Jade backed up into the short driveway of one of the homes along the road. Once she had turned the van around, she traveled the short distance to the front of the funeral home.

Crystal was out of the van first. As she pulled back the seat, Amber jumped forward. Her focus was on the large double front doors and she seemed oblivious to her sister. Her tiny feet carried her quickly up the stairs, her fine copper curls bouncing as she quickly moved toward the keypad at the left side of the door. A radiant smile spread across her face as her hand moved over the numbers in a rapid succession. The girls were unable to tell if she had actually hit all seven digits. They wouldn't wonder for long. A loud clicking sound made both girls turn wide eyes towards one another.

"Oh my God, this is it. We've really done it! We're in!" Jade spoke first.

"I'm scared!" Crystal grabbed Jade's and Amber's hands, trying to gain a little extra strength from their touch.

"You're never scared, well, at least not much." Jade's reassuring squeeze was intended to let Crystal know how much she admired her younger sister's outer bravado.

Jade dropped Crystal's hand and quickly moved toward the door. "We'll have to get this over with quickly. I'll go in and open the back-loading gate. Can you drive the van around the back?"

Crystal nodded.

"We can pull Dad onto the dock. There's an electric ramp that the caskets are loaded on. They take the bodies to the embalming room, so we'll only have to roll Dad a little way after we put him on the gurney. It'll be easy," Jade said.

"Okay, but hurry, the weather is getting worse." Crystal grabbed Amber's hand and pulled her back towards the van. Once inside they drove around to the back and waited for Jade.

Jade moved quickly towards the back of the funeral home where the morgue was located. The halls were dark except for a soft, red glow that came from security lights that lined the halls. Once down the hall she entered into a small, well-decorated waiting room, the place immediate families went to view the bodies and say a final farewell. A second door at the back of the room allowed Jade to enter the crematorium area that led directly to a loading bay. The bodies were brought here from the various hospitals or the medical examiner's office, usually loaded in body bags. Double doors led to a large cooler where the bodies were kept until they were embalmed, then buried or cremated. Large sliding doors were the focal point of the room, encompassing most of the back outer wall. Jade quickly ran over to the wall looking for a switch that would allow her to open the large loading door. She quickly found it and stood back anxiously waiting for the heavy doors to lift, and hoping Crystal and Amber were waiting outside. As the door rose, Jade could hear loud cracks of thunder as the impending storm drew closer. Large drops of rain began to pelt the outside of the building making a sharp 'pitter- patter' sound on the roof. Soon the storm would engulf them and few people would venture out on a night like this, making their detection less likely. The smell of the rain, along with the flash of the lightning as it streaked across the sky, was accompanied by loud cracks of thunder, rumbling across the black night. It was a fitting farewell.

Sam would soon be gone forever, except for the memories; the memories that the girls would have to deal with, each in her own way. Crystal got out of the van when she saw the door to the loading bay begin to open. She then settled Amber safely inside the loading area before she and Crystal struggled with their dad's body. Once Sam was settled at the top of the loading dock, the girls stood hand in hand, looking out at the storm-filled horizon. Jade hoped the tempest wasn't a sign of something more sinister for the future. With Sam gone what could possibly hurt them now?

CHAPTER NINETEEN

Jade looked at the crematorium as it began its final cool-down cycle. She thought how glad she would be when it was finally over, and she and her sisters could get out of this place. They had struggled with Sam's body, especially with getting him out of the van. Sam was a small man, well under a hundred and thirty pounds but the girls were small as well. Sam's dead weight proved to be a workout as they tried getting him up the stairs to the loading dock. Now they were victorious. Sam and his clothes, as well as a few other personal belongings, were just a few dying embers.

"Do you really think we can get away with this?" Crystal asked Jade.

"I hope so. We'll have to get our stories straight. Dennis and Veronica will most likely be over to the house." Jade paused for a few minutes to think things through. "Dennis is smart but I think he would have killed Dad himself if he could. We can only hope he believes our story. We'll have to wait and see which part of him wins out, the detective or the father. Let's hope it's the father." Jade prayed that Dennis wouldn't be too interested in finding out what happened to Sam and that he would accept their story at face value. Amber stood off to the side of the crematorium staring off into the distance. The hum of the silver chamber lulled her into her usual continuous motion, her fingers playing some song heard only by her. Suddenly, a loud click that preceded the opening of the front door could be heard, and both girls turned toward each other. They knew someone was entering the building and they would be discovered if they didn't move fast. Jade grabbed Amber's hand while Crystal took one quick glance around, making sure nothing of Sam's was left. *Shit,* Jade thought. *They'll hear the crematorium.*

The crematorium was still on and the timer said it would be off in less than four seconds. Would it stop its humming in time? There was no time to stand around and find out! They would have to hide fast and pray they wouldn't be discovered. The small nook with a carved desk and tick curtains draped the enclosure, framing the nook, and leaving a little room behind each drape. Jade dashed behind one panel while Crystal pulled Amber close to her and ducked behind the second. Just as the door to the crematorium room opened, the oven shut down. Not a sound was made as tall, thin man entered the room. It was the mortician, Derek Hanson.

Derek stood in the doorway surveying the room for a few seconds. Something was strange. He just couldn't put his finger on it. The storm outside diverted his attention as another round of thunder boomed overhead. The pelting rain was driven hard by the wind as it howled. Derek shook his coat, making several drops of water scatter across the lush carpet. Everything seemed fine. It must just be the storm. He moved over to the wall just off to the left of the crematorium where a security pad, hidden just inside a light switch, felt the light touch of his fingers. The tones from the number pad rang sweetly out into the empty room. There was no need to put on any lights. The red gleam of the security lights gave the room enough light. Derek finished punching in the security code known only to him.

The staff at the morgue was never allowed to run his precious crematorium. Suddenly the sleek chamber began to move forward, gliding smoothly over its hidden track. No one knew of the secret room below and no one ever would. It held his treasure; his great passion. Derek descended into the chamber below. Once again a red glow lit up the tiny room, spreading a fiery light around the room.

At the bottom of the chamber Derek went over to a stainless steel table that stood in the middle of the room. "There you are, my little princess. It's me, your older brother and lover. I've missed you so much but our time together is almost over. You'll have to spend just a little more time here before you retire to your fiery bed. Sleep my princess, it's almost over."

Derek bent over the table and looked into the face of a fair-haired angel. The young woman who lay on the table was no more than fifteen, a wisp of a girl. Derek put his cold blue lips on the tiny mouth of the pale girl. "Just a few more hours and we can make your cold little body heat up with a passion only you can feel for me." Derek ran his finger over the sweet, oval face of his young victim.

"You know you love me, and I'll always love you." Derek took the tiny hand into his large bony one, the long, skinny fingers, finding their way to her ring finger. "I just need this for a few hours." Derek slipped the ring from her finger. It was her school ring and he would need it, but only for a while. He had been lax in not handling the ring sooner.

He stood up, still having to keep his head bent. The room was small and Derek's tall, lanky form could not stand at his full height, without banging his head on the ceiling, only inches above the sliding track. As he started to go up the stairs he turned back once more to give a silent farewell to the young girl who lay on the cold, stainless steel table. Derek only had a few more things to do before he finished his precious ritual with his new love. He would take the ring back home and make a permanent mold of it. Then the ring would be added to his collection, which hung along the wall of the tiny room. The room smelled like embalming fluid, but he loved it. It was the smell of death. He never got tired of its pungent smell and it clung to him like a damp mist on a foggy night, soft but pervasive.

Once out of the room, Derek hit the keypad again. As he looked around once more, something seemed amiss. It was more a feeling than anything he could see, but after looking around again, everything seemed fine. He shook off the impression and went back out the way he came.

The girls could see each other from behind the thick curtains. Crystal made sure Amber kept her rocking to a minimum, and both older girls kept their breathing shallow. Derek had seemed to take forever before he came up from the room under the crematorium. All the girls could do was wait and hope he didn't need anything from the tiny desk behind the curtain where they hid. When they heard the final click of the front doors they let out a double sigh and let go of Amber's hand. Without waiting for her sister to catch up, Amber knew where she had to go. She quickly moved out from behind the curtain and sped over to the keypad. Instantly her fast, deft fingers found the exact sequence of numbers needed to open the chamber below. Again the furnace slid back, only this time it was Amber who went down the steep stairs into the scarlet glow below.

Jade and Crystal quickly followed, hoping Amber wouldn't touch anything she shouldn't. Amber went over to the corner of the room where the red light spread its cinnamon glow. Her only interest was watching the shadows she created as she moved her hands back and forth across the light. Jade and Crystal came to an abrupt stop as they saw a sight that left them speechless. Before them lay the body of a young girl dressed in a bridal gown. She was strapped to a steel table. Her lifeless body reflected a soft, pink glow as the light shone onto her fair hair. Both girls slowly went over to the table. The face that stared up at them was tiny and delicate, her mouth partly opened, her lips smeared with a deep, red lipstick. She looked dead and Crystal was the first to shake her bare arms. They were cold to the touch.

She was limp – lifeless. It was then that Jade noticed the large bruises that ran along the girl's tiny arms. There were small round burns on the back of her hands and Jade and Crystal knew what had caused them – cigarettes. Both of them had known their fair share of burns, a gift from their father. It was something they were all too familiar with. Jade lifted the hem of the wedding gown up over the young girl's legs. It was ghastly. The extent of the bruises and burns were horrific. Never had the girls seen anything like this. It was brutal beyond belief. There were tiny precise cuts all along the inside of her legs; only her face was untouched. The girls didn't need to see beneath the bodice of the gown to know that her small breasts would also be mutilated.

Jade and Crystal looked up at each other – neither could speak. Suddenly Jade let out a shocked, "Shit!" as she looked at the walls behind Crystal.

For a brief second Crystal was confused by what could have caused her sister more shock than the young woman who lay in front of them. She followed Jade's eyes. As she turned slowly, the hair on the back of her neck stood straight up as a chill ran down her spine. When she'd turned around fully, facing the wall, she too let out the only expletive she could. "Oh fuck! What the hell are these?"

Over a dozen newspaper clippings, with colorful, grotesque, pictures were stuck to the wall. Beneath each picture was an object; necklaces, rings, earrings and brooches; all personal items belonging to the young girls in the pictures. The girl lying on the table looked eerily similar to the girls in those pictures; tiny, perfect females, each wearing the same wedding dress.

One of the photos stood out. The girl in the photo was a tall, dark brunette, her body completely naked. Her breasts had been removed completely, while her face was mutilated with cigarette burns. She alone was different. A large X had been carved at the top of each thigh. Beneath the picture were several more X's, running along its border.

It wasn't until Jade looked at the locket that hung

below the picture and newspaper clipping that she felt her legs begin to buckle beneath her. "Shit, shit, shit, it can't be! Look at the picture again, Crystal, and tell me who you see. It just can't be her! I think I'm going to be sick." Jade held on to the edge of the table lowering her head, trying to keep the ground beneath her feet from rising up and hitting her in the face.

"Oh Jade, it's Charlotte!" Crystal's voice revealed all the pain anyone could feel when faced with something as horrible as the picture revealed.

Charlotte's last moments had been beyond belief, even for Crystal and Jade, who until now thought they had seen and experienced it all.

"It just doesn't make sense. She's the only one that's different. All of the other girls look like…Well, they all look like us. Each of the other girls could almost be our sister. Some of them may have a little more red, but Charlotte is a brunette and so much bigger than any of these girls." Jade was overwhelmed by fear and grief, but even so, she knew Charlotte didn't belong with the rest of the tiny young victims.

"We've got to get out of here before that freak comes back." Crystal began to feel a sense of panic.

The girls' attention had been diverted to the wall when they heard the soft moan. They stood motionless for a few seconds, unsure of what they had heard. When a second sound broke through the lips of the small girl on the table, Jade and Crystal returned their attention to the young captive. "Crystal, she's still alive, we have to get her out of here."

"We can't, we'll get caught! What will we do with her? Shit Jade, this is a real problem!"

"I know, I know. When we came up with this plan to get rid of Dad, how did I know we'd find this?" Jade looked at Crystal with all of the confusion and fear she felt. For one second she thought she should just grab both her sisters and run, but she knew she could never leave the girl. If the stranger was alive, they had to get her out, now! Time was something they were running out of; Derek would likely be back soon.

Another moan came from the girl, only this time much louder. Jade bent over her face and shook her shoulder. "Hello, hello, wake up. What's your name?"

The girl's eyes suddenly opened. Jade gazed into two perfect, blue eyes that were the exact same color as hers and Crystal's. The only difference was that these eyes were crazed with fear. The girl started to scream.

"Shush.... You're all right!" Jade laid a small, cold hand across the girl's forehead. "We're going to get you out of here."

The girl nodded.

"Let's sit her up and see if we can hold onto her and get her up the stairs."

Jade started to pull the small girl forward, while Crystal took the cue and slipped her arms under the small of her back. Suddenly the girl started to choke.

"She's going to vomit. Quick, lean her over."

Jade moved her over the table with one swift movement, supporting her by her shoulders, allowing for her head to fall between her legs. The long layers of the wedding gown caught the chunky, foul smelling, amber-colored vomit.

"Ugh!"

Crystal screwed up her nose while she tried to prevent

the girl from falling backwards. "That's a real funny smell, almost like ammonia or medication. She's been poisoned or something. Do you think she'll die?"

Crystal tried to hold the girl, but she wasn't much bigger than the stranger herself, so it was difficult. The balancing act between all three girls would almost have been comical, if things hadn't been so tragic.

"She's clearly been drugged with something. We've got to get her out of this dress – we'll never be able to manage her with it twisting around her legs." Jade started to undo the tiny buttons on the back of the dress. She could tell from the worn fabric that it was old and had been used many times, and judging by the number of pictures on the wall, more often than she cared to think about.

Suddenly the young girl went limp, falling back onto the table. Jade and Crystal struggled for what seemed like forever to slip the gown over the girl's shoulders, past her waist and over her hips. With a final hard pull they yanked the gown over her slim legs and tiny feet, tossing it to the floor. Together they pulled the unconscious girl up and off the table in one swift move. Both girls put all of the strength they had into the upward motion. It was a little too much and all three went sprawling forward. Together Jade and Crystal regained their balance, holding the girl between them.

"If we could get Dad up the stairs, we can get her up," Jade said, more to herself than anyone else.

"Yeah, but it took forever to get him up to the top of the stairs and it was a good thing he was dead because I couldn't count how many times we dropped him. This is different. Not only do we have to be more careful but we need to hurry in case that creep Derek decides to come back."

"Call Amber, she'll follow if we start to leave." Jade reminded Crystal.

Amber responded to Crystal's voice without hesitation. This was something only Crystal could do. If it was anyone else it could take a while. There in the dim red light of the secret room, the trio of girls struggled up the stairs with one little girl following, oblivious to the events that had just occurred. Finally all four were up the stairs out of the small chamber.

"Wait. I've got to go back down. I've got to get something," Jade said, giving Crystal a no-nonsense look, ensuring that Crystal wouldn't argue with her. She then went back down the stairs quickly, not bothering to wait for a response from her sister who now struggled to keep the naked body of the young stranger from falling face forward onto the carpeted floor.

Jade wasn't sure what drove her back; she only knew she had to go and rescue what was left. These small tokens were all that were left of the missing girls and somehow Jade felt she had to rescue them from the cold fiend who had snuffed out these young women's lives. She had difficulty finding enough room in her blue-jeans pockets, so she shoved a few of the items into her bra. She also decided to take the photos. She wasn't sure what she would do with the photos and items, she just knew she had to take them. It gave her a warm feeling of satisfaction knowing Derek Hanson would never touch these precious items again. Jade sensed he would become crazed when he found these items missing, and his secret chamber disturbed. Derek could go fuck himself and rot in hell. Jade bent down, picked up the crumpled wedding dress, and with all the strength she could muster; she ripped the gown in two and tossed it back onto the floor.

"No one will wear that gown again, you bastard," Jade whispered to herself and the image of the pale, evil mortician.

Within moments she was up the stairs, her arms around the strange girl, urging her sisters forward toward the door that would lead to the loading bay and freedom.

"Who would have thought," Jade whispered to Crystal, "that we would bring in a body and take out a body?" Jade giggled over the irony of the moment. Humor made the moment all the more surreal. Life was like a roller coaster. You never knew what was around the bend, but boy what a wild ride so far!

The door was just beginning to close when once again the girls heard a loud click from the front doors. They knew it was Derek returning to claim his prize. Shit, they only had a couple dozen steps to go and they would be out of this hellish place. Could they make it? The van was just outside the back door of the loading gate with the keys in the ignition. Jade and Crystal doubled their pace, rushing through the door. Any second now Derek was going to enter the room that had once held the treasures that he had gathered at such great expense. They stumbled down the stairs with the copper-haired girl, and then pulled her into the van. Amber followed like a well-trained terrier, happy to follow. Jade slipped into the driver's seat, checking to make sure her three passengers were at least safe inside with all the doors shut and locked.

"No lights. Let's just get the hell out of here!" Crystal said.

Jade accidentally stepped on the accelerator, causing

the engine to make a loud roar, heard even above the storm.

Derek was entering the crematorium room when he heard the sound of an engine roaring at the rear of the building. Someone was leaving. Had they been in the building? Did they know of his prize? As he walked toward the back loading area, he noticed the inner door was open. His heart picked up a beat. Once in the loading area, he became even more confused – the double loading doors were wide open. As he ran to the door, he saw the taillights of a van speed off into the darkness.

He glanced around only once before he ran back into the main room. The stainless steel machine was rolled back, exposing the hidden staircase leading to the room below. His long legs propelled him forward in seconds, and once he stumbled to the bottom of the stairs he screamed a long, blood-curdling howl of disbelief.

Gone! His bride, his love!

One more look around, and another scream ripped from his lungs. His head felt like it was going to explode. As he looked around the small underground chamber in disbelief, the realization that his world had been torn apart set in. Gone! Everything that meant more to him than life itself was gone. The newspaper articles, photos, and the souvenirs, all of it! The photos he had taken of each of his brides just before consummation of their marital rites. The pale, lifeless, angelic faces that usually stared out at him from the collage along the walls were now gone, leaving only outlines of glue and tape.

He felt inconsolable. Those rings and trinkets held the life essence of each girl, and without them he couldn't feel or touch their spirits. They had been ripped from his heart leaving him feeling sick to his stomach. His throat choked, threatening to close off his air, preventing it from reaching his lungs. He breathed deeply through his nostrils, sucking the lingering smell of his bride deep into his lungs.

A third primeval roar ripped from his chest, finding its release. At the same time that the sound of his scream assaulted his ears he dropped to his knees, feeling the loss even more than he thought possible. "Fuck, fuck, fucking shit, fuck!" Derek screamed. "This can't be happening!" He could hear the pulsing of his blood as it pumped through his veins. The pounding only added to the intense pain that engulfed his head. He bent over, grabbing the sides of his skull while applying pressure, trying to keep his head from exploding. That's when he saw it; the white, shimmering, satin dress. *No! No! It can't be,* Derek thought. The wedding gown lay on the floor, ripped from the back of his beautiful prize. He let go of his head, the pain temporarily forgotten as he bent to pick up the crumpled fabric. As he lifted it to his face, he noticed a second piece of shimmering satin. He picked the piece up. Torn apart, ripped like some unwanted child from its mother's breast. The once beautiful gown hung limply from his large hand. He bent once more to pick up another piece of fabric, gathering it into both hands and pulling it to his face, smelling deeply of its scent. The smell of his young bride lingered on the fabric, musky and light, better than a puppy's breath, innocent. Each girl had felt her skin next to this sacred fabric. Now it was torn into pieces. Part of the gown was foul with vomit, ruined. How would he ever find love now? Without the dress everything was hopeless. Derek felt his legs turn rubbery as he walked over to the stairs that led to the floor above. Once he ascended, he sank down quickly before his legs buckled. With his back next to the furnace he could feel the warmth as the heat penetrated his jacket. *What the fuck?* He thought as he stood up. The knowledge that the furnace had been used recently only added to his already confused state. Derek went over to the door and unlocked the airtight seal, hearing the soft whoosh as he swung it open. The embers were in the last stage of cooling but he knew that this couldn't be happening. He had cremated the last client early that morning.

There should be nothing in the 'belly of the beast,' but before him were ashes, more than he had ever seen before. One person usually left what amounted to the size of a medium cookie jar. His bony hands reached for a ceramic scoop. It was similar to a cat scoop used for kitty litter, but his was an expensive ceramic scoop, imported from Italy – only the best for his clients. It was used to sift out any bones, buttons, or teeth that might not have been consumed by the fire. It didn't happen often, the temperature in the crematorium was as high as eighteen hundred degrees and little escaped its all-consuming heat. But once in a while an object would survive the fire.

Whoever had used his machine had also taken his bride and his treasures. The van was familiar, but in the state he was in presently he had no clue as to whose it could be.

"Clink!" The sound of the ceramic scoop hitting the unexpected object startled Derek. When he pulled the small shovel from the oven, he could still see the glow radiating off the object. He quickly walked through a door off to one side of the furnace, to the embalming room. At the back of the room was a sink. He turned the tap on to hot and placed the object at the bottom of the sink. It sizzled as the water hit the object, sending a column of steam just out of reach of Derek's face. He turned the hot water to warm, and finally to cool, then cold. Whatever the object was, it would lead him to his enemy…the one who had snatched his prize and treasures away! At the bottom of the sink, a black, oval-shaped object lay innocently, awaiting Derek's inspection before giving up its secret. He held it in one hand while with the other hand he ran his bony fingers over the surface. Grooves could be felt on its now grainy surface. The back of the object had two protrusions, equally spaced. He knew instantly what it was. A belt buckle, the kind cowboys wore.

To the side of the sink he kept several compounds as well as a special light that could be used to magnify objects. He usually used it to examine photos of loved ones, in order to present them to their families as lifelike as possible. Often photos that the families brought didn't offer enough detail. The use of the magnifying light helped to clear up the smallest aspects. He dipped the buckle into a special jar with a clear liquid and held it between a set of stainless steel prongs. Once again, the object sizzled as the liquid came into contact with its silver surface. He dipped it a couple more times, making sure its surface was clear. After wiping it with a special cloth he held it under the light. Much of the surface was worn either by time or the fire, but enough was present for him to make out the stylized letters of S.E.W.

He ran the letters over in his mind. At the moment he could think of no one whose initials matched those letters. He placed the buckle on a pan next to the sink and washed his hands. Something was rattling around in the recesses of his brain. He had seen those letters recently, but where? Suddenly he saw it all. Everything was crystal clear. It was the girls this afternoon on the steps. He could hear them thanking him for his help with their mother's funeral and see them giving him a gift; a knife that had belonged to their grandfather or someone. He had only glanced at the knife briefly. He had been anxious to go home and prepare a special mold for the ring his bride was wearing.

Derek reached into his coat pocket and pulled out a small white box. He removed the lid, and there lay the knife gleaming up at him with the telltale markings flashing under the glow of the magnifying light. He held the knife under the lens. His flash of insight was rewarded when he saw the same stylized initials as on the buckle; SWE.

He walked calmly over to an old gray filing cabinet, one of several that stood along the wall. He opened the drawer and found the folder he was looking for; Walker. He flipped through the papers and found the photocopy of the visa slip that Jade had signed for her father, a man Derek had never met, but knew of. At the bottom of the visa slip was a name that would lead him to his enemy; Samuel Elliot Walker. The buckle was Sam's and so was the knife. The girls had paid him a visit so they could use his furnace. He remembered how fascinated Jade had been over the cremation process. It had to be Samuel's ashes in the belly of his pet. They had somehow figured out the key code and entered the funeral home. Now Derek knew a secret about them and he would use it to bargain for what was his.

CHAPTER TWENTY

The storm softened, leaving only a light patter of rain on the windshield. It wasn't until the girls turned onto a road that led away from the funeral home that they even dared to let out a sigh of relief.

As usual, it was Crystal who spoke first. "Holy shit. Now what? We barely escaped with our lives! If Derek had found us we'd all be Frankenstein's bride by now."

Crystal's dramatic outburst almost made Jade laugh, but not quite. "Look!" she responded. "If we don't calm down and figure something out we'll get caught."

Once again, a soft moan could be heard from the back seat. It was the young girl – she would need medical attention and they would have to figure something out. Jade pulled off to a side road, well out of sight of any passing cars. She turned the engine off and the soft sound of the rain made a pitter-patter sound on the tin roof of the van. It was a soothing noise that along with the dark sky and swaying trees, gave them a sense of safety.

"OK, let's think this through. We just burnt up our dead dad, who we killed, and rescued some girl from a serial killer, who's sure to be pissed off and is likely to kill us if he finds out who we are." Jade paused for only a second. Her blue eyes were becoming larger as their predicament became clearer. "We can't go to the police. We don't know who this girl is, or what to do with her. Shit! We're fucked and I'm still a virgin." Jade's voice was becoming higher and more hysterical as the picture of their predicament became clearer.

"Don't lose it on me now," Crystal broke in. "I'm in this with you, remember. We have a little sister to care for and we can't just leave this girl." Crystal looked at the young girl in the back seat. Her head was slumped forward, resting on her chest. She was naked from the waist up, with only a pair of white, sport briefs covering her battered body. Jade gave their young ward a blanket; one they always kept in the van. She wrapped it around her tiny shoulders, trying to stop the girl's uncontrollable trembling.

Amber sat next to the girl, unaware of what was happening. Her gentle back and forth motion did little to disturb the tiny victim, who drifted in and out of consciousness.

"She needs help and we can't give it to her. We'll have to drop her off at a hospital or something," Jade said. She was anxious to be done with things and get on with a new life, and this was certainly causing them some complications.

"Yes, you're right," Crystal said. "She'll be hysterical when she comes to!"

The young woman's bruises and cigarette burns were only a small part of what she had gone through. Whatever she had been drugged with was wearing off, and they would have to dump her soon before she could answer any questions and lead the cops to them.

"The hospital is ten minutes from here, we'll have to take our chances and hope we don't get caught," Jade finished, starting the van once again and backing onto the road.

The emergency drive-in at the hospital was a semi-circle. Jade got out while Crystal stayed in the van checking things out. It was nearly midnight and so far things looked quiet. Jade went in through the automatic double doors and found a wheelchair. They would need it.

"I'll need your help, Crystal," Jade said as she wheeled the chair close to the van. "There's a security guard just inside the doors. You'll have to create a diversion. There are also cameras and we have to make sure we don't get caught on film."

"How?" Crystal asked. "I don't know what to do."

"You go in first and act as if you are going to faint. Just get the guard to concentrate on you, not me. I'll wheel the girl in right behind you and hope the guard doesn't notice me. But make sure you put your hoodie up and I'll take her to the left, close to the seats that surround the intake nurse. I don't think they have a camera on the chairs, only on the nurse."

Jade could tell by the look on Crystal's face the last thing she wanted to do was to fall helplessly into the arms of anyone who carried a gun; especially after what had happened during the last few hours. The darkness and late hour of the evening, along with the storm, gave the evening a spooky feeling.

Crystal got out of the van, made sure Amber was buckled safely in her seat, then helped Jade put the girl into the wheelchair, all without saying a word. Then

Crystal pulled back her shoulders and marched up to the double doors where she stood and took several deep breaths. She gave one backward glance at Jade to make sure she was right behind her, with the small victim in the wheelchair. She lowered her shoulders, hung her head low, and went through the doors into the Emergency Room.

Once through, Crystal went over to the guard, grabbed onto his chest and then promptly sunk to her knees, still holding onto his shirt, and keeping her face hidden. The guard was taken aback by the young girl who seemed to be in need of his help, as he bent over to see what was wrong; Jade wheeled the chair past him into the waiting area, right beside the chairs by the intake nurse.

"Are you all right?" the guard asked, as he tried to hold onto Crystal, preventing her from falling to the floor.

"I have a very bad head-ache and I thought I was going to faint. I knew you wouldn't let me fall," Crystal answered, staring innocently up at the guard with her big, blue eyes.

"Here, let me help you to a chair. I'll get you a glass of water. Then we'll see if we can get someone to look at you." The guard guided Crystal to an empty chair beside a young woman with a baby.

When the guard left to get the water, Crystal looked around to see where Jade was.

Jade had already wheeled the girl into their chosen spot. Crystal had hoped they could just park the girl on the inside of the double doors and prayed someone would take notice and get her some help. She figured most people who come to emergency this late at night had enough of their own troubles without paying too much attention to anyone else. With Crystal's award-winning performance,

Jade had been able to slip past the guard unnoticed.

The shift from dark to light caused the girl in the chair to moan and shift suddenly as she drifted in and out of her unconscious state. The old blanket that Jade had wrapped around her was slipping off her shoulder. Jade pulled the blanket back up around her neck, hoping that no one would notice her in the process. She stood away from the wheelchair to see if anyone was paying attention to them, So far everyone seemed concerned with their own troubles. She looked around for Crystal, who was sitting on a chair next to a young woman with a crying baby. Just as she was about to approach Crystal, the guard came over to her with a glass of water. Crystal took the water and gave the guard a thankful smile. Once he was assured she was all right, he went back to his post at the emergency door.

* * *

Mandy was aware that her surroundings were different. She even felt safer without knowing why. This had begun when she'd heard the voices of the two girls. Their faces had drifted before her only a couple of times during the past few hours, although time was distorted and what had seemed like a few hours may well have been a few days. She could remember the echo of a soft feminine voice telling her she was safe and that "that bastard" wouldn't get at her again. Somehow Mandy knew it was true, and when the angels yanked that vile wedding dress past her hips she knew her ordeal was over. She allowed herself to sink back into the blissful state of unconsciousness where she could forget what had happened. There was a small part of her brain that received the signal to forget and let go of it all. She was safe and she need never relive these events again. Darkness claimed Mandy once again as the face of Ichabod Crane drifted before her mind's eye and the headless horseman galloped into the night.

* * *

Jade slowly stepped away from the wheelchair, leaving her small ward. The blanket that was wrapped around Mandy's body slipped once more, revealing one small, bare shoulder. Jade wanted to go to her side and pull it back up, but Crystal stopped her, motioning for Jade to sit in the waiting area while Crystal sat beside her. It seemed strange that there were only a half a dozen people waiting; it was usually a lot busier than this at the Herotin Hospital. But both girls knew if they were to go undetected they would have to sit and wait. They wanted to make sure someone would claim the girl. So far no one had even looked up. The clerk that did admissions was busy at the computer, helping an elderly couple enter their health care information. The girls suddenly felt anxious.

"What if no one notices her?" Crystal asked.

"Someone's bound to see her. No one's with her. She looks awful. If the blanket falls off of her shoulder, someone will see what happened. It's awful. No one could pass by and not cringe," Jade answered, looking around the room hopefully.

The TV in the waiting area was the only sound they heard beyond the occasional cough or moan. It was Crystal who squeezed Jade's hand and motioned for her to watch the TV. The newswoman was reading a report about a missing girl and the picture that was flashed across the screen was their victim. They read the name underneath the picture; Mandy Switzer. Both girls sat silently, intent upon hearing the rest of the news broadcast.

"Mandy Switzer, daughter of Judge Switzer has now been missing for almost one week. An inside source has linked her disappearance to over one dozen other young girls who have gone missing over the past six years. None have been found. They have all been between the ages of thirteen and fifteen. Foul play is suspected. Family members of the missing girls claim that their daughters would never have run away. They say the police have been reluctant to treat the cases of the other missing girls as anything more than runaways. We have reliable information that the case has been under investigation for a week, although no leads have been found." The dark haired newswoman then finished her report. "If anyone has any information, they are asked to call Detective Dennis Kortovich or Chuck O'Brian of the Chicago Police Department."

With the reporter's closing remarks, both girls looked at each other once again.

"Shit, she's a judge's daughter!" Jade exclaimed.

"Yes, and Dennis Kortovich is investigating," Crystal said. "What are we going to do?"

"Nothing. No one knows about us, and Mandy Switzer is in no condition to tell anyone about us either. No one knows about Dad. We just get away from here and keep quiet," Jade said.

At that moment, the admission clerk noticed the wheelchair with its patient sitting by the chairs unattended. She didn't remember anyone checking in with the young girl, so she got up and went around the counter to see if she could remember if she had seen her before. When the clerk got in front of the wheelchair, she lifted the girl's face up off her chest and as she did, the blanket fell the rest of the way down her shoulder, exposing the girl's tiny breast.

What the clerk saw caused her to scream. "Oh may God have mercy! Somebody get me some help! This girl is in real trouble!" The nurse pulled the blanket back up over the girl's battered shoulders.

Soon security guards and other hospital staff started pouring into the waiting room to see what the ruckus was about. This was the cue for the girls to leave. The commotion in the entranceway was beginning to look like a scene out of the television show *ER*, as hospital attendants, nurses, and doctors, as well as other patients gathered around the girl in the wheelchair. They stared in disbelief and horror. The body of the young woman was covered in cuts and bruises, but it was the hundreds of cigarette burns that covered her small breasts and abdomen that made them stare in disbelief. The diversion allowed the girls to slip out unnoticed.

CHAPTER TWENTY-ONE

When the call came in Dennis was fast asleep, trying to catch up on some much needed rest. The past year had been a tough one and Dennis had found himself unable to sleep as he got older. His dreams had taken a bizarre twist, leaving him drained and shaken. Just when things had started to get back to normal, he had begun to worry about Crystal, Jade, and Amber. Now this case of the missing girls had begun to haunt his nights. With one case solved another one would begin – that's how it was in this business. There was always enough crime to go around. The observations Dennis had made from the cold files led him to suspect that the missing girls were dead and there was another serial killer running around. Dennis hung up the phone and as usual, Veronica, a light sleeper, sat up wanting to know what was up.

"It's the Switzer girl, she's been found. Someone dropped her off at the hospital, beaten and half dead." Dennis pulled on his pants. "I've got to get there before the judge does. From the sound of things, she's in real bad shape and when she sees her parents she'll fall apart and that will be the end. If I'm going to get anything, I'll need to get there right away."

"I was beginning to lose hope. When this much time has passed, it's usually bad news," Veronica said, as she reached for her robe and got out of bed.

Dennis grabbed his housecoat from the back of the bedroom door and turned to look at his wife. He knew Veronica would head to the kitchen to make a quick coffee and put it in his thermal mug. A bagel would be quickly toasted and put into a bag. Veronica always made sure her family was fed and comfortable. He stood in front of the mirror. He needed a shower and shave but there was no time, he'd have to go the hospital first. For now, a quick splash of cold water and a pee was all he had time for. He would put on the clothes he had worn that day and hope the case didn't get away.

From the time Dennis and Chuck had left Judge Switzer's home almost a week ago, they had been going over the information in all of the files, trying to see if the last location of the missing girls could shed a light on who might want to abduct them. An all- point's bulletin had been put out on Mandy, along with her photo. Dennis and Chuck had questioned all of her friends, teachers, and the country club members. By the time all of the interviews had been finished, there didn't seem to be any one name that stood out as suspect. Now Mandy had been found and Dennis decided that getting to the hospital first, before the family, was his best chance at getting important information. He made a call to Chuck during the drive to the hospital.

"I'm sorry to bother you Shelley, but could you put Chuck on the line?" Dennis asked after waking her from a dead sleep.

"What's up, bud?"

"Mandy's been found. She showed up at the hospital wrapped in a blanket and nothing much more. It seems she is in very rough shape. The doctor who called said she had been drugged and tortured. I'm on my way now. Get Chuck to the hospital as fast as you can."

"He is on his way," Shelley said, as she hung up.

The drive took less than twenty minutes; there was less traffic at this hour of the night. Lightning lit up the sky, like a knife cutting through dark, velvet cake. As usual, the rain only made the night seem more ominous.

Dennis was ushered into the waiting room; the nurse said he would need to see the doctor before he could go in. Mandy was just coming out of a drug-induced blackout and they were monitoring her vital signs constantly to make sure there were no complications. He had been rehearsing in his mind the questions he would ask Mandy. He wanted to make sure he followed everything by the book.

When the doctor came up behind him he was startled out of his musing. "Not many people get to startle me and tell about it!" Dennis smiled as he held out his hand to the young intern, who quickly gave his back for a thankful shake as he introduced himself.

"I'm Dr. Grout." His freckled face was solemn. He was no more than thirty, but Dennis felt sure that this skinny, young man was able to give Mandy the care she deserved. "I'm so glad you're here, everyone's just sick about what's happened to Mandy Switzer, but she's finally coming around and I think she can answer some questions now." Dr. Grout motioned for Dennis to follow him to a private room that was just across the hall from the area where they were standing.

Two small florescent fixtures that hung over the bed lit the room. The rest of the room, by contrast, was dark and quiet. A nurse sat on a chair off to the side of the bed, keeping an eye on the monitors. An IV of saline solution was being pumped into Mandy's hand, helping to dilute the unknown drug that had been given to her during her ordeal.

"I've sent blood samples to the lab to test for toxic substances that she may have ingested. We should get the results back soon. I put a STAT order on them. I also took pictures of her body. I've never seen anything like it. She floats in and out of consciousness. She's really out of it. She was able to tell us her name. When we phoned the judge he told us to call you as well," Dr. Grout offered.

* * *

Mandy heard voices somewhere out there beyond a world of dreams to reality. She knew that she was no longer in danger, but at this moment she didn't seem to care to find out exactly where she was or why she was safe. Her small body felt as if it were being held down by a thousand tiny hands. Suddenly she was transported back to that place! Her heart beat faster while her blood ran cold. Her head was being held tightly to a cold surface by some unseen force that pressed against her face, its hot breath sickeningly close. The air felt as if it were being sucked from her lungs. A kiss! She remembered a wet, hard kiss. Words of love had been whispered nearby, but all she could remember feeling was fear. Flashes of pain, now gone, were replaced by a dull throb all over her tiny body. She remembered a face that was long, bony, and ugly. Yellow teeth, huge wet lips, the smell of something from the lab at school. Stuff she had used on that stupid frog. She drifted deeper and deeper to some dark corner of her mind; a place where anything could happen.

Suddenly a headless rider thundered down a dark, windy lane, its head tucked somewhere under its dark, billowy cape. All of the images swirled around inside her scrambled brain. The fear she had felt was gone, replaced by a drug-induced state of nothingness. She left the world of strange and crazy things, back to a place where only black nothingness and soft voices existed. Suddenly, all of the tiny hands were demanding that she sit up. They pulled and prodded her tender flesh; flesh that had been pinched and burned and would have felt a blissful nothingness if it weren't for the dull ache and those demanding little hands. How could those sweet voices demand that she sit up? Didn't they know she no longer cared? All she wanted to do was sink back into a state of nothingness.

Mandy wanted to forget as she melted into the pounding thump of the music and the dance. There she could abandon all of her youthful energy into the pulsing beat. She remembered drinking some pop and suddenly feeling ill. She had gone outside of the club that had sponsored the rave to get some fresh air. She bent over, feeling faint, when a large bony hand suddenly clamped down across her face. She saw no one until it was too late, as she began to sink to her knees. One deep breath and she was out. What happened later was too awful to bring to her conscious thoughts. She would will it out of existence. If that meant she would perish as well, so be it. She would never live with the memory of that face, that mouth, that man.

Mandy sank into blackness for what could have been

forever or only a second. Suddenly, the upward motion of her body being pulled forward by those tiny hands made her stomach rise from its depths to spill forward; an acrid, bitter liquid with chunks of some forgotten meal. It was the last meal she had eaten. She was a guest at her own bridal supper. She had been dressed in white. The monster had dressed her. He pulled the gown over her tiny breast, which bore the physical expression of his love – burns, slashes and bruises. He said he would stop if she would accept him, willingly. It made her feel sick.. This was even more of a nightmare than she could ever have imagined.

He had made it clear she had a choice; death or him – all of him. She would choose death. He hurt her for what seemed to be a lifetime just to see if she would change her mind. Finally he gave up. He said she was like all of the others and that she deserved to die and he would be only too willing to oblige her. He wrapped her up in a blanket and took her to some place that you could only believe existed in the movies. A cathedral of death! Mandy could remember the look on his face when he accepted defeat. The look of rage turned from a fiery hot eruption of all of the emotion a human could contain inside without exploding, to a cold, dead, dull acceptance of defeat. She was sure he had been in that state before. He would now allow for a final few steps before it would be all over. Mandy was sure death would be her only way out. Once again, she found herself sinking into darkness.

Then those pesky hands and soft voices started at her once again. Maybe she was dead and these beautiful voices and persistent hands belonged to angels. The hands were soft, tiny, but unrelenting in their insistence that she sit up. But no, you surely couldn't vomit in Heaven and Mandy was sure she had just vomited. She put as much effort as she could into opening her eyes. It wasn't as hard as she thought it might be. The light that shone on the three angelic faces bathed them in its soft pink glow. All of the faces looked alike; blue eyes, tiny noses, and soft curls, catching enough light to make their hair shine like jewels of ruby and gold. They were perfect and somehow they looked just like her. Maybe that's how it was in Heaven; everyone looked like you just so you could feel better and more at home.

Mandy suddenly felt the hands pull hard on her dress as she shivered from the cold air as it hit her bare breasts. It made sense. In Heaven you would have to dress like an angel, but these soft hands suddenly became hard and tore the gown from her body. She was sure she must have died and gone to Heaven, not the other way. She was much too young to have committed enough sins for Hell and these lovely faces were full of concern and compassion. She was being pulled up off of her cold hard bed of steel and dragged up several, steep steps. One of the angels held her against a warm, steel wall and then dragged her out into the cold night. The rain beat down on her for a few minutes and she knew she couldn't be in Heaven or Hell for that matter, because there was rain, wind, and cold all around her. A blanket was being wrapped around her tiny shoulders. She was still in the real world. She must forget. Forget it all. It was never really real. It couldn't be.

More voices; male, one, no two and a woman, lights overhead, tubes up her nose, in her arm. She could feel the heaviness coming out of her body and could make out a few phrases.

"Where did they park the wheelchair?" a male voice asked softly

"By the intake desk, we didn't see anyone near her," a female answered.

"How drugged is she, and how deep are her burns and cuts?" Dennis's voice was husky with concern.

"We started an IV, and as soon as we find out what she has taken we can take steps to counteract it. The burns and cuts are on the surface only, but there are so many. I'm sure they'll traumatize her," a female voice replied.

"All in all, we're making progress," a second male added.

"Can I speak to her?" the first male asked.

"If she comes around – she keeps going in and out."

Mandy's eyes opened once again. Wow! She wasn't in Heaven. She wasn't even dead. However she had seen angels and she had seen the devil! She knew she had. The angels' hands had placed her near safety, while the devil had marked her for his own. Mandy couldn't take any more memories. She could hear her name being called from somewhere above, pulling her back up from the abyss. She opened her eyes to see a handsome man with a kind face and a caring look sitting on the edge of the bed. He told her his name and said he had to ask her some questions – it was important. What could she really tell him? It was all a foggy dream.

* * *

Dennis sat on the bed calling Mandy's name softly, her hand resting like a delicate flower in his large one. Soon the young girl's eyes fluttered open. At first all Dennis could concentrate on was the blue of her eyes. His heart sunk as he noted their vacant stare. He could see the bruising on her neck as well as the marks and cuts along her arms. Dennis could get all of the medical information later. For now he needed Mandy's best recollections of the past several days.

"Hi Mandy," Dennis's voice was soft and reassuring. "My name is Detective Dennis Kortovich; I'm a good friend of your dad and mom." He paused, noting the moment of clarity and recollection in her eyes. "I'd like to ask you a few questions if you're up to it," he said, as he reached into his coat pocket. "I'm going to take notes and tape our conversation, is that OK?" He pulled out his small tape recorder, turned it on, and set it at the head of the bed as he spoke, never taking his eyes from hers. Mandy nodded. From his breast pocket Dennis pulled out his familiar black note pad and pen. He nodded to the doctor to stay and asked Mandy once again, "Ready?"

"Yes," came a weak reply.

"What do you remember?"

"Angels. Two. No three angels."

"What do you mean?"

"They rescued me."

"How?"

"They took me away."

"Away from where?"

"The ground. A man underground somewhere."

"Can you remember the location?"

"No."

"Who was the man?"

"I don't know."

"What did he do to you?"

Mandy squeezed her eyes shut and a tear slid down her cheek. "I don't remember," she said slowly.

Dennis sensed she was reluctant to go into the details of her kidnapping so he decided to leave that line of questioning alone. "OK. Can you tell me what he looked like?"

"I can't remember."

From her breathing it was clear that the questions were taking their toll. She either could not, or would not remember, but Dennis had to press on. "What things do you remember?" he asked, keeping his voice soft and reassuring.

"A bridal chapel with wedding music and a gown."

"Were you at the wedding?"

"Yes. I was the bride." Mandy's voice began to quiver. "We were the only ones."

"What did he look like?" Dennis asked, once again.

"A headless man – it's like a dream. I see a headless man on a horse riding at night. He has a sword and he's going to cut me." Mandy's voice was beginning to rise, hysteria just a breath away.

"It's OK. You're safe." Dennis tried to calm her, keeping his voice steady. He decided to try a new angle. "What about the angels?"

"They swore." Mandy gave a small smile.

"What do you mean?"

"The angels swore. Then they said I was safe and they took off the wedding gown. Then they swore," Mandy said looking a little more upbeat.

"What did they look like?"

Mandy closed her eyes trying to draw the image of the angels to her mind. When she opened them she smiled a brilliant, wonderful smile, like children do when they know they have the right answer. "Like me. They look just like me, but they're angels, especially the youngest one."

"How old is the youngest?"

"Young like me, she was my age."

"And the other two?"

"Like I said, just like me, but older."

Slowly, Mandy's eyelids drifted over her glazed, blue eyes. She was out once again. He would have to wait for a while before he could continue.

The doctor came around the bed to Dennis's side and motioned him to follow him back to the waiting room. "She'll be out for a while," he said quietly. "We can try again later."

Once they were seated in the waiting room across from Mandy, Dennis asked Dr. Grout about the extent of Mandy's wounds.

"She has cuts and bruises all over, but what is even worse is that some sick bastard took a cigarette and put hundreds of small burns all over her chest. It's awful. We've bandaged some of the deeper cuts and put special burn pads all over her chest, making it a little more comfortable. The wounds will heal, but I'm afraid she will still have scars."

"What about sexual abuse?" Dennis was almost afraid to ask, but it was better to get the answer before her parents arrived.

"No. She's still a virgin, but I've no doubt from the story she just told about a wedding that she was due to be someone's sex bride. She also has burses on the inside of her legs," Dr. Grout continued. "Whoever got her away from that monster did so just in time. Whatever drugs she was given, and we'll know which soon enough, sent her on a real trip. It will be a while before she sifts through that angel and headless rider stuff."

"Thanks Doc, I'll wait here for the judge and his wife. When they get here, can you bring them to me first?"

"Sure thing. Just relax, I'll be back soon."

Dennis sat down in a high-back chair, the kind that was made to sleep in. He could picture family members worried over the health of loved ones being able to catch an extra forty winks in a chair this comfortable. Angels and headless riders, the only clues he had so far. How much was real, how much was fantasy? He sure hoped he would be able to find out soon.

Dennis was replaying the tape recorder when he heard the sound of excited voices and purposeful steps coming from the hall. He could tell there were at least five people; four men, one woman. No. One more woman followed behind, trying to catch up.

He stood just as the superintendent, Judge Switzer, Dennis's partner Chuck, the doctor, and Mrs. Switzer came through the door. Behind by a few steps was Mrs. Switzer's mother, Marsha Stewart. All except the doctor looked relieved.

The superintendent was the first to speak. "What do you know, Kortovich?"

Judge Switzer spoke next. "Yes, how is she?"

Mrs. Switzer turned to the doctor with a pleading look. "When can I see her?"

"She's asleep again and I suggest we wait for a while. She drifts in and out." Dr. Grout tried to calm the excited bunch. "Every time she rests she gains a little more strength. Let's all sit down and go over what we know."

Once they were all seated, the doctor motioned for Dennis to start – he would fill in the medical information after. He was still waiting for a report from the lab.

"So far she's still pretty groggy. Whatever her abductor gave her was powerful enough to knock her out for a few hours. Whatever his final plans were, he didn't want her to fight back. She was found in a wheelchair in the emergency lobby. Other than panties, she was naked, wrapped in a plain gray blanket. The lab will run tests on the blanket when I leave here. No one saw anyone put Mandy in the lobby, but I was able to ask a few questions before she drifted off. I'll play the tape and you can hear everything first hand."

Dennis knew a full disclosure would be appreciated and once again a different insight to the questions and answers would help. Often crimes were solved by the astute observation of some small, overlooked detail. They just finished listening to the last of the tape when the nurse came into the waiting room and announced Mandy's return to consciousness. Everyone quickly filed into her room. Judge Switzer and his wife Lena were at her side in seconds. Her grandmother stood at the foot of the bed. The superintendent, Dennis, and Chuck stood back, giving Doctor Grout and Mandy's family room to gather round her bed. Once the hugs and tears were over Mandy tried to assure her family she was all right. It wasn't too long before everyone could see Mandy's small face was once again overcome by a wave of sleepiness. Her blue eyes began to close as she drifted off to sleep. Mrs. Switzer wanted to continue to stay at her daughter's side, unwilling to let her hand go. She stayed while they returned to the waiting room to continue their discussion of the tape as well as to get the final details on Mandy's condition.

It was Judge Switzer who offered the questions first. "What did she mean by angels and headless horseman and why was she naked?"

Dennis knew Judge Switzer was a loving, caring man, but at this moment his face looked like a thundercloud. He wanted answers and Dennis knew he would go crazy when he found out the condition of Mandy's body. When all of the information had been given to everyone present in the small waiting room, there was no one left standing. Everyone sat on the chairs scattered about the room, trying to digest the unfathomable information Dennis had given them.

They tried to make some sense of what, at this point, made no sense at all. All they knew for sure was that Mandy had been lured away from the rave several nights before. She had been beaten, cut up, and sadistically burned over and over, in a brutal attempt to accomplish something only the abductor would know. Mandy had been somewhere and because of her drug-induced state, she thought she had been at a wedding, where she was the bride. Three angels who looked just like her had rescued her. A headless rider had chased her, trying to strike her down with a sword. It was going to be Dennis and Chuck's jobs to sort out fact from fantasy, something that would take time and patience.

Finally, the doctor got the medical report from the hospital lab and he went over the report with everyone. Mandy had a deadly, mind-altering agent in her system and he had already ordered an antidote. Thank God, whoever found her had gotten her to the hospital when they did. It was only the intravenous that had been given to her as soon as she arrived that allowed some of the poison to be diluted enough for her to gain consciousness. She needed time and Dr. Grout made sure the family knew they could stay in the waiting room just in case she woke up again and asked for them. Dennis and Chuck decided to call it a night and return in the morning. Dennis had the hospital report and the old gray blanket in a plastic bag. He would drop the blanket off at the forensic lab before going home and trying to get a couple of hours of sleep. It would still be a long night and Dennis gave the judge his tape recorder with a fresh tape, asking him to record anything Mandy said. Everything or anything could be a clue. Once outside in the cool August evening air, Dennis and Chuck exchanged their personal views.

"Whatever happened to the other girls almost happened to Mandy tonight," Chuck said.

"I agree, and I'm sure the only reason Mandy's alive is that one or all of the angels are real. She was rescued by them just in time." Dennis gave the toxicology report to Chuck.

Once he read it through quickly, Chuck gave a low whistle. "She had enough shit in her blood to kill her if we hadn't got an IV into her in time. And whoever moved her got her to vomit and that alone made a big difference. Moving her also got her heart rate up before she lapsed into a state of unconsciousness. Mandy owes her life to whoever brought her here. It's our job to piece it all together." Chuck gave the file back to Dennis. "Let's meet in the morning for breakfast and go over it all once again before we return to the hospital."

Both men agreed and as they drove off into what

was left of the early morning, they thought about the other girls in the cold case files and could only guess at the horror of their deaths. With no bodies, it was still only guesswork.

All of the missing girls fit the same profile except one – Charlotte. Either she wasn't a part of these crimes or she would be the missing link. Either way, it would be her case that they would start with to see if they could find out why she was the only one different from the other girls, and how they all fit together. Both men hoped they could get some much needed sleep before they would begin the around the clock investigation of what was now one hell of a bizarre case. In a city where crime and death sometimes seemed commonplace, both men still found it difficult to understand the kind of man it would take to lure away young, innocent girls from their homes and then inflict untold pain and horror on their bodies before what was likely a brutal end.

As they left the hospital, each in their own car, they never noticed the old station wagon that was parked just off to the side of the emergency department.

* * *

Derek sat inside, his face hidden by the shadow of the building. As the detectives drove off, Derek pulled forward, turning in the opposite direction. He had seen the news about Mandy and his need to retrieve his prize and finish his task had driven him to the hospital in the hopes that he might be able to get Mandy back. It seemed that would now be impossible. They would likely have a police officer guarding his prize. Oh well! There were other plums to pick.

CHAPTER
TWENTY-TWO

Derek Hanson woke up the next morning to the sound of birds and bugs shouting out a discordant tune, despite the fact that all of the windows and doors of his tiny, acreage home were shut tight. The curtains were drawn to keep the morning light out of the dreary little farmhouse. The sound of the birds and bugs singing their morning song fell on deaf ears. The only thing Derek heard was the echo of screams and the sound of profanity from the night before ringing in his ears. "Fuck you, you freak."

Derek couldn't smell the clear fresh air; all he could smell was the lingering odor of vomit on the torn hem of the wedding gown as he pulled it to his long, bony face. An evil smile exposed his yellowed, bucked teeth. Flashes of her young, white body assaulted his senses, making it difficult to sort out what had happened, or better yet, what had gone wrong. Stolen, she had been snatched away from him just before he was about to consummate the wedding night.

Derek slipped into a world of delusion. From the day

of Lisa's death, he had tried to make his young victims see how much they needed him, like he always did on August twenty-fourth. Lisa, his little sister, the love of his life was gone and this young woman would take her place.

He had loved his baby sister from the first moment he saw her, the day his parents had been called by Social Services to come and pick up their new daughter. She was perfect. He had just turned seven and even then he had been too tall and thin. His bony features and strange looks caused him to feel isolated and alone. He too had been adopted and often he found himself wondering what kind of unholy union could have made the likes of him. Although at seven, all he could think of was how ugly his birth parents must have been, to give birth to a boy as ugly as him. The other children in school tormented him, calling him all sorts of names. The older children who beat and bullied him couldn't understand that his unusual height belied the fact that he was little more than a child. For the first seven years of his life he had felt isolated and alone. Now he would never be by himself; he had a baby sister and she would never leave him. She would love him forever and ever.

* * *

Derek shook himself out of his review of the past and drew the vomit-stained dress away from his face. He placed it gently on a chair that sat in the corner of a dirty, tiny living room, above the chair hung a picture of Lisa, his sister. The face that smiled down at him was the last photo taken, just before his mother and father had died. It was a terrible accident, but one that had been bound to happen, given the condition of the old boards around the well. Their deaths left him as the only guardian and family his little sister had. By then she was twelve and he was an ugly, gawky nineteen years old. As ugly as he was now, he looked even worse then. His skin was a mess with white, pussy pimples that covered his face. The light fuzzy stubble that covered his chin and upper lip made his face appear dirty. He was unable to shave often, due to the condition of his skin. He had always worn his hair long in an attempt to cover ears that were so large they protruded through the greasy hair. His buckteeth had a dull, yellow tint and when he spoke, spittle filled the corners of his mouth. Derek had always known he was adopted, but it become even more apparent as his little sister grew into a tiny, delicate beauty.

Lisa's blond hair, with its copper highlights made the natural curl look like spun gold, framing her tiny, perfect face. Her clear, blue eyes looked out under perfectly arched brows that were framed by lashes that touched their finely featured arches.

When she was very young, Lisa had adored him, but as time went on she too noticed that he was different. The more Lisa pulled away from him the more obsessed he became. At first he tried to bribe her with treats and presents. But after a while she rejected the bribes, forcing him to take out his pain and frustrations on small animals and the neighbor's dogs and cats. This behavior started his life-long obsession with death, which eventually would lead him to his present career as a mortician. Derek found his greatest pleasure came from causing small animals a slow, tortuous death. It was the cigarettes that gave him the biggest rush. The smell, the sizzle, the howls of pain from the helpless animals, gave him a sense of power that he had never known before. Often he would replace the real life image of the cat with the face of the latest bully, giving an extra rush to the torturous deed.

Derek took the picture of Lisa down from the wall. As he gazed at the lovely face in the frame it stared back up at him. He stroked her cheeks and caressed her hair as if she were still a living, warm being of flesh and blood, rather than a face in a cold, framed picture.

"It's your fault Lisa. If you had loved me, none of this would have happened."

The sound of Derek's voice was flat and emotionless like the heart that beat in his chest, a heart that kept his body alive, but never pumped life into his soul. "You could never love me and your betrayal made me do what I had to do. One day I'll find love. She will see what you couldn't. Being loved by me could have made you happy. I would have given you anything, but all you wanted was some pretty boy." Derek's face twisted into an ugly smile.

* * *

He remembered a time when Lisa had only been twelve and she had a crush on an older boy who took a fancy to her. The young man's name was Tim something or other, Derek couldn't remember his last name; after all, Tim meant nothing to him. Tim was only a temporary problem. He rode on the same bus as Lisa and often got off to walk her to the door and talk for a while after school.

Their parents thought it was cute and encouraged the relationship, hoping Derek would let go of his obsessive hold on Lisa. Derek tried to tell his parents that Tim wasn't any good for Lisa, but they only got angry with him.

"Derek, stay out of Lisa's business. She is old enough to decide who she likes and have as a friend. It's healthy for a young girl to have a crush and as long as Lisa sees Tim here, at our home, we don't see the harm in the friendship." His father, Elliot, stood close to Derek in a way that said he was willing to take him on if he were to argue any further.

It was late spring and Derek decided that he would quit arguing and take matters into his own hands. From the Hanson's house, the walk to Tim's home was about one mile. If you cut through the woods it was a shorter distance, even if the terrain was rougher. There was one spot where a stream cut across the property and the only way across was to step on several large stones. In spring, the runoff from the snow plus the spring rains made the stream much more difficult to cross. It was here that Derek decided to make sure that Tim never crossed the stream again.

Tim had stayed a little longer than usual talking to Lisa and the sun was going to set soon. Rather than walk the long way around, he decided he would go through the woods.

Derek had kept himself hidden from view as Lisa sat with Tim on the front porch. Tim held her hand, his face close to hers. Derek felt like taking a run at him and slamming his fist into his pretty-boy face. He held his impulse in check listening to Tim as he whined to Lisa about his dislike of Derek just before he headed home.

"Your brother hates me and I think he would rather hit me than to say hello. I don't know how you can stand having him hover over you so much. He never seems to leave you alone." Tim squeezed Lisa's hands, letting her know he was trying to understand the relationship and not judge it too harshly.

"I know Derek seems creepy, but it's mostly because he's lonely and I'm the only one he's got. He's never made any friends his age and so I'm the only playmate he's ever had. I guess he just can't see that I'm grown up now and need to have friends of my own. He's just afraid I'll get hurt," Lisa said.

Derek watched as Lisa looked up at Tim.

"It's more than being lonely and wanting to keep you to him-self. I sense something evil in him. It's not right the way he looks at you. It's like he wants to be your boy-friend. Don't you see it?"

"That's not nice to say. He's my brother. I don't like him that way. It would make me sick. I'm sure you're wrong." Lisa recoiled away from Tim.

"I still don't like him and he creeps me out. I have to go." Tim said, as he moved away from Lisa. "Just think about what I said."

As Tim ran through the woods Derek followed close behind, making sure Tim didn't see him. Tim began to pick up speed. *Does he see me?* Derek thought as he followed close behind. Derek could almost smell Tim's fear as he stumbled through the damp underbrush and long grass, trying to get to the stream. It was early spring and although the air was still cold, Derek saw a sweat break out on Tim's face. Soon he was running ahead to the stream where he had to slow his pace in order to cross safely. The stream was high and rushing in a torrent – one slip and Tim would be pulled under by the current. He carefully started to make his way across the stream, watching each step, making sure his footing was steady before advancing. He was halfway across when he looked up, stopping dead in his tracks. Derek stood in front of him, an ugly sneer on his long, bony face.

Derek's eyes were blazing, his breathing short and shallow. Staying ahead of Tim had required him to move at full speed. But adrenaline was pumping into his blood and Derek felt like a superhero. "Well, I guess it's just you and me out here." Derek's voice was low and menacing.

"Look Derek, I don't want any trouble. I just want to go home. So let me pass and I won't say anything to Lisa about you following me," Tim said.

"You think you're going to tell Lisa, you little fuck face! You'll never say anything to Lisa ever again. If you think I'm going to let a young bastard like you touch my little sister you got a lot of thinking to do." Now Derek was beside himself. Anybody who witnessed his temper would feel as if they were in the presence of someone who was totally out of control. He had used it many times to keep others at bay. When he was younger it was a defense mechanism to keep bullies from beating him up. But as he grew older his rage grew deeper and deeper. Soon he knew he was capable of killing. He encountered the bullies many times over the years and once, when they cornered him, he went berserk, striking out at the small group that had gathered to torture him with taunts and slaps. He went so crazy that all of the young boys ran away in fear. They never bothered him again. And it was the last time Derek had ever been afraid of anything.

"Look, just let me pass!" Tim tried to gain access to Derek's larger rock, hoping he could surprise Derek, knock him off, and get away as fast as he could.

Derek was tall and lanky, but the strength in his upper body and his added height was still no match for the younger, well-built teen. He would have to use intimidation as an advantage. He growled low, and then howled. It caught his prey off guard and then Derek had Tim by the throat and shoved him as hard as he could. Tim went down in the frozen water, shock running through his body.

Derek could feel the pull of the current and knew he had to get to Tim before he got to his feet. He jumped off the rock and stood over Tim's soaked body.

Tim's hands were behind him and he was flailing like a fish, trying desperately to get up off the stream's bed. "Get away from me you fucking freak!" he shouted.

Derek grabbed Tim by his hair, shoving him further back to the point where Tim was almost fully laid out. Then he used all of the strength he had and held Tim's head under the rushing water. "You cock-sucking, little scumbag of shit, don't you ever think you can threaten me or take what's mine, Lisa will never be yours and no little prick-faced kid will ever touch her!"

Derek held Tim's head under the freezing stream while he screamed obscenities at the struggling young man. The water was cold and every movement took all of the strength he had to hold Tim under. The cold was taking its toll, and slowly the will to fight drained from Tim's body and he stopped struggling. It was over. Derek was the victor. Now no one would touch Lisa again.

The next day when they found the body, the police ruled it an accident. They said Tim had slipped off the rock and his foot had jammed between two large boulders causing him to be pulled under by the rushing current.

His winter clothes prevented him from being able to pull himself up and free his stuck foot. Lisa had given Derek a look that said she somehow held him responsible, but she never voiced her suspicions. Even Elliot and Gabrielle Hanson had a twinge of suspicion, but quickly brushed the thought aside. Derek was strange and obsessive, but he would never kill someone. At least they hoped not. The police said it was an accident and they decided to leave it at that. It was a decision they would live to regret. As time went on, Derek's obsession with Lisa became even more apparent. Family photos became a nightmare when Derek announced that he would not pose for a photo. He was too ugly. They were already at the studio when he backed out so they had no option but to do the sitting with only the three of them. Lisa did a separate portrait, one that showed what an outstanding beauty she was. Derek had a huge copy made and hung it over his bed. More than once Elliot and Gabrielle overheard him talking to the picture in loving, obsessive tones. Something would have to be done with Derek, but what?

Derek was no longer afraid of his parent's dilemma of 'What to do with Derek?' They both unfortunately met with an 'accidental' death. That left him to make all decisions regarding him-self and Lisa. He no longer had to worry about his parents getting in the way, or anyone else for that matter.

* * *

Derek was drawn back to the present and as he focused on the picture of Lisa that he held in his hand. He was reminded of how little consolation it gave him compared to the warmth of her flesh and blood. "But everyone's not like you, Lisa. Others will see me for what I am, a man of power; power over life or death. I may not look like a god, but I am one, a fucking god!" His voice rose, spittle forming in the corners of his mouth. "No one can stand in my way of getting what I want. Not Mom or Dad or some young skinny kid who thought you were hot."

Derek began to put the picture back on the wall, pausing for only a second to place his protruding lips on the glass of the picture. He closed his eyes thinking of her white skin, tiny breasts, and perfect face. He would have her still, and take his revenge at the same time. "They tried to destroy what we had, but I'll get even. I'll get back my treasures and this time I will be loved!"

Derek finished hanging the picture on the wall and turned his thoughts to revenge. He knew who the driver of the van was. He had met her before. He had known about the family long before Jade had come up to arrange her mother's funeral. Jade had almost belonged to him. Derek had spotted her just outside of the high school, two years ago. She was perfect and he needed her to belong to him. It was the fourth anniversary date of Lisa's death…a death he regretted, but she had forced him to choose. He could lose Lisa to another in life, or keep her to himself, through death. There was only one way to keep Lisa forever, but Derek found himself driven to find a different ending, other than the death of his beloved Lisa. That was the beginning of his need to re-enact his last moments with her.

So far the story was always the same. Each one rejected him. But one day, one of girls would see him for who he was; a man to be loved who could love back. The first time Derek ever abducted anyone was on the date of

Lisa's birth, the second time on the date of her death.

He had continued the pattern ever since. The girls all resembled his beloved Lisa, and Jade was perfect. Her hair was a little redder than Lisa's but her eyes, face, and body were a perfect match. Derek knew she would fit the gown he had bought especially for his bride and that Jade would wear it on the day of his special event.

Three years ago, things had gone wrong. Derek had stalked Jade for months, something he always did. It made him feel close to his victims. He could never love a stranger. Derek knew Jade would be more difficult than the rest; she seldom went anywhere except to school and back home. Then things changed. Jade began to go out and visit a new friend, a tall brunette. This would make things easier. Jade finally came out at night and would walk home alone. Now he could capture her undetected, and make her his bride. Derek knew that after Jade visited her friend she would stop by the park and sit on the swing, watching the stars. The night he spotted her sitting on the swing set was a cooler than usual evening, even for the end of April. The black coat she wore was pulled up tight around her neck, an oversized hood pulled up over her head, she swung slowly back and forth, unaware of his slow deliberate approach. The evening was a dark, moonless bed of black. At times it was hard for Derek to see much in front of him. He followed the sound of the swing and the sweet sound of her voice as she hummed an unknown tune. He had a bottle of chloroform. It should be easy.

Jade was small, she looked the same age as his sweet Lisa was when she rejected him for the last time. Derek came up behind Jade, wrapping one long arm across her chest grabbing her left hand with his as he leaned over her body. Suddenly she shot up off the swing and tried to run. Derek held fast to her left hand as she swung around, falling hard. She started to scream. Derek had counted on the element of surprise to help him silence her with the use of the chloroform. Now she was a wild cat and much stronger than he had anticipated. Derek had to straddle her body and sit on her chest while trying to pin those arms that were now pounding him with all of their strength. Boy did it hurt and she packed one hell of a wallop. The screaming got louder, eventually attracting attention from a neighbor nearby who turned on a back-yard light, suddenly casting a glow across the park. The hood fell from the girl's face as she stared up at Derek, seeing him fully in the light.

The eyes that stared up at Derek weren't a perfect blue, they were a dark, smoldering brown and the hair that tumbled out from under the hood was a rich, dark brown. She saw him just as he saw her. It was wrong! All wrong and Derek knew what he had to do. He struck her hard across the face. Her jaw cracked from the force of the blow and she went limp as he shoved the dirty chloro-formed cloth in her face. Derek was angry. So angry that the cloth he pushed onto her face was delivered with such force that her nose crumbled beneath his large hand.

Fuck! he thought. This wasn't Jade. It was that tall bitch she hung around with. The kind that was popular and had always given guys like him the cold shoulder. Derek stood up, pulling her to her feet. She hung limply in his arms. He wasn't sure if she had been knocked out from his assault or if he had actually killed her, but he knew he had to get her out of the park. Derek was tall and skinny, but he possessed an unusual strength few would suspect at first glance. He bent forward pulling her toward him, and in one swift movement hoisted her easily over his shoulder. He carried her the same way a hunter carried a deer after the kill. However, Derek wasn't after this prey, so he felt none of the hunter's pride, only rage…the kind of rage one feels when the thing you wanted most in life has been taken from you, the kind of rage that needed to be vented on the object that had prevented him from fulfilling his needs. She would pay for being here tonight.

Derek didn't know what had gone wrong. How had it been that bitch of a brunette Charlotte and not Jade on the swing? She had ruined everything and he would skin her the way he had all those cats and small dogs over the years. It was wrong, all wrong and he would cut her with X's and cross her out the same way he would any useless unwanted thing. Derek swung her into the back of his old station wagon and drove off onto the black night. He could hear her breathing. She was still alive. She would regret that the blow to her face hadn't ended her life, right then and there. What he had planned would be a fate worse than anything he had ever done before. Skinning her alive would give him a great deal of pleasure. Charlotte would represent all of the popular kids that had ever tormented him and caused him so much pain. They were the ones who had made his Lisa see what a loser they thought he was. He would show her just what a loser could do.

Derek had taken Charlotte straight to the funeral home. He would not have her defile his chapel of love. She would not live long enough. Charlotte was laid out on the steel table in the hidden chamber beneath the crematorium.

"What do you plan to do with me?" Charlotte asked once she regained consciousness and realized she had been abducted.

"I never had any plans for you. You just happened to be in the wrong place at the wrong time and now you've wrecked my plan. You will pay for this." Derek put his face close to Charlotte's while he pulled her head back, yanking fiercely on her thick head of hair.

Charlotte spit in Derek's face. "You let go of me or else."

"Or else, what? You're tied up and it seems as if no one is here to defend you. It's just you and me. If you treat me well, maybe I'll let you go," Derek said knowing he would never let Charlotte live. Even if she did try to please him she wasn't what he wanted and there was no going back. This little game would have to be played out to the end.

"Look. I have brothers and they'll kick your ass. Now let me go."

"It's time to play a little game. It's called ashes," Derek said, as he lit a cigarette, dragging deeply.

"I don't smoke and you can't make me," Charlotte said screwing up her nose.

"You think the game is to get you to smoke? Shit, when I'm finished with you, you'll be begging to take a drag. No my sweet. I have a better use for this cigarette than to suck on it with you." Derek laughed with disbelief.

Charlotte gave Derek a cold stare and tried to pull her head from Derek's grasp. Suddenly Derek stood up dropping her head hard on the steel table. When he turned around, the cigarette was red hot. He pulled it from his mouth into his bony hand and placed its hot tip on Charlotte's face. She screamed out in surprise and anguish.

"This is just the beginning," Derek said as he touched the cigarette to her face again and again.

The screams that echoed inside the small chamber made Derek feel strong and powerful. It took several hours for Charlotte to finally die. She was a strong, determined young woman. When Derek put the knife to her breasts and started to carve them from her chest she took her last breath. But not before she made one last statement. "Fuck you. Rot in hell."

Derek went crazy. It was always the same. She would pay for her last insult. He carved Charlotte to pieces.

Over the next three years he had continued to abduct young girls, finding perfect replacements for Lisa. It had been a full six years since Lisa's final rejection and except for the brunette, he had loved over one dozen perfect girls. Next it would be Crystal, not Jade, who would be his new bride. Jade was now unacceptable, while Crystal was perfect. It would be Jade who would have to give him back his treasures and Derek knew she would willingly walk into his trap. He would have her sister for 'better or worse.' Derek knew the girls' secret. Jade would come out of love for her sister and for self-preservation. He knew what they had done. But first he would have to go shopping. His newest bride would need something beautiful to wear and Crystal would make the perfect bride.

CHAPTER TWENTY-THREE

Dennis and Chuck sat across from each other in Dennis's cubicle at the Area Three police station. Along the small wall were pictures of Dennis, Chuck, and his other partners. Some of the pictures were of the superintendent and Dennis at different events where the city of Chicago had paid tribute to the officers for a job 'above and beyond.' Dennis and Chuck had received many awards of merit. There were pictures of Dennis exchanging handshakes and awards of recognition with the mayor as well as many other notables, even the president, Bill Clinton. During the past twenty years Dennis had moved up the ranks, as had his partner. Dennis was one of the most decorated and respected police officers on the force, along with his favorite partner, Chuck.

Dennis hadn't joined the force until his late twenties. A former trucker, he had always had a lifelong interest in the Chicago police force and so his wife Veronica had finally convinced him to try out. His high scores on the written exams and his still youthful physical abilities had proven that age was no barrier. In many contests, Dennis often beat most of the other men who were much younger. Now fifty, he could still boast a slim, strong body, a contrast to his dedicated, but chubby partner Chuck.

At fifty-five, Chuck was packing around an extra thirty pounds and although it made him appear heavy, he was still able to pull off a good chase if need be. Chuck's easy nature and keen mind added a new perspective to Dennis's methodical, logical, and meticulous police work. They were a great team and even better friends. Chuck had what many envied, a will of steel with the nature of a saint. Dennis knew Chuck loved his job and woke up most mornings itching to get on with whatever case was at hand. He was still the kind of officer who liked to 'rush in, where fools fear to tread,' and Dennis kept him grounded from his usual maverick style.

"OK Chuck, including Mandy, what do you see when you look at these photos of our missing girls?" Dennis pointed to a string of pictures along a short wall to the side of his desk. The photos were placed in two rows, one picture on top of the other, making thirteen photos in all.

Chuck was looking at them all together for the first time. Until now, he had glanced briefly through several of the files noting their ages and addresses, only briefly looking at their pictures. "It's easy when you see them like this; they all look alike except for the brunette. She's the only one that stands out as different." Chuck was stating the obvious.

"Right and they are all thirteen to fifteen years old as well." Dennis went over to the computer and pulled off a printout. "Now here's something else that will seem unusual if these were just a bunch of runaways." He handed the list to Chuck.

"Holy shit, this confirms your suspicion that these girls were abducted." Chuck ran his finger down the list. "All of the girls went missing on either one of two dates and so far it's an even seven girls on one date and six on the others. The brunette must have been a mistake. There were two abductions on the same day. Mandy's disappearance was two days ago on August tenth, the same date as the other five, while the other six were at the end of April, on the twenty-ninth." Chuck put the list on Dennis's desk.

"These girls are probably all dead and whoever's doing this has done away with the bodies. We've never found even one girl or a single clue."

Dennis picked up the file that had all of the written reports. The one he held was Charlotte's. Dennis flipped through her file. "This is the only one that's different. So this is where we're going to start. She might not be connected at all, but we may find out what went wrong." Dennis looked up from the file at Chuck's earnest face. "If we're going to find out anything we have to either rule her out as having any connection at all, or find out why she's a part of this other bunch of girls. She went missing on the same date as six of the others, April twenty-ninth. But she isn't even close to the others in physical appearance. Let's see if we can find out what went wrong and who the killer was really after."

Dennis grabbed his suit jacket off the back of his chair and headed toward the door.

"What makes you think he wasn't after Charlotte?" Chuck was curious about Dennis's conclusion.

"It's just a hunch. But you know I could be wrong."

Dennis gave Chuck a friendly slap across the back.

"When have you ever been wrong?" Chuck followed Dennis out of the office door as they headed toward the staircase leading to the main lobby.

Dennis always took the stairs; it was one way to stay slim. Chuck didn't mind going down but coming back up was a killer, so he often took the elevator, leaving Dennis alone for his trip up the stairs.

Dennis knew Chuck was impressed with his ability to draw conclusions, often based on instinct and a gut feeling as well as the cold hard facts. But, if his gut went contrary to the evidence, he used his gut. It was a trait that would usually be foreign to Dennis's factual nature, but over the years he had learned to trust his intuition. This ability had helped him solve hundreds of cases over the years, giving him an almost mythical reputation on the force. If Dennis's guts said the killer had made a mistake and was after someone else, it was his job to find out whom.

Dennis and Chuck wove their way through the afternoon traffic, heading back to Ukrainian Village, Dennis's neighborhood, and the place where Charlotte was from. They were going to question Charlotte's mother and father. An appointment had been made for the supper hour. As they tried to find a place to park in front of the reconditioned walk-up, an old brownstone building that had been restored to its original condition, his area known as the Little Ukraine. Dennis gave Chuck the list of questions he had prepared, hoping Chuck would see if anything else should be asked. It was a double-check system that would maximize their efforts; after all two brains were better than one.

Mr. and Mrs. Kennedy were an attractive, middle-age couple who seemed eager to meet with Chuck and Dennis. Their greeting at the door indicated their anticipation of the detectives' arrival. Once they were seated it was Mrs. Kennedy who took up the lead.

"We were so glad to hear from you. When Charlotte went missing we tried to convince the police that she wasn't a runaway, but they acted like they didn't believe us." Mrs. Kennedy leaned forward, her pretty face showing both concern and relief with Dennis and Chuck's presence. "What is it you would like to know? How can we help?"

Dennis wanted to put the couple at ease; he could sense their pain at not having any answers about their daughter's disappearance. "We would like to start from the beginning and many of the questions may seem the same, nonetheless there might be something that was overlooked. We're hoping to pick up a new clue and follow it."

"Sure." Mr. Kennedy spoke up for the first time. "For us it still seems like yesterday. We'll do anything to help."

Dennis started on the list. "When exactly did you realize Charlotte was missing?" Mrs. Kennedy answered many of the questions; mothers were always aware of their children's comings and goings. "By around eleven that evening."

"Where was she going?"

"Nowhere, she had gone out with friends, came home, changed into some casual clothes and went out for a walk."

"Was that normal?"

"Yes, she liked to unwind by going for a walk, it

helped her sleep."

"No worries about her being out that late at night?" Dennis looked to see if they would object to any personal reference that they had done something wrong.

"No, after all, this is Berwyn and we always felt safe." Mrs. Kennedy continued; "When you don't drive, walking home at night or going for a walk isn't unusual."

Dennis continued to jot down notes. She was right, his own daughters had walked everywhere and he and Veronica had never worried. "Who was she with?"

"Several friends, I think I gave the original officer a list."

Dennis pulled the list from the file and handed it over to Mrs. Kennedy who quickly gave it a once over. "Yes, these were her closest friends. If they met up with anyone else, I don't know whom. I'm assuming the other officer followed up, but who knows?"

Dennis could sense her disapproval of how the first case was handled. "Can you think of any reason why Charlotte might run away?" He knew this would hurt, but he had to ask.

"No, like I said to anyone who would listen, she would never run away."

"Can you think of anyone who would hurt her?"

"Never in a million years! Charlotte was the kind of girl who was very popular. Furthermore, she spoke to and befriended everyone. There were all sorts of kids at school who felt she was a good friend and they came from all kinds of groups."

As a mother Mrs. Kennedy was very proud of the spirit that Charlotte had possessed. After several more questions, Dennis and Chuck stood to signal their departure.

"Before we go, is there anything else that you can add or think of before we go and question her friends?"

"No, I don't think so." Mrs. Kennedy turned to her husband.

"Can I see that list first?" It was the first time Mr. Kennedy had spoken up since they had exchanged their earlier greetings.

"Sure." Chuck handed the list to him.

Mr. Kennedy looked the list over thoughtfully. "Honey, there is one name missing, that new friend of Charlotte's. She was only here a couple of times, but it could be important."

"Who's that sweetheart? I'm sure I included everyone." Mrs. Kennedy took the list from her husband and gave it a worried look, hoping her mistake hadn't interfered with the return of their daughter.

"You know; that pretty little one with the copper-blond curls and blue eyes."

When Mr. Kennedy gave the description, Dennis and Chuck exchanged a knowing, but surprised look.

"Yes, yes, you're right, how could I have missed it? She was a new friend, but Charlotte took a real fancy to her." Mrs. Kennedy put her hand to her face in dismay at forgetting the girl. "Her name was Jade, yes, Jade Walker."

Dennis stopped writing on the pad. Blood rushed from his head, past his heart, into his stomach, making him feel sick. In a flash he knew his guess was right, the killer had never been after Charlotte, he'd been after a perfect little girl with copper, curly hair and beautiful blue eyes. Jade looked like all of the other girls – she was a perfect match. She could have been a sister to any one of the other dozen girls who had gone missing. The only lucky thing that had ever happened to Jade was that somehow the killer had missed her, and from the information, had gotten Charlotte by mistake. Dennis hoped Jade could offer him some answers.

Chuck and Dennis thanked the couple and excused themselves. They wanted to say out loud to each other what was rushing through their brains. They were onto something, and now this case was beginning to hit close to home.

Dennis wanted to get back to the station. He had a new computer program that could give him a geographic location of the suspect, using the locations of the crimes. Historically, murders committed by serial killers often occur in locations familiar to the killer. If you enter enough information into the program, the algorithm could provide a location within a five-kilometer radius that the suspect was likely to live or work. It wasn't a new theory, but coming up with enough data to get an accurate location was often tricky.

"What are you thinking?" Dennis asked Chuck once they were out of the driveway of the Kennedy home.

"I'm thinking that technology is wonderful and that we need to put all of the information into the computer and see what we come up with. What I don't understand is why no one else saw all of the correlations in these cases; the dates, the girls' descriptions, the locations. I'm sure we'll pin this bastard down soon. They always shit in their own backyard and the stench leads us to them."

Dennis knew Chuck was right and he felt that they would have to come up with the location soon. If the killer were unable to complete the abduction and murder of his latest victim, would he strike again? Dennis's gut said yes! He only hoped the killer hadn't found a new victim and that they would have a little lead time before anyone else was hurt. And then there was Jade. Was she an abduction gone wrong? Dennis felt that she was. The question was. Would she still be safe?

CHAPTER TWENTY-FOUR

Jade, Crystal, and Amber sat around the kitchen table. It was already late in the afternoon. Between last night and this morning, their world had certainly taken a dangerous turn.

"What the hell are we going to do about this mess we're in?" Crystal's tone was more an accusation than a question.

"By 'mess' do you mean the killing and cremation of Dad? Or finding out Derek Hanson is a serial killer? Maybe it's the part about that girl being a judge's daughter. Better still, what about Detective Kortovich showing up and asking questions about Charlotte?" Jade shot back with a fair amount of sarcasm in her voice, her face looking dark and stormy. "We're somewhere between a rock and a hard place. If we had told the police about what we found they would have discovered our reason for being in the morgue. Then Derek wouldn't be the only one going to jail." Jade dropped her defensive tone and let the worry of what lay ahead sound in her high-pitched voice. "But if we shut up, Derek will go on killing. After what we saw we can't let the bastard get away with it."

"I know." Crystal stood up and started to remove the dishes from the table. As usual, lunch was Kraft Dinner, Amber's favorite.

Jade looked at Crystal's drawn face, then at Amber's sweet, unworried one. She envied Amber her special condition. She was able to live in a world where there was no trouble, no reality. All she needed was a bed, food, shelter, and the love of her sisters and of course her toy phone; everything else took place in her head and who could understand what was going on in there?

Crystal looked at Jade, hoping for an answer. "We have to find a way to stop him, but how? We're in a real pickle, as Mom would say. When Dennis and Chuck arrived at the door, I thought we were under arrest. It took me a while to figure out what he wanted. When he said it was about Charlotte I was relieved, but worried as well." Crystal moved around the kitchen, while Jade watched.

Jade automatically started helping her sister with the clean-up. It felt good to be doing something normal. "The first time the police investigated her disappearance I was never even questioned, only her old friends. Did you see the way they both stared at us like they were seeing us for the first time? From the questions they asked, they know nothing about Dad, but they are investigating the disappearance of the girls."

Jade drew Amber out of the kitchen into the living room and sat her in a rocker to the side of the TV. It would keep Amber calm for hours. She just rocked and stared at whatever was in front of her on the television, often a game show. Crystal followed them into the living room and soon she and Jade were curled up on the couch trying to come up with a plan to get out of their predicament.

"Somehow I figure we're tied into this mess beyond our little visit to the morgue." Jade looked into Crystal's blue eyes and saw what Dennis and Chuck must have. "Did you notice anything about those photos we found as well as the pictures we were shown by Dennis?"

"No, they're just a bunch of missing girls and we are the only ones who know they're dead and who killed them." Crystal gave the answer she thought was obvious.

"Look again." Jade drew the pictures out of a shoebox that had been hidden under the couch. Inside were all of the pictures she had torn from the wall of the hidden chamber as well as the rings, watches, necklaces, and earrings that had belonged to the missing girls. She spread them out in front of Crystal; thirteen in all. "What do you see?"

"Dead girls in a wedding dress, except for Charlotte and shit she looks awful," Crystal answered defensively.

"There's more to see than that Crystal and we're a part of it. I can see it as plain as the nose on your face."

Crystal picked up each picture slowly trying to see what Jade saw, feeling stupid and frustrated for missing whatever it was she was trying to point out. "I give up," she said, throwing the last picture back in the box. "What is it that you and the cops have figured out that I haven't?" Crystal's voice was rising, her anger mounting.

"They all look like us!" Jade almost shouted, lowering her voice so she would not have Amber move from her chair. "Small, light, reddish hair, fair completion, curls, and blue eyes. We could all be sisters." Jade knew she was close to an answer.

"Shit!" Crystal picked up a couple of pictures at random giving them another look. It was time for a new perspective. "We do look like them, but what does that mean?" She was still confused.

"I've been thinking about it ever since Dennis and Chuck left and I began putting it together by the way they acted and looked at us." Jade changed her position on the couch, sitting back, and pulling her legs up under her chin. "I think that the night Charlotte went missing, Derek was really after me. It wasn't supposed to be her. It was supposed to be me." Jade rested her forehead on her knees, feeling sick about what must have happened.

"I was with her that night, a bunch of us were. I was supposed to stay for supper and then watch a movie, going home somewhere around eleven." Jade reflected back on that night trying not to feel the emotional impact of what was supposed to happen. "Mom called because Dad was going berserk, so I left early. I slipped out the back door and cut through the neighbor's yard, taking a short cut. I would usually go through the park but I was worried, so I took my chances cutting through several yards. When I found out the next morning that Charlotte was missing, her mom said she had gone for a walk and she probably visited the park." Jade turned and looked at her sister again.

"I think Derek must have followed me there and waited. When he saw Charlotte he must have made a mistake, somehow thinking it was me, but taking her. Or maybe Charlotte surprised Derek while he was lurking outside her house. Somehow I feel she was a mistake and he really wanted me. Look at the pictures. He's put X's all over her body and even cut off her breast and mutilated her. He's angry, but only with her. The others may have been hurt by him; but look at the way he's laid them out in the wedding gown – they look perfect. He's replacing someone with girls that look just like us and now we've walked back into his life." Jade looked up for a few seconds before continuing.

"Did you see the way he looked at you during Mom's funeral?" Jade turned fully toward Crystal, dropping her legs and placing her feet on the floor.

"He's after me now and I sure hope he doesn't know it was us at the morgue last night or he'll really be pissed, and boy we will be in trouble," Crystal said.

Jade took in what Crystal was saying and however fantastic it may have sounded she knew it was true. Two years ago Derek had meant to kidnap her and somehow got Charlotte. With their mother's death Jade and Crystal had once again came into view of Derek. With the killing of Sam and his cremation, the girls had stumbled onto Derek's secret. Crystal and Jade were now caught between a killer and the police. Jade laughed to herself. It was ironic that they too, were killers. The difference between them and Derek was survival. If their dad stayed alive he could have beaten them to death or at the very least, finally unleashed his unnatural desires on them along with the verbal, mental, and physical abuse. Jade and Crystal had no choice but to kill – they had killed for their and their sister's survival. Jade wondered what drove Derek to do what he had done. Did he have a choice, or was he driven by some unknown fear or frustration that forced him to unleash his unnatural obsession with young girls, that looked just like them? It felt weird trying to find a reason for someone to do what Derek had done. There was no way he could justify his killing of young, innocent girls. It wasn't life or death. It was an evil and unnatural obsession.

"I can't come up with a single idea about what to do; I'm just too tired from all of this. It was only the day before yesterday we killed Dad, and yesterday we got rid of him. Now we're in an even bigger mess. I just want to forget it all for a while." Crystal grabbed the remote and turned on the TV. It was her way of saying it was over at least for a while.

Jade knew they would have to come up with a plan, but she felt every bit as tired as Crystal, so she too just let things go for a while.

"The return of young Mandy Switzer has the police baffled. Reports from an inside source say that her arrival last night at the Henrotin Hospital is shrouded in mystery. Her rescue is credited to three angels. Our sources so far say there is no lead as to the identity of the so-called angels. We'll bring you more on the story as new details unfold. Let's turn to Charles Duncan for a report on the weather." The voice on the TV changed as the weatherman took over and gave the latest weather report.

Jade and Crystal turned off the TV and slumped over, feeling dejected. They were so drained of emotion, neither spoke, each caught up in the horror of their present situation. Would they now be an obvious target for Derek if he were able to put things together with the report on the news? For all the girls knew, Derek was already planning his revenge, but tonight they just needed some sleep.

CHAPTER TWENTY-FIVE

Derek awoke to the smell of vomit; the torn gown lay just beneath his long oversized nose while the scent of soured food, mingled together to make an unusual aroma. Derek had taken the gown with him to bed. It somehow gave him a sense of comfort. The smell and the feel of satin and lace along with the importance of the gown, gave him some comfort and he had finally drifted off into an uneasy sleep.

Images of young girls running, tripping. His hands striking them down, his body on theirs, tiny breasts, large hands, the moans and tears along with vile tirades, their language hurtful. Small hands tied to their sides while the smell of flesh burning, along with the scent of his cigarette, gave him that familiar feeling of power, screams, begging to be freed, calling out for their mothers. Their rejections of him along with his anger mingled with the smell of fear, again the white dress billowing all around him then splitting into pieces along with the flesh of the young girls. Blood everywhere, the white turning to crimson. Once he had regained his senses, the dreams fading, he lay naked beneath the dirty sheets of his bed for a few minutes before putting his feet on the cold, gritty floor.

Derek concentrated on what the day ahead would hold. He needed to get a new dress for his bride. Tonight it would no longer be a hard cold hand in his bed, it would be a copper-haired princess and this time he vowed he would make her love him, the way he longed to be loved, touched, and admired. He was a man and he knew if given the chance, he could prove it. Derek looked down, a frustrated look on his face. Damn his manhood, it always betrayed him. One touch and it went off like a new recruit with a trigger-happy finger – bang, bang, you're dead.

Derek pulled back the sheets and rubbed the white creamy liquid into his stomach. He liked the way it felt beneath his fingers, sticky, hot. Today Crystal would become the new bride, she was older than Lisa, eighteen, but her delicate beauty made her appear much younger. If she refused she would feel the full weight of his rage on her body. Alive or dead, he would have her. At this point in time Derek no longer cared how things played out; he was driven by something dark and unexpressed inside. He would not, could not, look beneath the rage he felt. Death would no longer be an option. She would have no choice but to accept him.

Naked, he walked purposefully. His feet felt the dirt on the floor, but he was used to the filthy condition of his home. The stale smells, the clutter of old newspapers, fast food cartons, beer cans, and unwashed towels. To him it was home and a part of who he was. The bathroom was small and dingy with only a stream of light finding its way through the unwashed window, over the tub. The mirror that reflected Derek's long, bony face was spattered with years of toothpaste, soap scum, and water stains. He no longer needed to see himself when he shaved and he liked things that way. Seeing his face in the mirror only made him feel that sinking, lonely pain. If he didn't see his face he could forget just what a cruel joke life had played on him. When he did manage to catch a glimpse of himself, he would curse his unknown parents and wonder again what unholy union had spawned a man such as himself. It was at times like this that he would feel a seething rage. He never asked for this life. It was death that he yearned for, and until that welcomed time came, he would visit death daily at the morgue, the only place he'd ever felt safe.

Grieving people were too full of their own pain to cause him any with their looks and whispers. At the funeral home he felt respected and powerful, full of an exalted self-importance. More importantly, the dead never judged him. Their lifeless bodies seemed to welcome his ideas and confessions. Derek felt safe confiding his secrets to them and often their faces would appear to him in his dreams, spectators to his fantasies and guests at his weddings. With his bride at his side they smiled their approval as he stood before the altar; confessing his love to his bride.

Derek dressed in the dark. The shirt he wore was a blinding white, the only object of clothing that made him appear professional. The clean navy-blue tie made the shirt appear even brighter. He had one dozen shirts. He had them dry-cleaned to a crisp, perfect look. It made his appearance just passable. Derek used an electric shaver, he hated the feel of water on his face and only showered once a week. He used a strong deodorant. This along with a clean shirt got him through the week. He pulled his long, greasy hair into a tight ponytail. He was off to go shopping, then to work and later—well…

* * *

Derek had passed the boutique many times, and he always found himself looking at the elegant window display. Every once in a while he would see a gown that would almost take his breath away. The little boutique specialized in affordable wedding gowns and once or twice he had been so taken with a dress in the window he found himself pulled into the store. He had to touch the soft fabric of the white designs and he would fantasize about some young innocent girl. It was nearly noon when Derek finally left the puzzled and exasperated clerk with his prize under his arm. It was wrapped in a clear, plastic specialty bag so that all of its beauty was visible through the packaging.

Derek could tell the clerk recognized him from his previous visits into the shop. By now she figured he was just a looker, and she only gave him a brief glance when he entered the shop. She had already gotten used to his unusual looks. When he finally approached her to see what she had in a size two, she was able to keep her face open and pleasant, making him feel relaxed and excited about his purchase. He proved to be a difficult customer. He obviously had a certain style in mind. Just when she had exhausted all of her sale skills, she remembered a gown she had in the back room. It had arrived first thing that morning and up until then she felt she was at a dead end. She thought the gown would be too expensive.

"You know Mr. Hansen, we had a wonderful gown arrive this morning and I have a feeling it might just be what you're looking for." The dark haired clerk's eyes were hopeful.

She returned from the back with a gown that almost stopped Derek's heart from beating. It was what he had always imagined his Lisa deserved. The style of the gown was very similar to the one that had been torn from Mandy's innocent body only yesterday, but it was also different. This was the real thing, not like the cheap one that now lay in a heap back at his home. His hands went clammy in anticipation.

The straps were thin and small rhinestones were set among the white pearls, where a tasteful sprinkle of the gems were arranged in an intricate pattern that dropped to the bodice. From below the bust line the waist of the dress dipped into a V, dropping to a full skirt that fell to the floor in a cadence of lace and satin. It was a strange combination of innocent style and sophisticated detail. The dress was meant for a princess. Could a prince who looked like a frog win his love's heart? He had to have the gown. Derek never even blinked or missed a beat when he heard the price of the gown, twenty-eight hundred dollars. He simply took the gown, twirling it around for a full view.

Derek's thick lips curled up over his bucked yellow teeth as he smiled a slow, wicked smile with white spittle forming at the corner of his mouth. He said nothing as he reached into his pocket and pulled out his wallet, removing his gold bank card to pay for the gown.

After Derek walked out of the store, the clerk let out a suppressed rush of air.

Poor bride who marries a man like that, I think I'd rather be dead, the clerk thought as she returned to her new inventory, getting the gowns ready for display.

It was now noon. Derek was so engrossed in his own thoughts and his pleasure with the purchase of the gown that he didn't look up until he bumped into a man who was sharing the sidewalk with him.

"So sorry!" came a familiar voice.

Their eyes met at the same time, each unaware of the other until they collided.

"Mr. Hanson, nice to see you, I hope I didn't knock you too hard. I just wasn't watching where I was going." Dennis held out his hand, noting Derek's hands were full. It took a few seconds for him to realize that what Derek held in his hands was a wedding gown. "Getting married?"

It was an empty question, but somehow automatic. Dennis knew Derek was single and he couldn't picture what type of girl would be attracted to the man. He shook off the uncharitable thought. The day was already very warm and it continued to be an unusually hot, muggy August. You could tell that tonight, when things cooled down, another summer storm would brew up from the lake.

The sweat on Derek's brow felt cold and a sudden chill engulfed his skinny body. He knew he had no answer for the detective, but he had to say something.

"No...No...um...it's not...for me. Oh uh...nope... it's...it's for a friend, yes. I'm picking it up for a friend. She's busy. It's a favor." Derek knew he sounded stupid, but he could not think of anything else to say, so he just stared at Dennis, waiting for him to make a comment.

"Well, I guess I'd better let you get going, it's pretty hot out here. I'll let you deliver that dress, it looks pretty special." Dennis saw the flash of jewels sparkle through the plastic.

Derek looked down at the gown and gave an embarrassed nod, color rising to his pale fact. "Yeah, I gotta go." His long legs carried him off as fast as they could.

Dennis continued to walk towards his favorite restaurant, and on the way he passed the bridal shop. He had seldom given the store a second thought. Now he stood in front of the window wondering what his encounter with Derek had been all about. One of two things came to mind; either Derek had a sweetheart and the gown was really for her, or he was a drag queen and the gown was for him. The mental picture of Derek as a

love-struck groom with some young woman standing at his side made Dennis shiver, even on this hot day. Then again, Derek's long, bony; body in a sparkle-studded wedding gown wasn't a pretty sight either. Dennis had to go into the store to solve the mental puzzle. It would drive him crazy if he didn't have the answer.

The tall brunette was exactly the kind of woman who would work in a specialty boutique. She was slim and classy, and her greeting was warm, yet professional. "Hello, how may I help you?" The rich tones in her voice matched the perfection of her stylish look.

Dennis got right to the point, flashing his detective badge while he asked the question. "There was a man in here that just picked up a gown for a friend. What can you tell me about him?"

"I can tell you the gown wasn't for a friend. I just

spent the better part of the morning showing him every-thing in the store. The one he finally picked was the most expensive one we had." Her professional demeanor had dropped due to Dennis's surprise visit and her tone of exasperation and surprise was evident from her statement.

Dennis was still confused. What could Derek want with a hand-stitched, expensive wedding gown? Who was it for? He decided to try his second choice of reasons for Derek's interest in a wedding gown. "What size was the gown?"

"Size two. He said it was for a perfect angel. He was adamant that she was very tiny and nothing bigger than a size two would do."

The name on the saleswoman's nametag was Clarisse. Dennis figured it suited her. She was definitely a classy Clarisse. He pushed further for something that would make sense. "What else can you tell me?"

"Other than the fact that the mortician makes an unlikely groom?" Her question was rhetorical; she con-tinued without waiting for an answer. "He said she was like a precious jewel. He described her as an angel, with ivory skin and reddish, gold hair that curled in ringlets to the middle of her back." Clarisse looked as though she found it difficult to believe anyone of that descrip-tion could really be willing to marry a man like Derek. "I always ask for a physical description if someone comes in to look at the gowns without the bride, although it's usually an overly anxious mother." She waited for Dennis to continue.

"Well, can you tell me what he paid for the gown?"

"Sure. It was just a little over three thousand dollars with the tax. He never even batted an eyelash, just paid with a credit card."

Dennis was quiet as he took a look around the elegant store with all of the beautiful white gowns, encircling the perimeter. It made him think of what the inside of a cloud must look like; white on white, or cream on white, soft, and beautiful like a dream. He thanked Clarisse for her trouble and left the store, his mind working overtime.

What the hell did Derek want with a wedding gown? He had obviously lied when he said he was picking the gown up for a friend. Dennis then pictured in his mind what his second options were; Derek in drag, what a thought. He almost started to laugh at the mental picture of Derek in a skimpy bridal gown. Derek was an ugly guy, but as a woman what a scary thought. Ugh! But a size two, never! He was definitely not the one dressing in drag, unless he had a twisted, emotional view of his body.

So what did Derek want with a wedding gown; one that was obviously important to him in some way? There was a nagging thought at the back of Dennis's mind. Mandy! She said she had been a bride at a wedding. Was there a fit somehow? Dennis decided he would have to follow the trail to whoever was supposed to be wearing the gown. Whoever it was, they would require a warrant in order to check Derek's home and office to see if there was a connection. It would be difficult. He had no evidence that Derek was involved with the missing girls in any way – just a hunch. He had no witness, nothing, only Mandy. Then suddenly the idea of the crematorium flashed before his mind. His heart started to pound. Dennis felt he was on to something as he once again got that 'gut' feeling. A chill shot through his body. He knew he had to somehow push for a warrant. It was as if someone's life depended upon it.

Dennis had been about to meet Chuck for lunch and go over the computer generated data when he ran into Derek. He would keep his suspicions to himself, for a while at least. It would be difficult to convince Chuck that just because a man had a dress fetish, it would make him serial killer.

The restaurant was just beginning to fill up when Dennis saw Chuck burst through the door. He looked excited and full of purpose.

"What's up?" Dennis asked. "You look like you just figured out who killed Kennedy, and you know the odds on that." It was a running game between the two of them on who was the best detective.

The Kennedy assignation was the ultimate case and they had each come up with several unique theories of their own over the years. If they ever discovered who was behind the Kennedy murder, both Dennis and Chuck were sure one of them would go missing. It was Gerald Posner who had written the definitive book on the presidential assignation, *Case Closed*, heralded as 'the best' by his peers, which had both men leaning toward his theory on who did it. However, no matter how strong the evidence, both men preferred their own theories.

"So confess, what is it you know, that I don't?" Dennis asked.

"The computer program finally finished compiling the data and came up with related vicinity for the suspect and I think you'll agree there are some key points that will help to narrow down our killer," Chuck said excitedly.

"Let's see. You talk. I'll read. It will make things go faster." Dennis took the printout from Chuck while he settled in.

A waitress came to the table with a note pad and a smile. "What will you have, boys? Why don't you surprise me today and take a look at the menu and live dangerously? Who knows, you might find something different." She was unaware that 'different' in a restaurant was something both men wanted to avoid.

Dennis and Chuck ordered their usual favorites from the waitress, Sherry, a middle-aged widow who was now a good friend. Chuck liked the chicken, a change from steak. After the last case they'd worked, he would no longer eat beef in a restaurant, only at home where his wife Shelley assured him it was safe. Dennis was a little braver and could still eat a good steak anywhere, even if he wasn't too sure how it was prepared. Even so, they both still had a lingering fear from that last case.

The burgers at Paddy's Family Restaurant were good, but Dennis felt the best were still at Moody's Pub on North Broadway, another of their favorites. Charcoal grilled, Moody's Pub burgers were always cooked to perfection. A quarter pound of beef that could almost make one forget that hamburger was the lesser byproduct of beef. Again, after that last case, beef would never be the same.

"OK, it goes like this." Chuck started his explanation as soon as Sherry left with the order. "All of the girls came from three residential districts; Oak Park, Bowyn, and Elmwood Park. The rave that Mandy attended was smack in the middle of the geographic area in the Newton section. It seems Mandy hung around the area at a few of the clubs and always went to the same place for the rave. So we have a similar geographic area for all of the missing girls. Now we have to look around for either a likely place for the suspect to live or work. We have a large business district as well as the usual community services, like churches and schools." Chuck took a deep breath and continued. "We can rule them out I think because the girls went to different schools and different churches. That leaves us a common place they might all go in the business area. The clubs, eateries, shops etc. But look at this hot point on the sheet. It's not even near the business section. It's near a fucking graveyard. The computer is pointing to an area that seems unlikely. What do you make of it?"

Dennis couldn't believe his eyes. The print out was done in 3-D, making the most likely point bright-red and at the highest elevation. This geographic profile was a computer program that was designed by a cop in Canada, and although it was a helpful tool, it was not infallible. The hair on his arms stood on end and goose bumps traveled up his arm to his neck, causing his ears to ring. This time he knew the computer was on target. Right in the middle of the hot area was a funeral home, and who worked there? Derek Hanson.

CHAPTER TWENTY-SIX

Jade was the first to feel the warm breeze on her face and hear the sounds of early morning burst forth to announce the beginning of a new day. She smelled the sweet scent of freshly cut grass and heard the sounds of a robin's chirp and the jays' awful two-toned screech. It was all very new to her because she had seldom allowed a window to remain open. Over the years, Jade had learned that Sam could turn into a screaming maniac at any time of the day, so an open window was out of the question. Whenever the screams could be heard to escalate into physical violence, the neighbors would call the police but without help from Jewell or the girls, these official interventions would only lead to more abuse, usually at times when the nosy neighbors were sleeping and wouldn't call the cops.

Jade heard the sounds of her siblings in the room next to hers. It was larger than the tiny room that held all of her precious belongings, but Crystal and Amber had always shared the room. Now they could all have a room of their own, if they wanted. Crystal had decided to leave things the way they were for a while, even though

Jade had pointed out the advantage of a room of her own. Crystal just wasn't ready to make any decisions right now. Besides, Crystal loved sleeping with Amber, it was the way Amber rocked herself to sleep each night that had helped Crystal put away her worries and drift off to sleep. Amber also felt warm and smelled like baby powder. For now Crystal just wasn't ready to give up that feeling of comfort.

Jade burst into Crystal and Amber's room with a big smile on her face, taking Crystal by surprise. Jade was always very serious, while Crystal was just plain angry. It had become more and more of who they were and now here was Jade with an entirely new look on her face.

"What's with you?" Crystal scowled at her sister. "You'd think you found the winning lottery ticket from the look on your face." Crystal got up out of bed. She needed a bathroom urgently.

"Hey, where ya going? I thought we could all cuddle and talk. It's still early and we can get up whenever we want," Jade said, sounding hurt.

"If I don't go pee you'll be lying in a wet bed. So move and let me by." Crystal sounded annoyed.

Jade knew Crystal really wasn't annoyed. She would like a morning in bed, just talking and hugging. But when a girl had to go it was best not to stop her.

"OK but hurry, I can't believe we don't have Dad in the house anymore and with such a beautiful day ahead I just can't seem to worry about getting caught, even if I should." Jade jumped into the queen-size bed, a gift from her mother to the girls on Crystal's thirteenth birthday. She cuddled into the warm body of Amber who was now doing her familiar rocking back and forth. Jade put her nose close to her sister's face. She too loved the clean, fresh, baby smell of Amber's hair and the feel of her soft skin.

"Move over and make some room for me you bed hog." Crystal jumped in next to Jade, her personal needs taken care of.

"I can't, Amber's almost in the middle of the bed. Besides, this bed is big enough anyway. Wow!" Jade continued. "Can you smell how wonderful the fresh air is?"

Crystal and Amber's bedroom window was also open. "I know. It's just wonderful," Crystal piped in taking a deep breath.

All three girls lay side by side, saying nothing, just enjoying the sun, the smells, and the feel of their warm soft, bodies as they cuddled. Jade and Crystal's thoughts were drifting back to all of the events of the past week, starting with their beloved mother's death and ending with Mandy's rescue. They had learned to almost read each other's thoughts, especially because of the fact that over the years their survival had depended on this ability.

"So, now that we're alone. What's next?" Crystal always wanted answers.

"We need to do two things," Jade said, becoming serious as she temporarily put aside her early morning mood. "First, we need a good story about Dad; one that we stick to no matter what." Jade sounded confident. "And second, we try to find out if Derek has figured out that it was us at the funeral home. And if so, we'll have to figure something out that won't get us caught, but might lead the police to him. Either way, we need to figure out a way to lead the police to Derek."

"So what do we do?" Crystal anxiously asked.

"We can stay near the house and wait for Derek to make a move or we can follow him and see what he's up to." It was all Jade could come up with.

"If Derek does know it's us, he's going to want that stuff back that we took from the funeral home," Crystal shot back.

With her temporary enjoyment of the morning, Jade had forgotten about the trinkets and photos. "We need to get the pictures and jewelry to the police somehow. Then they'll know the girls are dead, not missing. Maybe there are some clues in the photos that the police could use that might lead them to Derek or to the funeral home."

Crystal pointed out what Jade was already thinking. "Alright, so how do you suppose we get the stuff to the police without getting found out, smarty-pants? We can't just drop them off. Someone may recognize us or maybe they have video surveillance since they are, after all, a police department. We've had so many officers in and out of this house over the years, they are practically like family. We can't risk being identified."

"No problem, we'll mail the stuff," Jade said simply.

"What if they can track us from the package? It's easy for the police to trace things. Don't you watch CSI?"

"We'll mail it from downtown, that way the postmark will be from a different section of town," Jade said.

"Sounds good to me, now let's just cuddle and forget all this stuff."

Jade was satisfied with the plan and for now she felt safe in her sister's bed, in her own home with the two people she loved most. Jade missed her mother but at least she would never have to feel the sting of her dad's hands or hear his foul words, or have him grope her body.

Peace at last.

* * *

It was late afternoon and Derek was just finishing the final touches to an elaborate plan that would soon unfold and deliver a new, young bride into his awaiting, anxious hands. He had the perfect dress. It was even better than the old one, although he would never throw the torn gown away. It held their smell, all of the girls who had been objects of his obsession. He needed it to feel close to them. He felt that the new gown would bring him the luck that so far had evaded him, failing to bring him the love he needed.

* * *

Dennis Kortovich awoke early the next morning feeling anxious. He had dreamed a strange, but telling dream most of the night. The wind had howled and blown around him. The moon was bright, setting off the hangman's tree that was dead and withered as it reached into a cloudless, midnight sky. The headless rider thundered down the windy, moonlit, dirt road, suddenly stopping in front of the gnarled old tree. The white, ghostlike horse reared into the air, while the unholy rider waved his gleaming sword over his head. During the dream, Dennis was aware that he was dreaming, but it was more than that. It was as if he stood outside of himself – time and space having little meaning in this world of dreams. He was able to view the dream in much the same way he would have if he had been at a movie. However, Dennis was somehow in the dream and out of the dream as well.

The headless rider held his severed head under his arm, his cape flapping in the wind. As the rider thundered closer and closer into view, Dennis was suddenly shocked to see the gruesome face of the beheaded man, while the rider cushioned the head under his arm.

Dennis awoke with a start, his eyes wide open, he knew to whom the face belonged. Dennis had seen the face as a child. The face was on the Disney movie *Sleepy Hollow*. It was the cartoon face of Ichabod Crane and the flesh and blood face of Derek Hanson, the mortician.

Was it a premonition, a prophetic dream, or was this Dennis's gut instinct working overtime? He knew the day ahead would give him the needed answer. It was early morning now, but he felt the urgent need to dress and get going for the day. There was an idea that stood at some level in his subconscious brain, like a stalker hiding in the shadows, not willing to reveal him-self until just the right moment. Dennis felt the need for a cup of coffee and a fresh doughnut. Somehow the mundane was what was needed to coax that evasive idea into the light of day. He was well on his way to the station, his coffee half gone, with the remnants of his doughnut now only a few crumbs at the bottom of the bag, when the inspiration from the dream hit him. It was something Mandy had said.

Mandy had referred to a headless rider. She too had been struck at a subconscious level at how much Derek Hanson looked like the cartoon character of Ichabod Crain. Dennis's subconscious was trying to tell him something, like it often did. They had a saying in police work, "Ninety percent perspiration, and ten percent inspiration." Often it was that ten percent inspiration that made all the difference in a case. Dennis was sure of his interpretation of his dream, as well as his gut feeling that Derek Hanson was somehow involved in the kidnapping of Mandy Switzer and the other girls. He had little or no proof, only two small coincidences that tied Derek to the case.

The first; Mandy's description and his subconscious recognition. Second was Mandy's insistence that she was the bride at her own wedding. Running into Derek with a new wedding gown under his arm, cinched it. The gown had been a perfect size two, the same size as Mandy and the other missing girls. But it was Chuck and the printout that took Dennis's hunch and turned it into more than speculation. Whoever was killing these girls lived or worked smack in the middle of the hot zone and the only business in the area was the Greenhill's cemetery.

Dennis was sure Derek was somehow tied into this case but all he really had to go on was a hunch and a drug-induced dream of an extremely traumatized young girl, as well as a new investigative tool that had yet to stand up to scientific scrutiny. It wasn't much, but it was a start. He was sure that if he followed the clues to their conclusion he would be able to come up with some answers. So far he had more questions than answers and he was determined to see exactly if, or how, Derek Hanson fit into the still elusive picture that was beginning to reveal itself. Dennis hoped the revelation would happen before anyone else was hurt or went missing.

CHAPTER TWENTY-SEVEN

Jade, Crystal, and Amber were sitting around the kitchen table with the large box of cereal dominating the small table. The carton of milk was half empty and the sugar jar was off to one side, completely empty.

"We're going to need grocery money soon if we don't want to starve," Jade said, getting up from the table and going over to the fridge where she began to take stock of what would be needed to feed her family, now that it would be her total responsibility.

"I'll turn twenty-one in just a few more days and then money won't be a problem. I'll get my share of our inheritance and both of you will have access to the interest on your money until you're twenty-one, when you'll both get your share."

Jade wanted to make sure Crystal knew exactly how things would look, now that they were on their own. "Grandma and Grandpa were smart. They knew we would need the money while we were young so we could get away from Dad." She continued her inventory, going through the cupboards and side pantry. "If they hadn't been willing to give us access to the money until we were older, we would have had to endure Dad a lot longer. Without Mom around that would have been hell, but now we'll get Mom's share of the estate as well. We are very, very rich young ladies. The only problem is we are just a little-bit broke right now."

Jade looked down at the list she had written and realized that they would need at least a hundred dollars for food, as well as some gas for the van. "I'm sure we have enough beer cans and liquor bottles to cover our immediate needs. After I have seen Mr. Barrett, Mom's lawyer, and sign the papers, we should have it easy from then on."

Jade looked over at her two precious but hungry sisters as they devoured the last of the corn flakes as well as the milk. Even without the sugar they had finished eating everything in the box. "Crystal, if you help me load the bottles and cans into the van, I'll go cash them in and pick up enough groceries to get through the next few days."

Amber followed the girls outside to what at one time had been a carriage house and was now a garage of sorts. Inside, the family van sat next to Sam's old '88 Chevy. It was then that Jade realized they had another small problem. They had been able to get rid of Sam's body and personal things, but what about the car? If Sam had run off like they had planned to tell anyone who asked, and they figured few except Dennis would, then the car would have to go too, but where?

"Shit!" Jade's tone was more irritated than angry. "I forgot about Dad's car. Where can we dump it that won't cause any suspicion?"

Crystal looked over at Jade, indicating that the scope

of the problem wasn't that big of a deal. "Why don't we order a plane ticket over the phone in Dad's name and just leave the car at the airport?" Her solution sounded good to her and she had a satisfied smile on her face.

"That won't work. Once they figure out that he never used the ticket, the police will suspect foul play."

"Well then the bus depot. Anyone can buy a ticket at the last moment and they don't record the name for most of the destinations. We can buy one to Milwaukee and sign his name. You've perfected his signature, and as a matter of fact, most of the bills have been paid by you or Mom because he was usually too drunk or just didn't care, so why not the ticket?"

"You've got a good idea there," Jade agreed. "But one problem – when I sign it, I'm a girl not a guy. Then what?"

"Look, let's just try it. If they ask any questions, just pay cash." Crystal seemed annoyed. She hated solving problems. When things got tough she usually just got mad and started fighting.

Crystal was always the tough one and she seldom cried. For Crystal, problems were usually faced head on. If you had to, you lied and said whatever was needed to be said to end the problem or to make her opponent feel as if they had won. Her usual opponent had been her dad. Crystal had gotten so good at being able to look you in the eye, smile, and tell a whopping lie, that even Crystal herself could be surprised at just how quick and fanciful her lies could be. Maybe one day she would write a book, God knew she had a good enough imagination.

"Ok, I'll take the cans in first, and then I'll get groceries, after that I'll take Dad's car to the Greyhound bus depot and leave it there after I get a ticket. It may not be as hard as I think it is. Dad's card is S. J. Walker, Samuel Jackson Walker. If they ask, I could show them my ID," Jade said.

Jade's full name was Samantha Jade Walker. She was sure she could pull it off. They could make it look like Sam had had enough of them and left for parts unknown. If he went to Milwaukee, then he could go anywhere. Sam was about to become a missing person. It was too sad to think that in reality no one would miss him at all. As far as a person of flesh and blood, Sam had become something much less than human years ago.

* * *

Jade was finished with her plans for the day and was now sitting comfortably in the back seat of a cab. She had called the cab from the Dunkin Donuts. She didn't want anyone to trace her to the bus station. It had all been very easy. She had simply walked up to the wicket and had asked for a one-way ticket to Milwaukee, Wisconsin. The young girl who sat behind the computer had barely looked up. When she'd asked how Jade wished to pay, Jade said Visa. Next the girl asked for two pieces of I.D.

Jade decided to be brave and pulled out her driver's license. The girl glanced at her picture and asked what name she wanted on the ticket and the receipt. "Just use my initials, the ones that are on my credit card please." Jade's voice was smooth and sweet as she handed Sam's credit card over. The ticket was purchased, Jade looked down at her receipt and accompanying ticket. S.J. Walker was blazed across the computer-processed ticket. The Visa receipt was from an electronic machine as well. She had to sign their copy, but the girl never even compared signatures. Jade knew the signature wouldn't be an issue. She had signed her dad's card more than he had, with the same sloppy flair that Sam had developed in his writing.

Dad would soon be gone for good. Now all she had to do was get the ticket to the bus driver. There were three copies. One the clerk had kept, one was for her, and one had to go to the driver to ensure that his copy would get back into the bus's accounting system. It was easier than Jade had expected. The line-up for the bus was a sell out and as the driver began to let everyone board, Jade simply got in between two older women, and went on to the bus. When there were only a few more people to get on, she left the bus with a couple of women who looked like motherly types. They had assisted their loved ones to their seats and left the bus just before it was due to pull out.

Jade never looked back. The ghost of Sam sat somewhere on the Greyhound Bus and Jade wouldn't give her father's memory the satisfaction of a backward glance. Gone were all the fear, hate, and evil she and her sisters had been forced to live with. She took the extra copy of the ticket and the receipt, pausing for only a second to throw them in the trash. She would cut up the card when she got home. She and her sisters would make a celebration of Sam's final farewell. They would put the cut-up plastic credit card in an ashtray and watch it melt as it burned. Jade was surprised to find herself in front of her home. The cab driver asked her for the fare and she gave him her last twenty-dollar bill. The groceries she had gotten earlier would do for a few days, then she would see the lawyer and have access to all the money they would ever need. Jade smiled. Life was going to be great and they had just gotten away with murder. She felt no malice, only relief at having survived.

When Jade walked through the front door, everything seemed normal, and then suddenly she noticed the kitchen chair was turned over onto the floor and a broken coffee cup lay beside the vinyl chair. The hair suddenly stood up on the back of her neck. Where were Amber and Crystal?!

"Amber!" Jade called her name. There was no use in this, because although she understood her name, Amber could not or would not respond. She had no verbal skills and other than a whimper or a soft moan, she was totally unable to communicate verbally. As Jade moved up the stairs she heard the creaking of a rocking chair in Crystal and Amber's room. At least Amber was here, Jade thought. The hall was lit by daylight coming through the open bedroom doors. She looked into Crystal and Amber's room. Amber was rocking silently, staring at some unseen force above her head. Jade quickly checked her own room. Everything was exactly how she had left it.

Next, she checked their parents' room. Maybe Crystal had decided to take a nap in the king-size bed, which she sometimes did when her dad was not home. The room faced north and it was always a little cooler. The day was still very warm. Nothing! The room was completely empty. What could have happened to Crystal? Where could she be? Jade had never known Crystal to leave the house if she was caring for Amber. A cold, knowing chill swept over Jade's body. Crystal hadn't left Amber – someone had taken her and she knew who. It was more than a premonition. Jade could smell something. It was the same unusual scent that she had detected at the morgue. Derek Hanson had been there. Jade ran back down into the kitchen. When she looked around she was hoping she would be wrong. Maybe Crystal would walk in from the backyard and lay her fears to rest.

It was when she glanced around the kitchen for the second time that she saw it. The pocketknife they had given Derek as a ruse of gratitude lay neatly in the middle of the table. It was his calling card. Crystal had a date with death. Jade knew she would have to find Crystal somehow and rescue her from a man more evil than they had ever encountered. Even Sam hadn't been capable of the evil Derek had committed.

Jade's legs became weak and rubbery. She managed to slump to the floor before her legs betrayed her. They could no longer support her frail body. She realized she was no match for a killer like Derek. She had seen pictures of his handiwork. All of the girls had been beaten, tortured, burned, and murdered. Now Crystal was in the hands of this madman, and it was all Jade's fault.

She should never have left the girls alone. They had been so happy to finally feel safe. It was Jade's fault that they had let down their guards while knowing that a killer might be after them. It was a stupid mistake. Derek did know who they were and now he had Crystal. How could she call the police? They would find out about Sam. Derek would make sure of it. Jade knew her sisters needed her. If she called the police both she and Crystal would go to jail and Amber would be taken away. They had killed their father to protect each other; pure and simple survival. Now Crystal was in danger. Jade knew her sister would die at the hands of that madman.

She probably only had a few hours to get her sister back. Jade took several deep breaths. She had to come up with a plan to rescue Crystal and ensure they didn't go to jail. As she got up from the floor of the kitchen, a strange calm came over her – she'd be damned if she was going to let a man like Derek hurt her sister and she'd be damned if she was going to jail for killing a man like Sam. Damn them both! She'd send them all to Hell before she'd let any harm come to her family! She had endured enough. It was time to pick herself up, dust herself off, and go catch a killer.

A plan started to take shape in her mind. She knew she didn't have the physical strength to challenge Derek, but she was sure she could outwit him. A madman never saw the world the way it really was, only the way he wanted it to be. Jade would use all the survival instincts that she had learned over the years. Living with Sam had given her the resolve to carry her plans through and Jade knew there was only one man that could help her.

CHAPTER TWENTY-EIGHT

Derek had his beautiful prize beside him. She was presently bundled up in an old, musty blanket, her arms and feet duct taped. Crystal's mouth was covered in a large, multi-colored tie with cartoon characters on it, the kind you get at a Disney store. Lisa had given it to him when she was eight and Derek was fifteen. It had been his first tie and he had always used it to gag his victims.

Crystal was silent, unmoving, still out cold from the knockout drops he had put into the pop can that sat on the kitchen table. Derek had waited until he saw the old car pull out of the driveway with Jade behind the wheel, and it was exactly what he had hoped would happen. He had everything ready. He knew he could be much bolder than he had ever been before. The belt buckle from the crematorium proved that the girls were now parentless. There would be no one for the girls to turn to. No mother. No father. They were all alone with just each other and Derek knew first-hand that they had few friends to speak of. There had been almost no one at the funeral, only that detective, Dennis Kortovich and his partner Chuck, along with their wives and children. Derek wasn't too sure how close Dennis was to the family, but he had a feeling the relationship was professional, probably due to the investigation of the mother's death. He was pretty sure that the only ones who knew of Sam's death were the murdering little bitches and him.

Now Derek was about to pay them back for destroying his bridal gown, stealing his treasures, and rescuing his latest bride. He was about to seek revenge and the three sisters would realize what happens when you mess with him. He was a man who held the power of life and death, a man who knew death intimately. He smelled it, touched it, and drank it in every day. Death was his friend and they would all have to die. But first, there was to be a wedding.

* * *

Crystal could feel her lips as they pressed against her teeth. The taste of blood still lingered on her tongue; now swollen and dry. Her eyes were shut; they were much too heavy to open, but her senses were beginning to return. Her hands and feet had been bound, and her mouth was gagged so tightly that her teeth cut into her lip, drawing blood. She could smell something – it was familiar. Yes it was that madman! Derek Hanson. Crystal's heart started to beat faster. It only made the pounding in her head hurt more. All she could remember was that she had smelled that same chemical odor before she gulped down half a cola. Just as the room started to sway and turn black, awareness that she had smelled that same smell only twice before hit her. Crystal remembered smelling that same distasteful odor on the day they buried her mother and again on the day she and Jade had killed and cremated their father. Derek must have been in the house, but awareness came too late, Crystal's knees gave way the same time blackness engulfed her.

Now she lay beside Derek. Her head rested on his lap, and the smell from his clothing made her want to choke. She knew she was in real danger. Derek would be really pissed at Jade's and her discovery of his chamber and Mandy's rescue. She also knew he would want his pictures and treasures back. Crystal prayed Jade would realize that Derek had abducted her and would know what to do. She herself would have to stay calm and trust that fate, or God, would help her get away from Derek alive. She knew she would have to make Derek think that she was still unconscious until she could assess her surroundings. She felt overwhelmed by the fear of what may lay ahead and had to choke down the urge to vomit. Quite out of nowhere Crystal heard a tune in her head; it was her mother's voice, *Don't worry be happy*. A silly, tuneless song, it was one Jewell often sang to the girls when they were alone and it now repeated in Crystal's head. She could feel her mother's arms around her. It was the first time since Jewell's death that Crystal could sense her mother's presence. A warm glow enveloped her making her feel like she had as a child, when she rested her head on her mother's lap. The scent changed from a gross chemical smell to one of fresh laundry. That was when Crystal knew for sure her mother was with her to protect her from harm.

Jewell had loved doing the laundry and the scent of it at this time was a sign from Heaven. Often the girls would join Jewell in the basement. The best times were spent taking the sheets from the dryer, pressing the warm fabric to their faces, and smelling the clean, fresh scent. It was the scent of their mother and now at the most terrifying and desperate moment of Crystal's life, Jewell was here. She kept her eyes closed, hearing and smelling her mother's message of hope with every fiber of her small being. She would be safe. It was a promise that Jewell was singing in her ear and even though Jewell couldn't protect her children completely in life, she would protect them in death. Crystal heard that promise and let go of her fears. Crystal wouldn't worry and she just knew that one day she and her sisters would be happy.

* * *

Derek pulled his old station wagon up in front of his little house in the country. It was isolated, so no one would hear if Crystal woke up and made a fuss. He looked down at her as her face rested on his lap. He liked the way it made him feel; protective. Her small face was covered by a mass of golden, red curls that hid the tie that covered her tiny mouth. She was perfect and Derek knew this one would be different. This tiny girl would love him and become his bride. He would even invite her family. They had already received his calling card, a knife, so they would be expecting an invitation soon. Derek had sent it along with special instructions. He wanted all of his prizes and pictures. He needed them to relive each event over the past six years.

Each of his weddings had been unique and special and the tokens from each girl held their spirits. They were his brides and he loved each one as much as the first, his own true love; Lisa, his little sister. As Derek looked down at Crystal's face he could hear and see Lisa when she was small. She had loved him then, but as she grew older she began to shun him. At first he had begged her to love him, always trying to please her. As the years went on and Lisa had turned into a young teen, she began to voice her disapproval of his obsession with her.

* * *

"Leave me alone Derek, stop following me everywhere. The other kids call you creepy. They say you're a freak. At first I didn't believe them, but now I think they're right. You follow me everywhere. I catch you staring at me all of the time. And you're always touching me. I don't like it. If you don't stop I'll tell Mom and Dad and they'll make you stop." Lisa put her tiny hands on her hips trying to look strong. "I even heard Dad tell Mom he's worried about how you act around me, and he thinks they should send you away. You're close to twenty now, they don't have to let you live here anymore." Lisa sounded triumphant.

Derek saw Lisa's copper curls bob up and down as the fury of her anger and frustration showed on her face. Send him away! Never! Lisa was his! His parent had said so when they'd brought her home to him when he was only eight. He and Lisa were both adopted. They belonged to no one, only each other. He wouldn't let them send him away. He would make them understand how much Lisa meant to him. His parents would have to let him have her.

* * *

Derek got out of the car, breaking through the memories of his past. He had to get Crystal to the chapel. All was prepared and waiting for them. Derek picked Crystal up, his long arms engulfing her tiny body. Carrying her, he travelled away from the house toward a heavily wooded area. Once into the woods, he zigzagged through the dense brush in a way that would make it difficult for anyone to follow his footprints. There was no discernible path; Derek only went to his secret place twice a year; once on the date of Lisa's birth and once on the date of her death, each time with a new bride. Never before had he made preparations for extra guests. But this time was special.

Derek held Crystal in one arm as he bent forward and brushed away a few leaves that had fallen – soon summer would be at an end. Derek hated the thought of another winter. Winter was a lonely time of year. Only late spring and late summer held any joy for him. Once he cleared away the leaves he bent over and pulled on a large iron ring. A heavy metal door announced their arrival with a loud screech.

Once it was open, Derek descended the concrete steps that led to a large, round door that looked much the same as a door that would lead to a bank vault. No one but Derek's family had ever known about this place, it was a legacy left over from the cold war in the late '50s when the threat of a nuclear war seemed very real. It was a bomb shelter, built by his adoptive grandparents. He had never met them. They had died in the early '60s, leaving his parents the land, the home, and this relic.

Derek's parents had never told anyone about the shelter. They seemed a bit embarrassed at the fears of their parents, especially since at the time of its construction the cost of the shelter had been more than the cost of their modest little home. The shelter was a model to be envied by anyone's standards at the time. The large living quarters and storage area would have met their family's needs if a bomb had ever landed. But none had, nor would it be likely one would. Soon the shelter was forgotten until Derek had discovered it when he was ten. He and Lisa had played house in the shelter over the years. It wasn't until the children were much older; Lisa nearly eleven and Derek almost twenty, that his parents, Gabrielle and Elliot, discovered that the shelter had become a place to play. They did not approve and insisted their children not use it.

* * *

Gabrielle and Elliot had become aware of Derek's antisocial behavior and a few of his unsavory genetic quirks. Besides being ugly, Derek had a temper that could set off a rage when he didn't get what he wanted – he would rant and move toward his parents, his huge hands ready to strike. He controlled his rages when he could, but more often than not he would choose not to, preferring to see the fear on his parents' faces. They began to fear for their safety as well as Lisa's. One night, when his parents thought they were alone, they discussed the problem of Derek between themselves. The outcome was a decision to send Derek away to a university in another state. They had submitted Derek's application behind his back and they had just received his acceptance letter.

"Sweetheart, we need to decide how to tell Derek that he has to move out of state." It was Gabrielle who spoke first, the letter from the university in her hand.

"I know, but we need to figure out how to approach the subject so that it won't cause him to go crazy and do something dangerous. I haven't felt safe ever since they found that young friend of Lisa's in the river," Elliot said. "Somehow my gut tells me that Derek was involved. Derek hated him and I could see the rage in his eyes whenever the boy was here. It made my hair stand on end and now I fear it could be us in danger."

Elliot Hanson looked at his wife in a way that showed just how great his fear was.

"We had better not do it alone. We could call Larry O'Conner. He's a great cop and would be able to handle Derek if he goes off the deep end," suggested Gabrielle.

"Perhaps you're right. Derek may behave himself if Larry is here. He's a tough cop and nobody's going to mess with him." Elliot was sure it would go well if they had some backup.

Now Elliot and Gabrielle would have to tell Derek of the need for him to leave, but their fear of him made them hesitate. The only solution was to have a witness on hand when they broke the news and to hope that Derek wouldn't go berserk. Having a friend on the police force might make the unpleasant task safer. They would call Larry in the morning.

Derek's parents would never make that call. Derek had been in the house when the discussion was taking place. He had been out earlier, but he sneaked back in a little after Lisa's bedtime. He had slipped into bed beside Lisa, as he had done so often as a child, but now as a full grown man his feelings toward her were no longer those of a boy. As he pressed his large, awkward body next to her tiny, perfect form he looked down at Lisa's sleeping face. He could see the evidence of the young woman she was turning into. She would be his one day and no one was going to send him away.

The following morning after Lisa went to school, Derek put his plans in order. Both of his parents worked as freelance writers, so other than research and the occasional trip for seminars, they worked from home. Derek's father, Elliot, had gone out to the small barn to clean out a bunch of junk and get it ready to take to the dump. He never even turned his head as he heard Derek approach, continuing to move a bunch of stuff around and bent over in deep concentration. Elliot wasn't a big man and he barely struggled as Derek put the lightly chloroformed cloth up to his face, pressing with just enough strength to prevent his father from getting away. Derek knew it was important not to bruise the body in a way that would not be consistent with a fall.

There was an old abandoned well on the property that was usually fenced in. Derek had asked Lisa to help him remove the light fencing, saying that their parents wanted them to clean the weeds around the well so that it would be visible above the fence line. This way no one would miss the well and fall in. Later he told Lisa to put the fence back around the well because he wouldn't be able to get to it for a few days. He made sure that Lisa was busy when he told her. She would soon have to catch the bus to school.

"Why do I have to do it? I have go get ready for school. Why did we take the fencing down if you weren't going to do it today?" Lisa lashed out at Derek, feeling frustrated at having to do it just before the bus picked her up.

"Dad wants me to help him in the barn and I still have to finish up the cleanup in the garage. It only takes about three minutes to put the fence up so just do it and get on the bus." Derek hoped he sounded truthful and pressed for time.

"OK. But get out of here so I can get ready. You're always hanging around and getting in the way," Lisa said, turning back to the mirror, dismissing Derek in her usual manner.

Lisa suspected nothing and as usual she forgot to do what she'd been asked. That would make her the guilty one. Now his father lay crumpled at his feet. The chloroform was light and would only keep him unconscious for a short while. Derek knew a lot about putting animals under. His interest in death had driven him to make a makeshift morgue in the back of the shelter. He had learned many things about death and about how to preserve the bodies of dogs and cats. It would come in useful.

Derek had no time to waste. He had to get to his mother, the timing would be important. Gabrielle was at the desk when Derek came into the house. She never even looked up as he approached her. Gabrielle was small and getting her body to the well would be easy. Derek's father was just regaining consciousness as Derek approached him with Gabrielle in his arms. He placed his mother at his father's feet. Elliot was trying to stand up.

"What's happening Derek? I feel sick. What's wrong with your mother and why are we at the well? Where's the fence?"

"It's OK Dad. Mom's not feeling very well either. Just take her hand and see if we can get her to stand up. Don't worry, I'll help you both." Derek picked up the small form of his mother off the ground and placed her hand in his father's.

"This will be perfect – lovers to the end." Derek said, as he assisted his parents to their feet.

"What do you mean?" Elliot was beginning to see just how close to the well he was, and how unsteady he and his wife were.

"Walking can be dangerous and we all know how deep this well is. You will both be together forever, like all lovers should." Derek smiled as he spoke to his father.

"Why are you doing this?" Elliot was still too weak to run, but he knew what his son had planned for them.

"Why? You know why! You and mother were going to betray me and send me away so that you can keep Lisa from me. You said Lisa was mine and now you are trying to take her from me. I can't let you do that." Derek's voice was calm, belying the anger he felt deep inside.

Derek could see that his father was getting stronger and more alert by the minute and his mother was beginning to stir as well. There was no more time for talk. He gave both his parents a shove and watched as they descended down the deep well. The muffled thud assured him that they would now be spending eternity together.

The police ruled it an accident. When Lisa found out about the fall, she blamed herself for not putting the fence back up. She was inconsolable and suspected nothing. She became so distraught at the funeral that no one found it surprising when Derek told everyone she was depressed due to the death of her parents and had a nervous breakdown. Of course Derek was caring for Lisa as best he could. Soon no one was calling and even the kids at school forgot about her. Lisa was at Derek's mercy.

* * *

The loud clank of the door startled Crystal, causing a shock to move through her body. Derek felt the movement. He was holding her body next to his as he made his way into a large storage chamber at the front of the shelter. There was a huge tank in the center of the room, which held water that was pumped from an underground well when needed. It stood empty, filled with dust and mice droppings, having never been attended to over the years. The shelves along the walls were empty, except for a few boxes of candles and matches. At least a dozen empty cans of gasoline stood off to one side, the plastic containers a faded red. Their spouts were capped off. A generator large enough to keep several families going for quite a while stood off to the side at the back of the chamber. Next to the generator was another door, much like the first, leading to the living quarters of the shelter. Derek laid Crystal down next to the generator. He leaned over her now inert body and slapped her face firmly. It was not hard enough to make a mark, but had enough force to shock her into awareness. Her blue eyes opened suddenly and his pale eyes stared back.

Derek reached around to the back of Crystal's head and untied the Disney tie from her mouth. "Don't say a word, or scream. No one will hear you." His voice was calm and confident. This was his world and she was his guest.

Derek stood up; leaving a silent Crystal on the ground gazing up at him with what she hoped was a stunned, unaware gaze. She needed time to get her bearings and see where she was. Derek seemed satisfied that she was still groggy and half out of it before he stepped away from her to move toward the generator.

With Derek's back to her, Crystal was able to get a full look around. The room was dimly lit. A large lantern that dominated the center of the room gave off an eerie, candle-lit glow. She saw the tank, empty shelves, gasoline, matches, and a few other boxes of stuff, nothing that allowed her to guess where she was.

Derek started the generator and soon a low hum was heard and felt. Suddenly, the room lit up brightly as large florescent lights that swung overhead lit up revealing the room in its dirty, decaying form. Derek turned unexpectedly toward Crystal, catching her off guard as she gazed intently about the room.

"I see you've come around, my love – welcome home. You and I have a date with destiny and soon our guests will arrive. Come we must get ready."

Derek took one long stride toward her. He bent down, scooped her up into his arms and moved toward the second vaulted door. As he swung the door open, Crystal could once again smell the clean, warm scent of fresh laundry. Jewell was still with her. The knowledge gave her a great deal of comfort and strength, but not enough to prevent the gasp of horror that rushed from her mouth as she saw what lay behind the door, a sight that would shake her faith and weaken the resolve that she would need to get out alive.

CHAPTER
TWENTY-NINE

Detective Dennis Kortovich sat at his desk in total disbelief. In front of him were the pictures of over one dozen young girls, and all of them wore a death mask, their faces twisted white marble, showing the pain and horror of their last moments of life. Each girl lay on a stainless steel table, the same kind used by a medical examiner or at a morgue. The white wedding gown was identical in each picture. All but one of the girls had light, copper, curly hair that surrounded tiny, perfect faces. Only one girl was different, a beautiful, full figured brunette who had just celebrated her eighteenth birthday. She alone lay marked and naked on the table, her body mutilated by someone who had apparently been in a rage. Dennis knew he'd been right in his assessment. Charlotte had been taken by mistake. The killer had been after her friend, Jade Walker.

Along with the pictures of the girls were a collection of what appeared to be personal items; gold hoop earrings, a diamond-studded watch, a pearl and rhinestone necklace, a Snoopy watch, and pearl studs. The list itemized thirteen individual pieces of jewelry, each one probably belonging to a different girl. Dennis put his hands over his face and breathed deeply. The package had been left at the front desk. The sergeant in charge said he'd seen no one when it was delivered. He had gone to the back of the room for a few minutes to retrieve a few more pens for the front. When he'd returned, the large manila envelope with Dennis's name in large, black print was sitting on the counter. The sergeant had looked around to see if anyone was still in the lobby that might have left it, but no one stood out as the person who could have dropped it off. The lobby was full of an odd assortment of people, so it could have been anyone.

The sergeant had sent the envelope up to Dennis immediately. It had been marked as urgent and he knew Dennis was working on the abduction of Judge Switzer's daughter, as well as the other missing girls.

When Dennis finally pulled his hands away from his face he stared at the lifeless forms of the young girls. The envelope meant only one thing; someone knew who the killer was and he or she was trying to tell him something. But what? And why didn't they just say who the killer was and help him out? Dennis picked up the envelope one more time. Maybe there was something he missed. When he shook the envelope nothing fell out – empty. Wanting one last look, Dennis opened the envelope wide and looked again.

There was something stuck in the seam. He reached inside and pulled out a clipping. It was an advertisement from the Yellow Pages cut neatly around the edges, no more than two inches by four inches.

Greenhill's Funeral Home was the feature of the ad,

followed by the location and phone number. A picture of Derek Hanson was in the top right hand corner. It made Dennis feel faint – all the color drained from his face.

He knew it! Derek was somehow a part of the puzzle and someone was leading him right to Derek. But why not come in person? What were they afraid of? Dennis stood up, grabbed the photos, and dialed Chuck's cell phone. No time to waste figuring out why. Dennis had to get to Derek right away and see what role he had played in the murders of the girls.

Chuck agreed to meet Dennis at Greenhill's. Soon, Dennis pulled his white, Crown Victoria up behind Chuck's SUV just seconds after they both arrived at the funeral home.

Dennis walked toward Chuck as he greeted him. "Great timing. Thanks for dropping everything and meeting me here without an explanation."

"You know me, never a day's rest. We work till the job is done." Chuck rolled his eyes, indicating that this job would always be first, and the rest would wait. "What the hell's up? You sounded real shocked on the phone, and why were you at the station anyway?"

"I thought we were going to meet for breakfast and go over our notes to see if we could find a final clue to pull this together. The geographic profile confirmed a suspicion of mine, but I wanted to take the time to see if all of the pieces fit before I accused anyone. When I was at my desk, this was delivered to the station." Dennis said nothing more as he handed the envelope to Chuck.

"Holy fuck, where the hell did you get these? This is fucking unbelievable."

Chuck's already bright face got even redder, his eyes

nearly popping out of his head, and his face registering total disbelief.

"I have no idea. They were left at the front desk. No one saw who left them and this came along with the package." Dennis reached into his shirt pocket and pulled out the ad, handing it to Chuck who now leaned against Dennis's car.

"This is as good as saying Derek did it. What proof do you have?" Chuck knew it took more than the pictures and an ad to prove anyone, even a creep like Derek, had committed these crimes.

"I already had a hunch. I ran into Derek yesterday just before our lunch. He had just paid a whack of money for a wedding gown – size two. Then there was something Mandy said about a headless horseman. It didn't mean anything until I had this strange dream and then I got this package. What cartoon character does Derek remind you of?" Dennis was sure Chuck would see the resemblance.

"Shit if I know!" Chuck stared at the picture of Derek, drawing a blank. The last thing that he could think of after seeing the mutilated young women in the pictures was anything about cartoons. "OK Sherlock. So who does Derek look like?"

"Remember the Disney movie, *Sleepy Hollow*?" Dennis asked.

"Holy shit!" Chuck responded. "Ichabod Crain! He looks just like him, only uglier."

"Yes, Ichabod Crain and the headless horseman." Dennis's flat response made it sound as if Mandy's statement was obvious. "So far we have no real evidence, just a prophetic dream, and an envelope with photos of dead girls, jewelry, and an ugly guy with a wedding dress. All of the girls are wearing a wedding gown and I just know it's all tied into Derek."

"Who sent this to you and why?"

Dennis looked at Chuck, his jaw locking as he clenched his teeth and stroked his mustache. "I don't know Chuck, but whoever sent the envelope wants our help. I only hope no one else has gone missing while we're trying to come up with enough probable cause. Or that some other young girl is wearing that new dress."

CHAPTER THIRTY

Jade knew she stood no chance of facing Derek alone. She would need help. Dennis was the only one she could turn to, but she couldn't go to him in person. Jade knew she would have to come up with a plan that would lead Dennis to Derek, and allow Jade to find Crystal and rescue her before Derek did her any harm. She was just beginning to formulate a plan when she received a special delivery. It was an invitation to a wedding. The groom was Derek Hanson, the bride Crystal Walker. It would take place that evening and Jade was instructed to stay put, she would be picked up at seven. Jade was to dress accordingly and bring Amber. The pictures and personal items she had taken from the morgue were to be brought or Derek would make sure that Sam's ashes and belt buckle would find their way to the police.

Her only hope was Dennis. Jade knew it would be a trap and that she and her sisters might never get out alive. She had no idea where Derek would take her and Amber, but for once in her life she would have to trust someone. Dennis was the only one she believed in. He would find them. Jade only hoped it would be in time and that she would be able to find a way to save herself, Crystal, and Amber without Dennis finding out what had happened to Sam. The idea to send Dennis the photos and items came minutes after she received the invitation. Someone would have to know it was Derek who was killing the young women. She had no idea why all the girls looked alike or why Derek was driven to this madness.

The face of the girl in Derek's office came to mind. That was it! Lisa, Derek's sister – they were like her, exact copies. Whatever had happened to Lisa Hansen, Jade was sure she was about to find out. All of them were replacements for Lisa. Would she and her sisters meet the same fate as all of the other girls? If she had put her faith in the right place it would not be God that rescued them, but Dennis Kortovich, the only person Jade felt she could trust. If Jade and her sisters were to survive whatever was to take place tonight, Dennis would have to find them. Jade could only hope that wherever Derek would take them, a trail could be followed by a detective as good as Dennis.

* * *

Dennis and Chuck entered the large, bright foyer of the funeral home. The different shades of green and rose created a feeling of peacefulness and rest. It was a decorative theme that Dennis liked. The office to the funeral home was off to the right, the door was slightly ajar, and Dennis could hear a woman's voice talking softly to someone on the other end of the phone. She was assuring them that all of the details for an afternoon lunch would go well and there would be plenty of food.

Dennis and Chuck needed to get some answers

quickly. Once the woman hung up, Dennis knocked quickly on the door, a sense of urgency resonating from the knock. An older, middle-aged woman somewhere near sixty opened the door, a look of calm and serenity on her face. Dennis was sure she had mastered the look over the years. It was good for business. One needed to be calm when it came to matters of a departed loved one.

"Good afternoon, how may I help you?" The sound of her voice was low and soft, again very calming.

Dennis flashed his badge and held out his hand. She extended hers quickly, her grip even and well-practiced.

"My name is Detective Dennis Kortovich and my partner here is Detective Chuck O'Brien. We're from the Chicago Police Department. We're wondering if we could ask you a few questions about Derek Hanson." Dennis looked at the woman and knew from the way she held herself that she would find it difficult to answer questions without feeling compromised.

"How may I help you, Detective?" she asked, her face remaining unreadable.

"Where is Derek Hansen? Do you know where he lives?" Dennis asked.

"Where he is right now, I really couldn't say. He lives on an old farm about three miles from here, in Elgin. It's about a quarter mile off the main road. You may have to walk in. Derek doesn't keep the driveway well-tended and you may have to leave your car on the road. It would take quite a beating."

It was the only time Patricia Applegate showed any emotion other than serenity. Dennis and Chuck could detect the disapproval she felt on how Derek kept the driveway.

"I think he keeps the driveway that way so no one will visit him when he's not working. He's very reclusive." Her voice still held the tone of disapproval.

"Could you tell me anything more about Derek, especially these last few days?" Chuck offered this last question.

"Well," Patricia said with a measured tone. "Derek seems to have a rough time of it. Especially right now, late summer. I understand why. His family was killed in a home accident and his sister Lisa; she died around six years ago. He was devoted to her. His office is like a shrine to her. I think her death unbalanced him a bit. She's all he ever talks about or thinks about." Patricia paused a bit before going on, seemingly unsure whether or not she should share her views on Derek.

"I sometime think his love and devotion to Lisa is a bit sick. It even scares me at times." Patricia looked apologetic. It was as if her last observation was a bit on the gossipy side. She was a woman of integrity and Dennis could tell that it would take a lot for her to make a negative comment about someone.

"May we see Derek's office?" Dennis asked.

"I'm sure it will be all right. It's not locked so I doubt it will cause a problem." Patricia paused for a moment. "I would prefer however that you didn't go through his desk drawers without a warrant. I don't want any trouble. We do have to work together."

"That will not be a problem. We just want to look around," Chuck responded.

As Patricia Applegate swung open the door to Derek's office, Chuck and Dennis had to stifle back an urge to gasp and choke. In the middle of the feature wall was a quilted, framed picture that dominated the wall by its sheer size. The beautiful young women who stared at them with bright, blue eyes was a dead ringer for all of the missing girls. The girl in the photo was no more than fourteen, her delicate, pale skin surrounded by an abundance of curly copper-red hair. Her lips were rosebud pink, while her incredible blue eyes were surrounded by dark, long lashes; a delicate young beauty. Lisa was also the spitting image of Jade and Crystal.

"Shit!" Dennis was first to break the silence. "We'd better get over to Derek's right away and see what he's up to. Then we'd better check in on the girls and make sure they're all right. I have a feeling Derek's our man and Jade or Crystal will be next."

"No wonder we've never found the bodies. This guy can just burn them up along with any proof they are missing. No trace, no case." Chuck added his thoughts to Dennis, who nodded in agreement.

Both men barely said a formal goodbye to Mrs. Applegate who followed them out of the double doors at the front of the building. There she waved a final farewell with a look of concern crossing her face, breaking her usual look of controlled serenity.

It only took ten minutes to get to Derek's property line. The driveway was in worse shape than either detective thought it would be. Without a solid suspension, the Crown Vic would have taken a beating. They had left Chuck's SUV at the funeral home so they could drive together, review the evidence they had so far, and formulate a game plan.

"Chuck, we have no real proof. All we have is a purchase of a wedding gown, a guy who's ugly, looks like a cartoon character that you dreamed about, and Mandy who was half crazed from her ordeal, saw in a vision, whose dead sister looks like our missing girls. None of this is probable cause. Even the envelope proves nothing directly about Derek. The ad is only someone's guess that he's our man. Unless we find some evidence stronger than that to get a search warrant, we can't do more than ask a few questions and hope Derek says something we can use to arrest him." Dennis's running dialog was beginning to sound implausible even to him-self.

Dennis and Chuck removed their suit jackets, leaving them in the car. The day was very hot and the walk to the house would make wearing them much too warm. Without their jackets, their holsters with their guns were in plain sight. They were hoping that would be intimidating, just in case Derek was so unbalanced that he would attempt to give them a hard time. While walking up the driveway, attempting to avoid the potholes, both men noted the tall grass in the middle of the road was bent over. This meant Derek drove in and out. His car was obviously modified to handle the deep ruts. The weeds along the road gave off a sweet, pungent aroma that was somewhere between nice and too sweet. Still, the sounds and smells of summer made one wish you could take a walk in the country every day. As the men approached the old farm they both noted how run down all of the buildings were, especially the house. The front porch of the house looked like it would fall off at any moment. Chuck almost decided not to ascend the rickety stairs, fearing that the worn boards of the old porch might not support his excess weight. When Dennis and Chuck stood in front of the door, Chuck almost let out a sigh of relief. The porch was stronger than it looked and only gave way a few inches under his weight. The screen door was half off its hinges and bounced slightly, causing quite a racket when Chuck banged his large fist against its paint-peeled frame.

"Looks like no one's home," Chuck surmised after a few minutes of silence.

Dennis and Chuck looked around the yard and noted a patch of grass that was flattened and faded. It was obvious that it was the spot where Derek parked his car. It seemed from the silence of the house and the empty space in the yard, that no one was home.

"What's the chance that the door's unlocked?" Dennis looked at Chuck knowing full well an unlawful access could cause them problems.

"You know, anything we find inside without a warrant we won't be able to use in a case against Derek," Chuck said.

Dennis knew Chuck wanted to make sure they were on the same page. "Only if he knows we were here. Touch nothing, open nothing. If we come up with any evidence it has to be in the wide open, then we can get a warrant and come back."

Dennis was always by the book, seldom bending the rules. But when he did bend the rules a little right of center, he always made sure he never compromised a case. "Cross the t's and dot the i's" was a motto to be lived by. When Dennis put together a case it was solid and rarely fell apart in court. But at this moment, both men were more concerned with the package that had been dropped off and what it meant. They were sure that time was of the essence and that whoever had dropped it off was not about to become another victim of Derek Hansen's.

Chuck tried the door. It was locked, but the lock was simple. It would only take a credit card to get in. Both men put on rubber gloves. No prints, they were never here. Once in, they were overcome by the filth. The smell of rancid food and dirty clothes made them gag. Other than the smell of a decaying corpse neither Dennis nor Chuck could remember smelling anything as bad as the small house. Chuck called out from the dining room off the kitchen.

"What is it?" Dennis asked as he approached Chuck.

"Look on the table." Chuck nodded his head in the direction of the evidence.

There on the table taking up its full length were plaster molds. There were thirteen, well-defined indentations and it was pretty easy to identify what kind of objects would leave marks like the ones they were looking at. Dennis pulled the photos and list from his hip pocket.

He then referred to the list of objects, watches, earrings, and necklaces, even a headband. Thirteen molds, thirteen items on the list…all a perfect match.

"Wow!" Chuck's face became a bright red, betraying his excitement. "All of these molds match the list of items worn by our missing girls. He might as well have given us the bodies with his fingerprints on them."

"This evidence is enough to help us put him away for life. But first we had better get out of here and get a search warrant." Dennis left the molds on the table and continued his look around. "Be careful not to touch or move anything. If this creep gets wind of our being here before we get a warrant, this whole case could go up in smoke."

Dennis moved toward the back of the house where

the bedrooms were. "Shit, look at this." He motioned for Chuck to follow him into the larger of the two rooms. On the floor was the torn wedding gown, each piece tossed carelessly on an already cluttered bedroom floor.

"What?" Chuck asked as Dennis moved aside to give him a full view.

"It's the exact same gown as the one the girls were wearing in the pictures." Dennis's response showed his excitement at having found such conclusive evidence.

"Let's go. We need to get back here as soon as possible and it's never easy getting a search warrant. We can't even tell anyone what we've seen." Dennis was already down the hall heading towards the front door. "We're going to have to convince a judge that we have more than just a hunch to go on to get a warrant."

"Why don't we ask Judge Switzer first? With Mandy having been involved wouldn't that be just as simple?" Chuck's logic sounded good to Dennis, but it met with a disapproving look anyway.

"The problem with that idea is that Judge Switzer is too close to the case and his judgment could be questioned, putting the case in jeopardy. We're better off taking a little extra time and getting things right by securing a warrant from an impartial judge, rather than risking an unlawful search and blowing the case on a technicality. If we do this we do it right and get a warrant from an impartial judge. There can't be any accusation of prejudice in this case."

The thought of having the evidence so close and not being able to touch it or use it without a warrant was frustrating, but Chuck nodded in agreement. This case had to be handled correctly. As they left the house they made sure the door was locked and that everything looked exactly as it had when they entered. Dennis and Chuck were sure Derek wouldn't know if anything was amiss, the place was so filthy, but rather than take a chance, they did their best to secure the place and make sure all was as it should be.

Once they were in the car and well on their way back to the city, Dennis spoke up first. "We also need to check in on Jade and the girls and make sure they're all right. After what we've seen, I know one of them will be targeted next, either Jade or Crystal."

Dennis turned his vehicle onto the northwest freeway. In a few more minutes he would be at his office. Once he got his warrant, he would contact Jade and make sure everyone was OK.

CHAPTER THIRTY-ONE

Jade got a telephone call from Derek later that afternoon. She was to meet him at his place. Let no one know where she was going and be sure to bring Amber as well. If she did anything to bring attention to his place or leave any clues as to where she was going, Derek would kill Crystal immediately and come after them. If Jade wanted to keep her sister alive, she would have to do exactly as Derek told her.

Jade made a quick review of everything that had happened over the past week, hoping to gain insight that could help her face what lay ahead. Her mother was dead and although it was an accident their father was as responsible as if he had pushed her himself. Now, he too was dead at the hands of his daughters. Now Crystal was in extreme danger and Jade was feeling helpless. Their only hope was Detective Dennis Kortovich, and Jade had to make sure he could figure things out and somehow not discover their deadly secret.

Jade knew it was a calculated risk, but without Dennis she knew there was no hope. The clock on the wall was getting close to seven. The day was nearly over and she had less than thirty minutes to get to Derek's farm, to face what was to come. She prayed that she and her sisters would be able to get out alive. Jade needed to make one quick call before she and Amber left. Should she call the police station or Dennis's home? Finally she decided to call Dennis's home. Hopefully, Veronica would answer and she could pass a message onto her husband.

Jade dialed the number, her heart pounding. Timing would be everything. She would have to get to Derek before the police and hope that once they arrived she could come up with a plan to keep her and her sisters safe. If not, plan B was in Dennis's hands and timing would be everything.

"Hello." It was Veronica's deep, warm voice.

"Hi Mrs. Kortovich, it's me Jade."

"Hello Jade, nice to hear from you dear. How are you and the girls doing?" The tone in Veronica's voice went from professional to motherly in less than a heartbeat.

Jade hesitated for a moment, hoping what she said next would work. "We're fine, but I was wondering if Dennis was in."

"No, but I can get him if you want or you could page him."

"No...No just pass on a message for me."

"OK dear, what is it?"

The concern in Veronica's voice gave Jade a feeling of hope. She knew that Dennis and Veronica cared for her and her sisters and it made Jade feel less alone.

"If he wants more information about Mandy, you know the girl who was kidnapped, or my friend Charlotte, then I need him to come over to my house in about a half an hour. I have something important to show him, but not before 7:30. I won't be home before then; I have to run out for a while."

Jade hoped Veronica would pass the message on in time and that Dennis wouldn't come over till seven thirty. If so everything might work out.

"Of course, but Jade, this is important. Are you sure I shouldn't come over or at least get Dennis on the phone right away?" Veronica answered.

The tone of Veronica's voice reminded Jade of her mother's, all concern and love. Jade felt bad that she couldn't just confess everything and cry on Veronica's shoulder.

"No…just tell Mr. Kortovich to meet me at 7:30. And thanks. Thanks for everything. I'll talk to you soon. Bye."

"Bye dear," was all Jade heard as she put the phone down quickly.

With Veronica living next door, Jade did not want to wait to find out if a concerned Veronica would end up on her doorstep. It was time to face the devil and hope that the flames of hell wouldn't devour her and her sisters. Jade went upstairs to get Amber. They would have to leave right away if they were to arrive on time. Jade left the door wide open, allowing Dennis access to the house. The slightly ajar door wasn't noticeable from the street and someone would have to come up to the door to see that it wasn't shut, but Jade felt Dennis would know there was a problem with the house wide open and no one home. Once inside, the note on the table would lead Dennis to Derek's house, but not before she and Amber would have a chance to see if they could rescue Crystal. Jade hoped that she or the police could stop Derek before he killed again. The note was simple. It read:

Dennis; Derek Hanson has Crystal, we've gone to rescue her. Come and get us, but be careful or he will kill us all. He's crazy. I think he abducted the Judge's daughter Mandy and my friend Charlotte. I'm sure it was me he wanted, not Charlotte. Now he wants Crystal. Be careful. Jade.

Jade could never admit to all that she knew or it would implicate Crystal and her in their dad's murder. She couldn't afford to think of what would happen if the police found out about Sam, so she pushed it from her mind as she went out the front door to the van, with Amber in tow. The ride over to Derek's place seemed to take forever. While Jade drove she tried to keep her heart from sinking into her stomach and making her want to vomit. Once she came up to Derek's driveway she turned the van onto the narrow, weed-filled road. She had only driven a few yards when she realized the ruts and grass would make it impossible to continue. She stopped the van and took Amber's hand; the walk would help her gather her strength to face what lay ahead.

Amber looked like a beautiful doll as she bounced happily down the road. Her copper curls caught the evening's setting sun, like spider's silk when its web dances in the breeze, flashing the light of the day through its intricate silk-spun pattern.

The breeze was light and warm. August was in all of

its glory; the smells, colors, and clear blue sky. Within the hour, a soft blanket of midnight blue would descend on the little farm that lay just ahead. If a stranger were to view the two perfect young girls walking hand in hand down the rugged country road it would make a beautiful, innocent picture. However, the girls could never guess what unbelievable horrors lay ahead.

* * *

The afternoon had not gone well so far. Dennis and Chuck had been unable to secure a search warrant. They were at a dead end and hunches were not enough probable cause to search someone's home. Even the pictures and list weren't enough, because Dennis couldn't tell anyone what he and Chuck had found at the Hanson farm.

They were about to play the only card they had left – Judge Switzer. With Judge Switzer they could at least play upon his personal involvement. If they did get the warrant from him, it might compromise the case, but they were at a dead end and Dennis felt it could be their only hope.

When the call came in from Veronica, Dennis knew the girls were in trouble. He already suspected that Jade was Derek's real target when he abducted Charlotte, and now he knew his hunch was right. For now, Dennis and Chuck needed to get over to the Walker home. Dennis only hoped Sam wasn't drunk and unruly, or that the girls weren't being abused by that asshole. Dennis didn't blame Jade for not turning to her father for help. Sam was a useless piece of shit, and she was right to call him and Chuck for help.

Chuck and Dennis arrived a little before 7:30. By the

time they reached the front door their imagination was in full gear. With the front door ajar, there were no answers to their anxious calls as they entered the home.

Chuck was the first to send out a second round of calls. "Jade, Crystal, where are you?"

"Shit, shit, shit, I should have guessed!" Dennis stood over the table, reading the note.

"What is it?" Chuck was at Dennis's side leaning over his shoulder. "Wow!" The note took him off guard.

"Where's Sam? Maybe he knows something. He's probably passed out; let's hope we can get something out of him."

Dennis started up the stairs to see if he could find Sam. He was nowhere in sight. The master bedroom was empty and the closet door stood wide open. "Chuck, what's strange about this room?" Dennis stood off to the side, allowing Chuck a full view.

Chuck hated being asked these kinds of questions. Dennis was a master at seeing all of the details and Chuck lagged far behind in quick observation skills. "No time to guess. What is it?"

"The closet, look and tell me what you see."

"Clothes in a closet." Chuck's answer was bright, maybe a little too bright.

"OK I can see you're getting good at this," Dennis responded with the same over- the-top, overly cheerful tone. "What kind?"

"A woman's." Once again the sweet, bright tone in Chuck's voice meant he was being sarcastic.

"And?" Dennis played along, adding to the game.

"And, I don't know." Chuck gave Dennis a brilliant smile – he was done with the game.

"Where are Sam's clothes?" Dennis finished the exchange.

"Wow! What do you think it means?"

"Sam's gone."

"Another thing I noticed in the kitchen; there aren't any bottles of booze lying around," Chuck added, his tone once again professional.

"Well, there's no time to figure out what happened to Sam. We need to get to Derek's. The girls couldn't be lucky enough to have had Sam take off on them. And right now they're in real danger. Let's hope we can get there in time. They're no match for a man like Derek. We need to get there, now," Dennis said as he headed out the front door with Chuck close behind.

CHAPTER THIRTY-TWO

Jade stood with Amber in front of the rundown house wondering what to do next. Derek was nowhere in sight. It was Derek's game and all Jade could do was wait and hope she could learn the rules fast enough to win. Lives would depend on it; theirs. She pushed back the hope that Dennis would rescue them. It might boil down to her, against Derek.

A sound came from a bunch of trees alerting Jade to someone's approach. When she turned toward where it had come from, Derek was heading towards her after emerging from some tall trees and thick bush. Crystal was nowhere in sight.

Welcome to my celebration." Derek smiled, his large lips sliding over his yellow, uneven teeth. "I'm glad all of my little princesses will be with me to celebrate this important day. Come, take my hand, the evening is about to begin."

Derek took Amber's hand. She was only too happy to follow and was totally unaware of the danger she and her sisters were in.

The underbrush was thick and unruly. Derek deliberately kept the farm that way so that no one would suspect that less than three hundred feet from the house was a bunker that had become his cathedral of death.

Jade had no choice but to follow, even though the branches tore at her arms, leaving a few long scratches. She worried that the trees would assault Amber, but Derek was careful to make sure she wasn't hurt. When Derek came to a mound that seemed to rise out of nowhere, Jade realized just how much trouble they were in. How would Dennis find them in the middle of this thick, wooded area? Derek let go of Amber's hand and grabbed a hinge from what seemed to be nothing more than a rise on a mound. Jade was shocked to see that it was a doorway or hatch of some kind; an entrance to an underground chamber. Derek swung it open and pulled Amber in, and all of Jade's hopes vanished as she followed him down several stairs.

Jade was sure it was a bomb shelter. She had heard her father talk about the '50s, when everyone had been afraid of a nuclear bomb being dropped. Derek shut the hatch, blurring any hope Jade might have of Dennis finding them.

Once inside, Jade could see a large, round storage area shaped like a huge culvert. Empty shelves lined the curved walls, except for a few boxes of matches and candles. A generator sat at one end, running on full, and several empty gas cans were piled carelessly off to the side. A large door stood before them. The florescent light in the storage area cast a dim reflection on the door ahead and Jade had an uncontrollable urge to shout out, *And behind door number one…* It was an automatic impulse to lighten up what was becoming an even more desperate situation with every step they took.

"You and your sister will be my guests of honor. You're the only ones besides my own family and my other brides to see my cathedral of love," Derek said, giving Jade a toothy smile, swinging the second door open with as much flourish and flair as any magician performing his favorite trick.

Jade was transfixed by what she saw and heard. Before her was a huge cavern lit by hundreds of candles that stood on a variety of cast-iron stands. Dark-red, velvet tapestry hung from the walls, creating a heady feeling. Pictures of mythical demons and gods, reminiscent of a medieval castle's grand hall, covered the tapestries, making Jade think of a time long past when knights courted fair maidens. A plush, red and gold carpet, with designs of a mystical motif covered the ground. The most spectacular feature of the room was the large altar that encompassed the entire rear of the shelter. It featured a huge granite table that stood almost four feet high and at least six feet long. Behind the altar was a large cross, adorned with not a sculpture of Jesus but rather a strange-looking demon. The head was a goat, while the upper body and arms were of a man. The lower body was also that of a goat, its legs crossed with nails driven through its crossed hoofs. Both hands were impaled and a wreath of thorns adorned its head. When Jade looked into the face of the demon she was struck by the fact that rather than a look of compassion that was usually depicted on the face of Christ, this impostor stared at her with a look of utter contempt. It was as though all of the hate ever directed at mankind was embodied on the face of this goat-like monster.

Music assaulted Jade's ears. It was the eerie sound of monks chanting, the low hum beginning to drone even louder. It seemed as if everything was happening in slow motion. Her senses were so overwhelmed by the unexpectedness of the bunker that she knew her grasp of reality was fading. A flash of white caught her eye and when she realized who was lying on the altar, all of the blood drained from her face. "Oh my God!" she screamed. "It's Crystal and she looks dead. You bastard, what have you done to my sister?" She turned to Derek whose triumphant face said it all.

"No, she's not dead, only drugged." Derek started toward the altar. "A beauty rest. She'll come around soon. I timed it for your arrival."

A soft moan came from Crystal's lips. Derek stood above her. He placed his large hands on her small breast and continued to softly trace her entire body with his hands.

"She's absolutely perfect, they all were." Derek looked up at Jade. "You were perfect Jade. I almost made you my bride, but I got that foolish brunette instead. She fought me you know, and it wasn't easy. She was very tough, but I'm tougher and she wasn't what I wanted." His eyes narrowed showing his anger. He moved closer to Crystal, like a protective lover. "You messed things up for me and after I kidnapped Charlotte you were never available to me again. I stalked you for weeks before I finally gave up. Too much time had passed after the anniversary date of my dear sister's death. Then you showed up at the funeral home, but you were too old by then. But Crystal was perfect. Now she'll be my bride." Derek bent his head and put his wet sloppy lips on Crystal's.

Crystal could dimly hear voices, but it was like listening through a fog. The more she tried to move her head, the more her senses seemed to dim. The heavy mist swirled around her, weighing her down. It wasn't until she felt wet lips on hers and felt a hot tongue probing her mouth, making her choke, that she was finally able to become aware of her surroundings. When she turned her head to avoid the invasive tongue she saw her little sister, Amber, standing silently to one side, fascinated by the flickering candles that surrounded the altar. Crystal was able to look around a little better when the wet mouth left hers. It was then that she spotted Jade. "Jade!" was all she could whisper from her dry, drug-parched mouth.

"Crystal don't worry, we're here," Jade could answer back. But Jade had no way of offering Crystal any hope and she knew the tone in her voice betrayed her.

"Enough talk!" Derek moved away from Crystal who was already attempting to sit up. "I want to introduce you to my family. I know they'll love you all." He walked toward what looked like church pews; long, wooden, high-back benches that stood off to the right, directly in front of the granite altar.

As Jade and Crystal's eyes followed Derek they noticed feet protruding from a blanket of deep-purple velvet. Derek flung off the blanket in theatrical style. Screams tore from Jade and Crystal's throats as the mummified faces of the frozen figures were exposed.

The faces of the three mummies were grim masks of horror. The thin, waxy skin stretched across the bones, like paper on rocks. The hollow eyes of the trio stared wide-eyed, directly at Crystal. Frozen smiles stretched over decayed teeth. The hairstyles and sizes of the corpses revealed the sexes of the mummified guests. The tallest was a male; the second, sitting in the middle, was a woman, her hair tied back into a ponytail. The third body was tiny, her hair flowing in soft, rivulets of curls still holding onto their copper and red color. Neither girl had any idea who she was staring at, but from the way the bodies were displayed and preserved they must have meant a lot to Derek. For both Jade and Crystal, the piercing, fixed eyes of the figures brought waves of pure hysteria to their hearts.

CHAPTER THIRTY-THREE

As soon as Dennis and Chuck left to go to the Hansen farm, Dennis called into the main office and talked to the desk sergeant. He told the sergeant to call the other members of the special task force. Soon after Mandy Switzer had been found, Dennis and Chuck had put together a special task force to help investigate the missing girls. Hundreds of tips had been called in once the press got a hold of the story. It would take hundreds of hours of extra legwork to follow all of the leads. The detectives on the case were also dedicated and talented. They would need all the help they could get. Time was running out and both detectives felt a sense of urgency and a little fear.

Dennis was able to obtain a search warrant from Judge Heart based solely on the note that Jade had left. The team was to meet Chuck and Dennis just outside of Derek's property. Once they were all assembled and organized, they would storm onto the farm from several different coordinates and surround the small house. Hopefully Derek would be unaware of their arrival and they would be able to use the element of surprise to enable them to affect a rescue and an arrest.

By the time the task force had gathered the wind had picked up considerably. Dennis gave instructions to the men, and within minutes they were down the scruffy road surrounding the house from all sides. Dennis and Chuck were now at the south side of the house, just under the dining room window. The view from the window allowed him to see into the house and down the hall into the bathroom. There was nothing! No sounds, no one was walking around! The kitchen window was too high to peer through. Dennis waited several more seconds before he motioned to the men lying in the tall grass to wait. Finally he waved everyone forward. If they were to storm the front door, it would have to be fast. The front porch was so run down it would announce their arrival. While Chuck took the rear of the tiny house, along with three other men, Dennis took the front door with two veteran officers he trusted the most. The other four men remained in the fields, just in case Derek was somewhere else. As far as Dennis could tell, all of the outer buildings were empty.

The assault only took a few minutes. After calling out Derek's name and announcing that they were police officers, the task force broke in with full force. Once inside they were puzzled when they found that no one was around. Not the girls, nor Derek.

"Fuck, where are they?" An adrenaline-pumped Dennis approached Chuck from the kitchen.

Chuck and two other men were standing in the dining room, the looks on their faces mirroring Dennis's verbal outburst. "Shit! I don't understand it. Jade's van is on the road and Derek's station wagon is outside. Obviously they're not here, so where the hell are they? The outbuildings are practically collapsing on the ground so I doubt if Derek and the girls are in any of them."

Dennis looked at Chuck and the two other police officers for an answer. They had none. "OK let's make a thorough sweep of the area to see if we turn up anything." Dennis moved past the men and out onto the porch.

The wind had begun to roar through the trees making a loud swishing sound. Dennis shouted to the officers in the field to go over every inch of grounds on the old farm. After a full thirty minutes they had turned up nothing. Dennis, Chuck, and the other officers gathered on the rickety front porch that rattled with the wind as it tore over the roof, sending the occasional shingle whizzing through the air.

"They are here somewhere and we don't have a lot of time!" Dennis shouted over the wind to Chuck before turning to a young officer who had recently been promoted to a detective. "Ben, get on the phone and call the station. We need Lucy now! She's the only one who can help us find the girls, and tell Max Grant to hurry.

Dennis turned around and went back into the little house, which was now shaking and rattling frantically from the wind. "I hate this damn wind!" he shouted at no one in particular, leaving the rest of the team wondering if they should just stay on the porch or go inside. When a large branch from a tree slammed into the side of the house, shattering the window, the officers went inside.

"Make sure you touch nothing, unless you wear gloves. Let's gather and bag as much evidence as we can until Lucy gets here," Chuck said.

With that statement the officers began to get to work, filling the next half hour gathering evidence. Dennis went into the dining room where the plastic molds of the missing items worn by the girls, were found. It wasn't until they had bagged everything that seemed important that Dennis noticed a silver buckle among the leftover clutter. He picked it up, turning it over to inspect the intricate pattern carved into the front. Dennis noticed that the edges were charred, as if it had been in a fire. In the center of the buckle he could make out the initials. S--W was all he could make out, the middle initial was almost illegible. Suddenly it hit him, he knew who the buckle belonged to – Samuel Walker. Jade, Crystal, and Amber's father! What in hell was the buckle doing here? Dennis looked back down at the table. What else was under the pile of crap that filled the space on the table? A wooden box sat under a cloth. He picked it up and peered inside; ashes, nothing but ashes, but whose? He would have to get them down to forensics. They could belong to any of the missing girls.

There was the barking of a dog. *That was fast!* he thought as he placed the buckle in a bag and sealed the box of ashes. Once out on the porch everyone could see the uniformed officer running to keep up with a beautiful, German shepherd who seemed to enjoy being in the wide-open space of the outdoors, even if the wind threatened to blow her handler and her away.

"That was fast." Chuck was the first to greet the officer; he bent to put a gentle hand on the shepherd's head while the officer held the dog in check, signaling that Chuck was a friend.

"Good girl. We're sure glad to see you Lucy. We need

to find some friends real quick." Chuck scratched Lucy behind the ears, giving the officer a thankful smile.

Dennis was following close behind, and he held his hand out to the veteran trainer who was a long-time friend and colleague. "Max, good to see you. There's no time for details; we have to put Lucy to work right away."

Dennis turned back toward the house, motioning for Officer Grant to follow. As he neared the porch he handed the buckle and box to another detective. "Bob, get all of the stuff we've gathered together and secure it in my car. We need to make sure nothing goes missing. Stay in the car so the chain of evidence isn't broken."

Dennis turned to another officer, Terry Mahoney, a veteran officer with over thirty years' experience. "Terry, secure the house. Derek may return without our being aware. We still don't know what we're up against."

Bob, the young officer, nodded, took the buckle and box as well as several other bagged items from Dennis, and headed up the road to the car. Terry retreated into the small house while the rest of the officers waited for further instructions.

Dennis disappeared into the house, returning in a few seconds with a faded black jacket of Derek's. By the look of the collar and sleeves, which were worn and frayed it, was one Derek had worn many times. The jacket was also faded and in need of a good cleaning. Dennis approached Officer Grant who took the coat from him and placed it under Lucy's nose. Lucy buried her nose in the fabric, then sat down, raised her head and sneezed, a loud, wet, head shaking sneeze that caught everyone off guard.

"Boy, that's never happened before!" Max put the jacket back under Lucy's nose. Once again Lucy stood, put her nose deep into the jacket and once again sat back down, this time giving off two short 'achoos' into the air. The dog shook her head, lay down, and placed her paws over her nose as if to say *phew!*

"What the hell's on this jacket anyway? I've never seen her act this way." Max brought the jacket close to his nose and quickly held it away. "What's this guy do? The jacket smells like chemicals."

Dennis took the jacket and put his nose close to the sleeve. "It's embalming fluid. The guy's a mortician and obviously a sloppy one."

By now Lucy was standing, her tail straight and her nose in the air. In a few seconds she was pulling Officer Grant toward a large clump of trees that looked menacing as the wind rattled their tops.

Officer Grant turned to Dennis. "She's off and running. Let's go."

Dennis, Chuck, and the rest of the officers followed Lucy and Officer Max Grant, who were now disappearing into a thick clump of trees. Dennis knew somewhere deep in this wooded area they would find Derek and the girls. But would they be in time?

CHAPTER THIRTY-FOUR

Derek stood next to the grotesque forms of his family, a look of insane pride shining on his face.

"Mother, Father, Lisa, meet my new family; Jade, and of course the little one, Amber." He pointed to Jade who stood almost directly in front of the mummified forms, and Amber who still remained transfixed by the flickering glow of the candles. "And most importantly, my bride-to-be, Crystal Walker." He motioned toward Crystal with a gallant bow.

Crystal was now sitting up; her legs and hands were free, but the effects of the drugs were still evident. Her head hung on her chest. As the fog slowly began to lift from her drug-addled brain, she lifted her head from her chest just long enough to catch Jade's eye and let her know she was all right and getting stronger every moment.

Jade had been staring at Derek who seemed to be totally absorbed in his introduction of Crystal to his family, when she saw Crystal's head lift. She could tell Crystal was coming out of her drugged state. This was the first time Jade had been able to get a full view of Crystal and when she did a shocked scream escaped from her lips.

"Oh, no!"

Crystal's upper body and bare arms were covered with burn marks and tiny bruises. Derek followed Jade's eyes and outburst to its source, Crystal.

"Her condition is a necessary initiation in the art of love. And don't worry, she's still a virgin."

Derek moved toward Crystal, touching her tiny face with his large, bony hand. While he circled behind her, he made sure his hand never left her body. Finally he settled his hand on her copper, red curls. As Derek slowly stroked Crystal's hair, her eyes found Jade's once more, but now they were completely clear. A grim determined look crossed Crystal's face. It meant only one thing; Crystal was ready for a fight.

Jade knew they only had to find the right moment and hope they could overcome Derek, somehow getting away. Crystal had to stay alert and Jade had to come up with a plan. But first Jade needed to know what Derek had planned for them. "So what now? You have us all here. So how do you think you're going to get away with this?' The steely sound of her voice surprised even her.

"Who's going to stop me? You can't! Not even my parents could prevent me from having what I wanted."

Derek dropped his hand from Crystal's hair and put his long fingers on her throat.

"Lisa was my angel. She was too young to know what she wanted. If I'd only had enough time to show her the real pleasure of love, things would have been different. But she fought me. I had to burn some sense into her. Even then she resisted. Lisa said awful things, hateful things. I had to shut her up. Her neck snapped. I know she could have loved me if only she would have listened," Derek shouted, spittle forming along the edge of his mouth.

He tilted Crystal's head back and looked into her deep, blue eyes, his voice menacing. "But you'll listen won't you?" He bent his head over Crystal's face and placed his wet, hot lips over hers, once again plunging his tongue deep into the cool wet recess of her mouth. Crystal tried not to choke or pull away. The years spent with her father had taught her not to resist openly when he was in one of his drunken, obsessive moods. She knew that the less resistance she gave Derek, the more likely he would be to loosen his grip on her. If she was going to get out of Derek's reach, she needed to have him feel safe and in control. Crystal let her body go limp. Her eyes stayed wide open, never leaving Jade's face.

Jade knew that Crystal was terrified. But the years with Sam had taught them strong survival skills. Their motto with Sam had been, 'Say yes, wait, and get out of sight.' It would have to be the same motto with Derek. Show no resistance, wait for him to relax his guard, and then run like hell.

* * *

Derek liked the feel of Crystal in his arms. He liked the way Crystal melted at his kiss and touch. The others always fought. Crystal had been different from the beginning. He had made sure that all of the girls knew he was the boss. He gagged them and tied them to the table at first. Then he pinched and burnt his victims repeatedly, showing them he was the one in control and unafraid to use whatever means necessary to manage them. The others had struggled and made horrifying screams when he burnt their skin with his hot, searing cigarette or pinched them with his strong fingers, all the while telling them it was hopeless to struggle. They were his. But none of them had ever listened before. They struggled to the end. It was always the same. When he removed the tape from their mouths, a foul string of words would follow. When he pressed his lips to theirs they would bite and spit. Derek's efforts to subdue the girls always resulted in the same ending. He simply snapped their necks like he had done to the cats and small dogs that had resisted him over the years.

Sometimes he would drug the girls and take them back to the funeral home, hoping to give them one more chance to become his. When it became apparent that they were only going to resist, Derek did what he had to do. The 'belly of the beast' was their final resting place, a place where each would burn in hell. But Crystal was different. She welcomed him. She needed him. He could tell by the way her blue eyes stayed steady as he branded and pinched her tiny arms and chest. Never once did she let out a single peep.

When he removed the tape, all Crystal wanted to know was where she was and what he wanted with her. When he explained the way things were going to be, she seemed calm, accepting. Derek knew Jade and Crystal had discovered Mandy and he thought Crystal would be terrified of him. Instead she seemed resigned to be his.

Crystal was obviously the one Derek had waited all of these years for, a delicate little flower to call his own. Now she lay limply in his arms, welcoming his kiss and his touch. Derek felt an almost hysterical joy as the tears welled up in his eyes and he turned away from Crystal, facing the goat-headed God behind him, one hand still gripping her shoulder tightly. "You promised me a bride. All I had to do was be patient and you would deliver her to me." Derek's voice rose as he began his prayer of thanks. "Now a new life will begin for me, a life in which I can love and be loved."

The sobs began to tear from Derek's chest between his words of thanks, directed at the evil image. "Never again will I doubt you now that you have delivered my bride to me." The uncontrollable emotions and pent-up feelings overwhelmed him, making him drop to his knees.

This was it; Crystal knew it was now or never. Jade had moved over to oblivious Amber, who was still transfixed by the flicker of the candles as they danced across the multi-colored tapestry lining the walls. By the time Derek dropped to his knees, the girls were ready. The door leading out of the storage area was only a few hundred feet away. They would need to run like hell and hope they could run faster than the awkward but long-legged Derek, and somehow make it out of there.

Once Crystal saw that Jade had Amber's hand, she grabbed the bottom of the wedding gown, pulled it up to her waist, jumped from the granite slab, and began to run like hell. Jade was running just a few feet ahead, pulling Amber close behind. They were only halfway to the door when a gut-wrenching scream echoed against the walls, assaulting their ears. Derek was up off his knees, moving quickly in their direction. There was a look of total disbelief on his face for having been stupid and letting his guard down enough to trust them.

Derek's long legs allowed him to gain on them quickly. Jade reached the outer door first with Amber still in hand.

Just as she began to open the door she heard Crystal's screams as Derek lunged toward her, grabbing the back of her gown.

There was a loud rip as the back of the gown was torn away, the heavy fabric of the train preventing it from ripping further. It allowed Derek to hold Crystal in place until he could pull her to the floor with him.

Jade managed to open the heavy chamber door and push Amber through before closing it. Then she turned back to fight Derek off Crystal. At least Amber would be safe for a while, she thought, as she put all of her strength into a kick at Derek's head.

With Derek on the floor trying to subdue Crystal, Jade was able to get in another two big kicks at his face before his large hand encircled her tiny foot and brought her to the ground.

Crystal was tangled up in the volume of fabric of the gown as she twisted and turned, trying to get her feet free. Derek found it difficult to hang on to her as she writhed. Still fending off Jade's kicks and slaps, he grabbed at the folds of white material as they bunched itself up around Crystal's waist. "You fucking little bitch, I trusted you! I loved you! I would have protected and cared for you!" Derek spit out the words with all of the frustration and hate he now felt, a sharp contrast to the feelings of thankfulness he had felt moments before. "Now you two little whores will die just like the others."

Jade felt Derek's hand tighten around her foot, dragging her closer to him, his face only a few inches from hers. She stopped struggling for a few seconds, allowing Derek to pull with the same force but with no resistance from her. As he pulled her quickly towards him, a look of shock crossed his face just as the feel of her foot caught him full force on the bridge of his long, narrow nose. There was a *crack* as the bridge of his nose shattered from the force. Derek let go of Crystal, as a loud scream of pain passed his full, wet lips. The blood gushed from his nose out over his chin as his large hand smeared the blood onto his face.

Jade jumped to her feet and grabbed Crystal. The gown had to go. She spun Crystal around and pulled as hard as she could on the lower portion of it. It ripped only a couple more inches but it was enough. The straps of the gown were already over Crystal's shoulders; Jade pulled them down over Crystal's arms and continued to pull with all of the strength she could. The gown fell over Crystal's slim hips, crumpling around her feet. She quickly stepped out of the heap of white lace and jewels as Jade pulled her towards the door. Again they were only seconds away from freedom. Jade had begun to swing the heavy chamber door open when two large bloody hands lunged toward Crystal pulling her back. Jade was almost out when she felt Derek's hand give her back a violent shove. She fell forward, out of the chamber door and found herself sprawled out on the cold concrete floor of the outer storage area. The heavy door shut behind her, and her ears rang with Crystal's final screams: "Don't leave m..." before the hollow silence engulfed her.

* * *

Dennis was only a few feet away from Lucy and Max Grant. The dog's tail was wagging, her excited bark rising above the howling wind. They were now almost three hundred feet into the dense underbrush. The heavily treed path the dog followed was not well travelled, but there was still a path nonetheless.

Lucy was leading them to some unknown destination. She shifted from full gear into a sudden stop, the barking now an excited whining.

"They're here." Max turned toward Dennis, letting Chuck and the other detectives catch up and gather around Lucy.

There was a small rise, about three feet up, directly ahead. Dennis knew instantly what it was. "It's got to be the entrance to a bomb shelter, most likely built in the mid-'50s or early '60s." He turned to all of the members of the team. "The entrance is here somewhere." Searching for the door, he turned back to the mound. "Chuck, you and a couple of officers come with me. The rest of you stay here. There's no need to announce ourselves by making a grand entrance. We still need the element of surprise. So, quiet everyone. Let's go slow. We don't know what is behind the hatch. Just find it, now!"

Dennis, Chuck, and two other officers felt around the ground on the mound. It was Dennis who found the hard iron of the door's handle beneath his palm. He pulled hard and a metal door gave way, pulling up toward him, still covered in quack grass and a variety of other weeds. The light of the day was quickly fading as they descended the dark passage. After a few yards they found another entrance that opened into a large storage area. By now their eyes had adjusted to the dim light of the florescent bulbs overhead.

Dennis was both shocked and overjoyed at the sight that greeted him. Amber stood in front of him in the middle of the room and just outside of the large door lay

Jade in a heap, her feet up behind her and her belly flat on the floor. She looked up as she heard their approach. Her face was distorted with grief and fear. "Thank God you're here! Help me. Derek has Crystal and I'm sure he'll kill her. Hurry!" she screamed. Her voice broke as she regained her footing.

Dennis raced forward, covering the distance in a few long strides. He bent over and pulled Jade up, helping her to steady herself as she pulled away from the door. The room was growing ever darker as the generator ran out of fuel. Chuck was right behind Dennis and he pulled a lighter from his pocket and flicked it open to get some more light in the room.

"Get the girls out of here." Dennis turned to the young officer, the newest and youngest member of the team.

"Get your fucking hands off me," Jade spat at the officer as he started to put his arms around her, attempting to escort her out. "I'm not going anywhere without Crystal and you'll need me!" she shouted in frustration.

Jade's face was now lit by a couple of candles that Chuck had found on the shelves, allowing the eerie glow to show the look of stubborn determination on her face.

"And there's no time to argue. Take Amber, but I'm staying." Jade's chin stuck out in the air, her tiny face fierce with defiance.

"OK OK. No time to argue with anyone as angry as you are." Dennis looked down at Jade's red-rimmed, bright-blue eyes. He motioned to the confused young officer. "Take Amber. And get some more light down here when you come back. There are more candles on the shelves."

Dennis turned his attention once more to Jade. "OK.

Tell me what we're up against. What's behind the door?"

"It's like a church; candles, an altar, pews to the front and three special guests, all dead; Derek's family. I think he stuffed them like they do dead animals. It's almost like they're real." Jade was nearly breathless, her need to be of help overcoming her fear.

"Does he have a gun or a weapon?" Dennis could hear the young officer's return as he asked the question.

"No, none that I saw. I don't think Derek was expecting anyone but us girls and he felt we were no threat."

The room was now much brighter as more candles were lit and lined up along the half-empty shelves.

"Derek doesn't know you alerted us?"

"No, I wasn't sure you'd get my message, so I felt I was on my own," Jade answered back.

"Good, then we still have the element of surprise." Dennis turned to Chuck and the two other officers. "We need to get in the room without Derek's knowledge. Stand by, ready to take my lead."

Both men nodded as Chuck replied an audible, "Got it."

Dennis turned to Jade. "Do you think you can go back in and get Derek to concentrate on you while we try to get in and take him by surprise?"

"Absolutely." Jade's fear seemed to melt away now that Dennis and the other men were there. "There are tapestries along the wall, hung from the piping. They are about a foot away from the walls; you could slip behind them and make your way fairly close to the altar. That's where he'll have Crystal," she stated, sure that Derek would return to his original plan for Crystal.

"OK, let's go. It's up to you." Dennis put a firm hand

on Jade's shoulder to let her know that he would be right behind and he would get them out safely.

Dennis and Chuck pressed close to the wall in the outer chamber just to the side of the door. The other officers stayed just outside, ready to burst in at the first word from Chuck or Dennis. Jade grabbed the handle of the heavy chamber door and gave it a hard tug. It took all the strength she had to pull it fully open. The candles in the outer chamber had been put out; all but the one that Jade held in her hand. She hoped that Derek would concentrate on her and not detect any other movement.

As the door swung open, Derek turned towards the sound, not altogether surprised. Jade was a spunky little thing. She wouldn't give up easily. She must have taken Amber out of the shelter, he thought, as he noticed Jade's solo entrance.

Jade stood alone in the doorway. A candle lit up her beautiful face. For a second Derek didn't know whom he wanted more, Crystal or Jade. What the fuck! He would have them both.

Crystal was now lying on the altar, her tiny breast bare with the removal of the gown. She wore lacy white panties and a garter. Her white nylons were held up by their tiny clips, her feet shoeless. Crystal held on to her tiny breasts with both hands, hating the feeling of helplessness. Being half naked made her feel violated and close to hysterical. When the door had shut on Jade, leaving her alone with Derek, Crystal thought she would lose it. All she could do was to pray. But once again, she could smell the fresh scent of laundry. She knew she would be safe.

"I'm not leaving without Crystal. So I guess you'll have to have us both," Jade said seductively. She moved steadily toward Derek who was standing at the altar. Jade kept her eyes on Derek's, willing him to look only at her.

Derek's face took on a look of triumph the way a bully does when he's taken the lunch money from someone smaller and weaker than him. "So, you've decided to sacrifice yourself for your sister. How noble. So I'll let you. You're both perfect for me." His eyes never left Jade's.

Jade continued to move forward, focusing the candle on her face, holding Derek's attention. The music that played in the background continued its hypnotic chant. For a moment, Jade forgot that Dennis was somewhere behind the heavy tapestry, making his way toward Derek. Her eyes and ears were focused on the madman in front of her.

Derek put his hands on Crystal's neck, his long fingers pointing down towards her naked breasts. "The only way you and your sister make it out of here alive, is if you both give yourselves to me willingly," he commanded. He slid a hand down Crystal's chest and cupped her breast, squeezing her nipple hard. Jade heard a small cry of pain from Crystal as she turned her head to look at Jade.

Behind Derek, Jade saw a small amount of movement from the tapestry. Dennis was now directly behind Derek. All he needed was a diversion.

Jade knew it was up to her to get Derek to move away from Crystal before he could hurt her. She stopped, standing between Derek, who was only a few feet ahead, and his mummified family, who were only a few feet behind. She turned around quickly and moved toward the gruesome forms that sat silently on the pew behind her. Circling, she stood next to the figures of his mother and father, just between his sister and obsessive love, Lisa.

"Why not have all three of us? I'm sure Lisa won't mind. Oh, I forgot, she didn't want you any more than Crystal or I do. Maybe once again you'll have no one." Jade hoped Derek would forget Crystal and respond to her taunt.

Derek's eyes narrowed and Jade knew she was close to getting the response she wanted, but Derek's hands never moved from Crystal's body.

"What's the matter? Does the truth hurt? It must be difficult to be such a fucking freak. You want young beautiful girls, but we don't want you. You're just too fucked up to get it." Jade smelled the embalming fluid and whatever other chemicals had been used to mummify Derek's family. She was sure they would be highly flammable.

"You shut your foul mouth up or I'll kill your little bitch of a sister and then I'll kill you. When you are both dead I'll take you anyway," Derek sneered. "Death excites me. Your cold, lifeless body under mine is what makes me come, so don't fuck with me little girl, you'll never win."

Dennis had moved out from behind the curtain – he was only a few feet away from Derek. His gun was drawn and he was about to shoot Derek before noticed that the hand that held Crystal's breast right above her heart had a small, silver pocketknife in it. If Dennis made the wrong move, Derek could plunge it into Crystal's body in a second. He needed to get Derek to move away from the terrified girl.

Dennis froze, hoping Derek wouldn't turn around and see him. He would be forced to fire his gun and from the position of Derek's hand over Crystal's breast, he was unsure of the result. Crystal could die if he didn't get Derek to move away from her. Dennis would have to leave it up to Jade and hope her taunting remarks would get Derek to move.

Jade saw Dennis just behind Derek and the look on his face told her that he couldn't make his move on the madman who was bent over her sister. Jade would need to get Derek to move. The smell of the corpse that Jade stood next to made her look at the candle she held more intensely. As she looked up from the candle to Derek's face, she saw that he knew what was going through her mind.

"Noooo!" was all she could hear as she put the candle to the copper curls of Lisa's hair. Instantly, flames leapt and sizzled from the cotton-candy strands. Next, the mother too sizzled as flames started to flicker from her stretched skin. The father was next. Jade swung the candle to his clothing, hair, and face. Swoosh! The fumes and gasses from the bodies exploded, sending Jade backward onto her ass.

Derek ran from the altar, his knife still in his hand, Crystal now forgotten. His family was swiftly engulfed in flames. He had to do something to put them out. As he reached into the family circle to pull Lisa away from the soaring flames, the sleeves on his jacket caught fire instantly. Within seconds, his jacket was like a torch, the flames reaching up to his long hair. The look on his face was one of shock and terror. In his attempt to rescue his family, he had forgotten that the embalming fluid was formaldehyde and highly flammable. His jacket was always soaked in the chemicals, from his work at the funeral home. A scream of anger, contempt, and surprise, tore from his lips as his eyes bore into Jade's. "You Fucking Bitch!" The epitaph attached itself to the end of his gut-wrenching scream.

Derek's face was now a mask of contorted pain. Rather than run from the flames, he held Lisa's torched body closer to his. The flames were now rising well above his face. Jade could barely see his skin or hair through the flame's flickering, red fingers.

Derek moved closer into Lisa, his beloved sister, and put his melting lips into her now charred indistinguishable face. The air was finally choked from his lungs.

Derek and Lisa fell forward into the bodies of their family. The whole chamber was now lit by the fierce glow of the flames as they consumed the Hansen family. Dark smoke filled the room while the flames spread rapidly.

Dennis could see that the horrible scene in front of Jade had her transfixed. If she didn't move soon, the flames would engulf her, making Jade a part of the family's tragic end. With one arm firmly around Crystal's shoulder, Dennis took three giant steps toward Jade, shouting her name as he moved towards her. "Jade, move!"

Jade heard Dennis's command above the crackling roar of the flames that now danced along the walls of thick tapestry. She looked up and blinked twice. By the time Dennis was at her side, her arms were stretched out toward him. Dennis gathered Jade to his chest and turned toward the chamber door.

Chuck and the other young officers were only steps behind him. Chuck grabbed Crystal from Dennis and gathered her into his arms while Dennis held Jade firmly. Dennis and Chuck could do nothing for Derek and every second was needed if they were to get out of the black, smoke-filled room before all of the air was sucked out by the fire, which now shot flames over everyone's heads. The sparks fell dangerously close as they retreated. They ran to the metal door, closing it just in time, Derek's screams fading as the door shut. Dennis, Chuck, and Dennis, along with Jade and Crystal fell in a heap as they bolted through the outer storage area.

Dennis placed Jade on the dirt floor and turned to Chuck, who still held Crystal. With the loud thud of the closing door, the storage room became strangely quiet as the rest of the cops slumped to the floor, drained. Nothing was said for what seemed like forever, until Crystal began to cough, tears streaming down her face. It was partly because of the smoke, but mostly from relief.

Dennis noted that Crystal was still half naked. He nodded toward one of the officers who removed his bulletproof vest and took off his blue shirt, handing it to Dennis.

Crystal looked up at Dennis, and never had he seen such a look of relief mixed with confusion and fear. Her eyes turned toward Jade who was sitting on the other side of Dennis.

Dennis noted how Crystal and Jade exchanged a strange look that made him wonder if there was more going on with the girls than a near-death by fire. He felt that he should have seen a look that said it was over and that everything would be all right. Instead the look on their faces was more like their worries were just beginning. Maybe they were concerned about Amber.

"Your sister is all right. She's just outside the bunker." Dennis could see that this did little to lift their mood.

"Come on everyone, let's get going, the smoke is beginning to drift under the door," Chuck said.

Dennis gathered Jade up in his arms, her tiny body light and easy to move as she clung tightly to his neck.

Chuck took his cue from Dennis and scooped up Crystal. The whole group made its way out of the storage room into the passageway that led up and out into the black, star-filled night.

Dennis heard Lucy's excited bark as they drew closer to the outer door, the evening air caressing their faces with its welcome coolness and fresh forest scent. The wind was now little more than a brisk breeze. As if rehearsed, the group took a deep breath at once, releasing it slowly; their lungs welcoming the clear pure air.

"Let's get you girls home. Tomorrow we'll deal with the details," Dennis said.

Dennis gathered the rest of his team around him, giving orders to the men about a debriefing they would hold at the station after he got the girls home. He asked one young officer to run ahead and bring one of the cars down the rutted, bumpy road. The girls would be too tired to make the trek back. The ride would be rough, but it would be better than the walk.

Chuck and Dennis had seen to it personally that the girls got home and were safely put to bed. Veronica came over and rather than give her a blow by blow on how the rescue went, Dennis simply asked if she could stay. She nodded in assent.

"Just one more question before we go. Where the hell is Sam?" Dennis asked.

A look of fear and confusion spread across Jade's face. "I honestly don't know. He simply left a few days ago."

Jade looked briefly into Dennis's eyes before quickly lowering hers. There was a moment of silence between them before Crystal quickly interjected. "You know Dad – he hates us and with Mom dead we were probably too much. He just took off."

The sound of Crystal's voice held just a twinge of hopefulness. It didn't seem like it was because Sam was gone, but was more like the sound of hope that Dennis would believe her. Something was up and Dennis would have to find out what.

* * *

Dennis looked over at his partner. Chuck was leaning back on his office chair, swigging down the final drops of his strong, cold coffee. They had gone over all of the evening's details with the men. Their reports would be required quickly before the press got wind of Derek's death and his involvement with the missing and now known to be dead girls. It was over. Dennis, Chuck, and the team had put an end to an especially cruel and clever serial killer. So far Dennis hadn't mentioned his thoughts on Sam's disappearance, preferring to keep his unspoken suspicions to himself.

Chuck stood up and ran his fingers over the jewelry molds they had found at Derek's house. Items had been once laid into the soft clay, making the imprints of personal things that had once belonged to the young victims. Alongside them was the knife that had been held to Crystal's throat, as well as a belt buckle, ashes, pictures, and undeveloped film. All of the items held clues or proof of Derek's horrible crimes.

"Do you want me to take these things to the evidence room?" Chuck asked.

"No, I'll do it. Once they're signed in and tagged they'll never be seen again. With Derek dead and our testimony, none of these items will be needed for evidence.

I just want to be the one to put it all away forever. Maybe it's because I'm a father and I know how the families will feel when we tell them its over," Dennis said. He ran his hand over his face and stroked his mustache, a familiar move. "There is no hope that their baby girls will ever be coming home. I know how I would feel if it were one of my girls. I want to show the memories of the victims a little respect and spend a few more minutes getting this stuff ready for lock up."

Chuck could tell Dennis needed this time alone. The items would soon find their way into some numbered box, never to be seen again. Dennis was right. A little respect was needed before everything was put to rest. He nodded and left Dennis to perform the last rites.

Dennis leaned over the desk and picked up the small knife. Until now he'd had little opportunity to examine it. As he flipped it over he was startled to see that there was an intricate set of initials carved into its silver body: S.J.W. Dennis reached over and picked up the belt buckle that lay on the desk next to the molds. The exact same silver initials were carved into the buckle. In a flash of insight it suddenly became very clear to Dennis what had gone on in the last few days.

* * *

Jade and Crystal sat on the back step of their home while Amber was swinging on a hammock. Amber would stay on the hammock and swing for hours, only stopping if one of the girls came to get her. They couldn't believe what had happened so far that morning. Both of the girls had been too tired the evening before, so nothing about the past day had been discussed between them. They had hoped to get up early and discuss their story, getting the details straight before the police came to question them. But they had only just gotten up when the front door bell announced Dennis Kortovich's arrival. Both girls exchanged a fearful look before they had to answer the door.

His handsome face rosy and happy, Dennis looked fresh and relaxed, his clothes perfect, making him appear more like a businessman than a detective. His mood caught the girl's off-guard. They were expecting their crime to be discovered at any moment, and knew they could face a lifetime in jail for Sam's murder.

Dennis had a statement with him that he had prepared earlier. It was simple and it stated that the girls had discovered Derek's involvement with Charlotte's disappearance, which led in part to Crystal's subsequent kidnapping and Derek's blackmailing attempt, inducing Jade to join him at the farm, and his attempt to kill the girls at the bomb shelter.

It was straightforward and said nothing about Sam and other things Jade was sure Dennis knew, or questions she thought he would ask. What about the knife Derek had? And what about the buckle Dennis found at Derek's home? Most importantly, what about the ashes? Both girls knew the police now had all of the evidence. Would they ask more questions about where their father was? There was no way a detective as good as Dennis would let any of these questions go unanswered.

Both girls exchanged uneasy looks, waiting for the axe to fall. After each had signed her individual statement, Dennis said his farewells and got up to leave.

Jade walked Dennis to the door, still a little shocked at

how easy Dennis made closing the case on Derek seem. Dennis said it would soon be over. As he held the door open, looking intently into each of the girl's eyes, he could see two beautiful girls who had lived a cruel and bitter life. Sam had been as evil as they came. The Walker girls deserved a life free of fear and harm. They would have that now.

"By the way, I have a little gift for you. Open it after I'm gone." He thrust a small, wooden box into Jade's hand. It was wrapped in simple brown paper.

As the morning breeze blew softly across the porch, Jade and Crystal couldn't contain the tears that slowly slid down their smooth, young faces. It was over. They would never have to live in fear again. In the plain wooden box was their future and freedom. Lying in the ash-filled box were two silver items; Sam's buckle and knife. The morning light glittered off the intricately carved initials. All the girls could do was smile at each other through their warm tears.

Jade was the first to stand; the box rested in her tiny hands. She looked down at Crystal, her voice soft and contented. "It's over Crystal. Let's go bury Dad!"

BLOOD GAMES

Chapter One

The Chicago wind howled from the north, slapping the snow across the open field like a hockey player shooting at the net in a frantic last attempt to score. Detective Dennis Kortovich parked his Crown Victoria away from the howling northern wind, knowing that the vehicle would only give small amount of cover, his partner Chuck O'Brian followed close behind. A police cruiser had already arrived at the scene and two young officers were questioning a young man in a bright, red hooded jacket whom seemed to be freezing in the sub-zero weather. The January day was as cold as a whore's heart and twice as deadly.

"Put that young man in the back of the cruiser," yelled Kortovich shaking his head at the need to state the obvious. "He will be able to answer the questions if he's not half frozen." The wind whipped around Dennis's ankles trying to find entry into his warm boots as he moved around to the south side of the cruiser, to get a full view of the crime scene and knowing what he would find. The markers made it easy to focus on the bodies of a young couple. The male lay a few feet from the female, his body facing toward the young woman. His arms were stretched toward his partner in what looked like an effort to embrace her. She had her arms crossed on her chest, seemingly rejecting him even in death. It was obvious that the killer had posed the couple after he'd dumped the bodies in the open field.

Dennis looked away from the bodies as a gust of cold wind whistled past his head. The sky was heavy with bleak possibilities of even colder weather coming in from the north. The wind made it difficult to breath; it assaulted Dennis's lungs with its frozen fingers, its grip tight and unforgiving. God, how he hated these freezing Chicago winters, he thought as he moved closer to view the scene. As he stood over the bodies, Dennis began pulling off his winter gloves replacing them with latex ones. If he had to touch anything he wouldn't compromise the evidence. He pulled his fur-lined hood over his head and bent down over the closest body; the young women. Chuck stood off to the side, his notepad in hand.

"How many of these bodies do we have to find before we get a break?" Dennis said under his breath – his rhetorical question unanswered by Chuck.

Dennis examined the body of the women while Chuck made notes in the familiar black pad. The victim was young, under thirty and pretty, her long dark hair partially covering her face. Her makeup, once artfully done, was now a death mask of horror. The winter coat she wore was twisted around her body and looked as though someone had put it on after her death; the buttons were not in their correct holes. She wore a skirt, her legs a bluish hue from a night spent in the cold field of snow and ice. Her wrists had been bound and taped; marks could be seen where Jack Frost had laid his icy fingers. Her ankles also bore the marks of her assault.

"There's something different about this one." Dennis turned to his partner as he looked up from the victim. "What do you make of it?

Dennis could see a twinge of irritation cross his partner's face when he asked the question. It wasn't that Chuck didn't know the answer. Chuck was a great cop with well-honed observation skills, but Dennis knew Chuck wished he would just tell him what he saw and let him off the hook. Dennis liked to irritate his partner with his Holmes and Watson antics. It made solving crimes a lot more fun when his good-natured partner was put on the spot. Besides, it was a good way of thinking out loud and getting on the same page – not that they disagreed very often.

"As usual, this isn't where the murders took place; this is just where he dumped the bodies. There are no fluids around the bodies; everything is clean as a whistle. But the victim didn't put the coat on herself. It had to have been put on by her killer. It's the same MO as the others, but it's the first time the killer has gotten sloppy. If we are lucky he might be getting cocky. If so, mistakes will be made. There always are, eventually. Maybe we'll get a break and find a print on one of the buttons." Chuck made reference to the misbuttoned coat as he looked up at Dennis, the look of irritation still evident on his chubby face.

Dennis nodded in agreement. So far the killer hadn't made a mistake. However, whoever it was upping the pace. He had dumped more bodies over the past few weeks than he had since the crime spree had begun in early November. Once again the victim's throat had been cut clean by a very sharp object. As often as Dennis had seen death over the last twenty years, this was still a chilling and uncomfortable sight. He had seen death in all of its insidious shapes and forms, but it was something that he had yet to make peace with. These murders, however, were more depraved than the other homicides that Dennis and Chuck had dealt with in the past. Most of them had been gang and drug-related, with the occasional spouse offing his or her partner.

"Look at her ankles. It's the same. You can tell by the severe indentations that she was hung by her ankles before she was killed. The killer once again slowly slit her throat and drained all of the blood while she was still alive, bleeding her, like cattle at the slaughterhouse," Dennis said, trying to keep the disgust from his voice. "It's the same guy and we still haven't enough clues to even come close to one suspect."

Dennis reached over to the side of her coat to see if anything would be in her pockets that might help with the investigation. He pulled out several gum wrappers and a ticket stub from a movie house. The date on the ticket said it was from the night before. They would follow up later in the day to see if anyone at the theatre remembered the couple. A boot lay a few feet from the body; it had fallen off when the killer had dumped her. Her handbag lay at her side. Dennis touched her frozen face; her skin almost seemed translucent, pale beyond imagination. He didn't have to look at the girl's companion to know that he too had come to the same grisly end.

"The crime scene investigative team will be here in seconds, they can go over the scene for fibers and prints. All of the other victims have been clean. No evidence that can be traced back to a suspect. With all of our victims from out of town, it's impossible to link them to one common suspect," Dennis said as he walked over to the male. "They look like they had one hell of a scare just before their deaths. I'm sure they were aware of what was happening just before he slit their throat. It would be terrifying to come to this kind of an end."

Chuck stood by as Dennis bent over the young man and continued his summation. "I'm going to assume that they were drugged just before their deaths. The coroner said all of the other victims but the first had a dose of Halcion just prior to their murders. It would have knocked them out long enough for our killer to tie them up without a struggle. Still, by the time he slit their throats they would have been fully aware of what was happening to them," Dennis said as he pulled the coat away from the young man's chest, reaching inside the jacket pocket and pulling out a small bag of soil.

"It's the same killer alright. He's left his calling card once again. What the hell is he trying to say by planting a bag of soil on each of the victims? This is one crazy bastard and we had better catch him soon." Dennis placed the bag of soil back in the victim's pocket while a team of investigators descended on the area. He stood and greeted the senior member of the team, a woman by the name of Corrine Wilson.

Corrine Wilson was a tall brunette with more curves than the Indianapolis 500. She was close to the same age as Dennis, fifty, but her face was holding up well. Strong features with smooth, wrinkle-free skin, made her a shoo-in for a Dove commercial. Corrine's bulky winter coat covered up her abundant chest, an embarrassing distraction for Dennis. He always found himself straining to keep his eyes on her big, baby blues.

"What have you got, Kortovich?" Corrine asked as she drew closer to the scene.

"The same thing we've had for the past four months," Dennis said as he moved closer to Chuck, allowing Corrine to view the two victims now behind them. "More bodies than clues."

Corrine gave Chuck a friendly nod, and turned her attention to Dennis. "I'm about as sick of this as you are. It's starting to get embarrassing. My reputation is on the line."

As Corrine moved closer to the male victim the rest of the team started to take photos and scour the scene. She had been recently promoted to head investigator of her forensic team. A bright, energetic woman who had been divorced for almost a year, she had earned Dennis's respect. At almost six feet, Corrine could look a man straight in the eye. It made her seem powerful and in charge of her environment, qualities Dennis liked in a woman. He respected her ability and had enjoyed working with her in the past. But recently he felt as if her energy had taken a strange shift toward him and he still hadn't been able to figure out what was different.

"Look, let me do my job," Corrine said in a professional tone. "It's still early and I'm sure I can get the basics done by the end of the day. If you're up to it, we can meet for a drink and go over the preliminary report. The medical examiner will need a little more time with the bodies, but I'm sure I can get you photo, print, and fiber reports as well as a toxic screen. The soil analysis shouldn't take all day either. We have all of our resources working 24/7 on this one."

Dennis knew she was right and that everything the department had was being diverted to the multiple bodies that had been turning up all over Chicago.

"Call me as soon as you have anything and I'll see where I'm at then. If we have time for a drink, fine. If not, just scan and send me the report on my cell," Dennis said, noting a strange look crossing his partner's face.

Dennis would have liked to ask Chuck what the look was about, but members of Corrine's team were moving in on the male victim's body. It was time to leave and let the investigators do their stuff. Besides, Dennis was beginning to feel a little warm, even on this subzero winter day. As they moved away from the scene he turned around to take one last look. Corrine was still standing where he had left her, the look on her face intent. Dennis thought maybe a drink would be nice, after all this case had turned into a nightmare and Veronica, his wife, was used to his working around the clock.

Dennis Kortovich was one of Chicago's finest detectives. With nearly twenty years of service, his reputation for detail had made him irreplaceable when securing a crime scene. It was his ability to see the micro and macro of his surroundings that always amazed his partners. Dennis's notes were meticulous and he seldom forgot a conversation or an interrogation. He could recall hundreds of small details of cases long past; an ability many of his colleagues envied. His first partner, now deceased, used to say, "When in doubt, ask Kortovich," knowing that Dennis always had the details and answers well at hand. But lately Dennis felt he was slipping, and this case was beginning to make him doubt his long years of service and the department's recognition for his ability to solve crimes on good solid work and observation skills. He had never been one to hang his reputation on hunches. Give him the facts and only the facts.

"Well what do you think?" Chuck's brisk baritone voice broke into Dennis's thoughts. The strange look was still on Chuck's face.

Dennis decided to ignore the look. Chuck had been his partner for the past four years and Dennis knew when to just leave things alone. Chuck's square face and evenly placed features gave him a familiar look. Everyone felt as if they had met him before, and they had, in the imaginations of their youth. His thick hair hung over bushy brows and full rosy cheeks. Dennis figured that one day, twenty years from now, when Chuck hit seventy, he would look into a mirror and realize that if he ever grew a beard he could pass for Santa Claus. His stocky build and barrel chest would eventually succumb to gravity and become a paunch – definitely a Santa Claus stand-in. Dennis smiled. He really liked the guy. So far Chuck was his favorite partner and as such was a frequent guest at his home. Veronica, Dennis's wife of thirty years also had a soft spot for his chubby partner and thought it was a shame that he was single. An extra plate was always set at the table every second Sunday, with an occasional female guest thrown in for flavor. Veronica hated to see a sweet guy like Chuck stay single and she was determined to find him a good wife.

"What I think," responded a frustrated Dennis, "is that there are too many bloody bodies and it's starting to make me sick." He removed his latex glove as they moved closer to the Crown Vic. "These are numbers ten and eleven and the hell of it is, we still haven't a bloody clue what the hell is happening. Who? Why? Not even one suspect. It's now the end of January and we're almost four months into the investigation and we have nothing. Meanwhile the superintendent and mayor are having a shit fit." He pulled the front door of the Vic open.

Once in the car Dennis pulled his warm gloves back over his frozen hands before pulling away from the scene of the crime. His foot pushed all the way down on the gas causing the car to veer to the right, just missing the police cruiser with the witness. He had instructed the officers to bring the young man to the station. He and Chuck would need to handle the questioning of the witness themselves. Every 'T' would have to be crossed and every 'I' dotted. There was so much heat coming from above they couldn't afford to miss a beat. Dennis knew that his usual calm was beginning to crumble. This string of murders was just about the biggest and toughest case the city of Chicago had ever seen. A full task force had been pulled together after the fourth and fifth bodies had been found and it was Dennis who had been put in charge. Six more bodies later and he was feeling like a man going down for the third count in a boxing match, KO'd out cold for the match.

"So, what is it we know so far?" Dennis asked Chuck, wanting a brief overview of all that had happened to date.

"The first body was discovered alone; the next two were a young couple found together; then numbers four and five, all within two weeks. Except for the first, all of the victims were found in pairs." Chuck flipped through his notes as he spoke. "It was early November when the first body was discovered and it is now three-quarters of the way through February and these two make the body-count eleven." He summed up what they both already knew. "Our killer is getting bolder. He is killing at a faster pace. If he starts to get too cocky he may start making mistakes. Till then we are out in the cold." Chuck looked over at Dennis as he continued. "These latest two victims must be a yuppie couple. Their clothes were expensive; matching mohair dress coats. Rolex watches. The male's suit was Armani. Other than the gash across his throat, I'd say he was a real catch." Chuck rolled his eyes and then gave a small laugh. "Neither of them could be over twenty-five and from the looks of them I'd say they have a hefty paycheck in order to afford to dress the way they do. We'll get more information once we run a check on their ID and prints. Before the end of the day we should know everything we can about them."

He slapped his notepad shut. "There hasn't been any forensic evidence to go on so far and the killer seems to have knowledge of police procedures and the way we collect evidence. He or she has the ability to cut a clean, precise incision along the neck much like a butcher or meat cutter. It's hard to say what kind of knife made these incisions. We'll have to get the M.E. to nail that down. All of our victims are thirty or under. There is also a small bag of soil planted on all of the bodies except the first; an indication that the first killing was done on an impulse while the others may have been planned. All of the victims had the same contents in their stomachs and were killed within hours of their last meal." Chuck finished, without the benefit of his notes. "What do you think the odds are that eleven people could be killed and all of them would have the exact same meal?"

Dennis answered, "Slim, to none. But it seems each of them ate their last meal in their hotel room. I think the killer may have sent them the meal. Either they knew the killer, or it was an unexpected gift from a stranger. Never look a gift horse in the mouth. I'm sure the victims ate the meals without ever knowing who sent them." Dennis hoped he was right.

"If not, the killer would have to have stalked his victims first, something that seems unlikely given that they were from out of town. What information did you get from the ID in the women's purse?" he asked, knowing Chuck had made note of the information once the forensic team had arrived and processed the purse.

"As usual they're from out of town; New York. Pretty soon word is going to get out and no one will want to come to Chicago," Chuck answered, referring to his black note pad. "It seems someone wants to kill off our tourists and it isn't good for business when they turn up dead. This makes visiting Florida look like a walk in the park." Chuck was referring to the carjacking's and murders that had plagued Florida years before. "Whatever else we find out will have to wait until the reports are finished. I'm sure Corrine will be only too happy to fill you in on the rest of the details over a drink." Chuck's tone was solicitous, and the strange look returned to his face.

"What the hell do you mean by that?" Dennis asked,

irritated by Chuck's tone.

"I think Corrine is going above and beyond the call of duty, doing a rush on the reports and then inviting you for a drink. Why not just email you? Information and refreshments seems a little out of line don't you think?"

"What's out of line? I think this case has us all spooked. Corrine has been the lead CSI in this investigation from the beginning, and I for one am grateful that she has been willing to pull all the stops and get us the information back so quickly," Dennis said defensively.

"Why not invite me? I'm on this case as well. Let me assure you she wanted only you to meet her for a drink, and I'm not invited." Chuck's tone was sharp. "Hasn't she noticed you are married?"

Dennis knew Chuck was usually easygoing and enjoyed a good laugh at anything that would embarrass Dennis, but the usual humor was lacking in his tone at the moment. He would likely get a laugh out of seeing Dennis uncomfortable at the thought of having a drink with a female colleague if it meant more than a work-related event, especially a female with all of the abundant talent displayed by Corrine. But Dennis was sure it was just the heat of this case that had prompted Corrine to extend the unusual invitation. "Look, I'm sure she assumed you would come too. After all, we're a team. Why would she want to meet me alone? Corrine knows I'm married and she has never been anything but professional."

"Corrine has been divorced for more than a year, maybe she's lonely?"

"There are lots of single guys. I'm not the one to fill her lonely nights." Dennis gripped the steering wheel tightly as he maneuvered through the traffic.

"Are you sure of that?" Chuck asked, letting his question hang in the air.

Dennis tried to ignore his partner, saying nothing in response to Chuck's question. Things had been different lately. He had been wondering about life and hadn't come up with any answer that seemed to make sense of how he was feeling. There was a restlessness that seemed to gnaw away at the pit of his stomach. He loved his wife and he loved his job. But somehow each day seemed a little flat. Maybe it was that each day offered more questions than answers; questions about his personal life and these crazy murders. Dennis had chalked his restlessness up to his inability to solve this case, but the fact was, he had been feeling this way for a long time.

Veronica, his wife was going through her own change of life. It had forced her to move into the spare room, an arrangement that didn't make intimacy easy. And as usual, she was as busy as ever. It seemed as if they had been drifting apart for the past few years. Often weeks went by before they connected. Dennis knew he loved his wife, but he seemed to be asking the same question lately. *Is this all there is?* He hadn't been able to find the answer.

"Look. Right now all I need is a hot cup of coffee and not a hard time from an old fart like you. I'm not about to get into trouble with Corrine or anyone else on the force," Dennis said bluntly, hoping Chuck believed him.

With an obvious end to the conversation Dennis continued to wind through the late morning traffic, his thoughts turning back to the case where it seemed safe. Thoughts of murder were a lot more comfortable than thinking of having a drink with a woman like Corrine.

He pushed all thoughts of Corrine from his mind.

This case was getting to everyone and was now considered a 'heater,' a high-profile case. The press was all over it like gaudy makeup on a prepubescent teen, and the more murder victims that turned up the more the press piled it on. By now it would take a carving knife to peel away the muck and get to a likely suspect. Because the blood had been drained from the victims, every cult and weirdo in the city was on the carpet for the murders. But so far nothing had turned up. The teams of investigators that Dennis had assembled to help solve the case were frantically chasing down every lead they could find. Chicago was a city with a raw underside and if you wanted to find something that suited your fancy, from the weird to the wacky, you didn't have to go far to find it. And these killings qualified as just about the most bizarre case Dennis and Chuck had ever seen.

After the first three bodies had been found it hadn't taken them long to interrogate many of the satanic cults and devil worshipers in the hope of finding a clue, but so far nothing. Now even the sickest members of the night world of Chicago were trying to give the police a helping hand.

The murders were bad for business and many of the after-hours clubs had seen a decline in attendance because of the series of shocking murders. The detectives would have to dig a little deeper into the habits of the many night crawlers of Chicago to find out what the blood might be used for. And it was tough enough dealing with the usual thugs, let alone a killer that left his victims looking like they had made a trip to a slaughterhouse.

* * *

It was now bright out; the clouds had disappeared as the sun shot gold beams of light on the frozen marshmallow world. Chuck could see Dennis' reflection in the window as they passed a large grove of trees. At fifty, Dennis was what one would consider good-looking. Not great, just good; square jaw, straight nose, gray eyes, and medium-brown hair. Once it all came together he had an 'All American' look. His moustache covered a generous mouth and the dimples in his cheeks gave him a slightly 'Magnum' look. His broad shoulders tapered into a narrow waist. Chuck envied him the fact that he never worried about his weight, a worry which was a fact of life for Chuck. One of the most outstanding characteristics about Dennis was how neat he always was. As detectives, they wore their own style of clothing, but Dennis seemed to put it together better than anyone else. You couldn't really say he was a fashion plate but he usually wore his clothes in a way that made everyone else look slightly out of date. Maybe it was because Veronica bought his clothes for him, but he managed to make them look better than anyone else. He could have been the CEO of a Fortune 500 company. He looked as if he came from money, but Chuck knew that was far from the truth. He just had good taste and a way of standing out in a crowd. Maybe that was why Corrine had asked Dennis out for a drink. Chuck had a bad feeling about the invitation.

Lately Chuck had seen his partner fall into a slight case of the blues. It had started right after Dennis's fiftieth birthday. Veronica had thrown him a small birthday party with close friends and family. She was usually a great hostess but for some reason the party seemed half done, something out of line for the normally vivacious Veronica. And neither Dennis nor Veronica seemed to connect. This wasn't the usual loving couple that Chuck had learned to envy. It would be terrible if Dennis were to go through a mid-life crisis. Chuck decided he would have to keep an eye on his friend and make sure he didn't do anything stupid at this point in his life.

Chapter Two

Once back at the station, Dennis and Chuck headed for the conference room that had been converted into 'Command Central' for the special task force assembled for the multiple murder cases. As he swung open the double oak doors he was still impressed with the expensive furnishings in the room, a result of a recent renovation. The superintendent had been able to twist a few arms to get the quality furniture, not the usual cheap crap they were used to. The twenty-foot, solid mahogany table was rounded at either end, giving the illusion that the table was oval. Thick padded leather chairs were drawn neatly up to the edge of the table on either side; sixteen in all. Currently there were only eleven detectives assigned to the case, but more could be added as needed and often the superintendent or the mayor would sit in on updates. Along the south wall, directly to the left, was a huge, whiteboard. Written on it in big letters were all the key words that tied this baffling case together. In bold capital letters it read:

TIME OF DEATH: Three to six hours from

last meal.

All of the victims ate the same meal: steak, potatoes, salad, along with dessert and wine.

METHOD OF DEATH: Hung by heels, throat slit, and blood drained from body, traces of Halcion in stomach.

PROFILE OF VICTIMS: All under the age of thirty. Victims were all from out of town; upper to middle income. First victim single, white female. Other victims white couples.

OTHER COMMON DENOMINATORS FOR ALL VICTIMS: None apparent so far, may have been random. Killer probable didn't know his victims.

B.O.S.F.O.B.

This cryptic code of initials stood for 'bag of soil found on bodies.' It had been agreed upon that no one would speak about the soil beyond the confines of their team for fear of alerting the press to this valuable clue. Pictures of the victims lined the west wall. All had been taken post mortem. Pictures of pale human beings, all with a different story, except that they had all died the same way. But why? Dennis hoped that he and Chuck would find the answers to that question soon. If not, the body count would continue to climb.

* * *

Chuck was ready to go home to bed with his report

finished. He liked to keep the

paperwork simple, while Dennis was methodical and meticulous. They had been going around the clock and Chuck could sleep on a dime. Dennis on the other hand, couldn't.

"Go home, Chuck. There's nothing to do until today's report is in. I'll head home in a few hours as soon as I'm done here."

"You don't have to ask twice. Call me when you hear something. I'm bushed and can hardly think straight. Half of my nights are spent seeing our victims swinging from their heels with blood gushing from their throats. I sleep better in the daytime. Let the ghouls deal with these murders – for now I am just going to forget about what kind of sick mind comes up with these kinds of killings." Chuck grabbed his heavy winter coat as he went out the door.

Dennis was just about to call it a day and head home when two veteran police officers who had been assigned to the case, came into the boardroom. Both were in an animated discussion about another case they were currently working on. They followed calls generated by the press and Dennis's case was their primary investigation while the death of socialite Margaret Mendoza, the wife of lawyer Jackson Mendoza, was their secondary case. At the moment, most of his team had several unsolved homicides to deal with in addition to Dennis and Chuck's case.

Margaret had been the daughter of Robert Grey, one of the richest men in Chicago and the great-grandson of one of the original Rubber-Barons. Grandfather Grey held the majority of control over the rubber industry, which sold raw material to the tire-manufacturing companies, making him a very rich man and one of influence. It was a shock to Robert Grey when his only daughter fell in love with the handsome Jackson Mendoza. Mendoza was a third generation Colombian, who was rumored to have ties with the illegal world of the Colombian drug lord, General Zaragoza.

"I don't care what you say. Mrs. Mendoza would never have gone to a doctor like Clarence Fielding. She's probably never even been on the south side of Chicago, let alone gone to the office of that loser." Detective Ferine O' Donnell sounded miffed and irritated at his partner who seemed unwilling to let the discussion end.

"Who knows what these rich socialites will do? And maybe it's like the husband said, she didn't want her friends to know that she wasn't feeling well. I can understand that, especially in a town that 'tells it all' like Chicago," Detective Patrick Getty shot back.

"Hey, don't you two have something better to do than argue about how the rich get medical treatment?"

Dennis welcomed the diversion. He liked the two officers, who were ten years his junior. Ferine was well over thirty-something, a man whose rugged good looks had most of the female staff drooling over the 'Irish Stud' every time they came into contact with him. He was often the butt of many of the other officer's clumsy sex jokes. After all, Ferine was single and could get laid anytime he wanted. At this point he seemed less interested than he had in the past, the result of a crush on one of the new female rookies, who so far wouldn't give him the time of day.

On the other hand, Patrick was bald and a little paunchy, the result of a fifteen-year marriage to a wife who was rumored to be a gourmet cook. From the look of Patrick's protruding belly, Dennis felt the rumor must be true. Patrick was a man of great humor and joy, which made him one of the most popular lunch and after hours' drinking partners on the force.

"Hey Dennis, I didn't see you there. I was so busy trying to knock some sense into this lazy partner of mine." Ferine turned toward Patrick and gave his shoulder a friendly punch.

"What are you still doing here? It's OK to go home once in a while you know!" Patrick said as he approached Dennis.

"I was just heading out when you two loudmouths came busting in. By the way, what's the argument about?" Dennis always found it amusing to watch the volatile but loving chemistry of the two partners.

"It's the other case we're working on, the death of Margaret Mendoza. Her husband told us that she had two doctors." Ferine said. "One has been the family doctor for over thirty years, and apparently she had a second doctor for the past three months, a Doctor Fielding. But he's a scummy low life who has a major drinking and drug problem and I can't see why a classy dame like Mrs. Mendoza would even go to the south side, let alone to the grubby office of this slime-ball. It just doesn't make any sense, yet he was the last one to treat her before she died. My partner here is giving me a rough time and says no one can figure out the rich." Ferine gave Patrick an evil look. "Besides, I think there is something fishy going on and that there is a tie in on our case to the new doctor. It all just seems too convenient to have a new doctor and then die so suddenly."

"Hey I didn't say I didn't agree with you, I just said who can figure out the rich? They sometimes do some strange things. If this Mrs. Mendoza were anything like what her friends say she was, I agree. She wouldn't go to a man like Dr. Fielding," Patrick said, a wicked smile crossing his face.

"I think I'll let you two boys figure things out on the Mendoza case without me, I have enough on my own plate. By the way, how are things going on the phone leads?" Dennis hoped something would have turned up that could lead them to even one suspect.

"Every nutcase in Chicago has us running all over the place. Half of the weirdoes and mental patients have confessed to being the killer, especially the ones with a fascination for blood. They think that they have killed the victims by sucking them dry, but none of them know about the soil so we've had to rule them all out."

Ferine aimed his answer directly at Dennis and turned his back on his partner letting him know he didn't appreciate the rough time he had been given in regards to the Mendoza case.

The team of men and women that was assisting Dennis and Chuck with the case had been sworn to keep the information about the soil secret. It was only spoken of among the members. It would be the one thing that would help them to determine if they had the real killer. Often in high profile cases they would have some unbalanced 'son of a bitch' confess to the crime. It was only the small details that could confirm or deny if the confessor were the real killer. The press was often their biggest problem. If too many details were published about the case then the confessor could fool the cops into thinking they had the murderer, often letting the real killer go free until he struck again. The result was egg on the face of the investigating officers. The details about the bags of soil were guarded within the investigation circle, and Dennis hoped it would stay that way.

"All right, I have a bunch of other leads on my desk. If you two could follow up on as many as you can, we may turn something up."

"No problem. We have a lot of delay time on the Mendoza case. We have to get access to the medical records of Mrs. Mendoza and the husband is giving us a rough time. We talked to the original doctor and you could tell he wanted to co-operate with us but he can't unless we get a warrant to get access to his records. We're just waiting to get a request petition before a judge," Ferine said.

"Well good luck but I'm out of here. I'll see you both at tomorrow's briefing. Let's hope someone on the team turns something up."

Dennis grabbed his coat and left the two detectives still bantering different theories back and forth. They were a great team and debate seemed to be what held their ten-year partnership together.

Just as he was getting into his car, Dennis received a call from Corrine. The report was finished and she wanted to go over it with him. Veronica was still working in her salon. She had been a stylist for over thirty years and after selling her chain of salons, she went home based and had never been happier. After all, getting to work was just a step away. As Dennis looked at his watch he figured he had time to meet Corrine at O'Malley's for a drink and still be back for supper with Veronica and his daughters,

Natasha and Katrina.

As he walked into the bar shortly afterwards, he noticed several other officers that he knew. It seemed strange to be meeting Corrine at a bar. It was the first time he had ever met with her outside of the crime lab. Still, it was work and this case was different from all of the others. Everyone needed more than a drink to get through this one. What harm could a few drinks be?

He knew even as he asked the question of himself that he was wading ankle deep in water that was rising fast, and he was without a lifeboat. Was something about to bite his ass? He hoped not. How far he was willing to go before he was pulled under, he still didn't know. Hell, he loved his wife. Corrine was a colleague and he had no idea what she was thinking. All she wanted to do was to give him some information on the case. He was making stuff up in his mind that he had no business thinking.

Dennis shook off his thoughts and tried to stay aloof. He had a job to do and it was up to him to stay focused. As he walked up to the table where Corrine was sitting he noticed that under her bulky coat she was wearing a low cut, V-necked top that exposed her abundant chest. The smile that greeted him showed even, white teeth. Dennis hoped he could stay focused. He cursed himself. What was happening? He'd never felt so disconnected.

"What's up Corrine?" he asked, as he sat down beside her.

"I wish I could tell you we'd found something different with these two but I can't. It's all pretty much the same; still no prints or fibers. I even got the toxicology reports back from the lab – Halcion, like all the others," Corrine said, looking sheepish. "I shouldn't have called you out again tonight. I could have e-mailed you the reports but this case has me so frustrated I needed a drink and I hate to drink alone." Her voice was soft and apologetic.

Dennis knew how Corrine felt. This case was taking its toll on him as well. Something was different about how he felt about life, his family, and his job. He didn't want to look deeper. It would mean making the right decision and right now Dennis didn't feel like doing the right thing.

Chapter Three

The Beef Chateau, one of Chicago's best-known steak-houses, was full of the sounds of success that Saturday night, back in early in November. Waiters and waitresses were dressed in the famous red and gold of the Beefeaters' sixteenth-century guard regalia, setting the tone for an authentic glimpse of the past. The eager young men and women hustled to pick up their plates loaded with hot potatoes, salad, mushrooms, and thick slabs of home-made bread smothered in sweet garlic butter before they went to the hot sizzling grill to pick up their individual cuts of beef, cooked to perfection.

Back in the kitchen, plates clattered and silver reso-nated with a low-pitched 'clickity-clack' the way heavy cutlery sounds when it's dumped onto cooling trays fresh out of the dishwasher. The atmosphere was upbeat and it had a rhythm and pace that was unique.

The owners of The Beef Chateau, Lexy and Bara, had found a surefire recipe for success. Everything was brought in fresh daily except the beef. It was cut and hung in a huge meat locker at the back of the twelve thousand-square foot restaurant for a full twenty-eight days of perfect aging. Lexy Cohen and his wife Bara had lived for well over six decades and for more than forty years they had been in the food business. It was only in the last ten years that they had come up with the idea behind the Beef Chateau. The problem with most eateries was that the menu had too many items and spoilage often ate away at profits. The Beef Chateau featured steak, steak, and more steak. Everything was streamlined. Their prep chefs had it down to a science.

Every night things came together like a symphony; the movement, flow and rhythm reaching the crescendo around nine when the crowd in the restaurant would hit its peak. The number of out of town guests often rivaled the locals and The Beef Chateau had developed an international reputation. Grade A Prime Cut Beef, the finest in the world. Grain fed, it had a taste like no other and the citizens of Chicago loved it. But it was the secret to the special steak marinades prepared by Brian Bentham, Lexy and Bara's head chef that soon became the most sought-after secret recipe in town; a combination few could beat.

The Beef Chateau was located off of Columbus Drive not far from the Goodman Memorial Theater. This had added greatly to their success with a large before and after theatre crowd.

Lexy looked around the dining room at the end of the evening, feeling a great deal of pride. November was a great month for business and Christmas parties were well underway. The red and gold décor seemed to be especially appropriate at this time of year. As a good Jew his reason for loving Christmas was mainly due to the increased dining traffic, but some of the sounds and spirit of the season flowed over into his joyful soul, making him especially happy during the holiday season, and Hanukah was also his favorite time of year.

Everything about Lexy made you think of circles. His round head, big blue eyes, round button nose, full round lips, round, wire rim spectacles, round shoulders, round tummy sitting atop short legs, all seemed to add to the impression of a big butterball. Even his temperament was well rounded; always smiling, he seemed to enjoy each minute with just the right level of excitement or dismay.

Most of the staff had been with Lexy from the beginning. And a few had even followed him from his very first venture forty years ago, a specialty deli. His maître d' André was now a little over sixty and Lexy remembered how young André had been back then and still seemed to be now. As he looked back at the many years he had been with André, Lexy hoped his old friend would be with him for many more. One more look around. As usual everything seemed perfect. Chairs were tucked neatly under the tables, white tablecloths, stemware, and coffee cups were all in their correct places. Everything was clean, crisp, and perfect – lights out.

Next Lexy waddled over to the kitchen where his wife Bara was overseeing the final cleanup. Once through the double swinging doors his eyes were assaulted by the bright lights of the kitchen. All was quiet. The dishes were piled neatly in stacks of forty covering a long row directly behind the huge cold and hot preparation area. Stainless steel gleamed from everywhere. When the late morning shift arrived they would fill the huge cooler trays with fresh crisp lettuce, shredded carrots, green onions, bacon bits, and all of the other items needed to complement the steaks. Huge row of deep silver trays ran along the south wall near the prep station, full of over a dozen different dressings, all made fresh by the head chef, Brian Bentham. His secret recipes like the steak marinades were unique to the Beef Château.

"There you are my little dumpling," Lexy cooed to his wife Bara as she rounded the corner coming from the office at the rear of the restaurant.

"Where did you think I would be? Ten years and every night you find me here checking out the kitchen to make sure everything is clean and put away. Did you lock up the cash and transfer the debits to the bank?" Bara launched back at Lexy.

"What else? Every night I do the same thing and every night we have this same conversation."

With that final remark, Lexy kissed Bara on the forehead, slipped his arm through hers and headed for their coats at the back of the restaurant. Like clockwork it was always the same. As they donned coats and gloves, Brian Bentham, the head chef, emerged from the meat-cutting room.

Lexy knew Brian still had another two or three hours of work left. He had to finish cutting hundreds of steaks, some with the automated processor and dozens more by hand. Only the very best cuts were good enough for their clientele. Next Brian would prepare his special marinade. Most of the steaks would soak in his 'world famous' secret recipe for up to forty-eight hours while they were kept in a special cooler to ensure their freshness. Brian was the best chef the couple had ever had and they loved him like a son. It had taken several years for him to open up to the couple and even after a decade of service he still seemed guarded. But Lexy and Bara knew Brian was giving them all that he had of himself and they were grateful for him being a part of their business.

"Another great night," Brian said as he came forward to give his customary hug to Bara. "Drive carefully and I'll see you both tomorrow."

Brian stepped back and gave Bara a loving look. "Are you losing weight? I swear you're at least ten pounds lighter than yesterday. If you don't watch it you'll melt away to nothing and then how much fun will it be to pull your chest into mine." Brian winked down at Bara.

Hugging Bara was great. At only five foot two inches, she was almost as wide as she was tall. With a full, forty-eight inch chest that felt like a soft cushion when you pulled her into your arms for a hug, she was a wonderful pillow of a woman. Bara still had a beautiful face surrounded by thick, naturally curly hair, cut above her shoulder and dyed dark. Her hair framed her clear, creamy-white skin and made her bright blue eyes seem almost bottomless when her intense gaze fell upon you. Dark brows and long lashes made it difficult to pull your eyes away. Forty years ago she had a real beauty but now she was a bit of a dumpling, although still beautiful.

"Oh you bad boy, you tease me so!" Bara laughed, beaming like a schoolgirl as she looked up into Brian's handsome face.

"You know I love you and think you're the most beautiful woman in the world and I never want you to change. So just stay the same so I can get the best hugs in the world." Brian squeezed a little harder making Bara give out a happy, girlish squeal.

This completed a customary ritual that ended every night just before midnight for the past ten years. Although the evening's custom remained the same, tonight would be an exception. Tonight Brian's life would change forever.

Once Lexy and Bara left through the back door, Brian pulled the deadbolt back, locking the door securely. He usually set all the alarms but tonight was different; he would have to open the front door for a special guest set to arrive very soon, so the alarm would be of no use. As Brian walked through the kitchen toward the double swinging doors, his thoughts turned to the past, to a day he would never forget, a week before his ninth birthday. It was the day his life had been altered forever, the day his mother left. At least that's what his dad had told him but Brian never believed it. Not then, not later, and not now. He knew with all the heart and might a little boy could possess that his mother would never have left without him. He knew his father's secret and he had learned to hate himself for keeping it. He'd never told anyone back then and now it was too late.

Brian still remembered that night so long ago when the police showed up to investigate. His dad had made his story sound pretty truthful. She had run off with her hairdresser, Max Fielding, who was also missing. All of the stuff in the hairdresser's apartment was gone, but the lady who owned the salon where Max worked said he would never leave without his paycheck, so she had called the police. She told them he had been friends with Brian's mother and that's when they came to investigate and talk to his dad.

The taller cop introduced his partner and himself

when his father came to the door. "Mr. Bentham, I'm Officer Crain and this is Officer Butler."

"We have had a complaint about a friend of your wife's who's gone missing and we were wondering if Mrs. Bentham was in and could answer some questions."

Brian stood behind his father when the door was answered. His heart beat faster, waiting for his father to give an explanation.

"Don't hold your breath, Officers, you won't find my wife here or that slimy hairdresser, seeing as my wife ran off with him last week. He can have her. She's nothing but a slut. The whore was dicking him for the past year and now she's gone off with the bastard." Joe Bentham's face was a twisted mask of contempt.

"Do you have any idea where she is or if you will hear from her?" This time it was the second cop, Butler, asking the questions.

"I haven't a fucking idea but if you'd like to come back next week who knows? Till then, I've got nothing to say about where she is. She can go to hell for all I care; no-good bitch left the kid and me. Now I gotta do everything myself."

"Well, if you hear from her, will you have her call us?" Butler said handing a card to Joe.

"If I hear from the bitch I'll pitch her ass onto the sidewalk."

"If we don't hear from you within the week we will have to come back and reinvestigate."

"Fine!" Joe slammed the door in the officer's face as he turned toward his young son slapping him across the head as he passed by heading for the kitchen to get a beer.

"Don't even think you know anything. Your mother

left for a faggot hairdresser. She never loved you and she never loved me. They will never find her, she's gone for good, and no one but the devil knows where she is."

No one asked Brian where his mother was. No one cared what he had to say; the little boy that was left behind; the little boy that knew where his mother's suitcase was and all of her things: The box filled with her jewelry and all of her bathroom stuff. The stuff she would never leave without. And he knew she would never leave without him. No one had asked about the secret place in the basement behind the wall; the place only his father was supposed to know about. The place where his father kept 'those' magazines and the videos he would watch late at night. Brian had prayed the officers would ask him a question but they never even looked at him.

They came back a couple more times, but Brian's father managed to convince them that she was just another runaway wife. And each time they ignored the little boy who stood by his father, his eyes pleading to be asked about the secret place. He couldn't tell and they never asked. He was just too scared to cry out that his dad was a liar.

At night in his dreams he did cry out for his mother's arms. But it was his dad who jerked him from his sleep, shook him hard, and told him to stop crying like a baby. It was his dad's fist that slammed into his face and twisted his hair while telling him no one cared. Not about him or his 'fucking' mother. Brian could smell the stale whisky on his father's breath from an evening of drinking. He never forgot the stale smell of his father or the sweet smell of his mother.

* * *

Brian was startled out of his dark glance at the past by a loud rap at the large oak door at the front of the restaurant. As he swung it open, he knew he was about to cross a threshold that few ever had, and once having done so, he could never turn back.

Standing outside the door was a beautiful, tall redhead. He had spotted her earlier that night and had asked Sherry, her waitress, if she was from out of town. She was dining alone and often that meant a visitor to Chicago, of which The Beef Chateau had many. Sherry confirmed his suspicion.

As was his often his custom, he went to the customer's table to welcome her, making sure the food was to her liking. While he engaged her in a conversation, he felt as if a dark cloud had lifted from his brain and suddenly he knew he had a solution to a problem that had been keeping him up after his late-night shift. Long nights and little sleep were taking their toll. He had felt a strange surge of power as he approached the woman's table. He knew that women found him irresistible and he hoped his charm would hold for the invitation he was about to make. It was in the instant that he introduced himself that he knew that the dark side was about to take over. After all, hadn't his father told him often enough that he was no good?

"Hi, my name is Brian Bentham, and I'm the head chef. I hope the meal is to your liking." He leaned over to get a whiff of her perfume.

She seemed flustered that he had come to her table and he planned to take advantage of the moment. Brian took her hand after a formal shake, refusing to let go. Her hand was cold – his warm and he could tell she felt a connection in the instant that they touched. Her face went red and she lowered her eyes, unable to keep contact with his piercing baby blues.

"If you're not doing anything later I would love it if you would come back and take a private tour of the restaurant. Please don't think I'm being forward; it's a custom to ask a special guest back each night and share the secrets of the marinades and dressings. And tonight I can't think of anyone more lovely to spend the rest of my evening with." Brian flashed a brilliant smile few could resist.

He hadn't known if anyone would fall for a line like that but she had and now she stood just inside the door. Brian locked the door behind her just before he took her coat and flashed one of his most glorious smiles.

* * *

Gloria couldn't believe her luck. She was in Chicago for a week staying at one of the better hotels just a few blocks away. Gloria was from New York, working for a promotional company featuring a new computer disk business card. She knew the electronic card would be a great success. She had been pitching the disk to a high-level brokerage firm for the better part of a week. With the sale closed she was ready for a little rest and relaxation. Tonight would be special; an evening she was looking forward to. The Beef Chateau was one of the best restaurants in Chicago and she wouldn't have missed eating here for the world. As it turned out, the food wasn't the only great thing being offered.

When the head chef came to her table she didn't know what to expect. His long legs, lean body, and broad shoulders were magnificent, but it was his face that made her heart stop. Blue-black hair, dark skin, and flashing blue eyes made her heart flop once. Then he smiled and her heart did a second flip-flop. His even white teeth covered by a full sensuous mouth, made her feel weak in the knees. He was glorious and he wanted her; she could tell by the way his eyes seemed to devour her. There was a moment when their eyes met that she thought she could see a flash of light. She got a feeling unlike anything she had ever felt before. It was like Brian was having a sudden realization, as if a solution to an unanswerable problem had suddenly been solved just by looking into her eyes. It was intoxicating and now here she stood in front of him. Hopefully there would be more than wine and a secret sauce. Hopefully there would be sex. Great sex if the looks this man gave her, were any indication.

* * *

"Welcome Gloria. I wasn't sure you would take me up on my offer. It's the first time I've ever invited anyone back. It was just a line when I told you I did this every evening. This is really my first time."

Brian took her coat as he guided her into the dimly lit interior of the restaurant. He could tell by the red glow starting to run up from her chest to her pretty face that Gloria was excited and flattered by the attention he was showering on her. He knew he had her in the palm of his hand.

"No problem, I was hoping tonight would be something special too," Gloria said, her breath catching in her throat.

"More special than you will ever know." Brian guided Gloria into the recess of the restaurant knowing tonight would be delicious, simply delicious.

* * *

It was easier than he had ever dreamed. Cattle were more difficult to lead to the slaughter. The rest of the evening had gone exactly to plan. With the chit chat over, he had gone in for the kill. The final drops of blood were now just dripping slowly over her chin. He spun Gloria around once, looking objectively at his delectable sacrifice. She hung limply from her ankles, the strong ropes cutting into her flesh. Swinging from the meat hook, her hands dragged along the cold concrete floor, still bound by the duct tape. Gloria's red hair dragged softly against its cold surface. Brian had drained all of the blood from her body. He had to hold her head to one side to ensure that the flow of blood would leave as little mess as possible. She had been alive and fully aware when he brought the small automatic blade to her throat. She had struggled for the first few minutes and it wasn't until near the end that she stopped jerking around. As the blood drained into the plastic bucket, Brian was excited by the amount he had collected.

He would be able to make a wonderful batch of his secret marinade with this warm, red elixir. When he was finished he poured some of the blood into a new marinade pan. He thought it was nice to have the bright, shiny, stainless steel pan used only for this sacrifice. Gloria would never know it, but her blood was needed like air. It had become as important as his very breath and

Brian knew he could no longer live without it. They say once an animal has a taste for blood, it can no longer go without. Brian now knew it was true. The thirst for blood and the sense of well-being it gave him had driven him to do what he had never thought possible.

* * *

Brian had spent the first hour of the evening sharing with Gloria a wonderful white wine, Kaiserstuhl 98, and asking all sorts of questions. They sat in the front of the restaurant, music softly adding to the sense of romance Brain was trying to create. Did she have any family in Chicago? Friends? When was she due back? Where did she work? Did she have to check in back at the office? He tried to get as much information as he could – after all he knew how important it would be if he wanted to get away with the murder.

Murder. He had never imagined that one day he would do to someone what his dad had done to his mother. Kill. He had imagined the murder of his mother in his head a thousand times. How had she died? Strangled? Stabbed? Shot? Was it an accident? No! When his dad moved the other woman in, Brian knew his father had planned it. The bitch was still living in his house years later, sleeping in his mother's bed and he still hated her. But he hated his father even more. "Like father, like son!" No! Never! He just had to do this. It wasn't personal. He just needed the blood. Everything in his body yearned for the feeling he got from devouring what was forbidden.

When Brian felt he had enough information to complete his plan, he invited Gloria to take a tour of the restaurant. Opening the cooler door he knew she would find the meat-processing room, fascinating.

"This is where we cut the steaks," Brian said as he welcomed her into the room. "Come over here and I'll show you how everything works."

He walked into the middle of the room where a very large wooden block stood. Overhead a rack of knives hung, each one a special tool for the carving of the steaks.

"We cut our steaks here. But it would be much too difficult to cut them all by hand so I have the help of an automated processor," Brian said as he turned around and opened a small door off to the side of the wall. "It's tucked in here and runs on a special arm."

He pulled the round, saw-like apparatus from its small chamber. It looked like a small buzz saw and ran on a pulley that would allow Brian to maneuver it with exact precision. He walked over to a large set of doors that was off the right of the room. He opened it and showed Gloria a room full of trays stacked on dozens of shelves. They were wrapped in layers of what appeared to be cellophane.

"This is a flash freezer. It hits sub-zero in seconds. We can freeze our extra steaks and they will still be as fresh as the day they were cut. This process makes it impossible to tell that the meat was ever frozen once it is thawed," He said with pride.

Once out of the flash freezer, Brian moved Gloria closer to the middle of the cutting room. On the meat table he had a wooden mallet used to beat and tenderize some of the cheaper cuts of steak. In an effort to give Gloria a kiss, he turned Gloria so that her back was against the table. She moved in closer, her head turning up to receive his lips. Brian knew he had her.

As he slipped his hands up her skirt to the warm recess of her body he knew he would be able to enjoy her in more ways than one – sex and murder, an intoxicating mix.

* * *

It was finally over. Now he had to make sure that the cleanup and disposal of the body was meticulous. He knew what to do. After he had enjoyed the warmth of her body Brian's hand closed in around the mallet. Gloria lay face down on the wooden table. As Brian withdrew from her body he had the mallet in his hand. Before she knew what was happening he brought the mallet down upon her pretty, red head. She had no idea what had happened. By the time she came to, Gloria was bound by her ankles with rope, and had been hoisted off the ground by a hook that usually supported a hind of beef, her hands bound by tape. Her mouth was also taped shut. Brian had heard enough from her pretty lips. Why spoil the moment now by listening to her pleading for her life? He preferred to stay aloof. He simply swung Gloria around, bringing the automated blade to her throat. He knew how to slaughter his prize and take advantage of the blood her body would provide.

The terror Gloria would feel in the moment would provide a wonderful mix of hormones, a very powerful combination. Once Brian soaked his steaks in the special blend of wine, blood, and herbs he knew that the human blood would provide a special kick. He would once again get that unique feeling. But first he would have to make sure he cleaned up. There would be no evidence. Brian knew what to do.

As he laid Gloria out on the floor, which he had covered with bubble wrap, he stroked her face and kissed her lips once more. Cold. He carefully washed her hands with warm soapy water. Finally he brushed her hair with the brush he found in her purse, afterwards placing it back in her handbag. He made sure that there would be no fibers or hair from his body found on her. After he had hit her with the mallet, he had dressed himself in a full, white, disposable body suit. He usually used them in order to keep the cutting room hygienic, making sure that the beef that was served would never have a human hair. Now it would protect him from leaving any clues for the police. Next he carefully examined her lifeless body to make sure there was nothing on her clothing to tie her to the meat cooler or to him. He ran a large piece of tape over her dress, panties and private parts, making sure he removed any of his hair that might have attached itself to Gloria. He had made sure he wore protection when he came inside of Gloria. No DNA. The rope fibers around her ankles were a standard issue, the kind you found at any hardware store – nothing unusual there.

The floor of the cooler was unpainted and washed twice daily with a water-soluble detergent: the kind of soap common to ninety percent of all commercial buildings, again, a tough lead to follow. The cops could follow the smallest clue and Brian would try to give them as little as possible to go on. He knew that the contents of her stomach would be examined and he would have to be sure that no one would suspect that her last meal had been at The Beef Chateau. He would be sure to dump the body a few days later, but for now a little hocus-pocus.

He had a sure fire way of confusing the police. If they

could pin down the time of death they could trace the murder back to the restaurant but he had a way to baffle the police and he knew he could get away with it. He dragged her body into the special freezer.

Brian wore his latex gloves, the kind you find any-where. This would prevent him from contaminating the body and leaving any evidence. After he laid the body in the center of the freeze zone and closed the door, he turned the dial slowly. She would be frozen in less than thirty seconds.

The process was called 'flash freeze' but in reality it took a little longer. He had removed the bubble wrap before placing Gloria in the freezer. It couldn't stand up to the sub-zero temperature that was needed to freeze the body quickly. Once done, he re-entered the cooler and gently rolled the body onto the wrap. Frozen, she needed to be handled with care. Again he examined the floor to make sure it was spotless. He didn't want any evidence that the meat freezer might give the CSI team that he knew would eventually investigate.

Brian would have to load the frozen corpse into the back of his van. He would then take the body home with him and put it into his empty deep freeze before dumping it a few days later. He would have to lay out a clear plastic tarp over the van floor to ensure that fibers would not be found in the wrap, nothing that could lead the police back to him. Now all that was left was to load the body into the van, lock it up tightly and return to the restaurant to finish his evening's work. Later he would plant the rest of his evidence to lead the police on a wild goose chase.

Printed in Canada